THE MAUSOLEUM

Recent Titles by David Mark

Novels

THE MAUSOLEUM *

The DS Aector McAvoy Series

DARK WINTER
ORIGINAL SKIN
SORROW BOUND
TAKING PITY
A BAD DEATH
DEAD PRETTY
CRUEL MERCY
SCORCHED EARTH
COLD BONES

* *available from Severn House*

THE MAUSOLEUM

David Mark

This first world edition published 2019
in Great Britain and the USA by
SEVERN HOUSE PUBLISHERS LTD of
Eardley House, 4 Uxbridge Street, London W8 7SY.
Trade paperback edition first published
in Great Britain and the USA 2019 by
SEVERN HOUSE PUBLISHERS LTD.

British Library Cataloguing in Publication Data
A CIP catalogue record for this title is available from the British Library.

ISBN-13: 978-0-7278-8872-3 (cased)
ISBN-13: 978-1-84751-997-9 (trade paper)
ISBN-13: 978-1-4483-0210-9 (e-book)

This is a work of fiction. Names, characters, places and incidents
are either the product of the author's imagination or are used fictitiously.
Except where actual historical events and characters are being described
for the storyline of this novel, all situations in this publication are
fictitious and any resemblance to actual persons, living or dead,
business establishments, events or locales is purely coincidental.

All Severn House titles are printed on acid-free paper.

Severn House Publishers support the Forest Stewardship Council™ [FSC™],
the leading international forest certification organisation.
All our titles that are printed on FSC certified paper carry the FSC logo.

Typeset by Palimpsest Book Production Ltd.,
Falkirk, Stirlingshire, Scotland.
Printed and bound in Great Britain by
TJ International, Padstow, Cornwall.

'Three may keep a secret, if two of them are dead.'

Benjamin Franklin

PROLOGUE

October 2, 2010

The voice is brittle. Raw. The words sound as if they are being scratched into sandpaper with a coffin nail.

'. . . *yrja alttawaqquf . . . yrja wade hadd laha . . . ich habe keine informationen . . .*'

The sounds rasp up and out of the old man, grinding into the dead air around his face. It seems that some invisible force is pushing on his chest. The utterances spew onto the front of his paisley pyjamas. They froth onto his stubbled, red-veined chin. They spill into the bristly caverns of his big pink ears and rain upon a woollen blanket that has taken on the appearance of an unwrapped shroud.

'What's he saying?' asks the elderly lady in the high-backed chair beside the bed. She is in her early eighties. Beneath her tights, her legs are swaddled in bandages. Her feet are clad in mauve slippers, cookie-cutter holes snipped out to accommodate matching bunions. She wears a pleated skirt and pale blue jumper. She has a pleasant face and kind eyes.

'It's almost sad. You feel so helpless. They look at you like it's your fault – like you should be able to make it stop. You end up feeling angry at yourself and at them and then at the whole world. You sometimes wish it would all just end.'

'The whole world?' asks her companion, who stands at the foot of the bed and leans on the mattress, her hands planted either side of the old man's feet.

The lady in the chair watches her companion's mouth as she speaks. She is deaf in one ear and has grown used to reading lips these past few years. She has a habit of imitating the words of the speaker while they talk so it seems that the room contains a faint echo.

'The pain,' she explains. 'The suffering.'

'Seems a silly wish to me. You don't get to pick the bits

that you like in life. You agree to the whole lot. Pain and
suffering are part of it. And if you want to know what he's
saying, he's asking for it to stop. Asking for the pain to end.'

'It will soon,' says her companion.

'Too bloody soon. His Arabic's terrible. German's good.
Wherever he is in his mind, he's not having a good time.
Wouldn't be eligible to serve these days. You talk in your sleep
and you're out of the service. There were experiments with
shock treatment to try and prevent it, back in the 50s. I read
the files. Horrible.'

'I do wish you wouldn't tell me these things,' says the
woman in the chair, shuddering. 'Hands hurting, are they?'

Her friend scowls then looks down at her hands as if they
are enemies. Her knuckles are twisted and swollen so that her
fingers spread out and twist like the roots of an ancient
hawthorn. 'Anybody who tells you pain is all in the mind can
take a running jump,' says the woman. 'Pain is in the bloody
nerve endings.'

Despite the suffering they cause her, the woman still wears
her rings. There is a diamond and a gold wedding band on
the third finger of her left hand, and a modern, Aztec-style
twist of silver on her thumb. She has long white hair and a
thin, sharply angled face. Her eyes are lapis-blue. She wears
a fitted white jacket over a clinging blue top and smart, neatly-
pressed trousers. She is a handful of years younger than her
friend but could easily pass for sixty. She looks younger still
when she smiles.

'I should have switched to a typewriter,' she mutters, sighing.
'Or a computer. Writing by hand will kill your joints. Damn
things.' She glances at her friend, an incongruous and impish
smile chasing the anger and sadness from her face. 'They're
not nearly as ghastly as your legs.'

'Ooh, you've a nasty side to you,' smiles her friend. 'You
could twang a raw nerve like a violin string, you could. My
legs don't hurt. They're just annoying.'

'They're bloody horrible to look at.'

'I know. Our John says they look like those sausages you
get abroad.'

'More like a pair of nylons stuffed with haggis.'

'I've never liked haggis.'

'You tried it?'

'No.'

The silence stretches out for a moment. Neither feels compelled to talk. They have been friends for a long time.

The younger woman screws up her face. Tastes the air. 'It's supposed to smell of disinfectant and boiled cabbage in places like this. I can't smell anything at all.'

'It's nice. I enjoyed my last stay.'

'You're not meant to enjoy it, Flick. It's a hospital.'

'Not really. It reminds me of that B and B where I stayed when I was down in Bournemouth. Nice people. Lots of chatter. A few people who don't know what day it is . . .'

'Sounds lovely.'

'Aye well, it was good enough for us,' says Flick. 'I tried abroad. Didn't like it.'

'There's a lot of it, I've told you that before.'

'Well I didn't like the bit I saw. We've been through this before, Cordelia.'

Cordelia rolls her eyes. She looks back at the small, frail figure in the bed. She fancies she could pick him up and carry him and he would weigh no more than a sack full of bones.

'Shall we wake him?' asks Flick, cautiously. 'It seems wrong, somehow. I know we've come a long way but it was different just talking. It seems wrong being here. I don't feel like I should.'

Cordelia scratches her forearm and the scent of her fruity, floral perfume fills the small, comfortable room. This is a pleasing space in which to die. The walls are a sunshine yellow and hung with pictures of local landscapes. There is a TV mounted on a stand in the corner of the room and though the curtains are closed, the window by the far wall usually offers a view of the front garden. Cordelia would like to open the curtains. Outside, a light rain is falling from a grey-blue sky. She enjoys such weather. It reminds her of home.

'It's now or not at all,' says Cordelia, quietly. 'The nurse said if we can steer him onto the right path, all sorts of recollections might pour out. He might have fooled them into thinking he doesn't know who he is but that's only because they don't know the truth of him. He's been so many different people it's no surprise he's in a muddle. But here, at the end, I have a feeling the centre of him, the truth of him, will want to make itself heard.'

'I don't know if I want to know. Not really. Not now we're here.'

'We've waited half a bloody century, Flick.'

'But look at him. Whoever he was, he's not him any more. People change . . .'

'We can't make him suffer any more than he already is,' says Cordelia, gently. 'Whatever he can see in his dreams, he's in his own hell. He would thank us for the reprieve.'

Flick turns to look at him. She seems to be considering her own mortality, her own mounting frailty. 'Don't ever let me get like that,' she says.

'You already are,' says Cordy, and her face splits into a smile that her old friend shares.

They take a moment. Pause; revelling in this last, final instant in which they can still walk away. They are two figures upon a clifftop, leaning forward into the wind, held upright by a gale that could drop without warning. Then Cordelia walks to the side of the bed and leans over the decrepit figure who fits and cries and prays in his tortured sleep.

'Wake up,' she says, and closes her fingers around his nose, flinching a little at the contact and the pain the action causes joints. 'We have questions. You have answers. And if you keep pretending, I'll bury you. I'll put you in the ground, just like the body in the blue suit.'

Beneath her hand, the old man coughs. His breath is warm upon Cordelia's wrist. She applies more pressure and his fragile body twists. Only when he seems about to burst do his eyes slide open.

He looks up at the white-haired, blue-eyed figure, lit from behind by a glowing golden bulb.

He smiles the smile of a man who had expected to wake in Hell.

CORDELIA

October, 1967

I was lying in a grave the first time I met Felicity. It was the day the storm came. The clouds were a mound of dead doves; all grey and purple, silver and muddy white. Made me think of foxgloves pulped against stone. It would be a week before we saw blue again. A week before the clouds rained themselves out. The Tyne rose six feet that fortnight. They had to evacuate half of Haltwhistle. Bones rose from the churchyards like worms.

I wasn't uncomfortable, lying there, looking like something the earth had winkled out. It was out of the wind, protected by the branches of the big laurel tree that stood sentinel over the oldest headstones. I liked such spaces, at the time. I liked containment. Manageable environments. I would have dug a hole and crawled inside it if I knew anybody well enough to shovel the dirt back on top of me.

I breathed in. Damp grass. Mud. That high, meat and camphor whiff of unloved furs. I experienced the sudden sensation of coming back to myself. I realized I had drifted off again. Not asleep exactly – just absent. It felt like I was dying in increments, dwindling into nothingness, like a name in an unread book. What had I been doing? I flexed my fingers and felt the reassuring weight of the novel, sitting on my belly in the place where Stefan used to like to plonk himself; a jockey on his mother's belly, giggling while I jiggled him . . .

I adjusted my position. My clothes were sticking to my skin. Grass prickled at the skin of my wrists. A long-necked daisy had grown between the fingers of my left hand. I wondered how long it would take for the earth to claim me. I had a vision of myself, semi-consumed, a risen hump of grass, cow parsley and buttercups, split into sods with the gravedigger's spade. I shook the image away before it took hold. I found myself staring out at the little grey mausoleum that stood at the rear of the churchyard. Were I a painter, this would be the section of the landscape that I would have chosen to paint. Cosy, in a Gothic sort of way. I envied the building its indelible pocket of gloom, shielded as it was by the purple leaves of an overhanging tree. Moss grew on its walls, as if the stone was a living thing that somehow provided nutrients. I had seen swifts flitting in and out of the elaborate eaves.

Upper Denton. That was the name of the village. A mile south of Gilsland. A place at the edge of things. It was shaped like a crucifix – the cross section formed by a straight grey road that ran parallel to the train tracks. Three houses at the top of the village and a couple more sloping away down the hill. Ragged outbuildings and crumbling barns. Then the church. Beyond that lay the river and the trees and endless miles of nothing at all.

'Oh Jesus, Joseph and Mary, I thought you were a ghost!'

I didn't move. Didn't make a sound. I'd heard her approaching. Lain still as a housebrick and hoped she would pass right on by.

'Are you well? Oh my goodness, I'm shaking!'

She was one of them. A local girl. One of the tribe. A girl from the borderlands, the place between pages; tucked into the margins between two northern counties and a stone's throw from the Scottish border. A Gilsland girl. As much a part of the landscape as the cow shit and tumbledown stone walls.

She'd jumped like a startled cat when she saw me. Literally jumped. Both feet off the floor and one hand rising to her face. The other held a small bouquet of carnations, which she was crushing against her damp jacket like a child with an ice cream.

'I'm so sorry . . .' she began.

I stopped her with a shake of my head. I couldn't abide feebleness. Already I felt I knew what she was. Could imagine her running a neat little home, peeling potatoes, picking elder-berries, scrubbing medicated shampoo into some pale-skinned little ruffian's hair. I drank her in a little more. She was older than me. Mid-thirties, though with the fashions in that place it was never easy to be sure. Women started dressing like their grandparents as soon as they pushed out a child.

'You gave me quite a start,' she said, all fussy. Her accent was local, a low, self-conscious marbling of Geordie and Scot. 'Have you fallen? Can you hear me? Are you not well? I'm Mrs . . . well, I'm Felicity, really . . .'

I probably shrugged. I certainly didn't have the energy to smile. Just looked at her, over the top of my book, and wondered if she was going to say any more. I didn't want company. Hadn't wanted company in a long while. Didn't even know if my sore throat and cracked lips would allow for conversation.

'It'll be Mrs Hemlock, am I right?'

She wasn't going to accept silence, that much was clear. But I wasn't about to jump up and thank her for acknowledging my existence. I was enjoying being rude. Made me feel like I was back at university and so full of anger and ambition that it sometimes made me want to tear at my clothes and skin. I was like that, then. Maybe I still am.

I shifted my position a little and managed a tight smile. The action felt unnatural to me, like putting on a dress that used to fit and finding it suddenly uncomfortable and restrictive. The air felt wrong around me. It was as if there was burning metal on the breeze. I didn't know if I was too hot or too cold; a wet baby beneath a thick woollen sheet.

'I was just enjoying the quiet,' I said, aware that my mouth opened more precisely around my words than her's did. I sounded posher. Richer. Better bred.

'In a graveyard?' she asked, looking baffled at the notion. 'On your own?'

'Nothing to be scared of in a graveyard,' I said, in the tone of voice that had always made people think of me as a little fond of my own opinions. 'There's nothing here that can hurt you. We're the only people in history to think of bones as unclean things. There are cultures where people dig up their ancestors every year. Dress them and take them for a celebration. We're the ones who decided there should be a dividing line between life and death. Other people think of it in shades of grey.'

She nodded. Gave a tight smile. It was a well-meaning gesture, the sort you give a child who has just drawn a picture of an eight-legged cat. 'That's nice.'

We both fell to silence. Something buzzed, fatly, by my ear. I felt the tickle of tiny creatures scurrying across my skin. At length, she tucked her elbows in to her sides and drew a circle around me with her eyes. 'That's a grave you're laying on.'

'I know,' I said, oddly pleased. 'Victoria Asbrey. Died in 1717, aged 100, though I have my doubts that they kept proper records. She was probably much younger.'

'She was a Reiver,' said Felicity, jerking her chin in the direction of the grave. It was a mannerism I associated with men – hands in their overalls and giving directions with grunts. 'She was a hundred when she died. Says so on the headstone, look.'

'A Border Reiver?' I said, and winced at having asked a silly question. I wanted this woman to know how clever I was. I had always needed to be the brightest in the room.

'Rough people,' explained Felicity, quietly, in case they overheard and took offence. 'Fighters. This whole area is Reiver country. Used to be, anyways, though if you throw a rock in the air it'll hit somebody with a surname from one of the old clans.'

'I've studied the Reivers,' I said.

'How?' she asked.

'I'm sorry?'

'How did you study them? They're long gone.'

'Read about them, I mean. In books.' I waved the novel I was reading. It was probably an Orwell. I liked Orwell a lot in those days.

She continued to stand there, staring at me. Now she had recovered herself she seemed disinclined to move on. Behind her the sky was an ugly grey, like wet limestone. Her coat was buttoned up to the top but she looked cold, as if she was suppressing a tremble.

'I'm not a big reader,' she said. 'My husband likes cowboy books. And films. I try to read but I fall asleep.'

'You're reading the wrong books,' I said, primly.

'Yes?' She seemed interested in the idea. 'You can tell me which are the right ones.'

I gave her a little more attention. Angled my head, enquiring whether she wanted any more of my time. The wind played with the long grass. The birdsong was shrill, a plaintive whistle, like a drowning sailor calling for help.

'Do you know all the occupants?' I asked, waving generally in the direction of the next headstone. It was a sandstone affair, its letters semi-obscured by wind and rain and time.

'Not all,' she said. 'Most of these are before my time though I recognize a lot of the surnames. Mam's in a family plot, you see. All the newer burials these days are back in Gilsland. St Mary Magdalene. The new church, we call it, though it's been up more than a hundred years.'

'Your family's from here, then.'

'Oh aye. Dad says they built the place around us. Reckons we helped put up the Roman wall. I'm Denton, now, I suppose, but I hope I'm still Gilsland.'

I didn't let myself laugh. Gilsland was roughly a mile back down the railway line – a village of a few hundred inhabitants clinging to the remnants of Hadrian's Wall. Its only other claim to fame was a sulphurous spring, rumoured to produce long life among those who held their nose and drank its waters. The village had experienced a boom two decades back when men from the ministry arrived and declared they were going to transform countless acres of virginal peat bog into a modern RAF base. They did so, at colossal expense. Brought wealth and workers to the place. Tested the rockets that might one day have flown to the moon. Broke the sound barrier so often that the locals got used to their windows rattling. Then the government lost interest. The plug was pulled on the space race and the workers went away. The money that locals had earned in the good times was sunk into subsidising family farms and paying the rent on properties they could no longer afford. People stopped visiting the tourist sites. Dr Beeching even closed the railway station. Gilsland began to fade.

'You'll maybe know Dolly,' said my new friend.

'Dolly?' I asked. This was the most I had spoken in months. I was torn between craving a return to the silence, and continuing to lose myself in the warm comforts of her inane prattle.

'Little woman,' she explained. 'Lives in the house by the turn. She's got normal hands but no arms. Do you know who I'm talking about? She's a dinner lady at the school. She said you'd had a natter a few weeks back. You said you might come and give a talk at the school.'

I had no memory of the conversation. All I could recall was a short, stout woman who had said something about me coming to the school and talking to the pupils about what it was like to be from somewhere other than there.

'Would you want to talk to the children?' asked Felicity. 'Your neighbour, Mr Parker – he talks to the schools. Our Fairfax is a regular too. You might have something worth hearing.'

I considered my new acquaintance properly. She had a nice face. Her teeth were white and even and she was wearing no make-up. Her hair was the brown of varnished wood. She was wearing clumpy brown shoes and her skirt reached past her knee. I would never have spoken to her had she not spoken to me first. I'd have laughed at her type at university. Would have sneered into my drink and made fun.

'I'm not sure I'd have anything worth hearing,' I said. 'I don't know the area. Not really. And I'm a bit lost, to tell you the truth.'

'Lost? Like, you don't know the way home?'

I wished it were that simple. I wanted to tell her how it felt to be me. How it felt to be bereaved beyond enduring; to have one's insides scraped out with a spoon like a turnip carved out for Halloween.

'What's your family name?' I asked, out of forced politeness. 'I'll check the headstones.'

'Eagles,' she said. 'Though I've married a Goose. There aren't many women can say they've gone from an Eagle to a Goose and never flown. My John says I'm bird-brained, but he doesn't mean it nasty.'

She waited for me to smile at her joke and I obliged. I lowered my book. Marked the page. Readjusted myself against the hard stone.

'You're from the Zealand place,' she said. 'Farm over the river. Mrs Winslow's.'

I nodded, watching as her features realigned themselves.

'I was so sorry to hear about your son,' she said, looking down at the ground. I think her lip even quivered. 'Horrible. Just so sad.'

I kept staring at her. I think I did it unkindly, so as to make her feel uncomfortable. I was full of venom, back then. Angry at everything. Hateful and spiteful. I was surrounded by so much blackness it felt like I was swimming through ink.

'Thank you,' I said, quietly, though my expression didn't change.

'How are you coping?' she asked, putting her head on her own shoulder so she looked briefly like an injured chicken. 'I wanted to come and bring you something but John said you'd no doubt have staff for that sort of thing. Are you on the mend?'

I gave a short, harsh laugh. It was a ridiculous question. My child was dead. The child I'd changed my life for. The child I'd given up everything to keep. Every day it felt as though I were wearing damp sheets around my skin and that my throat was being slowly dammed with smooth, cold stones. My existence was sorrow; my every thought an agony.

'Not well,' I said, and my face twitched. Just one rebellious muscle, high on my cheek, pulsing like a tiny heartbeat.

'How old was he?'

'Just under two.'

'Awful,' said Felicity. She sniffed, smearing the heel of her hand across her nose and eyes and shaking her head at herself as if in reprimand.

Tears have always undone me. I'm not one for crying. I can't see the sense in it. I never feel any better for having squeezed out a few tears. But other people's weeping is impossible to endure. I find myself overcome by pity. I pulled myself up without thinking about it. Before I knew it I was standing in front of her and offering a handkerchief which she took with a grateful smile.

'I'm sorry,' she said, shaking her head again. 'It's just so sad. I thought of you, up that place on your own, having to go through it all. I cried a bucketful when my husband told me.'

'Do I know him?' I asked. 'Your husband?'

'No, no. But your neighbours, Mr and Mrs Parker, they let people know what had gone on. It's a small place, even with the airfield and people passing through. People hear things quickly.'

I thought of the Parkers. Her, with her serious face and eyes like Roman coins. Him, with his bad wig and his hunched shoulders in a suit three sizes too big. They'd descended on me after the doctor left. Could they do anything? Did I need help? Was there anything they could get me or anybody they could contact? I'd wanted none of it. They'd never taken the trouble to get to know me or my boy while he was alive and there was no chance I would let them have a part of his death.

'Is your son buried here?' asked Felicity, quizzically.

'He was cremated,' I said. 'I scattered him places he liked.' I gestured around me, remembering his little plump legs kicking at the air, laying on his back and smiling, gummily, with a face he had yet to grow into, on the brown summer grass at my side. 'I scattered him here.'

'Cremated?' asked Felicity. There was something like disapproval there. Something else, too.

'It felt right.'

'People get buried around here. I'm surprised I didn't hear. That sort of thing can be a scandal.'

I felt my expression change. Forced myself not to let the temper out. I didn't know this woman well enough to give a damn about upsetting her but I knew that if I started shouting, I might never stop.

'It's nobody else's business,' I said. 'He was my son.'

'I'm sorry,' said Felicity, suddenly looking aghast at having spoken so freely. 'Truly. You and your husband must have been through so much. And with him being away so often . . .'

I nodded, sparing her the embarrassment of having to finish the lie.

'I'm Felicity,' she said. 'Mrs Goose, really.'

'Felicity,' I said, surprised. 'I knew a Felicity at university. Flick, we called her. Do you get Flick?'

Her face broke into a beam. 'Never! No, I get the full title, or Phyllis, to those who think the name's too fancy. Flick! Well, I never.'

'I'm Cordelia,' I said. 'From *King Lear.*'

'Where's that?' she asked, interested.

'No, the play. Shakespeare. The name's from there.'

'Oh,' she said, and did not seem to realize she should be embarrassed at her lack of knowledge. 'Mrs Hemlock, yes?'

'I'm fine with Cordelia. I haven't got used to the Hemlock yet.'

'It's funny, isn't it? Having a new name. I still get mine wrong and I've been married thirteen years.'

'And your husband?'

'John. Works in Carlisle for the corporation. Two children. James and Brian. Brian's a little so-and-so. Could charm the skin off an apple. You've probably seen him in your garden. He knows you've got goosegog bushes and he's the sort to help himself.'

'Goosegogs?'

'Gooseberries. Mrs Winslow's father planted them years back. They still yield?'

I looked at her like she was speaking a foreign language. She started talking quickly then, as if to spare me the embarrassment of not knowing.

'Grand old place, the Zealand Farm. Went there when I was little. Day out with the school, I think. Mrs Winslow played the piano for us. She was already on her own by then. Grand old woman. Strong as an ox. Worked until she couldn't stand and then took to her bed and gave orders the rest of her days. Shame her son couldn't take it on but I'm sure your husband's going to do right by it. Must get lonely up there though. Cold, too. A bugger to heat, I'm guessing . . .'

I let her talk. Stefan had been dead seven months. I don't think I'd exchanged more than a handful of words with another soul in that time. I wrote letters to family but couldn't bring myself to read their replies. I gorged myself on food and drink or starved myself as my mood dictated. My face had begun to look unhealthy, like meat left out in warm weather. When I did take the trouble to brush my hair I would find whole clumps of it wrapped around the brush. If I dressed myself in

more than a blanket it was in Cranham's discarded clothes –
big, patterned shirts with extravagant cuffs and collars; rugby
shorts so big I could fit my whole body through one leg-hole.
I floated around the house like a leaf on the breeze, wafting
into empty rooms and nudging against the great thick walls
and ancient bannisters; knocking pictures askew with careless
movements, hugging myself in the dark behind thick, dusty
curtains; cuddling my knees in front of a dead fire.

It took me an effort of colossal will to emerge into fresh
air. Took small walks to the pretty places Stefan and I had
enjoyed. Dragged myself down muddy tracks and over damp
wooden stiles to look upon waterfalls and deep pools of
whisky-coloured water; breathlessly clawing my way up steep
riverbanks to stare at landscapes that had made my baby smile;
mosaics of so many different greens and browns; the houses
and farms arranged as if a giant hand had scattered them across
the landscape.

'. . . but you went to university, you say?' asked Felicity,
when she finished a lengthy monologue on the various people
who had showed an interest in the Winslow place before
Cranham had bought it.

'Classics,' I said, and realized I might have to add a bit
more. 'Nuffield. Oxford.'

'Oxford? That's a good one, yes?'

I smiled, not unkindly. 'It is, yes.'

'They let women go, do they?'

I let my surprise show. 'Why wouldn't they?'

'Don't know,' said Felicity, and seemed to mean it. 'Just
seems a man sort of thing. You must be very clever.'

I wasn't sure what to say. What was the right story to tell?
That I was one of only three females on the course? That I'd
had to fight twice as hard to prove myself? That I was seen
as a tea girl by half the faculty? Or should I tell her how I'd
ruined it? How I'd let a married man become the only thought
in my head? How I'd become infatuated? I was Byron's lioness;
a creature of undiluted passion, driven mad by a desire to
possess and be possessed. I had thrown myself at him. His
protestations and dismissals were twisted by my imagination
into declarations of eternal love. I left him no choice but to

have me. He did his damnedest to resist but I was young and my skin was soft and my mouth was hot and in the end it would have taken more strength than he possessed to resist me. He cried afterwards. Sat on the edge of the bed with his head in his hands, weeping at what he had done. I see myself there, now. Laying on my back with a triumphant smile on my face and a warm, pleasant pain between my legs. I had done what I set out to. I had earned him. Taken him inside myself. His tears spoiled the moment. I told him not to cry – that he had done nothing wrong. I wanted it. I had forced it. He had earned the right to some happiness. I've never forgotten how he looked at me. At the disgust and the anger and the sheer contempt in his eyes. I had trapped him, he said. I'd ruined everything. He did not want this. Never had. I was a whore. A tramp. I was repellent to him . . .

'I didn't finish the course,' I said, briskly. 'Baby came along.'

'Oh well, at least you must have learned something, eh?' said Felicity. 'And you're married now so it doesn't really matter anyways.'

I wasn't sure where to start with Felicity. Wasn't sure how to begin re-educating her. I didn't know whether to let her ignorance go by unremarked, or to analyse her every statement to see if she could possibly mean the things she said.

'Dulling over,' said Felicity, looking at the sky.

We both looked up. I hadn't noticed the change but she was right. The sky was a leaden grey and the clouds that were tumbling in from the east were black battleships. The birds had fallen silent.

'Spot of rain,' I said, extending a hand.

'You walk here?' asked Felicity.

'I don't have a car,' I said.

'Of course you don't have a car,' she said. 'A bicycle, I meant.'

'No. I just walked. You?'

'I'm only up the road. White house at the top of the lane. Two minutes. You'll never make it back to Winslow's.'

'It's fine. I don't mind the rain.'

She looked at me as if I was mad. 'There's going to be a storm. You get caught out in it, well, it's not the rain you have to worry about. It's the lightning.'

I dismissed her fears, screwing up my face as if to say that such a thing was a needless worry. Above, the clouds twisted upon themselves, like milk being poured into black tea. I heard raindrops begin to hit the leaves. Felt droplets of water fall as footsteps upon my skin. There was something in the air; a static and charge. The hairs on my arms began to rise like sails.

'Come to my place,' she said. 'You can wait out the storm. I have a nice apple cake. The children are at school. I would be worried sick letting you walk.'

'I'll just pop in the church,' I said, waving at the sturdy grey oblong with its flat roof, leaded windows and thick walls.

'Is it open? It's always locked. Fairfax is the warden and he lives two doors from me. You're just as well popping to my place.'

I was torn. Part of me was enjoying this sudden moment of human contact. Felicity was a warm, kind and generous soul who wanted to keep me safe from the storm. What did it say about me if I refused? Yet the idea of a warm, comfortable family home filled me with dread. I would never have such a thing myself. I would never know such a life.

'Here it comes,' said Felicity, and she raised a hand above her head. She was still holding the flowers and seemed to realize it. 'Here, give these to the grave you've been laying on. I'll get more for Mam.'

For a moment I felt as though I was inside a tin shack and somebody was banging upon it with a bat. The rumble in the sky was a colossal thing. God moving furniture in the heavens. I ducked my head into my shoulders. The shiver that passed through me was primal; a fear that would have seemed as familiar to the Romans who stood on the nearby boundary wall as it did to me. It was a feeling that the ground was about to split; that some almighty force was preparing to plunge His fists into the ground and pull up the earth's foundations.

'Come on,' said Felicity, and to my surprise, she took my hand. I found myself smiling, grinning inanely, as I was led briskly between the ancient graves that stood out of the long damp grass and the untended wildflowers like boulders from the sea.

'Oh goodness, here it comes . . .'

I gave a shriek as the skies opened and a deluge like I had never witnessed tumbled down. It was as if somebody had flipped the earth; as if the sea had become the sky. I felt as though I was running through a waterfall. Felicity kept hold of my hand and we staggered up the shingle path towards the rusty black gate. Felicity wrenched it open and turned to tell me to hurry.

I felt the lightning strike rather than saw it. I experienced a sudden moment of light and heat and power at my back, as if somebody had suddenly opened the door of a furnace behind me. I spun and lost my footing, dropping painfully to one knee and my hand was wrenched from Felicity's. I lay there, twisted and sprawled, watching the deluge beat down upon the tiny church and the ancient tombstones, flattening down the grass and thistles, ragwort and cow parsley. Then came the sound. A noise like the cry of a dying beast; a keening wail that grew to a scream before climaxing in a crack that hurt my ears.

I looked up to see the ancient laurel split in two. It tore down the middle as if somebody were ripping a photograph. For a moment the trunk was two perfect halves. And then they fell. The branches were still tangled together and both halves of the trunk fell in the same direction, collapsing downwards with a dreadful crescendo of splintering wood.

It missed the church. Fell at an angle that would later be seen by the faithful as an act of God. Instead it stamped down into the churchyard with an impact that made the ground shake and one of the stoutest arms smashed into the stone roof of the little crypt that had stood there for three hundred years. The construction was not much bigger than a garden shed. It was surrounded by rusty iron railings and there were ornate carvings above the rotten wooden door. The whole edifice collapsed as if made of cards.

'Oh,' said Felicity, in my ear. I will always remember that. That sudden, simple exclamation. She had her hands under my armpits and was dragging me upright while her feet battled for purchase on a path that was already becoming a river.

We both saw it happen. Both watched as the crypt came apart in an explosion of stone and ancient timbers.

We knew there would be bones. Knew that if we did not look away we would see ancient skeletons and grinning skulls.

But the body that tumbled onto the grass was dressed in a dark suit and had a full head of hair. The face that looked at us had staring eyes and the mouth was open as if in surprise. Were it not for the unnatural position in which he lay, folded in on himself and twisted as if dropped from the sky, he may have just as easily been sleeping.

I turned to Felicity and saw the horror on her face. Her mouth was open and I wondered if her scream was lost to the sound of the wind and the rain and the settling stones.

She looked at me, then. An accusing, puzzled glare. Looked at me as if I had done this thing. I had brought this ugliness into our lives. Then she dragged me upright and grabbed my wrist and tugged me through the storm.

I had to look where I was going. Had to try and find my feet as I splashed through the path and felt the earth pull at my boots as if hands were reaching out from the earth.

I took a last glance at the body as I splashed through the lychgate. The pummelling of the rain ceased for an instant. When it slashed back down it was with the precision of a blade. Through the rain I saw a man in blue. Dark hair. Neat brown shoes. A greenish-brown satchel wrapped across the torso. Then he was lost as I tore my gaze away, searching the pock-marked road for patches of ground where I might keep my feet. I ran. Thought of myself first. Thought of my boy's ashes after that. Felt a wave of something inside me as I pictured the dust of my baby being washed away like sand.

FELICITY

Transcript 0001, recorded October 29, 2010

Is it working? Is it on? Cordy, is it working? I just speak, do I? I feel silly. I mean, where do I start? And it seems wrong. I mean it was all about the recordings, wasn't it? That's what made it all happen. I just, I don't know. I did one of these for the Oral History Society but they just wanted to know about the village and the nuclear tests and what it was like in the old days. This is private. But I know. I know it needs to be told. Have you got my notes? My reading glasses are over there . . . All right, that day . . . I'd been shopping in the morning. Fish. Eggs. Bread. Flowers for Mam. Usual. Some of those chocolate mint balls for the boys. Why do I remember any of it? Then there was the graveyard. You startled me. The church. The storm. The body. All of it . . . I can't get my breath. Cordelia, please, can we turn this off? I'll start again when I've got my breath. I feel dizzy. Please. Cordy, please . . .

Transcript 0002, recorded October 29, 2010

It's an odd thing, harking back. Half the stuff you remember as you are now and half of it you remember as you were then. You remember being upset with your parents when you were eight and they blamed you for setting fire to the outhouse when you were taking out the hot ashes. But in the memory, it's you as you are now. So you understand your parents' point of view, 'cause you're a grown-up and you've had bairns yourself and you know the frustration and the expense and the fear. But you're still feeling like a bairn at the same time. You remember the feeling of unfairness. Temper. You were being blamed for something that was an accident and could have happened to anybody. You remember the tears on your cheek and the hard hand off your bare backside and the shame that sliced into you like skewers into a side of pork. So you're both people. You then, and you now. So when I remember '67; when I remember that time, I always feel a bit bad because the way I used to think, the bad way, is still a part of me. And I feel awful for how I must have appeared in that moment. For looking at her the way I did. As if she'd done it. As if she'd brought the storm and knocked down that tree and made me look at that man, all mangled and twisted like that. How could it be her fault? How could it be anybody's, 'cept for the nasty bugger who had left him there like a bag of rags and rubbish? Am I making sense? John tells me I'm hard work. Reckons he could bottle me and sell me as a headache.

I thought it was a tailor's dummy. Honest I did. One of those big dolls you get in the windows of the shops in Carlisle. I thought somebody had dressed one up and put it in the Kinmont crypt for a game. That's what I tell myself now, anyhow. Maybe I didn't think that at all. Maybe I knew straight from the off what I was looking at and I've made the rest of it up. Maybe not. I'm blathering, I think. Wittering on, John calls it. Pushing my dinner around the plate. He says that too, and I like that description. Acting like I'm eating, but not actually eating. That's maybe what I'm doing now. Making noise without saying anything. I'm sorry. I'll try again . . .

I'd seen her a couple of times before. Cordelia, I mean. Striking lass, she were, though it pains me to say it, given how fond of herself she can be when she's dolled up to the nines. Weren't always as slim, mind. She were massive with the baby when she moved in to the old Winslow place. Big enough to be carrying twins. She was a delicate thing underneath, you could tell that at once, but with the baby she were carrying – well, she looked like a house-end. Even so, John had said she was a balm for the eyes and he wasn't wrong. Looked like somebody from a magazine. Eyes like forget-me-nots and her lipstick were a colour me mam would have called 'brazen'. Carried herself a bit fancy, if I'm honest. Sniffing the clouds, as me mam used to say. Bit fond of herself, though if I were half so pretty as her it would be a struggle to get me away from the mirror. But I don't like to judge and you can't know a book from its cover so I never joined in when anybody made fun or said she were a bit too bloody haughty by half.

Can't have been easy, I thought. Only young and married to a man twice her age who was never here and who'd left her there to deal with that great old place up on the hill with nowt but her babby for company. She was probably lonely. And you could tell from the clothes she weren't familiar with our part of the world. I wouldn't even know how to describe what she was wearing when we spoke that first time. It had me in mind of a monk's habit from the horror films; like a sack with a hood, except it stopped above the knee, and she was wearing white long socks and boots shiny as a tadpole. Her hair was a city style. Fringe at the front but shoulder-length at the back and sides, and she'd done her eyes so they looked like a cat's. She was glamorous. That's the word. The sort that men reckon are flaunting themselves, though they don't mind enjoying the show. The sort that women don't feel safe around. When John said she were pretty it was no different to him telling me he'd seen some nice flowers or a rare bird, but I'll admit there were times when I could have slapped her with the frying pan for the ease with which she looked so bloody good, and the way she could just, well, turn it on and off. She could make men go weak at the knees when she tried, though it always seemed to kill a little part of her when she did so.

It were wrong of me to look at her like that. I know that now. But you can't help it, can you? Instinct, I mean. No different to when I jumped out of my skin after seeing her laying there in the old grave. Looked to me like she were a corpse herself, laying there on top of the spot where those old bones were sunk in deep. What's the word I'm looking for? Sacra-something? Sacrilegious, that's it. Seemed sacrilegious, her lying there, though I don't worry overmuch about going to church. Wouldn't swear in a church, mind. Wouldn't laugh at a joke about Jesus. Just because you stop believing in Father Christmas doesn't mean you go and board up the chimney.

Looking back, I can understand well enough. Her baby were there. Scattered on the wind. It was somewhere she could feel close to him and who was I to deny her that? She might have been a snooty sort but nobody deserves to lose a bairn. Not like that. When she lost him it were the first time I'd heard anybody in Gilsland say a kind word about her. Up 'til then she were pegged as a snotty cow. Nose in the air trying not to breathe us in. That were the story, any road. Stayed up there on a farm she couldn't work, playing with a baby who looked nowt like his father. And the father were no sort of man. Great walrus of a man. Something in London, so we were told. Worked for the government doing one of those jobs they do in the films. A bowler-hat-and-umbrella kind of job. Not short of cash and happy to spend it. No great brains on him, according to our John. Said you could charge him whatever you liked and he'd pay. Reckoned people up here were honest and decent and wouldn't try and charge more than they thought was fair. Daft apeth learned he were wrong, in time. Lads fleeced him down to the bone. But they did the work he paid them for. Made the old place habitable. Decorated inside and out. Tidied the garden and the pasture and hacked back the apple trees so she could see the view across the river. She didn't even offer them a cup of tea. Just sat with her baby on her knee, reading to the little lad from a book, as if he had the first blooming clue what she was saying. When he died, story changed. After that people were saying how lonely it must be up there on her own. Saying how she idolized the little man. How they'd seen her in the post office and her eyes were so dark it was like she'd been working down a mine. I should have gone up there then, I suppose. But you don't like to, do you? Don't like to put yourself forward.

It half stopped my heart when that tree came down. I was never good with my nerves. Flighty, Dad always said. *Neurotic*, according to John. I didn't need a name for it. I just suffered with my nerves. Didn't like heights, or the dark, or being too long on my own. That didn't make me a pushover. I still had a tongue like an adder when my blood was up. Always made sure I put myself on the side of the road where the cars were coming from if I was out with the bairns. Looking back, I'm flabbergasted at myself. Anybody who knew me would have expected me to scream like a trumpeting elephant and then go into spasm. But I didn't. Maybe it was the water running over my shoes or the leaves that were slapping me in the face and tangling in my hair but it just seemed a lot more important to me to be doing something useful than standing there and being an extra problem. We couldn't stay there. Had to get indoors. Church was closed and the barn and garage back up towards the railway tracks were so flimsy we used to joke that a big bad wolf could blow them down. We had to get home. Up a muddy road that was turning into a river; the water chuckling over rocks and the ruts left by Fairfax's tractor.

'There's a man,' she said, looking up at me. Her eyes were wide. She looked young and frightened and no matter who she's turned into in the years since, there'll always be a part of me that remembers what she was in that moment. Always be a part of me that knows how soft she is inside the shell.

'We have to go,' I said, and dragged her onto the track. Weren't like me to be bossy like that. I were a follower by nature.

And she starts on at me. 'The man . . . the man . . .'

I knew she wouldn't move if I didn't say something so I promised her we wouldn't just leave him there. 'We'll tell somebody,' I said, all calm, like she were a toddler needed soothing. 'Please. It's getting worse.'

I had to hold my hand in front of my face. The air was full of flying twigs and stones and leaves. They felt like bullets as they hit my hand. Pushed me back like a man.

'That house,' shouted Cordelia, and she had to repeat it so I could hear her over the wind. She was looking at the grey cottage that stood outside the churchyard. 'Let's go there . . .'

'No,' I said, and I swear it felt like my insides were just ice and gravel. There was no bloody way I was going in there. I'd rather have been naked in the storm.

'Keep going,' I said. 'My house is just up there.'

I couldn't explain it. Not then. Not over the sound of the storm. However bad the rain got, we wouldn't be going in Pike's house. He was more dangerous than the lightning. His house looked like he did. Damaged. Battered. Moody. If a house could be a bastard, that'd be the one. I can see it in my mind's eye, clear as what I'm looking at now. The rusty bones of a tractor and plough stood in the overgrown front garden and there were tattered bedsheets hanging in the windows instead of curtains.

It was like climbing a mountain. The road to my house were never that steep but the wind was pushing us back and every step made my knees hurt and my breath catch in my throat. I hadn't even realized I was holding her hand! It felt strange, looking back to check on her and seeing her fighting along behind me like she was a child and I was her mam and I was taking her somewhere she didn't want to go. She looked really small like that. Huddled into herself, her arm in front of her head, clinging onto me for dear life. Maybe that's what made me strong. It got us up the hill anyways. I've never been so pleased to see my own front door. The thing nearly came off its hinges when I opened it, slamming open like it had been kicked by a giant. We fell into the house like we'd survived a shipwreck, soggy clothes and muddy boots and all. It was like we'd been thrown into the hallway by the sea.

We just stood there for a moment, once I'd slammed the door behind. Just leant against the bannister and the wall and got our breath back. I don't know if I was crying or if my eyes were just wet from the wind but when I think back I remember her all sort of fuzzy, as if I was looking at her through somebody else's glasses. She looked every bit as bedraggled as I did. Looked like she'd swum to my door through a river and a hedge.

'I thought I was going to be blown away,' I said, tearing off my coat. I wanted it all to be normal. Wanted to close my eyes so tight I could wipe out what had just happened. Water was running down my neck and I was soaked to my vest. I had fears of a chill. They always went to my chest. Spent half my childhood slathered in goose grease and wrapped in brown paper in front of the fire. Weak lungs, the doctors said. Strong heart, said Mam.

She pushed her hair back from her face. Wrung out her ponytail onto my carpet. I almost told her off for that. Almost asked who she thought she was. But she was already speaking.

'There was a man,' she said. 'In that crypt. The stone building under the purple tree. The laurel went right through it. There was a man. A body.'

I shook my head. Can't really say what for. It just felt that one of us should be saying something different. If one of us disagreed it would be more likely it wasn't true.

'That's the Kinmont Mausoleum. Been there for centuries. Of course there's bodies.'

'That was a man!' she said, and even as the rain and the wind battered the house it was the screech in her voice that went through me. 'He was . . . fresh!'

'He couldn't be. Who would put him there?' It was a daft question but it summed up my head in that moment. The idea was madness.

'We have to go back,' she said, and I saw her move towards the door.

'In this?' I goes. 'Are you mad?'

Her face twisted into something I didn't like. Her smile was like a gargoyle's, all leering and boggle-eyed. 'Mad? They think so. Some do. Maybe all. But I know what I saw. We can't just leave him there.' She stopped herself and I saw something else on her face, as if a fish had come to the surface to feed and then disappeared again without leaving much more than a ripple on the surface. 'That's his place. Stefan's. My boy. He liked it there. We played . . .'

I don't think it was in her to cry. She never did seem the type. That's maybe the closest I saw her to squeezing out a tear. She held onto them like they were gold.

'Come on, we'll get dry, wait out the storm and then go and tell someone. Whatever we saw will be easier to get a gander at when the rain stops.'

She seemed like she wanted to protest but then her teeth started chattering and she gave in to a shiver and suddenly the idea of tea and a fireside didn't seem so awful. She took her coat off in the hall but carried it with her to the sitting room, dripping water all the way. When she pulled her boots off she wasn't wearing socks. Her feet were pale, swollen things. They made me think of the eggs we made at Easter; hard-boiled in ferns and leaves and onion skins with mottled patterns all over their shells.

It always felt nice opening the door to the sitting room. We kept it warm. There was always a fire going in the big, old, wrought-iron cooker that had been there since they built the house a hundred years before. The heat would hit you like a wall. And I'd usually have baked. It would smell of pastry, or apple cake, or warm scones, mixed with whatever I was stewing for John's tea. It was all meat and pastry and crumbs and warm air; all laundry powder and starch.

'Look at it,' I said, mouth open, staring at the window. The rain was coming down so hard it could have been a mirror. I knew the view from that window so well I could have drawn it from memory but I could barely see it for the waterfall that was cascading down the window. My garden seemed to have been turned into a swirl of wet paint and the fields beyond were just a great soggy wedge the colour of new moss. 'We're going to be swept away.'

I handed her a warm towel from in front of the range, opening the oven door so the heat from the coals would pump another little cloud of heat into the room. Our clothes started to steam. I wanted to strip off, down to my vest and tights, but I couldn't do such a thing in the sitting room and it would have been rude to go upstairs and leave her by herself. So I stayed soggy. Towelled my hair and filled the kettle and rummaged in the good tin for the posh biscuits. Laid out the cups and saucers we'd only used a dozen times since we wed. Listened to the kettle rattling on the cooker top and the rain against the window. Those five minutes stretched like dough.

'You know what we saw,' she said. She had put copies of the *Hexham Courant* on the sofa and was sitting on them primly.

'Let's not think about it right now,' I said, and it sounded rather a hopeless thing to say. 'Do you want a change of clothes? I don't know what will fit but you'll catch your death—'

'I don't care,' she snapped. 'It doesn't matter. We need to—'

'Warm socks,' I said, too loud. 'I'll get you some of John's. I knit, he darns. They'll warm you through. Do you not wear socks in Oxford? Is that not the done thing?'

She looked at me like I was a mad person. Looked down at her feet, as if answers might be written on her mottled skin.

'I don't think about it,' she said, and the answer seemed to come as a surprise to herself as much as to me. 'I don't think I've worn socks since Stefan died. I don't know why. I don't know why I do most of the things I do. I can't use the machine we have and I got tired of scrubbing them in the sink. It didn't seem important.'

'You'll get chilblains,' I said, relieved to be onto a subject in which I was an expert. 'They're horrible things. Your feet split open like they're a sausage skin. Dad used to say you should soak your feet in a bowl of your own pee first thing in the morning, but it's not nice, is it? Nobody wants to see their father up to his ankles in his own water. It's not a position you want to be in when the doorbell goes.'

She gave a tiny laugh at that. Some colour appeared in her cheeks – two red circles, high on her perfect cheekbones, like you used to get on dollies.

'I can show you how to use the washer,' I said. 'It just takes practice.'

She managed to keep the smile on her face. Didn't speak again until I poured out the tea. She didn't say how she wanted it so I put two sugars in and a splash of milk. She didn't hold it by the handle the way I thought she would. Made a spider of her hand and held the cup by the rim, drinking through the gap between forefinger and thumb. I swear she may even have slurped.

'Coming back to life,' I said, and felt a little proud for having helped.

She ate two slices of apple cake. I think she didn't know she was hungry until she took a bite. Then it was like she remembered what food was for. She kept sniffing the air, as if trying to suck John's dinner from the oven. If I'd had it to spare I'd have offered her a plateful but John did love his liver and onions and there would have been merry hell to pay if he'd come home to find I'd given it to the pretty lass from over the river. He was a kindly soul but he worked hard and didn't deserve to be coming home to an empty plate.

'Can we talk about it?' she asked, quietly. There was steam rising from her damp clothes and she was making little nervous fists with her toes. I worried she was going to wear a hole in the carpet.

'We don't need to,' I said. 'Not until the storm . . .'

I stopped talking when I heard the back door going. We didn't hold much with knocking or standing on ceremony. People announced themselves by name and came straight in the back way. I was over the moon to hear Fairfax call out from the hallway.

'Fairfax coming in,' he shouted. 'Somebody forgot to build an ark!'

He pushed open the sitting room door. Stayed on the threshold of the room. He was wearing his green boots and thick cord trousers, shirt, tie and pullover. He was holding his green jacket over one arm and had his sodden cap in his hand. He looked startled to see Cordelia sitting there with her bare feet and bare legs, her soaking top clinging to her in a way that I hadn't thought of until I saw it as Fairfax must have done.

'Hello there,' he said, straightening up a bit. The old dog was nigh-on seventy but he made an effort of pushing the strands of ragged hair back across his patchy scalp and removed his spectacles for long enough to wipe the raindrops from their lenses and smear the drop of moisture from the tip of his nose. 'Get caught in it, did you? Aye, they said it would be bad but I weren't expecting this. Haven't known it come down like that in years! Cats and dogs and cows and sheep. Siling down!'

Cordelia shrank into herself a little. Looked to me like the air in the room had changed.

'This is Mrs Hemlock,' I said. 'From the old Zealand Farm. Mrs Winslow's.'

He nodded. Already knew. 'Still got the greengages at your place?' he asked. 'Did some work for old Mrs Winslow and she always said help yourself. Makes a tart kind of jam,' he said, then his long, loose-skinned face broken into a grin as he thought of a joke. 'Not a jam tart, though! Ha! I'll remember that!'

'This is Fairfax,' I said, before he could show me up any more. 'Mr Duke. Lives in the house yonder.' I smiled at him, the way I always found myself doing. 'He's a pest but he's harmless.'

Fairfax looked indignant. 'Harmless? How dare you. I'm still a danger. I'm a wounded lion, says I. Ferocious, in fact. Sharp of fang and lethal of claw.'

Makes me sad and happy all at the same time, thinking of him now. Forty years and I can still see that look on his face. Can't remember me own mam's face without looking at a photograph but I remember Fairfax, all pleased with himself and grinning; his little tape recorder always shoved under somebody's nose and comb-tracks through the Brylcreem in his fine hair.

'He has two of his own teeth left and he can't fasten his own shoelaces without help,' I said, grinning, and suddenly the storm seemed like something that had happened long since. 'Tea, Fairfax?'

'I won't say no,' he said. 'Permission to come aboard?'

'Boots off,' I said, refilling the kettle and peering out through the glass. The rain had eased off a touch but it was still torrential out there.

He started kicking his right boot off with the toe of his left. Leaned in the doorway, one big old hand on the jamb. Then she said it. Said what I hoped she would keep to herself.

'A tree came down in the churchyard, smashed through the old crypt. There was a man. A man in a blue suit and shiny shoes. He was dead.'

Fairfax stayed as he was. Stayed staring at the toe of his boot. Said nowt until I started cursing because the kettle was overflowing and soaking my sleeve.

'Tree come down?' he asked, eventually, straightening his back. 'The old laurel? Crying shame. Planted back in Reiver days, I'll bet.'

Cordelia's eyes burned into my back. I could hear temper in her voice. Temper at us. At Gilsland folk. Northern and daft and set in our ways. The sort of people who didn't want to know. The sort who didn't ask and didn't tell and minded their own bloody business. I think she hated us, then. I could feel it. Pure flaming loathing, like the tip of a poker. If I'd stuck my tongue out the spit in my mouth would have sizzled on the air.

'We don't know what we saw,' I said, as brightly as we could. 'But aye, yon tree made a right mess. Crying shame for the Kinmonts.'

'Not many of 'em left,' said Fairfax, one boot on and one off. 'Last of them is up at Greenhead and they won't have money for repairs. Maybe a whip-round, eh? I'd best assess the damage. My job, after all, though there ain't much wardening to be done when the church ain't being used.'

I heard her stand. Heard the rustle of her clothes and the crinkle of paper.

'I'll show you,' she said, flatly. 'I'm warmed through. I'm fine. Come with me and I'll show you what we saw.'

Fairfax gave a sigh. Rolled his eyes a little. 'Hold the tea, Felicity. The lassie wants me to get another soaking.'

'Lassie?' she asked, cocking her head.

'Stay where you are, miss. I couldn't live with myself if you got hurt. I'll pop down and have a gander and if there's owt as can be done I'll go straight to Samson's. Sgt Chivers drinks in there afternoons. We'll have him back up in a flash.'

'I want to go,' said Cordelia, though she sounded as though she could be persuaded to stay by the fireside.

'You stay,' he said, not unkindly. 'I can take a soaking. Easing off now anyways. And I've got the Roadster out front. Top's up, don't fret. Tractor's in barn too. It's only weather. Don't panic.'

I wasn't sure what to say. Didn't know whether I wanted him to go and see or to stay where he was and keep the whole thing uncertain. I suppose, looking back, I knew what he was going to find. There had been a body, right enough. Fresh enough I'd still have got a stew out of the meat on him and not worried about it being off. I've never thought of that moment without crying. Not 'til now.

'Don't go out in that silly little car in this weather. And only if you're sure, Fairfax . . .'

He smiled at me. Slipped his sock back into his boot and pulled on his hat and coat. I'd known him since I was a girl. Dad's friend. Bit of a rascal. Bit of a joker. Lost his boy in the war and aged about twenty years overnight. He'd become a bit crooked, as though he were carrying more weight on his shoulders than he was built for. But he always found the strength for a smile and a joke and he always made me feel like I was doing all right.

'Keep the pot warm,' he said, turning away. 'Be back before you know it.'

We waited for an hour and twenty minutes. I remember that exactly. I'd forgotten that the clock in the sitting room had a tick. I'd stopped hearing it. But I heard it count out every second of those eighty minutes and by the time I lost my patience and went to grab my coat, we were both ready to rip the thing off the wall.

The rain had lost some of its fury and the view from the

front door looked fresh and clean, as though everything had been scrubbed with wire wool. The road down the hill was a stream and there were fresh lakes by the edges of the road; deep and black as a wishing well.

We didn't speak as we tottered down the hill. I heard her footsteps through the water and I'm sure she heard mine. Heard my own breathing, and hers.

'Fairfax!' I shouted, pushing back through the gate.

I think I shouted it again, but perhaps I only got halfway through the word.

The tree had brought down more than the crypt. It had flattened half a dozen headstones and crumbled them like biscuits. The branches had dragged down a handful of smaller trees and their roots were now pushing up through the earth like giant snakes. I thought of fairy tales: a great tangle of thorns and worms and bones. It made me shudder. Made me want to turn away.

I felt her push past me. Saw her run to the mangled collection of rock and leaves and earth. Saw her reach out and jerk back as if electrocuted.

She turned to me with her mouth like a bullet hole. I had no answer for the question she asked with her eyes.

'I don't know,' I said, and meant it. I had no idea where the body had gone.

I think I left her there without saying another word. Walked back up the hill in case Fairfax had popped home for his car or a change of clothes.

John was waiting for me on the front step. Solid and straight, like a rock in a stream. I'd have run and kissed him if he held with that sort of thing. But something in his face stopped me. Something told me that my heart was about to get a fright.

'It's Fairfax,' he said, and he couldn't keep his eyes on mine. 'Went off the Spadeadam road. That daft car folded up like a penknife. Nivver stood a chance.'

CORDELIA

I called it my *nest*. Cushions from the sofa, laid out in a circle in the parlour. The scratchy woollen blankets from the guest bedrooms. The sheets from my own bed and the soft, velvet curtains I had found in a hamper beneath the windowsill in the attic. I dragged them all into the sitting room a couple of weeks after Stefan died. I arranged them like a wren positioning twigs. Made a circle of linens and drapes. Wove myself a comfortable, padded little sanctum on the bare wooden floor. I lit the space with a single oil lamp, feeling oddly proud at knowing how to fill and light the old contraption. Sat there, exhausted and manic, panting in my small, dark room, lit with the kind of glow beloved by painters and poets.

I kept the curtains closed but there was always enough light to read by. The only picture on the wall was a pencil sketch of a stately home and the shadows cast by the light sometimes conspired to make it seem as if the grand old place was lived in; as if a splendid family were holding riotous gatherings within its great walls. I liked to make up stories for that house. Imagined myself and Stefan and whichever man I saw fit to allow, gliding down polished stairs, my white-gloved hand unsullied by dust as it stroked the varnished wood of the bannister. I saw myself as Jane Eyre. As Cathy. Saw myself as every heroine who had inspired me in happier times. Sometimes I felt as though the world within that picture was more real than the one I inhabited. Every so often I imagined waking up behind the glass; a collection of pencil strokes and smudges.

That night, the night that Fairfax died, I don't think I even lay myself down. I sat in my nest like the only survivor of a catastrophe – the only passenger in the lifeboat, sitting up and staring into the distance as though hoping for land.

Within my nest I had grown used to sleeping for hours at a

time. Before Stefan died I made do with what I could. That's
a mother's lot, I suppose – especially with a child who doesn't
like to close their eyes. When he was alive I slept the way a
hungry man eats, gorging myself when opportunity arose, then
surviving on just enough scraps to stay upright. After his death
I feasted on sleep. Stuffed myself on it. Slept in a place of such
utter blackness that to wake felt like breaking through ice.

That night I knew there would be no sleep. I was too
energized to consider closing my eyes. 'Het-up'. That's what
Felicity called it. Said I was going to do myself a mischief.
Honestly, I think she'd have put leeches on my pulse-points
to try and drive the demons from my spleen if she hadn't been
in such a state herself.

Harking back, I remember the feeling of anger. Was that it?
Would anger do it justice? Perhaps it was something else. Some
feeling I cannot articulate. It makes me smile to think how that
failure would have angered me, back then. It was so important
to me to know what every word meant, and to be able to use
them in conversation without jarring. At Oxford, few things upset
me more than hearing an unfamiliar word. I remember when
Samuel, an MP's eldest son from a leafy borough in Surrey,
referred to his rooms at King's as his 'phontistery'. He'd said it
with a flamboyant sweep of his arm; adoring himself, a lesson
in confidence, a vision in his black velvet jacket and tangerine
chiffon scarf, with his dark curly hair and dead-eel pout. My
face had betrayed my lack of knowledge. He looked at me like
I was an infant. Pouted, patronisingly, at the silly girl who had
bumbled her way into the same college as so many more enlight-
ened souls. I made it my business to use the word in conversation
the next day. Learned its meaning. *A thinking place.* Samuel
heard me say it. Smiled that mocking smile. I still remember
the red circles of burning shame he brought to my cheeks. They
made a game of it, after that. Made up words and dropped them
into conversation, winking at one another as I scribbled them
down, desperate to open a dictionary and improve myself. They
probably thought they were just being funny. Didn't realize I
would have taken a hundred slaps from hard hands in place of
that one sensation of being a fraud; an imposter.

Samuel would have known the word for how I felt that night

as I sat in my nest and ground my teeth, grabbing blankets in my fists and sucking on my cheek until it hurt. Was it temper? Fury at being doubted? Sadness, even. Fairfax had seemed such a likeable man. Perhaps it was the sting of disappointment. I had glimpsed something other than the darkness of my constant grief. As the body tumbled onto the damp grass I had experienced something ignite within me. It was as if an ember had suddenly erupted in a dead hearth. For that heartbeat, as the rain battered down upon me and I looked upon the limp and broken corpse, I forgot Stefan. For that solitary tick of the clock, I escaped from the mire of my own grief. It felt like being thrown free of a burning car.

I'd seen him. Of that I was sure. He'd worn a blue suit. He had dark hair and polished shoes and he wore a khaki bag on a strap. His face was white and angular, like dough pulled into points. Not old but not young. A man. A dead man, hidden in a crypt alongside ancient bones.

'That doesn't matter now,' Felicity had said, as she snivelled into her sleeve. 'Fairfax. It's horrible. We should never have made him go out . . .'

I couldn't stand it. Not the self-pity. Not the weeping and the stooped shoulders and the shaking hands. I'd stayed in that churchyard an hour, looking for a body that shouldn't have been there. Only gave up when the rain started up again. Knocked on Felicity's door. Her husband opened it. A little man, with square shoulders and bandy legs and a lipless knife-wound of a mouth. He knew what had happened. Felicity had told him. He'd invited me in and offered tea. Handed me a towel. Told me what had happened to Fairfax. It seemed extraordinary. Two hours before he had been standing in the doorway of the kitchen. Now he was a mangled thing on a dirty, rain-lashed road.

'Sergeant Chivers will be up to talk to Felicity when he has time,' said John. 'He'll want to know what the old sod was thinking, driving in this weather in that daft bloody car. Should nivver have bought it but he wouldn't be told.'

He hadn't said it accusingly but Felicity had heard it as such. She'd given in to more tears. Shuddered and wailed and said it was all her fault.

'The body,' I'd said. 'He went to go and see the body we told him about. And now the body's not there.'

'This is the body in the crypt, then,' said John, and his expression was hard to read. 'Don't think on that now. Can't have been nice. Must have been a shock.'

I hadn't known how to respond. I think I looked a little petulant, like a child about to stamp their feet. What did I actually want? What would I have asked for if given the chance?

'The body's gone,' I said. 'There are old bones and scraps of clothes and bits of coffin under the branches of the laurel but the body we saw – it's been moved.'

He'd shaken his head at that. Flicked a finger at Felicity, as if to tell me to say no more that would upset her. I'd wanted to shout at the ceiling. Wanted to start smashing things. I think he saw that in my eyes. Saw that I wasn't going to be pacified with tea and the warmth of the kitchen.

Chivers never came to my door. I sat in the kitchen all night, waiting for the lights of his car to illuminate the blackness beyond the glass. Nobody came. The silence was absolute. I angled the chair so as to be able to hear the telephone if it rang in the hallway but it stayed maddeningly silent as the evening wore on. I had changed out of my damp clothes when I finished my long, soaking trudge back up the hill. I'd wanted to put on nothing more than a bathrobe or to simply wrap myself in a blanket but I had expected Chivers, and perhaps even a detective or two. I'd expected questions. Gentle probing. Conspiratorial glances and intelligent eyes. So I dressed smartly: a person to be taken seriously. White woollen polo-neck sweater and a black skirt. Even found my wedding ring at the bottom of the cutlery drawer and slipped it on. It was too big. Slid around on my finger like a hula hoop. I kept it on nonetheless. I was a married woman. I'd been to university. I'd suffered bereavement and I'd seen more of the world than any of them. If I said I'd seen a body then I was damn well to be believed. Nobody came. Nobody came the next day either. I rattled around the house, floating aimlessly into rooms I barely remembered having visited before.

It would have been a perfect home for somebody who actually wanted it. Three storeys high, with five acres of land, sitting halfway up a hill with a view across the tree-lined valley and the sound of the River Irthing occasionally bubbling up through the silence to soak into the old stone walls. It had stood for a hundred years and bore the mixed tastes of each of the previous inhabitants. Some of the rooms looked little changed from Victorian times with their high ceilings and dusty chandeliers, picture rails and ornate fire-places. Others were homely, as if a smaller, cosier residence had been crammed into the interior of the stately shell. I had made little impact. The books that had threatened to over-whelm my living space at college took up barely one shelf of the colossal library and the framed pictures of the Parisian jazz bands that had looked so sophisticated when I was nineteen seemed faintly ridiculous hung against floral wall-paper in the master bedroom with its sagging four-poster bed. Cranham had bought the place at auction. Took it lock, stock and barrel. Paid over the odds, no doubt. Stuffed hand-fuls of cash into the pockets of locals and told them to make it habitable. Probably held their handshakes a little too long; that little smile twitching in the corner of his eye. It was wrong of me to think of him in anything but affectionate terms. He had saved me, though by God I resented him for that. Took a woman who was carrying another man's child and offered her a home and an income. Had no interest in what I got up to or who I got up to it with. Just needed a wife and child and a cover story so his family and colleagues would stop questioning him about when he was going to find a wife. Needed one, if he was going to become a parliamen-tarian. Couldn't let the truth get out. Couldn't tell the world that he had as much interest in women as a fish does in aeroplanes. He liked men. Rough, dirty-faced, hard-skinned men. Kept one, almost as a pet, in the Knightsbridge flat where he slept on the nights he wasn't reclining on soft sheets in some luxurious hotel or another. He was a kind man, in his way. Did right by me when he really didn't have to. But we both knew what our marriage was for. He would have come to the funeral, had I given him the chance. There was no service. Just the cremation and my own mumbled words as I scooped up handfuls of what used to be my son and tossed them onto the breeze.

CORDELIA

I t was gone six when my patience snapped. I wasn't going to sit and wait for a knock at the door any longer. Wasn't going to stare at the telephone. I wanted answers. People should want to ask me questions. I had things to say.

The pub the locals called Samson's stood just beyond the railway bridge on the Northumberland side of the village. The geography of the place still makes my head spin. Gilsland is split in two by a boundary line that deposits half in Cumbria and half in Northumberland. The two sides have different councils. Different rules. Different attitudes, if you can believe such a thing. The Northumberland half thinks of Haltwhistle, Hexham and Newcastle as the nearest big towns and cities. On the Cumbrian side it's Brampton and Carlisle. Families divided from their neighbours only by an adjoining wall can pay different taxes and receive different services. And cutting across that invisible boundary line is the remnants of Hadrian's Wall – a risen scar, a lesson in the brutal efficiency of conquerors who reached Gilsland and decided they had probably gone as far north as anybody really needed to. It was a place on the edge of things – fragmented, disjointed. More past than present.

I had been in Samson's once before. A friend from university came to stay when I was seven months' pregnant. She wore a lemon-yellow raincoat and a tartan beret and in the sweat and cigarette fug of the bar we had felt like something from the circus as we sipped our pints and bathed in the silent glares of men who had no desire to see two young lassies in their pub and who resented having to hold in their farts for the sake of two silly girls. We'd found it funny at first. Drunk an extra pint just for bad. But the fun of it didn't last long and we were both pleased to leave, closing the door on the roar of angry words that followed our departure.

I was shivering by the time I reached the front door. The rain was still coming down in waves and my umbrella blew itself inside out as a military vehicle on its way from the RAF base tore past me and sent a puddle up my legs as far as my waist. I looked bedraggled and pitiful as I pushed open the door and walked into the main bar with as much bravado as I could muster.

The little man who pushed past me did so while doffing his cap. He was one of the few I was likely to recognize. His name was Parker and he lived in the house next to my own. He was an unsightly little fellow, with a hunched back and lips like lugworms. His wig looked like a squashed cat. Stefan had laughed at him without malice the first time he spotted him in the neighbouring field. I'd shushed him, but not with any gusto. Parker was a vile little imp: all twisted limbs and mottled flesh. He'd been there beside me when Stefan died. Trying to help. To be kind.

'Your pardon, Mrs Hemlock,' he said, knuckling his cap. 'Are you well?'

I was a bit startled by his closeness. I had a sudden memory of the past winter, when Stefan first fell ill. The Parkers knocking at my door. Could they help? Could they hold my hand as my son breathed his last? I swear, if I'd had a gun I would have killed Parker and his mousey little wife for no other reason than temper.

'There's a stag,' he said, and I heard the trace of his accent. 'We're looking for whoever hurt it. Left to bleed, it was. A terrible thing. Terrible.'

I looked past him at the other drinkers in the bar. Parker had been sticking a reward poster to the wall beside the counter. It was offering a tenner to anybody who could help find whoever had butchered a stag and left it to bleed to death on the forest floor out at Greenhead. That was typical of Parker. He saw himself as somebody important. A toff – that's what he'd have called himself. He had nothing against hunting and wouldn't have objected to a pack of hounds tearing into a fox, but he disliked the notion of somebody sticking a knife in a stag and letting the poor bastard bleed away.

'If you need anything,' he said, and his wormlike lips stuck together like wet jelly sweets as he spoke. 'Audrey and I – we're there for you. Whatever you might need.'

I gave him a little nod, my own lips unconsciously pressing together as I did so. He saw me mimicking the action and he looked sad for a moment, as if he had looked in a mirror and it had laughed. My heart softened at once and I was about to invite him to stay: to say an overdue thanks for the help he and his wife had given last year. But he was already shuffling past me. I reached for his arm and he turned to look at my eyes with such intensity that I feared my thoughts would be visible on the back of my skull.

'You don't have to be lonely,' he said, quietly. 'Not when there's people who would do anything to be your friend.'

I glanced around, wondering if we were being listened to. Everybody had their heads down. They were keen to see the back of Parker. He may have given plenty of money to the village but he was not really one of them. He read great big textbooks that he ordered from overseas and gave lectures at schools and village halls all over the neighbouring towns and villages. He liked the sound of his own voice, but more than anything else, he was difficult company. He didn't like to talk about the football or what was in the newspapers or whether Big Jim Cotteril really had killed a bull with a shovel out at Cumwhinton. He wanted to hear about people. Their private lives. Their relationships. Were they happy? Did they regret their decisions? What did they want from the future? Talking to him was like a job interview and the men of the village found it uncomfortable.

A moment later the door banged. Parker was gone and I was alone with the handful of drinkers who had made the journey to Samson's. The weather had kept the crowds away. Two men stood drinking at the bar and a fat man I recognized from the post office queue was seated at one of the square tables. He had a tube of glue unscrewed in front of him and was attempting to fix flights to a set of darts. He looked up as I approached the bar. Gave me a once-over. Decided I wasn't more interesting than the task at hand.

'Evening,' said the man behind the bar. I found out later his name was Stubbs. He was tall and sixtyish, with a ruddy face and an assemblage of risen, gnarled warts across his neck and forehead, as if he was in the habit of resting his cheek against a toad. He seemed friendly enough. A different man to the last time I was in.

'I was looking for Sergeant Chivers,' I said, and to my shame, I think I tried to make my accent sound more like the locals. I jerked my head a little too, like Felicity, pointing with her chin.

'Be in if he can,' said Stubbs. 'Roads are bloody awful.' He winced at his use of bad language in front of a woman. 'Apologies,' he said. 'What'll it be?'

I looked at the two other drinkers. Neither seemed remotely offended by my presence. The pub was no bigger than Felicity's kitchen. The walls were that yellowish-white that bald men's pillowcases go after a year or two. It smelled of cigarettes and mud; of wet clothes dried in damp rooms. Of spilled beer and burnt fat. There was a mirror behind the row of spirits behind the bar and the only other decoration on the walls were a collection of horse brasses, a picture of a ship that was hung so wonky it appeared to be trying to correct the waves, and a dartboard that seemed more holes than cork. Somebody had written 'Macker's a Puff' on the blackboard beside it.

I wasn't sure if I wanted to stay. I'd got myself ready to talk to Chivers. Had my whole speech planned. I wasn't ready to deflate yet. Wanted something more.

'We have an American whisky,' said Stubbs. 'Nice with a drop of lemonade. My wife's a fan.'

I found myself liking him. Gave him a smile that he seemed to like. Propped my elbow on the bar as if I had done this before.

'Had a shock, I'll bet,' said Stubbs, putting a glass in front of me. It was filled to the brim. I took a sip. It tasted of vanilla fudge and I nodded my appreciation.

'A shock?' I asked, reaching into the pocket of my leather coat for my purse.

'Yesterday,' he said, nodding in the direction of Denton. 'Put your purse away. There's a dozen drinks in the till for you already. There was a collection when you had your sadness. Nobody knew where to send flowers so they just put you a drink in if you ever came down the hill.'

It felt like there was something blossoming inside me. I pictured closed roses opening to the sunrise. I just nodded. Something between a grimace and a smile gripped my features and I took another long swig of the sweet drink.

'The wife was going to bring you something,' he said, resting large hands on the bar top. 'Wasn't sure what to bring. We were all sorry to hear. Bad business.'

'Thank you,' I said, tightly.

'What was the nipper's name?'

'Stefan,' I said, blinking rapidly, nails leaving crescents in my palms.

'You foreign, then?' he asked, chattily.

'No. I just liked the name.'

'First Stefan for me,' he said. Then he jabbed the air. 'Tell a lie. There was a Stefan in Holland, I think. I drove a wagon in the RAF. Celebrated the end of the war in this tiny place in the middle of nowhere. Street party like you wouldn't believe. Met a Stefan then. Trombone player, I think. Hard to remember. I'd had a few.'

I wasn't sure what to say. This was conversation. This was how grown-ups spoke. I realized how few such chats I had ever had; how few times I had spoken just for the simple exchange of stories and the passing of the time. I always wanted something, even if just to show off how much cleverer than them I was.

'Bad news about Fairfax,' he said, breathing out. 'I heard you had a wee chat not long before. Up at John Goose's place in Denton. Poor old soul, eh? Shouldn't have been out in it.'

There was no reproach in his voice but I sensed the other two drinkers subtly shift position so they could hear. I recognized one of them. He was a well-built man with curly black hair and lips like slugs. The shoulders of his checked shirt were soaked a darker hue than the rest of it and a faint steam rose from him, as if from compost.

'That's what I wanted to see Sergeant Chivers about,' I said. 'I thought he might have been up to see me.'

'Never rushes himself, our Chivvy,' smiled Stubbs. 'Takes an hour for a thought to reach his mouth, though that's 'cause it has to travel the half mile from his arse, if you'll pardon the language.'

I grinned. It might have reached my eyes. 'So he will be up, you think?'

'Don't know, love. What you got to tell him?'

I took another drink. Gave it two breaths of thought. Shrugged inside myself.

'When the storm hit a tree came down. Smashed into one of the old crypts. There was something inside. That's what I told Fairfax. He went to see. Next I heard he'd had an accident.'

'Aye, God rest him,' sighed Stubbs, shaking his head. 'Spadeadam road. The way that rain came down it's no wonder he got himself turned around, though you'd think he would be able to find his way in pitch bloody darkness given how long he's been here. Word is he was off to go and tell the vicar of Magdalene about the damage. Floods pushed him up the wrong road. Lost control going over the brow towards the base. Slammed on but skidded and went straight through the glass. Couple of lads from the base found him there. Bad state he was. Right mess.'

I closed my eyes. It was a horrible thought. I'd barely known him but I knew he would never have been out on the road had I not pushed him to go to the churchyard. Was he trying to impress me? He'd enjoyed looking at my legs. Had seemed a cheerful, playful sort of man.

'It's awful,' I said, and nodded when Stubbs enquired if I wanted another drink.

'Been through a lot had Fairfax. Lost his son at the tail end of the war. Was a wireless operator who should have been miles from danger. His boy were a soft soul. Bad eyes and a weak chest but he signed up rather than be called up. RAF, same as me, though we were never anywhere near one another. Radio station he was in took a direct hit. Fairfax were broken up, you could tell that, but he kept it in, like you had to. Dealt with it the right way. Crying shame. Had a gift for words did his son. Reckon he would have been a writer if he'd made it back. Fairfax would have been proud as you like. If you ask me that's the only reason he took it up himself. Helped him feel close, if that doesn't sound too feeble.'

I wasn't sure what he meant. Told him so.

'You must be one of the few he never talked to,' said Stubbs, with a laugh. 'Quite the scribbler, was Fairfax. Wrote a couple of little pamphlets on the history of Gilsland. Another on walks along the Roman Wall, which made him few friends, I can tell you. Last thing we need is even more people up here. We're at capacity.'

I looked around at the empty bar. Raised an eyebrow.

'Was he good?' I asked.

'At what?'

'Writing.'

He scratched his chin. Shrugged. 'Good at asking questions. Always jotting stuff down, like a journalist in a film. Needed a hat with the word "Press" in it to complete the look. Wanted to do a book on the people of Gilsland. Said it had a fascinating history, which I don't suppose I can argue with. Always asking if he could pop over for an interview. That's what he called them, his chats. Interviews.'

'What was he working on?' I asked, and while the snobbish part of me was eager to dismiss his efforts as the works of an amateur, I still found myself eager to read the results.

'Something on the old camp,' he said, sucking his lip. 'POW place up the road. All gone now. Was a big old set-up in its day though. Hundreds of Germans. Thousands maybe. You must know this, love, you can't not have heard.'

I found myself embarrassed. Temper flashed, as it always did when I found myself not knowing the answer to something.

'I've not become encyclopaedic, no,' I said, and immediately heard myself sounding like a snooty cow. I softened my face and tone. 'I'm interested though.'

'There's books and stuff. People remember. Some of the prisoners even stayed. Married local girls. To be honest, Fairfax would have been the one to talk to, if you do want to know.'

I looked down at the varnished bar. Drew a stick man in some spilled beer. It looked twisted, like it had fallen from the sky.

'Here's to Fairfax,' said Stubbs, who had pulled himself a pint of muddy brown ale. The other drinkers joined him in a salute and they spent the next few minutes talking about what a menace he had been with his questions and his jokes and the pride he had taken in a car he had bought which so ill-suited the local roads.

Hearing about the dead man's life only made me regret his death all the more. I sipped at the next drink. Took off my coat and hung it over the open hatch that led behind the bar.

'We don't get many ladies in on weeknights,' said Stubbs. 'Nice to have a pretty face instead of these ugly mugs.' He gestured at his regulars, who obliged him with harmless scowls. 'You were in before, weren't you? You and some lass dressed like a daffodil. Busy night, that one. Sorry if you didn't get to see the place at its best. Not everybody's so forward thinking.'

There was a sharp laugh from the man with the black hair.

'Aye, there's a couple of cavemen, right enough. Couple who reckon a lass should be home and not in here with the likes of us.'

He turned to me as he said it but there was nothing unpleasant in the way he looked at me.

'Changing times,' I said.

'Pike doesn't think so.'

Stubbs pursed his lips and blew out a lungful. Took a cigarette from the packet in his shirt pocket and lit it, blowing out a lungful of smoke and resting his elbows on the bar as if settling in to tell a story.

'You know Pike?'

I shook my head. I may have heard the name but couldn't be sure.

'Lives next to that church you like. Scruffy place.'

My memory filled with pictures of the tumbledown cottage with the holes in the roof and the sheets at the windows; the peeling paint and rusting machinery on the scrap of lawn.

'Lives there with his old mum. Reckon they built that house around them and when it falls down he'll still be inside. Bit of a terror is Pike, if you don't know how to take him. Banned him from here a dozen times though it's never good for trade. He just tells the regulars what'll happen if they come in drinking when he's not allowed. I always end up inviting him back.'

'I don't think I've seen him.'

'He'll have seen you, love. Always got his eye on a pretty lass, if you'll forgive me saying it. Got himself in bother as

a younger man. Too young to fight in the real war but he was
in Korea. Came back a bit damaged. Told us one night that
the ladies over there weighed no more than a kiddie. Couldn't
do a damn thing to stop you – even those who tried to.' He
raised his hands, aware that this was probably no topic for my
company. 'Sorry love, mouth running away with me. Don't
be worrying, you're a married woman, which means you're
not his type. And if you ask me he prefers fighting to courting.
Had a couple of fiancées but he'll never go up the aisle.
Wouldn't get past the wedding guests without seeing somebody
who needed a punch. We had some of the Irish in a few months
back. Good lads. Maybe a bit full of themselves but no harm.
Their accents upset Pike. He asked one of them to keep it
down and they apologized. Then the volume started going
back up again. Pike doesn't ask twice. Took the stick he uses
for killing trout and clubbed Paddy on the back of the neck
so hard it's a miracle his skull didn't break. Tore through the
lad's mates like they were dolls. He's a devil when his temper's
up. Chivers would have needed a vanload of coppers to take
him in and even then I think he'd have been too scared to try.'

'What happened?' I asked and in my mind I started counting
the number of steps from Pike's front door to the site of the
broken crypt.

'Nowt happened, love. Paddy went home with a bandage
on. We sent a bottle of whisky to the house he was staying in
with his mates. Sent the Heron to have a little word with Pike.'

'The Heron?' I asked, confused.

He smiled at me. 'You don't know anybody do you? Heron's
what we call Trevor Halpin. Used to be a gilly at the castle,
looking after his lordship's lakes. Big lad. Didn't take to being
talked down to. Not an ounce of anger in him but has a good
sense of right and wrong and knows when a person deserves
a thump. Probably the only person who can keep Pike from
being Pike, though if I were the Heron I wouldn't sleep well,
knowing that mad bastard were holding a grudge. He lives
where he pleases. Old barns and empty cottages you wouldn't
keep pigs in. Helps himself to his lordship's salmon and takes
it personally if any bugger kills a deer with owt other than a
clean shot. And he can tek Pike.'

'That's why you call him the Heron.'

Stubbs grinned. 'Can tell you've been to university.'

I stayed for two more drinks. Bought a round for the other drinkers. My coat was almost dry by the time I slipped back into it.

'I can walk you home,' said the dark-haired drinker, who had admitted to the name of Ray. 'I doubt Chivers will be in now. Probably found himself somewhere dry or followed the smell of chips and got a feed. We'll send him up to you. I'll walk you back.'

'I'll be fine.'

'Lot of people passing through,' he said, seriously. 'You must hear the roar of the rocket.'

'From the base? Sometimes.' I had a flash of memory and smiled at it. 'I used to tell Stefan it was a dragon.'

'Aye, maybe. They don't drink in here so I can't say what sort of lads they are. But I don't like the thought of you going back out in that rain. Not on your own.'

'I've been here two years. You've never worried before.'

They looked at me like I was mad. 'You've never been in here before, love. Never been ours to worry about.'

'And now?'

He shrugged, as if the answer was obvious. But I didn't let him walk me home. I didn't feel the rain as I smiled in the darkness and trudged through the downpour up the hill. My head was full of mysteries and questions.

The air base.

Pike.

A writer's father, dead on the Spadeadam road.

I slept soundly that night. I didn't wake. Didn't hear anybody lift the latch on the back door and move through my house. Didn't feel the eyes of an intruder, staring upon me with the intensity of sunlight through glass.

That knowledge came later, when I looked at the muddy footprints I had left on my route through the house and saw them overlaid with boot prints that dwarfed my own.

FELICITY

Transcript 0003, recorded October 29, 2010

My friend Janet came with me to sort out Fairfax's things. John had offered but he would have been more hindrance than help. It's not a job for a man, that sort of thing. They get sentimental. Start telling you that this and that has got to stay and before you know it you haven't so much got rid of the rubbish as rearranged it. And Fairfax had plenty rubbish to rearrange.

'Bloody pigsty,' muttered Janet, looking around the living room and pulling that face she used to use when the farmers were spreading slurry on the fields.

'It's clean,' I said, sticking up for him. 'Just cluttered.'

'Aye,' she goes. 'Cluttered with muck.'

It were hard to argue. It looked like somebody had left a window open during a hurricane. If I hadn't known him I'd have thought it the house of somebody not right in the head. It was like he'd been stealing other people's rubbish just so his own had company. Empty cans, papers, post, dirty mugs, plates that looked like those things artists hold while they're painting. Books and newspapers and folders that spilled their sheafs of writing paper onto the mucky carpet like a lorry shedding its load. The unit by the wall that used to display little figurines and thimbles was now a dump for notebooks, all brimming over with pots of pens and brown cardboard tubes stacked like logs. There was a pair of women's shoes on the windowsill. And the dust! I could have run my finger through the air and it would have turned black. I were embarrassed for him, truth be told. Sad he'd let it get like this. He'd always looked smart enough when he popped in. Maybe a bit crumpled but his socks matched and he didn't smell bad. If I'd known he were living like that I'd have offered to give him a hand. Poor old soul. Was that why he kept popping to my house? Had he been escaping from the mess? Hoping I'd take pity on him and offer to show him how to live right? I felt tears pricking me eyes at that. I thought I'd cried them all out the night he died. Cried for him, and for Cordelia's baby, and for those poor sad bones and scraps of clothes in the churchyard. Cried for myself too. Cried for telling lies.

'You don't think he's been robbed, do you?' asked Janet, all dramatic and loving it.

'What would they take?' I asked. 'There's no gaps in the mess, is what I mean. It's not like anything seems to be missing.'

'He must have had money. That car . . .'

'He spent all he had on that car,' I said, shaking my head and feeling bad about every bloody thing. 'He said as much to our John. Bloody silly thing to buy.'

'Well . . .' she goes, 'he's paid the price right enough.'

I had to turn away before she saw me bawling. Found myself getting all upset again and remembering the house as it had been when I were a girl. Before the war. Fairfax's son, Christopher, ten years older than me, sitting at the dinner table, leaning his head on his arm as he scribbled furiously onto page after page of lined paper. Fairfax kept throwing him proud little glances. His mam worked around him, putting out plates and dishing up meat and veg and talking to me mam and dad as if it were the most normal thing in the world to have a nigh-on grown man sitting writing stories at the table on Christmas Day. I always wanted to ask what he was writing but Dad had told me not to bother him. I never did. Never found out what he saw in his imagination. That was the bit I cried for when we heard he'd died. Never getting the chance to ask.

'Did you know it were getting like this?' asked Janet, looking around her at the mess, and I thought it sounded a bit harsh, the way she said it.

'No,' I said, and I had me dander up enough for it to come out in me voice. ''Course not.'

I hadn't been in Fairfax's place in an age and I hadn't been in the living room since I was a girl. His wife were still alive then. Enid. Big bull of a woman who walked like a man and only had two fingers on her right hand. We always wanted to know whether it had been an accident or if she'd been born like that, but it felt wrong to ask. Dad once joked that she'd been born giving a V-sign to the world but Mam told him off for that. She told him off for a lot. Enid died in '51. Not much of an age. Didn't look like herself any more neither. Had shrunk a little. There were a lot like that, back in the forties. People who just withered and folded inwards. Got smaller, as though they were moving away from you. It were loss that did it. Loss of something precious. Christopher, in her case. Hit her hard when her boy didn't come back from the war. Went grey in the space of a week, and I don't just mean her hair. Something went wrong with her insides. She was buried in the same plot as her son.

'I don't know where to start,' said Janet, hands on her hips. She looked like a teapot in a cosy. 'Where would he keep it?'

'I never asked,' I said, and got one of her nasty looks as reward.

It was common practice in those days to keep an envelope full of your important bits and pieces somewhere safe – just in case you suddenly upped and died. It was just manners, really, and a way of ensuring nobody went through your things after you'd gone and made snidey remarks about the dust on the top of the wardrobe. It never contained very much, as a rule. Maybe an insurance policy, if you had one. A copy of your will. Deeds to your house, if you owned it, and Fairfax did. Maybe even a letter, if you'd had the courage to write one. Always seemed a bit ghoulish to me, that. How would you even start it? The devil in me always thought it would be fun to leave a note just saying: *'Dear Snooper – I'm standing right behind you'*, though I never told anybody that as they would have thought me awful.

Anyways, Janet was moaning. Wittering on. Mumbling about not having the time for this and how she were never that fond of the nosy old bugger anyway. Janet had a good soul but there were limits to how long her acts of charity would last. She had a habit of losing patience without any prior warning. One wet Sunday she'd thrown a carving fork at her eldest son while washing the dishes, just because he'd asked her one too many times whether she knew where something was. It had stuck in the wall beside his head, juddering like a terrier's tail. Then she'd gone back to cleaning the pots. The holes were still in the kitchen wall. She wouldn't paper over them. Liked them to serve as a reminder to her husband and bairns that their mam could only be pushed so far.

We worked in silence for a couple of hours or more. We heard wind and rain battering the windows and the roof. It had been damn ugly as we crossed the road. Sky was grey and purple. Put me in a mind of trout just out the freezer; stiff and sad and dead.

'Church will need a new warden,' said Janet, while she pushed stuff about half-heartedly and watched me work. Never was subtle, our Janet. Even at school she had a way of asking questions that made you feel like she had you in thumbscrews.

'Don't think there were much wardening involved,' I said, on my knees by the sofa, sifting through a great stack of crinkly yellow copies of the *Hexham Courant*.

'Title's important though,' said Janet. 'You think your John might like it?'

'He's busy enough,' I said. 'Not really a one for church anyways. And it's a job for somebody from Denton. Gilsland at a push. He's Brampton.'

Janet accepted that. There was only nine or ten miles distance between our house in Denton and his family place in Brampton but they were miles that mattered. It would be years before John was thought of by the blokes in Gilsland as anything other than an outsider. They even gave me a bit of grumble for moving from Gilsland to Denton when I got wed, and that were under a mile. Always seemed odd to Cordelia, all that stuff. She couldn't understand why boundaries mattered, especially in a place twisted around a 2000-year-old wall and then split into different counties by civil servants.

'You never got me told,' said Janet. 'Fairfax. I heard tell he'd been at yours, though there were nowt unusual with that. Did I hear right? Went to go and inspect the churchyard in the middle of a storm and shot off in his car like a bullet from a gun. Poor old soul. You think his head was going a bit?'

I felt a bit funny at that. Nervous, like – as if I were being interrogated. We'd been friends since before we could talk. Our mams were close as sisters and they raised us the same way, though if I'm honest, I don't know if I would have picked her as a best friend if there had been more to choose from. Knowing she was my age always made me feel like I was getting old because, God love her, Janet was never a looker. She was short and round and looked to me like a clay sculpture that had been sat on just before it went in the oven. She had the manners of a tinker, too; forever sniffing back snot or ramming a finger in her ear and rummaging about. She were a burpy person too, and I'd never liked that. Always seemed to be fighting a battle with a bit of trapped wind. Even belched during her wedding vows. I blushed for her but she thought it were funny and at least the man she were marrying could see what he was letting himself in for. I rarely lost my temper with her, though sometimes I would give her one of my looks and she'd know she was going too far. John says I have an impressive 'look'. Reckons if I glared at a plucked chicken for long enough it would be ready to eat.

'He'd come to see if I was all right,' I said, and realized I was talking to her backside. She was bent over, pulling the tops off the tubes from the dresser and fiddling about with the contents.

'Got caught in the storm, had you?' she asked, over the swell of her bum. It was like talking to a bloody armchair.

'Been to Mam's grave,' said I, matter-of-fact about it. 'Met the lady from up the hill. Mrs Winslow's old place.'

She turned at that. Flared her nostrils.

'That snooty thing? Married to the great fat man?'

'You know who I'm talking about,' I said, in no mood for her games.

'Spent a fortune on that place and she doesn't deserve any of it,' sniffed Janet, and her head went further into the rubbery folds of her neck. 'You seen the old orchard? Like a jungle. And there were a decent enough turnip field came with it. Just left it to rot, she did. Could have offered it out if she didn't want it. But that would mean speaking to the likes of us.'

I found myself offended on Cordelia's behalf. 'She doesn't know farming, Janet. And her husband works in London. She's all alone up there. And she's had her grief.'

Janet softened a little at that. 'Aye, were a tragedy. Where did she bury him? Family church, was it?'

I said nowt. Didn't want to tell her she'd had her son cremated and scattered among the headstones like confetti at a wedding.

'What was she like?' asked Janet, standing up. She was holding a map and squinting at it.

'Like?' I asked.

'Snooty, was she? Bet she was.'

'She was fine,' I said. 'Bit stand-offish but she's been through a lot. She's lonely, I think, though she doesn't know it. She's been to university, y'know. Got a good head on her shoulders.'

Janet gave a shake of her head, like a dog trying to dry off. She wasn't impressed.

'Tree came down near you, I heard.'

I felt it in my chest. A tightening, like somebody was pulling at the straps of my bra.

'It did,' I said, and hoped she'd shut up about it. 'Crashed down on the Kinmont tomb. That's where Fairfax was heading, so they say. To tell the family about the damage.'

'In that weather? On the Spadeadam road?' Janet wasn't having any of it. 'He must have had a bang to the head.'

'Got himself muddled, I reckon,' I said, and I suppose I meant it. 'He took a shine to Cordelia. Maybe he was trying to play hero.'

Janet's features went pointy. She was cross. 'Cordelia, is it?' she asked, in her fake lah-di-dah voice. 'She was in your house?'

'I told you, the storm came down.' I don't know why she were being such a cow about it. I tried explaining. 'She would have got drenched walking all the way back up to her place.'

Janet sniffed and gave the map more attention. 'Well, you know her better than I do so I couldn't say whether she can handle the rain or not.'

I got myself a bit flustered. Janet turned her shoulder to me, just like she did at school when I admitted to playing with somebody else while she had been at an uncle's house over the summer. She didn't like to share me.

'What you got there?' I asked, trying to lighten the mood.
'Map,' she said, pettily.
'Where of?'

She thrust the map at me. Her look said I might as well
take this as I had already taken everything else, whereas life
had given her nothing but slaps and cow shit. She loved to
tell people she'd only been put upon the planet to be shat
upon. Our John had a reply to that. Said it were nobody's
business what went on in another couple's bedroom.

I turned over the map. Saw more of Fairfax's spidery writing
on the other side. I couldn't make much of it out but he seemed
to have been copying out of a reference book. The words 'Le
Tanneur' were underlined and he had scribbled a drawing of
a stick man hanging from a rope in one of the gaps between
his sentences. I found myself reading before I could tell myself
to stop.

'. . . *born 1910, Limousin area, links to Alsace region,
apprenticed to a leatherworker . . . arrests for theft, violence,
sex assault . . . jailed for knife attack on suspected love rival
. . . freed by Vichy Government. Trained by Milice due to local
knowledge. Excelled in interrogation. Witnesses to incident in
Tulle describe "dispassionate" way in which he used burning
coins on the skin of victim. Left victim alive . . .*'

I tried to stop reading but I found myself entranced by the
words.

'. . . *fled in 1944, three weeks after D-Day. Captured by
Maquisards. Evidence to suggest he was disfigured in the
traditional manner . . . large swastika carved into skull . . .
last seen in 1946 in rural Normandy . . . thought to have been
killed by Resistance or living under assumed identity after
collaboration with security forces . . .*'

I felt cold all the way through. Didn't know whether to
throw the map down or start a fire and toss it on the flames.
The words were ugly.

'What's this bloody thing?' asked Janet, looking behind the
sofa and dragging out a large, butter-coloured box. She put it
on the table and opened the clasps. 'Typewriter! Well I never.
Fairfax as a secretary, eh? I'd never have given it credence.'

I looked at the object she was staring at. It was a nice

looking bit of kit; white, circular keys and a black body, all
oiled and greased and expensive-looking. It had the name
'Remington' stencilled on the front.

'He typed, did he?' asked Janet. Then she looked around
at the bundles of paper with their scribblings in ink. 'Well I
never. Why all this scrappy writing, eh? Why not just type it
all up?'

I stared at her as she pressed the keys. She fiddled with it
the way she would have fiddled with any object she had
discovered. None of it mattered to her. She was here to poke
about, and so far, nothing she had found satisfied her curiosity.
I didn't like the way she played with it. Didn't like the tension
between us. So I let myself down good and proper. Blurted it
out like a kiddie with a secret.

'Did you hear what we saw?' I asked. I tried to make it
sound juicy – to get her back on side.

Janet took a moment, as if deciding whether the gossip was
worth changing her face for. In a moment she decided it was.

'Aye, Sally in post office said when the tree came down
there were bones and all sorts came out. You must have had
a fit with your nerves.'

I nodded, quick and urgent. 'There were more than that,' I
said, and suddenly I felt excited, like I was about to run a race
or go to a dance. 'One of the bodies that flew out – seemed
like it hadn't been there long. And there hasn't been anybody
buried in the Kinmont grave for nigh-on forty years. This
bloke had on a suit and new shoes and he was carrying a bag.
There was still meat on his bones. And his face! I swear, had
I known him I could have recognized him – that's how far
from a skeleton he was.'

Janet moved closer. There was a flush of colour in her
cheeks and she dropped her own voice; delighted.

'And you told Fairfax?' she asked, and her mouth went
into an 'O', like the end of a trumpet. 'That's what he shot
off for, I'll bet. Went to find Sergeant Chivers. He might
have been up at the air base. Spends a good bit of time up
there, according to my Maurice. And if Fairfax was wanting
to play hero . . .'

I nodded, twisting the map in my hands. I felt hot under

my vest. It was sticky in the room, despite the storm. It was
that muggy, unpleasant heat that makes your hair stand on end
and everything tastes funny. Had I done right? Was there any
wrong to be done?

'I feel so guilty,' I said, hoping she'd have some nice words
for me in return. 'He was only out driving in that silly car
because of what I told him.'

Janet weighed it up and seemed to decide there was no sport
in being a cow. 'He wouldn't have shot off to tell the Kinmont
lot without seeing the damage for himself,' she said. 'So there
must have been something to see. So why haven't I heard
about a body being found in the graveyard?'

I heard the crinkling of paper as I twisted the map into a
Christmas cracker and unfolded it again. I couldn't shut myself
up now. Had to keep talking.

'There was no body when we went back to check,' I said,
dropping my voice. 'The tree had smashed through the tomb
and there was stone and mud and bits of all sorts on the ground
but whatever we'd seen, it was gone.'

'You've told Chivers this?'

'I kept it a bit vague,' I said, and if I were the type to blush,
my cheeks would have burned.

Janet nodded. She reckoned I'd done right. 'Best off out of
it,' she said. 'Could have been anything and if you're not
certain then you don't want to go putting yourself forward.
Not if it cost old Fairfax his life.'

I must have looked like I was going to cry at that because
Janet immediately took a step forward and rubbed my arm. I
took a handkerchief from my sleeve and wiped my eyes and
nose. 'It was frightening,' I said. 'Horrible. Horrible.'

Janet nodded. I could see her struggling with herself. She
wanted more from this story. Wanted some other delicious
titbit.

'Cordelia was convinced,' I said, almost whispering.
'Wouldn't be told. Convinced, she was. Ready to swear blind
we'd found a body. But it's a graveyard. I mean, there's bound
to be bodies. And what do I know about the freshness of
corpses?' I shuddered at the sound of the word. 'It could have
been a hundred years old and just looked like that because the

crypt had stopped him turning mushy. Who are we to say?'

'True, true.' A smile split her face. 'Imagine if it weren't old, though. Imagine if it were a body. Like in the films. And you'd stumbled on where he'd been stashed.' She got playful then. Started being the bully she could be at school when fancy took her. 'He might have been watching! Whoever stashed him there. Might have seen what you saw. Ooh, Felicity, you could be in bother.'

I put my hands over my ears. Suddenly I was seven years old again and she was telling me where babies came from and I was crying and begging her to stop. She didn't when we were kids and she didn't then. Kept right on. Kept teasing. 'You heard anything from your friend Cordelia these past couple of days? Like you said, she's up there alone. And she's the one who wouldn't let it drop. Funny place is Gilsland these days. All those people passing through, and who knows what goes on at the base. Sometimes it's what you see which gets your eyes closed permanently . . .'

'Stop it,' I said, and I suddenly felt like I was coming down with a chill; all shivery but hot and sticky.

'Maybe that's what happened to Fairfax,' said Janet, revelling in it. 'Saw what you saw and got himself in bother.'

'No!' I yelled, and it sounded loud in that little muddled room.

Janet stopped and her face reddened. She'd been mean and knew it, but as ever, her embarrassment became temper.

'You're a soft soul, Felicity. Was just playing with you. I've no time for this now anyways. I've got children to feed. You sort this out if you like but when I said I'd help I didn't know I was clearing up a bomb site. I'll see you in the week.'

I didn't speak as she left. Just stood shivering and feeling wretched. I didn't like being such a weakling but Janet had always enjoyed seeing how long it took to pull my hair before tears came to my eyes.

I went back to tidying. Sorted the stuff into neat piles and took the dirty dishes to the kitchen. Put the map back in the tube without really taking any notice of the words or the place names. I went to the kitchen and washed the pots and poured the milk away. Couldn't face upstairs. Didn't want to see the state of his bedroom or breathe in the aroma of an old man's privacy. Stayed downstairs. Made a pile of useful foods from the fridge and loaded them into a fruit box to take home. I could smell Fairfax in that kitchen no matter what I did. Could smell the man I knew and not the sloven who had left the filth in the other room. I had a sudden memory of him, leaning against the metal draining board, notebook in his hand, asking me questions about my memories of Dad. Memories of school. Of seeing the work crew from Camp 18 fixing fences out towards Low Row. His pencil was a blur. He looked happy and sad as he wrote, like he was enjoying it but knew the enjoyment came from a sad place, if that makes any sense. He wrote to feel close to Christopher, but that was as close as he would ever get.

I spent a few moments in the pantry. There were jams in there from a decade back. I recognized my own handwriting on the damson jelly label from '61. There were tins of meat and trays of eggs. A barrel for biscuits full of crumbs. Tea. Tins of baked beans, stacked like mortars. A first-aid box, issued in wartime. I thought there might be plasters inside. Maybe gauze. I used to burn myself on the cooker a lot and if he had any spare ointment I knew where it would find a good home. I opened the box. The keys stared up at me like treasure. A great bunch of them, like somebody would carry on their belt in a castle. Church keys. Crypt keys. Keys to the outbuildings in the church grounds.

Maybe a whole minute went by as I stood looking at those keys. I'm not sure my brain has ever worked as fast. I don't even know where the impulse came from. I just suddenly had a flash of something I didn't know I knew, like when you look at your husband's crossword puzzle and somehow just know the answers to the questions and you daren't tell him in case he thinks you're calling him a fool.

I took the keys. They were cold and heavy and there was mud on the body of the biggest one. I slipped them into my sleeve. They made a bulge like a muscle and felt cold against my skin. I closed the door to the pantry, pulled on my coat, closed the back door and stood on the back step like a thief. The rain had eased but the road was not far off being a river and I knew I would get wet to the knees just walking back to my own front door. Might as well turn right at the junction instead of left. Might as well hurry down to the church while John was at work.

When I tell you this was out of character I don't want you to think I'm exaggerating. I swear, this was so unlike me it felt like I had just decided to fly to the moon. I don't even know what I was planning. Perhaps I had been bitten by the bug of excitement and needed to do something daring. Maybe I liked that feeling of my heart beating in my chest.

The rain started coming down again as I fumbled with the lock of the church. It was set in an iron casing, sunk into wood so weathered and worn it could have been a timber from the ark. There was no doubting which key would open the church door. Nor any protest from the lock as I turned it. The lock had been well-tended. Oiled and frequently used.

I pushed open the door to the church as if I was breaking into a torture chamber. I stood in the doorway for an age. Felt the cool air on my hot, damp cheeks. Stood in that great rectangle with its wooden pews and its distant ceilings, vast flagstones and its dark shadows. The stained-glass windows offered almost no light and there were no switches on the wall but instinct made me reach out to the recess by the door and close my hand around the waxy candles. I found matches too. Lit myself a feeble torch that turned the half-black air into a golden circle of red, purple and yellow.

There were footsteps on the dust of the floor.

Almost sleepwalking, shivering so hard that the candle was fluttering in my hand, I followed the footsteps to where they became lost in a big old smudge of different patterns. Fairfax had kneeled here. You could tell just by looking. He'd eased himself onto his side by the third row of pews. I peered forward, squinting. Felt around in the old wood of the pew. A keyhole. A mouth set in the wood. I found a likely key and slid it into the gap. It opened as easily as the door.

I reached inside.

The papers were ragged. Crumpled. Even in the half-dark I could see they had been blackened and singed. They had been saved from fire. They still smelled of smoke.

Why did I take them? I still don't know. But the words that
I read on those grey and yellow pages changed me so deeply
they may as well have been carved into my heart with a blade.

EXTRACT. TR 046.

I recognized the boy strapped to the bonnet. I don't think I knew his name but he was familiar to me in the way . . . that somebody you see every day on your way to work is familiar to you. Almost enough to nod hello to. The sort you can't instantly place if you see them out of context. I was looking at him with my head angled, unconsciously mirroring the way he was looking at me. He wasn't really alive any more. He wasn't dead either but the way he looked; the absence in his eyes, none of that looked like life. It was Milice work. Favre's work. They stood beside the men in uniform. Shadows. Three or four of them; blobs of oil among the grey of the uniforms. Torturers. Killers. Zealots. We feared them more than we feared the Germans. They had chosen this life. Opted to kill their own kind.

'Move. They are staring. Come. Come.'

I was still gazing at the Maquisard's face. Freedom fighters – that is how they have come to be known. The Resistance. Good men. Brave men. But this was no man. He was no older than me. But he had not eaten so well nor enjoyed the comforts of a warm bed or a hot bath. He had lived hard. There was dirt on his face beneath the dried blood. He was already filthy before they started hurting him.

What can I remember? I don't know the words for it. Confusion, more than anything. Some fear, but not the way you would think. We didn't know what was going to happen. Nobody did. It was just the noise of the half-track's treads crunching over the stones – those boots brisk and neat as the men in uniform closed off the streets. Our questions were muted. We asked each other – not the intruders. We whispered in one another's ears. Did anybody know? Had anybody done anything wrong? Had somebody told lies?

The officer who spoke was dark-haired. Round-faced. He didn't close his mouth all the way when he wasn't speaking, *as though his jaw had been broken at some point and improperly set. Mother would have told me off for hanging my mouth open like that. Would have called me a panting dog.*

He didn't seem angry. Even looked like he admired the village. Glanced around admiringly, as if he was holidaying and found himself pleased with his choice of destination. He was shiny and clean. The men he led were not. They looked bloodied and exhausted and they looked at us with eyes dark as the treads of the tank.

'For every one of my men you have killed, we will kill three Maquisards,' he shouted, in the silence of the square. 'You will tell me you are not Maquisards. You will tell me there are no Maquisards here. You will feign ignorance and spit on the ground at the mention of their barbarous deeds. And many of you will be telling the truth. But the truthful ones will pay the price for the lies of the others. We will offer no mercy. If we shoot a child, we have stopped them growing into an enemy. If we kill a woman, we have stopped them breeding a new generation of swine. Tell me, now, who are the Maquis among you. Speak up and you will have my thanks and forgiveness. Keep quiet and you will die. We have rope and bullets and my men have lost brothers. They long for blood. It will be yours if you do not speak.'

We did not speak. Not for minutes. Then Mayor Geroux stepped forward. We have no Maquis, he said. Let the women go. Let the men pay the price if blood was what they sought. Let the women and the old men leave. Let the children leave . . .

The officer shot Mayor Geroux with his pistol. He was still talking when the bullet entered his head – punching a black hole into his top lip. The back of his head blew open like an aerosol thrown on a fire.

That was when the boy on the front of the car woke up. He started shouting curses. Angry, bitter, spiteful noises that seemed to come from beneath him; as though he were a mouthpiece for Hell. I think they'd have let him die easy if he'd just kept his mouth shut. But he was proud and he was foolish. That was when Favre came forward. We didn't even know he was there. But even as the mayor lay dead on the ground it was the presence of Favre that made us shake with fear. His reputation was that of a monster. He had been a leatherworker before the war. A good one at that. Rumour had it he had been born in a little village in the Dordogne. Others said he was a German by birth but had grown up in France with Jewish parents whom he butchered before he was fourteen years old. We never knew what to believe. He was just the name in the darkness; the handprint on your window. He was in prison when war broke out, I've learned that in the years since. When the Vichy Government decided to establish the Milice they did not discriminate against men with blood on their hands. Do you know of these men? They were the Nazis' hired sadists. The Milice were brutes. Rapists, killers, torturers. And Favre was the best of them. He could make people talk. Could make them tell things they did not know that they knew. He went to work on the Maquisard in front of us with a leatherworker's knife. The boy withstood for a long time. Then Favre asked for a brazier full of coals. We watched as he heated a handful of coins in the fire. One by one he seared them into what was left of the boy's skin. When he whispered his confession into Favre's ear, Favre nodded to the captain. He had given them the town. The distant place where six hundred men and women would die amid the flames.

That was when the screaming started.

That was when they opened fire.

Please, Fairfax. Let me stop. I need to rest.

End of session.

CORDELIA

I've never really understood people's reactions in moments of fear. When I was a child and had one of my nightmares I never suffered from any compulsion to run into my mother's bedroom and snuggle down with her in some warm, perfume-scented cocoon. The notion never occurred. I would just lay there. I'd pant sometimes, until I got my breath back. But I would never pull the covers over my head. I simply waited for the fear to go. Mother would have been little use in a crisis anyways, and there was little chance that she'd be the only inhabitant of her bed. She never lacked company.

So when I saw the footprints by my bed there was never any question of dashing from the bedroom and running for help. Where would I even go? The nearest house was further up the hill, and I'd barely exchanged three minutes of conversation with the occupants since moving in. The Parkers. They had cows and sheep and some time ago they had asked if they could use a field that belonged to my house as rough pasture for a new breed they had invested in. Were willing to pay. I'd said yes because I could see no merit in saying no, and the money they paid in advance was a handy little extra on top of the monthly allowance my husband wired the post office on the third of each month. I'd managed to save a decent sum. I don't know whether I'd begun to think of it as my escape money by that point. That would come later.

It was Mrs Parker who had come to make the enquiry. A small woman of around fifty years old, she wore her smile like a poorly-fitting shoe. She was all teeth and creases. I'd answered the door with Stefan on my hip and she had barely glanced at him. That had set me off immediately. How could she not want to fuss him? How could she not long to wrench him from my arms and cuddle him close; make him giggle with tickles and clucks and pretend to eat his fat little legs like an uncooked loaf?

She had introduced herself with a handshake. Told me we were neighbours. Told me that her husband had tried to buy the farm and the house after Mrs Winslow died but that he couldn't match my husband's offer. Was I supposed to apologize? Was I supposed to feel sorry for her? I didn't even offer to make tea. Kept my attention on Stefan and played the harmonica on his stubby little fingers. She made her offer and I accepted with little more than a shrug. I didn't expect cash. But it felt nice to hold some. Felt oddly comforting to have a fist full of clean, warm notes that nobody else knew was mine. She must have read that in my face. Saw that I was for sale. That was the first time her smile reached her eyes.

I remember sitting up in bed, looking at the boot prints. Whoever had left them must have known they would be seen. No effort had been taken to wipe the floor. I climbed out of bed and followed them back down the stairs. The intruder had ventured into several rooms. They had spent time in the library. I found one large print in the centre of one of the white pillows I had used to build my nest. They had been in the kitchen and pantry. I don't know if they took anything. I had never counted the tins of food or the jars of jam or the eggs, tomatoes and stale loaves that were delivered, without my asking, to the doorstep each Monday morning. I presumed the food parcels had been arranged by my husband or his benefactor. I had no interest. Told Stefan they were gifts from the faeries at the bottom of the garden.

I dressed at a leisurely pace. There was much yawning and stretching and considering of myself in the mirror. I dressed as if taking my clothes off; the inversion of a striptease. Had I dressed quickly I would have felt as though I were in a hurry to leave the house and I would have found such a display of panic unforgivable. So I changed my outfit several times. Brushed my teeth for longer than usual. Applied a little make-up for the first time in months. I didn't do it for anybody else's benefit. It was all for my own. I wasn't going to be scared. Wasn't going to let anybody think they had intimidated me. I wanted anybody watching to see a woman who had been through more pain than they could imagine and who could laugh off a midnight intruder with a carefree toss of their hair.

It was nearly eleven when I considered myself fit for the day. I lit a fire in the stove and put two thick slices of bread under the grill. Opened a packet of coffee and began the complicated act of brewing a pot. It had been months since I had performed such actions and there was something reassuring about doing a task that had once been so familiar. Stefan used to watch with fascination as I played with the complex chrome and silver percolator that I had received as a wedding present and the opening of which had been the only part of that ghastly day in Hounslow that I had actually enjoyed.

I revelled in the rich aroma of the ground coffee beans. Gave an audible sigh as I poured the scalding water onto the brown dust and let the water infuse with the rich dark flavour. Pressing down the plunger on the cafetière was the most splendid moment of all; a kind of reverse Excalibur – a returning of the sword to the stone. I drank it black, like we all did at university. Ate my toast with a thick smear of rhubarb and ginger jam. I even switched on the wireless for a little while, though that was one act of defiance too far. Stefan and I used to listen to the wireless. We would dance and clap and sing to the songs. It was too much without him. The pain sat like undigested food in my chest and I switched it off at the plug.

When I had finished I washed the dishes and left them to drain. I watched the rain as I worked. The deluge had eased off into a fine mist that hung in the air like dust in a colossal cobweb. The sky beyond was the colour of white towels washed with black shirts. The fields and trees, the strip of road, the pebbles lining the drive; the damp air had made them all somehow liquid and as I watched I began to imagine that if I simply stretched out a hand I would be able to swirl the colours into a pattern; smear the landscape into nonsense like damp oil paints.

I was checking my reflection in the mirror above the kitchen table when I heard the brass knocker on the big front door boom three times. It was such an unusual sound that at first I struggled to place it. My visitors had been few in the time since moving in and even fewer since Stefan went to sleep. For an instant I saw the footprints by my bed. Could my visitor have returned? But if so, would they think to knock? Was it a diversion? Was somebody else sneaking up to the back door while I was preoccupied at the front?

I opened the door to a man I recognized from the village. He always touched his cap when we passed one another in the street and had once told me Stefan was a 'fine handsome lad'.

'Mrs Hemlock,' he said, and as he smiled he showed off a mouth that contained only a bottom set of dentures. His top teeth were entirely missing. 'I'm Carl Nixon.'

We took each other in. My hemline was above the knee and there was a good few inches of pink skin on show before it disappeared into my boots. With my red tunic dress and black ribbon holding back my hair, I have no doubt he enjoyed the view of me a lot more than I did of him. He was tall and clad in overalls and wellington boots that looked as though they had been left at the bottom of a cliff where a thousand seabirds nested. He had curly tresses that he parted on completely the wrong side for the natural inclinations of his grey-black hair and his face had that ruddy, weather-beaten hue that always makes me want to advise a large pot of cold cream and a bag of ice.

'Can I help you?' I asked, and I made the effort to say it with something other than cold disdain in my voice.

'I saw Ray Pellew,' he said, and I noticed how his bottom lip protruded to accommodate his dentures. It made his accent hard to read. 'He said you were asking about Fairfax – God rest him – in Samson's last night. He said I might be able to help.'

I glanced at his boots. It was impossible to tell if they were the same size as the treads left by my bedside.

'How, exactly?'

He wiped his hands on the front of his overalls. I realized his clothes and hair were damp but I had little wish to invite him in.

'It was me got Fairfax into the writing, like. Told him a few local yarns.' He looked away as he said it, embarrassed. 'Ray said you were asking about it . . .'

'I'm not sure I was asking, exactly,' I said. 'It's just, I saw him shortly before the accident and I thought we might have got on. He seemed a nice man. And I feel bad that he was helping me when he died.'

Nixon looked at me from beneath bushy eyebrows. Seemed to be trying to work me out like a crossword.

'I feel bad meself. Shall we feel bad together?'

Pity got the better of me. I invited him in and he stopped on the step to remove his boots. I snatched up a newspaper from the stack by the coat rail and made sure I placed the wet boots down on their surface. I would have a chance to compare the prints later.

'I was in the kitchen,' I said. 'There's coffee.'

He followed me down the hallway to the kitchen and nodded appreciatively at the aroma of the fresh coffee. He looked at the percolator as if it was a part of a rocket ship. 'That's snazzy,' he said.

'Wedding present,' I said, gathering a mug and sugar bowl from the pantry.

'You got married down south then,' he said, as though the present made this much obvious.

'Registry office,' I said.

He looked up from his examination of the percolator and endeavoured not to let disapproval show. 'Not a churchgoer?'

'No.'

He stayed silent a moment, debating whether or not he would risk his mortal soul if he accepted a cup of coffee from somebody who hadn't said their vows in front of a vicar. His taste buds got the better of him. He heaped a spoonful of sugar into his mug. Stirred and took an appreciative swallow. 'Excellent,' he said, grinning, and for a moment I saw that he had once been a handsome man. He pointed at the kitchen table. 'May I?'

I nodded and he sat down. I stayed leaning against the drainer. I poured the last dregs of coffee into my own mug. I heard the clock tick fourteen times before he spoke.

'Fairfax was my friend,' he said. 'All my life.'

'I'm sorry for your loss,' I said, and I think I meant it, even as I found myself competitively comparing the level of our bereavements. He'd lost a friend? I'd lost my whole damn heart.

'It was a horrible shock,' he said, staring into his coffee cup. 'We'd only just talked the night before. Not that that was unusual – my wife says we're like a couple of fishwives.'

I didn't want to interrupt. I knew he had something he felt he needed to say and even if it didn't have anything to do with the dead man in the blue suit, the least I could do was listen.

'You're a Gilsland man?' I asked, and endeavoured to make it sound like something one should aspire to.

'Born in Baggarah, up the road. I'm Gilsland now.'

I nodded, as if I understood the geography. I knew from a framed map in a guest bedroom that the local place names were a lesson in the versatility of the English language. Baggarah was just one of the tiny hamlets with names that made Stefan and I laugh. There was Low Row, Greenhead, Runner Foot, Bush Nook and Blenkinsopp, all within a few miles of one another, though I would never have been able to point in which direction any of them lay. I always thought of 'Baggarah' and 'Bugger Off'. I still do.

Nixon took a deep breath, preparing to dive in. I gave him a smile, and it seemed to help him get his words in order.

'He were born two years before me so I think he were like a big brother in a way. It was him talked me out of signing up in the Great War. I were full of zeal for it. Wanted to serve me country and see the world. Fairfax got wind of me lying about me age. Dragged me back from the recruitment office in Haltwhistle by the scruff of me neck. Gave me the beating of me life. Didn't practice what he preached though. Signed up himself in '16.'

I let my surprise show in my face. 'He fought in the first war?'

'Never spoke of it, though he dug halfway to Hell in those trenches. Fusilier. Saw things a man shouldn't see.'

'He came back to Gilsland?'

Nixon noticed the surprise in my voice. 'You're thinking that after seeing the world it would be madness to come back to a little place like this. I understand, love. But think of it t'other way. You've survived a war that blew your mates to bits. You've seen what human beings can do to one another.

Wouldn't you want to be somewhere safe and comfortable
with the people who care about you? Wouldn't that be more
appealing?'

For all the admirable textbooks on war and sociology that
I had read, it was Carl Nixon's simple words that first made
me actually stop and think. He saw it in my face.

'It's not all bad, is Gilsland, love. I know it must seem
confusing to a newcomer but it's cities that are the odd ones.
Real people live in places like this, love. Communities.
Streets where people know your name and what you're up
to. Streets where you can share a pint with somebody whose
grandad used to play football with your grandad. If that's
to be scorned I'd rather be on the receiving end than dishing
it out.'

I shook my head at that. 'I've never scorned any of you,' I
said. 'I'm just not part of it. I haven't said a word of insult
about any of you.'

He shook his head. 'It's a small place. All it takes is a letter
you've mailed a friend to accidentally rip; to maybe need a
replacement envelope . . . maybe somebody in the post office
casts a glance over the contents to make sure nobody's spilled
their tea on your words to a friend. And the next thing everybody knows what you think. Everybody knows you reckon
there are more teeth than brain cells in our heads and that our
mums and sisters are the same people. Then it can be harder
for you to be welcomed.'

My mouth was wide open. How dare they! How dare they
read my private post. How could they hold words written in
confidence against me? That would be like holding the contents
of somebody's diary against them.

'I don't know what you mean,' I said, teeth clamped and
cheeks burning.

'That ain't what I'm here for,' said Nixon, patting the air.
'Owt you may have said don't matter none anyways. When
you lost your little lad – that wiped the slate.'

I glared at him. 'That's all it took, was it? If I'd known I'd
have let him die months earlier.'

'Don't be like that. Look, just listen, yes? I wanted you to
know about Fairfax. About his writing.'

I folded my arms, stewing like strong coffee. I wanted to kick him out. To tell him to get back down the lane to his inbred neighbours and friends. And yet I needed to hear him out. I gave the slightest of nods. He breathed out, relieved.

'Fairfax's son, Christopher. He died right at the tail end of the war. It half broke Fairfax though he never let it show. Saved his tears for when he'd had a few drinks and even then he resented every single tear that he let spill. Saw each one as a failure. Missed his boy like you would miss a limb, love. It was me got him into writing. We used to talk about how his son would have become this incredible writer. Like a Hemingway – a soldier turned storyteller. He would have been great at that. His death was needless. A tragedy, right at the end of the war. He had no business dying. Life had such big plans for him.'

I softened my gaze. Told him to carry on.

'Fairfax was a lost soul without his lad. The house he lived in, that were owned by his father before him so there were never no mortgage to pay and he didn't need much money in his pocket for the things he liked. Worked here and there, doing a bit of farmhand work or as mate for a mason or a plumber or two. Reliable hand and because he were so good at being friendly to folk he were never short of work. But he was empty inside – anybody who knew him properly knew that. It was me told him to start writing. Late fifties, this was. We were having a drink and nattering and sharing stories and he came out and said that all this stuff should be in a book. Said if Christopher were alive he'd be writing it. Would show the world what this little pocket of the world was really like. I told him he should do it. Do it in his boy's honour, like. We had a toast to that and I don't think I thought of it again. Next thing we're in Haltwhistle to buy some spark plugs for a tractor and he comes out of the stationery shop all pleased with himself. He'd bought this beautiful, leather-bound notebook. Honestly, it were so smooth it were like polished wood. Got himself a fountain pen and umpteen pencils. All the stuff, like. Pleased as punch, he was. Said he was going to do it. Would dedicate it to Christopher. Would write about the history of the village but more about its people. Its character. I hadn't seen him like that in so long I told him it were a grand idea. Get to it, I said. Start with me, if you like.'

I found myself smiling. I only had one memory of Fairfax and it was of an old man half in and half out of his wellington boots in Felicity's doorway. I preferred the picture Nixon painted for me. He was grinning. It was nice to think of the moment he had found that smile.

'I spread the word, like,' said Nixon, smoothing down his shirt front with his big red hands. 'Had a few words in a few quiet ears and said that Fairfax wanted to get people's memories down on paper and not to pull his leg too much about it as it meant a lot to him. We're not always good at sharing our secrets but people did their bit. Started telling him their stories.'

He stopped for a moment and swallowed. His throat seemed dry. I got him a glass of water and placed it down in front of him. He thanked me with a nod.

'You're wondering what would be worth saying, I'll bet,' he said, smiling.

'No, actually,' I said. 'I know a bit about the history of the area. That was one of the reasons I was keen to come here.'

He seemed surprised. 'You chose Gilsland?'

I moved my head from side to side like a pendulum, indicating that this was a complex question. In truth, my husband had simply wanted me to be somewhere out of the way. He gave me the option of a dozen houses from rural locations and told me to pick the one I liked. I was in no position to ask for something less remote. If I chose not to go through with the wedding he would simply find somebody else and I would be back on the streets with a swelling belly and nowhere to go but down. I picked a thatched cottage in Somerset but the owner wouldn't sell to anybody but a local. Gilsland was my third choice. Mrs Winslow's lawyers had no compunction about selling to a man from well beyond the village boundary. They wanted the best price and in my husband, they found a rich fool willing to pay it. When I first moved in it was with a sense of excitement. I wanted to know all about my new home. Read up on its history and the seemingly endless violence and bloodshed that had scarred the landscape. But the novelty wore off. My extravagant home became my prison.

My loneliness became exhausting. Nobody visited. Nobody called. And when Stefan was born there wasn't a soul from the village who bothered to come and wish us well. I grew to hate the village and its people. After he died, I hated everything.

'You go in any village you'll hear stories,' he said. 'I've no doubt you could stick a pin in a map and find folk who would swear blind their village were the centre of the universe and the most fascinating place on earth. Maybe not just a map. Maybe an atlas. I'll put money there are men and women even out there in Australia who reckon the history of their little town is worth a book and Australia's no older than the wagon I've got in the barn.'

He must have seen impatience in my expression because he gave himself a shake, as if exasperated with himself.

'I was the first man at Spadeadam,' he said, looking down. 'It wasn't Spadeadam then, mind. Wasn't an RAF base splashed all over the papers for being a waste of millions of pounds. Was just miles and miles of bog. Don't blame me for it but I took the government land surveyors to see the site. Years back. Proper men from the ministry. Men like your husband, I've no doubt. Of course we didn't know it then but they wanted a rocket site. I can see why they liked it. There was nothing of any value there – just a wasteland. When we surveyed it we were probing with rods that go down forty foot. We didn't get near the bottom. There was a plane came down there during the war. It's still there. Be a bloody puzzle for them archaeologists, eh?'

'Fairfax wrote about RAF Spadeadam?' I asked, confused.

He began to look agitated, though whether it was with me or himself I couldn't tell. As he spoke, a shaft of sunlight briefly speared through the glass at my back and he raised a hand in defence as it blanched the pink from his face.

'He spoke to every bugger,' said Nixon. 'I swear, late fifties this area was booming. Workmen from Scotland and Ireland. Men from the RAF. Surveyors, solicitors, inspectors. And everybody had been told to keep their mouths shut. Bet you struggle with the thought of that, eh? But we were under orders – you don't speak when you've been told not to. So there was all this guessing. What were they building, what would it become. There were nigh-on three years of guessing before it came out. Some big shot from London came up and wouldn't keep his mouth shut. Just came oot with it, like. It was going to be a rocket site. They were going to try and reach the moon.'

I nodded, smiling and waiting for more. I knew the story. The Blue Streak programme had been a failure of colossal proportions. Millions upon millions of pounds went into the doomed attempt to get a Brit into space. They'd have had more luck with a ladder.

'We'd hear the rockets morning and night,' said Nixon, looking at the pattern in the wood of his chair. 'Shook the ground sometimes. But it gave the local lads a good living and it brought people in and Fairfax was always the first in line to buy them a pint and pick their brains and get their stories down in his notebook . . .'

'Even outsiders?' I asked, confused.

'That was what surprised me,' he said. 'Seemed like he'd lost sight of what he was writing. Seemed like he had just got into the habit of nosing about. He was forever asking questions.' Nixon stopped. Sucked his lower lip. 'It wasn't a good time to be nosey. Not when there's war still in people's memories and the Russians were after every secret they could steal. Somebody from the base must have reported his interest. He was white as a sheet after they had a word with him. Some men in suits, that's what he told me. Told him to stop nosing.'

I waited. Raised my empty cup to my lips and then put it down again. Looked at his feet, clad in mismatched socks, and wished I had known his friend.

'What are you saying?' I asked.

'There's no profit in asking questions, that's what I learned from Fairfax. You understand?'

I stared at him, suddenly realising where this was going.

'Are you trying to frighten me?' I asked, angry. 'Because if that's what you're trying to do then you need to be a lot scarier . . .'

He hit the table. I expected the mug to jump but he pulled the blow at the last and it ended up being a feeble slap at the wooden surface.

'I heard you was asking questions,' said Nixon, infuriated with the way the conversation had played out. 'Ray said you walked in the bar last night bold as brass. And John's wife Felicity, she told him you spoke about a body on the grass at the church. Says that's what Fairfax was doing when he crashed that blasted silly car.'

'And?'

Nixon screwed up his face; wrinkles forming into mountain ranges at the corners of his eyes. 'He bought that car because it looked like a drawing his son had done. Did you know that? He would do owt to feel close to that lad. It were years ago the men in the suits told him to stay quiet but when I heard he'd died, that was the first thing I thought. I knew it were silly – my wife said as much. But when Ray said you'd seen him and that you were acting suspicious . . .'

'Is that what I was doing?'

'There's stuff you don't know,' he said, and his breathing was heavy. He was scratching at his hair as if ants were biting his scalp. 'Do you know about the camp? About the lads during the war? The stories Fairfax heard – they were too much for him to publish, I reckon. Too raw. He'd got to the stage where he wasn't asking questions for a book – he was asking questions for the sake of it. He wanted to know everything about people. Had got it in his head there were all these secrets to be unearthed.'

In truth, I knew very little about the camp he spoke about. I knew a POW camp had been built a couple of miles from Gilsland during World War Two but that was as much as I had read.

'It weren't just a few soldiers, love. These were the senior Nazis – the U-boat diehards who had been Hitler Youth. It was a De-Nazification Camp. They came here as prisoners to learn how to be anything but a Nazi. They worked the land round here. Went out in work gangs. Some of them stayed. When the war ended they were allowed to go home or they could do what many did. Married a local girl and made a life. There's a gadgie works the dust carts in Brampton. Bit of an accent but other than that you wouldn't know he weren't a local. The war ended and times changed but Fairfax, well . . .'

'He'd lost his son,' I said, understanding what Nixon was trying to say.

'No, I don't mean he held a grudge,' said Nixon, shaking his head. 'The opposite. Sought them out. Asked questions. Always scribbling.'

I suddenly felt cold, standing in the window with my wrists touching the cold metal. I moved into the centre of the kitchen and didn't feel any better for it. I was as agitated as Nixon. I wanted him to tell me what he thought.

'If you're concerned there was something more to his death, you should tell Chivers,' I said, bluntly. 'He might listen to you.'

He scoffed at that. 'Chivers? Man's a jobsworth. Does as he's told and can barely lever his fat arse out of his car. He wants it easy. Always has.' He screwed up his face again. 'I'm talking to you because you're not from here. Because you've got no reason to think there was any explanation for his death other than an accident. And yet you seem to. You think there's something to dig into. And maybe that's got me thinking. I don't know. Maybe I just wish my friend hadn't died.'

He turned his back on me at that, manoeuvring himself so I was looking at his shoulder. 'Maybe I just want you to ask a few questions, like Fairfax would.' He spun back to me, narrowing his eyes. 'You said you saw a body. After the tree fell.'

I pressed my lips together. Nodded.

'And it weren't there when you got back?'

I shook my head.

'And Fairfax had been there in the time you took your eyes off the site, yes?'

'Yes.'

'So Fairfax might have moved it,' he said, cautiously.

I stayed silent. Listened to the ticking of the clock. Shivered, as if I was staring at my own grave.

'Why would he do that?' I asked, at last.

'I don't know, love. And I've been here long enough to know that people are happy to say nowt. Sometimes you'll see a pike take a perch in the tarn. You'll see teeth and fury and blood and scales. And a moment later there's not a ripple on the water. That's here, love. People are happy to wait for the ripples to drift away. But I need to know if there were scales in the water. I need to know if a pike took a perch.'

I heard myself breathing. Heard the tick of the clock change its rhythm and realized I could hear my own heart. Nixon looked at me for a moment longer than I was comfortable with. Then he gave a nod and rose from the chair.

'I'll see myself out,' he said, quietly. He looked as though he was about to reach out and shake my hand. Then he stopped himself, as if the action would be wrong.

'His notebooks,' I said, unable to help myself. 'They might make for interesting reading.'

He stopped in the doorway, smiling a strange little smile. 'If you knew where he kept them, love, you'd know every dirty little secret in the village.'

'He never showed you what he wrote?'

'Not a word,' said Nixon. 'But I swear to God, there are those would kill to get their hands on a few pages. And then there are those who would put a match to every page.'

I was still standing there when I heard the door close. Still standing there when the next streak of sunlight pierced the cloud. Still standing when it winked out, and pitched me into darkness.

FELICITY

Transcript 0004, recorded October 29, 2010

*D*on't hunch your shoulders. That's what me mam always said. We're prone to a hump, the lasses in our family. Mam's started when she were not much past fifty. Looked like a question mark by the time she died. I always try to hold myself straight, though you don't want people thinking you're looking down your nose. Takes an effort, remembering. Some people never manage it. They grow old staring at their shoes. Spend their dotage walking along looking like they've dropped a tenner.

Were hard to keep my head up that day. Rain was falling straight down and every drop seemed to be looking for the back of my neck. I were probably wearing the headscarf that John had brought back from Carlisle. Nice silky material, all gold and red, like a fire. No bloody good in the rain but it was better than nothing and if I'm honest, I think I liked being the only splash of colour in that sea of grey. The sky looked like a coalman's bathwater and the streets had rivers in every gutter. The leaves had been falling for a couple of months so there was no end of muck and mulch being carried in the gullies and it didn't take long for the drains to fill up. Even at the bus stop by the post office I could hear the River Irthing, gurgling and mumbling like a sleeping drunk.

'You think it'll come?'

Pat had to ask it twice before I realized she was talking to me. My head was full of Fairfax. Full of footprints in dust and crumpled pages that smelled of smoke. Full of dead Frenchmen and hot coins.

'Got your head in the clouds, Felicity? Be careful, you'll drown.'

I told myself to smile. I'd always got on with Pat. Weren't her fault she were born a little hard of thinking.

'Sorry Pat, load of things on my mind. What was you asking?'

'Brampton bus,' she said. 'Think it'll come?'

'Came last winter when we had five feet of snow,' I said. 'It'll manage rain.'

She seemed relieved at that, as if I were the wireless and given her some official bulletin. In truth, I wasn't sure. Didn't even know if I wanted it to turn up. I should have spoken to John first off. Told him what I'd found and what I'd read. Should have walked up the hill and knocked on Cordelia's door. Mrs Green in the post office said she'd been at Samson's the previous night, bold as brass. Asking questions. Giving Chivers a pasting behind his back. She wasn't letting it drop. She should know what I knew. She should at least be allowed to give me her opinions on the scraps of paper I'd found hidden in the church floor. She'd been to university, after all. Had a good big brain. I think I was just frightened of seeing the look on her face. I hadn't supported her. Had been too busy snivelling and trying to make it all into a lie.

'You'll be needing some bits and bobs, I'd imagine,' said Pat, huddling back into the protection of Debbie's cottage opposite. Some days Debbie would let you wait in her house until the bus came. Today she hadn't poked her head out the front door. Pat and me were soaked to the bone.

'This and that,' I said, and wondered to myself why I was being vague.

'Aye, I'm short of that meself.'

Pat was in her early sixties with a face like yesterday's rice pudding. She was small and round and had worn the same burgundy overcoat for as long as I'd known her. She was a hard worker though. Her husband, Keith, had taken ill a few years back and their son had no interest in taking on the family joinery business so it had fallen to Pat to make ends meet. She cleaned at the school and for a few of the big houses out towards Lanercost. Polished the silverware and glassware for the big fancy club on the Longtown road. She usually cycled but the weather had made that impossible. She needed the bus to come. Needed to deposit her savings in the Brampton bank before Keith could find where she kept them and limped his way down Samson's.

'Oh, there she is,' said Pat, suddenly, under her breath. She raised a hand and waved at Mrs Parker, who was emerging from the post office with an empty basket over her arm. 'I wonder if her halo keeps the rain off.'

'She's a kindly soul,' I said, not really paying attention. 'All those letters to write. Food parcels to send. She's one of the good ones.'

Pat gave me a look like I was daft.

'Short memory, Felicity,' she said, a bit harsh for my liking. 'Might be a saint these days but she were a terror when she were a girl. That poor brother of her's had to bugger off to university just to avoid her. That were a daft thing to do cos he barely came back and he ended up shot to bits in the war. She can send letters and butter and bacon to half the starving families in Germany and she'll still always be that nasty cow from the big house as far as I'm concerned. Anyways, Germans are doing better than we are these days. All the POWs are making a fortune over there. What's she still bother with them for, eh? They may have worked her farm but I reckon twenty-two years later it's time to pack it in.'

'Maybe she's being kind,' I said, and it sounded feeble. I blushed a little and turned to the street, where Mrs Parker was climbing into her expensive car. As usual, she had a face worse than the weather.

'Kind? She's maybe doing penance. She'd have been in the poorhouse if not for her husband and his bright ideas. More to the Swiss than yodelling and cuckoo clocks, believe me. He aint pretty but he's interesting. Gave a good lecture at the Women's Institute, which you'd have known if you bothered coming along.'

I turned my sigh into a cough and then shivered, exaggeratedly, as a silence began to stretch between us.

'I were sorry to hear of Fairfax,' she said. 'They say it was sudden.'

'Aye,' I said, and it sounded too much like a shrug to be decent. 'Janet and me were opening the curtains at his place this morning. Was all I could do not to run out the door.'

'Was a good man,' said Pat, nodding approval. 'Knew him

since I can remember. Always had a twinkle in his eye. You find the envelope?'

I shook my head. 'Don't think the bugger ever planned on dying. The place is a pigsty.'

'No wife these past years,' said Pat, shaking her head at this sorry state of affairs. 'Kept himself smart though. Always shaved and scrubbed.'

'That silly car,' I said, falling into the easy back and forth.

'Bought it for Christopher, if you ask me.'

'Aye, that's what everybody said. Maybe he just wanted it for himself. Either way. Least he died driving something he was proud of.'

Pat considered this. 'You think he would still be alive if he had a more sensible car?'

'I don't know much about cars,' I said, wiping rain from my face. 'But you can still die if you drive a tank. Sometimes accidents happen.'

Pat nodded her head in agreement. 'Was a shock for poor Ern,' she said, widening her eyes.

'Ern?'

'Ernie Glendinning. Works at the base. He found Fairfax, did you not know?'

I thought back. Had John told me? Had Chivers mentioned it? Did I even ask?

'Aye, he'd taken a late lunch and was heading back for the afternoon shift. Saw the car there in the middle of the road, windscreen smashed. Got out in the middle of the gale and found Fairfax on the road. Sorry sight, so I heard. Went right through the windscreen after he hit the tree.'

I closed my eyes. Couldn't help but picture it. The Spadeadam road was a desolate place; a curled grey rope dropped into acre upon acre of forest and bog.

'He got some of the men down from the base soon as he found him,' said Pat, pushing herself further back into the wall as the rain redoubled its efforts. 'He was already gone. They called Chivers from the base. Harland came and towed the car. Ambulance came from Haltwhistle. You'll be looking after the arrangements, I presume.'

Would I? Had that already been assumed? I supposed there

was nobody else. I was the closest thing to family that Fairfax had.

'Was the car damaged though? I mean, if he went through the windscreen . . .'

'Knowing the details won't bring him back,' said Pat, looking down the road in the hope of seeing the sturdy, familiar shape of the bus. She sighed and checked her watch. 'I'm starting to worry about getting back.'

'You haven't got there yet.'

'The bus will come. But what if there's no bus back? I'll have to stay over with Meg and that'll lead to blood on the walls.'

I managed a smile. Pat and her sister had never seen eye to eye, though when I said as much to John he told me it were due to the fact that Pat was a wee thing and Meg was a tall, long-limbed creature. We would have never said it in company but there was always a few suspicions about whether their mam had stayed entirely faithful to her old fella when he was away in the merchant navy before the first war.

'Who you got today?' I asked.

'Mr and Mrs Dolan at Talkin. He'll pick me up in Brampton but said he wouldn't come all this way. Thinking of the mud on his Rolls Royce if you ask me.'

'Is that what he drives?'

'I don't know. Looks posh though. Not as posh as the brothers drive at the hall though. He hasn't got their manners neither.'

I didn't push her on that. Nobody asked what went on up at Kirklinton Hall but it was fun to tilt your head and put an ear to the wind and snatch the few whispers that drifted east. The hall had been a stately home and a private residence for the gentry during its long life. A hotel during the war and then flats that nobody wanted. Then some Londoner with plenty of money got his hands on it. He put in a glass-floored ballroom and turned it into a private casino. Spent a small fortune filling it with the sort of luxuries you would find in a sultan's palace. Rumour had it there were dancing girls who wore nowt but feathers and that there were no shortage of local farmers had gambled away their children's inheritance while lasses with

lips like a folded quilt whispered in their ears. I had no wish
to see the place but I'd have washed all the dishes in Denton
to know which locals had crossed the threshold. Rumour had
it that the two well-dressed brothers from the newspapers were
regular visitors. It was only a couple of years later that the
brothers got locked up and the place went out of business.
Turned into a wreck within three or four years. Last I heard
about it, some lad from Longtown was on the wireless, remembering how he and his mates used to break in and steal the
furniture when it was all boarded up. Got a phone-in going
on Radio Cumbria. All these reformed bad boys telling the
world how they used to use priceless old antique wardrobes
as rafts on the Eden.

'Wonder if Fairfax's book will be published now he's gone,'
mused Pat. 'Would be nice to see what he's actually been
working on all these years though I feel like crying knowing
he'll never see it on a shelf.'

I shivered. Felt somebody walk over my grave. Held my
elbows in tighter and clutched my handbag tighter, as if I'd
seen a stranger on a country road.

'The house is full of old papers and scribblings,' I said,
shaking my head. 'If there is a book among that lot it will be
the size of a sideboard when it's typed up. Loads of notes and
mile after mile of handwriting. I don't know what will become
of it all.'

'Be sad to see it on the fire,' said Pat.

I shook my head, hard. 'That won't happen. I'll read every
word, given time.'

'Make sure you only glance at my boring old stuff,' said
Pat, laughing. 'Honestly, it will put you to sleep.'

'He interviewed you?'

'Interviewed every bugger. Spent plenty time with me and
my Keith. Must have been ten years ago he got round to me.
Asked questions he already knew the answer to, like where I
went to school and where I lived and where I met Keith. His
pencil was a blur. I don't know what he got out of it. I talked
to him about both wars though I felt uncomfortable about it.
He was off fighting in the first one and his son died in the
second so why he'd want to remember, I don't know.'

'What else did he want to know?' I asked, and the query sounded unfamiliar on my tongue. It suddenly struck me as odd how rarely I asked such honest questions.

She scratched her head. 'Wittered on about the drama society during the war. The athletics team from the camp. They built the first 400-metre track in this country, did you know that? Some of it's still there. You ever go up the castle? You can see the old buildings. Old cells too.'

I realized I was chewing my lip. Did it matter? Was it in some way connected to the words beneath the church floor?

'Why did he ask you about it?' I said.

Pat screwed up her face. I swear, her lower lip almost touched her forehead.

'I think I were just there to make it chatty,' she said. 'You know my Keith. Ask him how he is and he'll tell you "fine" – even if there's an arrow sticking in his forehead. I get him talking even if it's just by correcting the bits I get wrong.'

'And what did he want to know about from Keith?'

'Well you know as well as I do that his father was a master mason and afore the sickness, Keith was no slouch. They did a lot of the work on the big buildings around here. Manor house, castle, vicarage, churches.'

'Churches?'

'Of course. Magdalene and yon church at Denton. Out Longtown way too.'

'What was he asking?'

'Designs. Whether he still had old draftsman's sketches and whatnot. Then he got onto talking about the camp.'

'The POW camp?'

'O'course. Keith and his father were among the contractors who put the place together. 'Twere just a field, if you remember it. Next thing it had to accommodate thousands of men and not all of them were happy to be out of the war. Some wanted to keep scrapping. Fairfax was asking Keith about what he saw. About the men who came. Where they were from. What countries. What languages. What uniforms. Honestly, this went on an age.'

'And this was years ago, was it?' I asked, unsure of the relevance.

'Aye well, Fairfax started his research around the time the Romans left but there were never a time when he weren't pestering us for little bits we might have forgotten.'

I stared at the stream that gurgled in the gutter. Watched a clump of leaves spin and twirl on the current. My brain felt like that – as if all I could do was give myself up to the direction of the wind.

'Did he ever mention a Frenchman?' I asked, and the words were away into the air before I could suck them back. 'Ever ask questions that made no sense . . .?'

Pat changed her face. Hardened it a little. 'What you asking for?' she snapped.

'I'm not,' I said. 'Not asking. Just wondering. Some of his papers mentioned a little place in France. Seemed important to him but who's to say? And Fairfax never interviewed me, y'see. Just wondered why not.'

'Oh,' said Pat, and the tension went out of her. 'Well, you're as best being in the group of lucky ones. There'll be no shortage of folk worrying about what Fairfax did with their words.'

'It was just a local history book,' I said, shivering as the rain finally found a route from the tip of my spine to the bottom of my left leg.

'Aye, but there's some history you probably shouldn't speak on. Nobody wants other people reading what they did in the war or what they thought about the prisoners working their land or those who stayed and married the locals. They're personal thoughts. And Fairfax did push, God rest him.'

As she spoke, I felt, rather than heard, the approach of somebody behind me. There was no sun to cast a shadow but I suddenly felt somebody at my back. Then I smelled him too. Dogs and dark places – like a bleeding Alsatian at the back of a cave.

'Hello Felicity,' said Pike, as I turned.

He wasn't smiling. Pike never smiled. He was saving up for new teeth, so he said, and in the meantime he preferred to hide the black stumps that were stuck in his gums like bits of charcoal pushed into rotten fruit. His nose was halfway across his face, like he were trying to sniff his ear, and his eyes were sunk deep in his head beneath the sort of brow that made me think of a shark. He was wearing his camouflage coat and his ginger hair had gone black in the rain.

'All right Pike,' said Pat. 'How's Mam?'

'Still alive,' said Pike, still staring at me. 'Still bane of me bloody life.'

'She's tough as old boots,' said Pat, and God bless her, she moved to stand beside me. Everybody knew that Pike was not to be left alone with a woman or a kiddie. 'You're a good lad to look after her as you do.'

Pike finally gave her his attention. He wasn't a big man. Maybe that were his problem. He was always making up for the fact he wasn't as big as the other blokes. But he had something. Some viciousness. He'd always been the same. Even at school he was uncontrollable. He'd say nowt at all for weeks on end then one day just go and bite the headmaster or start carving words in his bare legs with his pocket knife. Scared the life out of all of us. Parents too. His dad had run off when he were just a baby. Left him and his mam in a house that was already falling down a century before they moved in. They had animals but didn't seem to know what to do with them. Sheep and cows and a family of ducks lived in the house with him, I swear to God. Great holes in the roof that the rain came through. Three different vicars tried to help them but they didn't want none. Didn't need charity and saw nowt wrong with how they lived. Pike poached. Took salmon, trout and deer. Made friends with the lads who built the air base and always seemed to know how to get his hands on cheap cigarettes or cases of bargain booze. Grew up to be a man to be feared and word had it that he knew people in Newcastle and Belfast who would be only too glad to hurt people if he asked them to. Not that Pike would ever ask. He preferred to do the hurting himself. We'd never had cross words and he'd never put a hand on me but I still remember what I saw him doing to himself the first time I went to put flowers on Mam's grave. Curtains open, shirt off, watching me walk past his door to the church, big leer on his face as I held my carnations and skipped through the puddles. I've never told anybody that. Don't know why I'm telling you.

'I were sorry for Fairfax,' said Pike, to me. 'Sorry about his car as well.'

I suddenly remembered Fairfax telling me about that. He'd found Pike admiring the new vehicle. Had spent twenty minutes talking to him at the kerbside – a pleasant enough chat about tyre pressure and engine sizes and whether it were wrong to buy a German car.

'There'll be a funeral,' I said. 'Maybe at Denton.'

'Don't like funerals,' said Pike.

'Well, that's up to you,' I said, and suddenly didn't care whether the bus came or not.

'I liked Fairfax,' said Pike, jerking his head. 'Talked to me like a person.'

'And how does the rest of us talk to you?' asked Pat, and her body language suggested she was ready for a dust-up.

'Who's getting his machine?' asked Pike, ignoring the question.

'Machine?'

'Tape player with the microphone. I saw him sticking it in plenty faces.'

I turned to Pat, confused. She nodded, understanding better than I did. 'Aye, he were a menace with that. I never liked speaking into it. Like having a telephone conversation with yourself.'

'I'm sorry,' I said, colouring. 'What machine?'

'He had one of those recorders,' said Pike, and I glimpsed the ruination of his mouth. 'For recording stories, he said to me. Thoughts and memories. Asked me to say my name into it then played it back to me. I didn't sound like I thought I would.'

'I never saw it,' I said. 'Why didn't I see it?'

'Like you said, he never interviewed you.'

I looked from one to the other. The mulched leaves in my brain had come to a standstill, wedged against the kerb. I needed to push. Needed to make things happen.

'Never mind the bus,' I said. 'I was daft to bother. I'll leave it.'

Pike shrugged. Put a hand in his pocket and brought out a carton of Player's Medium. 'Your John still smoke these?'

I nodded. Took the pack and managed a smile. 'Give my love to your mam,' I said, and couldn't look him in the eye. He nodded. Started trudging away up the road.

'You really off?' asked Pat. 'You're already soaked.'

'I was daft. I'll get home. Start on Fairfax's place properly,' I said.

'Aye, well, if you find owt saucy just bin it off. After you've showed me, of course.'

We parted on a shared grin. I walked slowly. Saw one or two faces flicker at windows as I trudged up past the old vicarage and the clumps of Roman wall that stood out from grassy tufts like wrecked ships. Gilsland. The place I grew up and which, on that day, looked like a photographic negative – as though the whites and darks had somehow switched and all the colour had bleached into the soil.

I started running when I reached the Denton road. Didn't stop until I had reached Fairfax's place.

I was still panting, still soaked through, an hour later – sitting in an avalanche of paperwork holding the memories of people I had known since the cradle. My head was fizzing with secrets and stories.

Looking back, that's when I accepted it. That's when I let myself believe that somebody had killed my friend.

CORDELIA

Old age takes the veneer off people. The nice get nicer and the mean get meaner. That's one of Flick's sayings and she mutters it when I'm in one of my moods. She has the right to say it, given she's been too bloody nice by half for the past eighty years. I'm not so comfortable with it. I don't think I've ever been nice. I have kindness in me and then sometimes I have an impulse to do something absurdly generous. But I'd be the first to admit that there's a mean streak in me. I know how to catch a person off guard. I can see somebody's frail supports and weak joists and I always seem to know just where to insert the lever. I was only in my twenties back in '67 and still hadn't worked out how to use that particular skill in a way that turned the world in my favour. I just knew that more than a handful of people had referred to me as a nasty piece of work, and the nuns at school felt they had cause to bless themselves more often in my company than in anybody else's. *Wicked*. That was the word I heard most. Wicked.

I was musing on wickedness as I tramped up the Featherstone road. Wondering whether or not I was bad all the way through. At school, when I suggested that the Good Book was so full of punishment and violence that it could as easily have been written by Satan, I was thrashed so hard that the scars are still visible on the backs of my legs whenever I flush pink.

I was their troubled case; their difficult charge. Me, with my big brain and my endless questions and my refusal to be fed their regurgitated scraps of wisdom like I was some sort of feeble baby bird. They were pleased to see me depart for the grammar school and they, in turn, rejoiced at my leaving for university. I had never had friends. No champions or trusted confidantes. So I never asked the questions aloud. I still chewed on them like gum. Still mashed them into a tasteless blob with the molars in the back of my head. What was I for? What did

I matter? Why had I been made? Christ, but I was a tedious specimen back then.

It took me almost an hour to get anywhere near the castle. It was pushing four p.m. by the time the low-hanging clouds delineated into a child's drawing of a fortress: a landlocked battleship of turrets and columns and pencil-shaded walls. I was still trudging up the winding grey road. The river surged to my right, already a couple of feet higher than the last time I had visited. Then it had been a spring day and Stefan had spoiled the trip by grizzling and sweating against me and refusing to walk even a handful of steps. He wanted to be carried. Wanted to loll against me like a roll of carpet. Wouldn't eat or drink and refused to be comforted. Refused to be my little prince. The sunshine did not seem strong enough to have caused him such distress and I grizzled back at him for spoiling our adventure with his ungrateful mewling. We didn't get to see the castle properly. Didn't get to watch the rainbow trout in the shallows or drop sticks from the small stone bridge. I marched him home. Arrived angry and sweat-soaked, impatient and sore. He was dead four days later.

'Watch it, lass!'

I turned sharply. A green farm vehicle had pulled up next to me. I hadn't heard the tyres on the wet road for the sound of the raging river. The driver was leaning his head out of the window; the solitary windscreen wiper wagging like a happy dog's tail. I must have looked at him sternly because he pulled a face and motioned with his hands for me to calm down.

'Dint see yer till I were almost on yer. What yer daeing out in this?'

For a moment I saw myself through his eyes. A city girl in all the wrong clothes; soaked to the bone and shivering in the half light, trudging up a road towards a castle that offered no promise of warmth or welcome. I softened my face, grateful for the interruption.

'I wanted to see the camp,' I said. 'I think I picked the wrong day.'

He smiled. He was maybe forty but it was hard to say for certain. Handsome, if you liked the sort of men favoured by Renaissance painters. He had pale skin and a full beard, pale eyes and long features. He had a woollen hat perched on top of his dark hair and was wearing blue overalls beneath a brown leather coat. I didn't recognize him.

'The camp? POW? Not much to see, love.'

I squinted at him. The rain was still coming down. The sides of the narrow road were running with brown water and the bushes by the stone walls were sinking in on themselves; collapsing like cardboard. The rain seemed to hang in the air. It felt like walking through a fishing net.

'Just a bit of a history project,' I said, trying to seem like it didn't matter, even as I stood shivering in the rain. 'I wanted to know more about the camp.'

He smiled. Looked at me like I was charmingly mad. 'You need a television, love.'

'I have one. Can't get it to work.'

'You have an aerial?' he asked. 'Up proper? Should pick up the signal, love.'

I smiled again, hoping he wouldn't push it. My husband had sent me a splendid television in a wooden case. All I had to do was get a local in to set it up for me. The only picture it had ever shown was my own reflection, puzzled and frustrated and cursing my own incompetence. *Feckless*, that was the word for it. I was utterly devoid of *feck*.

'Am I going the right way? I know it's through the castle and into the next field but I haven't seen any signs.'

He laughed. Showed me a pointed pink tongue, protruding over his bottom lip like a terrier's. 'A sign? No, love. You'll be lucky to see owt anyways. Bulldozers took it down years back. Not the sort of place you want to mek a fuss about.'

I could understand that. Nixon had said as much. A few mounds and a couple of outbuildings; some peculiar shapes in the grass. I felt suddenly silly; abruptly aware of the folly of setting out to see this place for such an absurd reason. I'd seen a corpse, of that I was certain. Fairfax had died not long after I alerted him to it. Fairfax had a son who died in the war and he had a habit of asking questions. Through design or accident, Gilsland sat between two edifices that had a vested interest in keeping their secrets buried: a Prisoner of War camp a couple of miles up the road and an RAF base on the other. It only made sense that I go and poke around. What the hell else was there to do with myself? But the idea of saying that to anybody else suddenly made me flush with colour. I was doing nothing but getting wet and looking silly.

'Yer far from home?' he asked.

'Back in Gilsland,' I said.

He looked me up and down. Put a couple of pieces together in his head. 'You'll be Mrs Hemlock,' he said, and tugged at the imagined brim of his hat.

'Cordelia,' I said, surprised.

'I'm Loz,' he said. 'Loz Gladwin. I've got farm at Park Burn. Near as neighbours to the castle, like. I were sorry to hear of yer sadness,' he said.

'Thank you,' I said, and realized I had started to appreciate the simplicity of the sentiment. People genuinely were sorry for me. They wished it hadn't happened. Is that not the truest expression of regret? I filed the thought away. I would chew it over at leisure.

'Is it through the castle then?' I asked, squinting into the rain.

'Aye, ye can see what little there is if you ye push on down this road and go through the courtyard and over the wee wall. Go through the next field and ye'll see where the river widens. There's about eighty head of beef in there though and I know ye won't see owt worth the walk.' He paused and looked at his watch. 'If ye hop in I'll show you in the dry.'

Instinctively I shook my head. I had been told too many times of the dangers of getting into cars with strange men. I thought of the sisters. I was a wicked thing; a product of desire and illicit, sticky fumblings. I had been made from a wanton act. I was not a creation of love but of temptation and lust. I heard such accusations throughout childhood. I knew of my wickedness. Knew how filthy a thing I was. Knew what I would become if I did not keep my heart open to God's love and my legs closed to the attentions of weak-willed men.

'I'm fine, thanks. I can only get so wet, can't I? And my skin is waterproof.'

He looked at me oddly then gave in to a huge laugh that ill-suited his delicate frame. So too did the idea of him working in a manual job. He looked slender and flimsy, like fine porcelain.

'Love, I can't let ye gan on in this weather. And I swear, ye'll be home quicker and without yer death of cold.'

He could see me pondering it. I was soaked. Frozen through. My teeth were chattering and my hands were so cold that I was struggling to feel their tips. If this man meant me harm he would be able to get me into his vehicle without much of a fight. And he would have to be a very opportunist killer to be driving down this road at this time in the hope of finding a lone female.

'If it's no trouble . . .'

'Please, ye'll be daeing me a favour.'

Decision made, I walked around the front of the vehicle. There was black mud and torn grasses snagged in the grill. A streak of rusty red on the broken headlight. He leaned across and opened the door and I gratefully climbed inside. It smelled of outdoors brought in. Damp earth. Wet leaves. The tang of gunpowder and wood polish.

'There's a flask under yer seat. Get it in ye.'

I did as he suggested. The thermos was a red tartan and warm to the touch. I poured thick brown liquid into the plastic cup and took a slurp just as we set off. I scalded my lip but laughed it off. There was brandy in the coffee and it warmed me as if I had swallowed hot coals.

'This some sort of tribute to Fairfax then?' asked Loz, sitting forward in his seat as the wiper carved a sail of visibility in the cascading water. I shot a glance at him. He wasn't looking at me. Was focussing hard on the road ahead.

'You knew Fairfax?'

'Aye, course. Everybody knew Fairfax. Were a sickener to hear on it. Tellt him that car were a fool's toy but he wouldn't be tellt.'

'Tellt?'

He glanced across. Narrowed his eyes as if doing sums. Then snapped his fingers. 'Told, I means. Sorry love. Ye must think we all talk like cavemen, eh? Where ye from yersel'?'

I stared ahead at the road. Watched the castle growing larger.

The rain had darkened the stone and cleaned the windows and it was hard to believe the fortress was hundreds of years old.

'Nowhere in particular,' I said, keeping it vague. 'I studied at Oxford. Nuffield.'

'Aye? Get a good job off that, did ye?'

I finished the coffee. Savoured the richness. 'I didn't finish,' I said.

'No? Married life call, did it?'

'Something like that.'

I could feel him watching me. I became aware of the scratchiness of the seat covers. Felt prickly and agitated as my clothes started to steam.

'Fairfax,' I said, changing the subject again. 'You asked if I was doing a tribute. What did you mean?'

Loz swung the vehicle right through a gap in the hedge just before we reached the main entrance to the castle. It looked deserted. There were no vehicles in the courtyard and the curtains at the windows I could make out through the rain all hung askew or were entirely missing. We ploughed on, into the neighbouring field.

'He were the local history fella,' shrugged Loz. 'Always asking questions and scribbling away. Planned a book, so he said. Were gonna be the width of a kerbstone if he ever published it. But he were good to talk to. Liked knowing what ye thought of things. Liked yer stories.'

'What did you and he talk about?' I asked, jolting suddenly as the vehicle clunked into a dip in the surface of mud and grass and rock.

'Family,' said Loz. 'Who we were, what brought us here, how long we'd had the farm.'

'The camp?' I asked, gently.

'Oh aye. We dug a lot of it out so only made sense. Keith Tanner's old father did the construction work but me and mine cleared the fields. I were mebs eighteen. Mebs more. Were a rush job but the ministry paid handsome.'

'And Fairfax was interested in your memories?'

'Aye, like I said, he were always after a tale.'

'What did you tell him?'

'He knew most of it,' said Loz, taking a hand off the wheel

to rub his chin. He didn't look strong enough to control the big car. 'Opened in '44. Garrison for the Yanks. Didn't have that many pass through, thank God. Then they went off for D-Day and the prisoners started arriving. Italians at first and then we started getting the serious buggers. Real hard-case Nazis. The ringleaders went to Nuremberg and it felt like every bugger else came here. Black, grey and white. That was how the camp commander divided them up. Thousands of the sods over time. The Black Nazis were the ones you had to fear and I don't mean black like the colour of their skin. I mean that's how they was labelled, like. The Black Nazis were the ones who believed in Hitler to their bones. These were the U-boat crews and the Western Front heroes who had worn the brown shorts and shirts and Heiled Hitler all their lives. It were up to the camp to make them decent people. How did you do that, I ask? But it worked, near enough. Treated 'em fair and they appreciated the respect they were shown. Was a decent enough place. They got good meals and a nice view and went out to work the land. There were a couple of escapes and the odd pagger now and again . . .'

'Pagger?' I said, gripping on as we swung left moments before we were going to plough into the churning white-peaked waters.

'Fight,' he said, apologetically. 'Odd scrap with the locals and between themselves but they were just people really. We got letters from a few lads after they went home. Said how much their time here meant to them. They went home to all kinds of hell. There won't be many folks around here that didn't get a letter or two from somebody they used to know. They wanted food parcels and the like. Berlin was just rubble. No work. There were plenty who envied the lads who stayed.'

'And there were lots of those?'

'No shortage. Married a few of the locals. Even wrote home to tell family they should come and give our part of the world a try. Your neighbour for one.'

I was about to ask him to elaborate when he suddenly hit the brakes and the vehicle slid to a halt on the soaking, muddy grass.

'There ye are,' he said, waving a hand. 'Not much, like I said.'

I followed the sweep of his arm. He was right. There were long, rectangular humps in the grass and a handful of tumbledown outbuildings but if I hadn't known what once stood there I would have presumed it was no more than the ruins of a farm.

'Shame to knock it down but it looked wrong when it were empty, as if we were waiting for trouble to start again and wanted to be prepared. Brought a load of workmen in and dismantled it all in a few days. Some of it's ploughed back into the land and some of the stone went to prop up other buildings or put up walls. There's not much goes to waste up here, love. Up there, that were the barracks. And ye can mebbe see the shape of what used to be the church and theatre.'

'Church and theatre?' I asked, surprised.

'Aye, like I say, they made the most of their time. People here showed them the first kindness they'd known for a long time. I'd like to think none of 'em went home a Nazi.'

I sat in silence, watching the rain scythe down into land that had known the rhythm of so many different soldiers over so many centuries. The thought nearly took my breath away. I found myself thinking of Picts in furs and blue woad, battling the red-and-gold splendour of the Roman invaders. Saw the blonde hair of the Vikings who brought hell from the seas. Began to see the ceaseless surging of invasion and repulsion; a tide of men in different uniforms, clinging to different gods, flinging themselves upon this landscape like waves upon a shore. I sensed bones beneath my feet. Felt light-headed at the torrent of blood that had been spilled upon this quiet, pretty place.

'We get 'em coming back,' said Loz. 'Old inmates. Proper association now, y'know. Organized trips about once a year. Men who were prisoners here – they come to see old friends and soak up the air they remember so fondly. Doing OK now. It could turn your stomach if ye let it, the way Germany's pulled its socks up. Ye wouldn't know they'd lost the bloody war. But then ye see the lads and their families and ye realize it's all just luck, really. Who knows what we'd have said if a Hitler had cropped up here, eh? It's all an accident, I suppose. We were losing the war for a long time, remember that, love.

It could all have gone different. It could be me going to visit some rural POW camp in Germany and remembering the good times.'

I glanced at him. He looked a little deflated. His eyes were dark.

'Did you say all this to Fairfax?'

He barked a one-note laugh. 'Aye, he had a way of getting you talking did Fairfax. Sometimes you don't know how you feel about things until after you've said them and then you find yourself agreeing with your own words.' He glanced at me, half-smiling. 'That probably sounds mad to a university girl.'

I shook my head. 'I never know what I think about things. I tell myself I do but it's just bravado.' I sniffed. Shivered. Wondered why I was telling him this. 'It shook me up, what happened to Fairfax. I don't know, maybe I just feel as though I've missed out on somebody who would have been good to know. Maybe I was wrong to try and stay out of everybody's way. Maybe I could have made a friend.'

He considered me and I saw myself reflecting in his eyes. Saw the twin outlines of my ridiculous self.

'You're young to be so clever,' he said, at last. 'And aye, ye'd have got on with Fairfax. Ye'd probably have reminded him of his boy.'

'Christopher? I've heard he was a writer.'

'Aye, he were a good lad. Looked a bit soft but he weren't. Put Pike on his arse.'

'I've heard of Pike . . .'

'Off his 'ead, he is. And he liked winding Chris up. Chris were quiet as ye like but Pike pushed him a bit far and Chris nearly took his head off. Took half a dozen of us to get him off. Pike took it better than ye'd think, to be honest. Didn't burn the house down or cut his head off the way you'd have feared. Got on OK with Chris after that. Not exactly friends but some kind of respect if nowt else. I reckon Pike were as upset as any of us when Chris got killed.'

'Did Pike go to war?'

Loz gave a grin. He took the thermos from me and poured himself a drink. 'So he says. Certainly went away for a couple

of years and came back more bloody off his 'ead than before
but for all we know he could have been doing a stretch in
prison. He says he don't like to talk about it but he talks an
awful lot for somebody so keen to be silent.'

I nodded. Eyed Loz's cup. He passed it to me without a
word. His finger brushed mine as I took it from him. His skin
was rougher than I expected, like a cat's paw. I found myself
wishing that mine felt the same; that I was somebody who
knew this land and worked this land and bore its scars and
callouses upon my hide.

'Harvest moon,' said Loz, suddenly. He was looking past
me, at the darkening sky. 'Be a hell of a view from your place
tonight if clouds lift. I've seen 'em red as blood, love. But
weather like this, it'll look like a bruise. I'd best get ye back
before God pulls the curtains closed.'

I found myself smiling. I liked this man. Wondered what
he thought about me and then instantly despised myself for
thinking it. I found myself becoming flustered.

'It was kind of you,' I said, more high-pitched than I wanted.
'That you stopped, I mean. Some men I know would have
waited until they saw me passing a big puddle then driven
through it at ninety.'

'This thing doesn't do ninety,' he said, and the shadows in
his face lifted as he smiled. 'I likes the company. I likes a
yarn almost as much as Fairfax did and it does ye good to
hear a stranger's thoughts. Stops you becoming an inbred
simpleton.'

I bit down on my lips, wondering if he was quoting
something I had written. He turned away from me, squinting
at the darkness. Sheep were moving in the grey and purple
air like storm clouds.

'I sent him a few decent tales,' said Loz, putting the vehicle
in reverse and looking over his shoulder as he began tearing
backwards across the field. I got a whiff of him. Sweat and
baking, peat and gunpowder. I found myself wanting to curl
up in the pocket of his shirt.

'Tales?' I asked, settling back into the seat.

'Aye, stuff ye hear in the pub, blokes with a story to spin.
Some on the road, some at the sales.'

'Sales?'

'Cattle market. Always told them to have a chat with Fairfax.'

He span the car in a wide arc and started making for the castle. I found myself enjoying a fantasy. Had flashes of running up the stone steps through the rain; laughing and shivering in the echoing hallways; standing goose-pimpled and pink in a darkness lit only by the golden flames of a great open fire; wrapping ourselves in blankets and one another and watching the branches and coals burn to ash. I felt silly at the girlishness of it but could not bring myself to will the vision away.

'. . . charver out Glendue Burn, couple of miles away.'

I realized I hadn't been listening. Cleared my throat and made a theatrical pretence of cocking my head to better hear what he was saying.

'I missed that,' I said, and felt the reassuring whirr of a real road beneath the tyres.

'Bloke I sent Fairfax's way,' he said, not minding repeating himself. 'Thought he were one of the old POWs to be honest but he were French, not German. Not that yer'd know it, like. Just a flicker of an accent. Got himself turned around and was heading for nowhere at all when I stopped to pick him up. Grateful for the lift but quiet as a mouse til I got him talking. Birdwatcher, he said, and I suppose the binoculars and the bag were a give-away, even if the suit made him look like a bank manager who'd got lost. Had this contraption with him too. Recording birdsong, so he said, which aint my idea of a party but must be nice to listen to. Said he were recording it for friends back home. Real sounds of the English countryside.'

I could hear the river again. Could hear the roar of dirty brown water tumbling over rocks and shifting the stones with a movement that seemed to contain purpose and threat.

'Really?' I asked, keeping my voice calm. 'That's interesting. I'm sure Felicity mentioned seeing a man with a bag . . .'

If he thought my probing suspicious he didn't show it. Just kept on chatting.

'Aye, he said he were working in Carlisle and took the train out here because he'd heard there was some rare bird. Walked from the station so this were early in the year because Beeching hadn't bloody closed it then. Asked me if there were anywhere to stay for the night and I told him to tek his pick. Since they killed off the rocket programme there's plenty people eager to rent out a bedroom for the night.'

'Where did you take him?' I kept my voice steady. Didn't want to rush it or make too much of what I was beginning to suspect.

'Dropped him in the centre of Gilsland,' he said. 'Told him the food at Bridge Inn was worth his time. He was going to make his way to one of a couple of addresses I'd mentioned but to be honest it were Fairfax he wanted to see by that point.'

'Fairfax?'

'Like I said, I always sent Fairfax the blokes with the best stories though I don't know if this charver was one of them. He asked me if there were somebody in the village who could help him identify somebody. Asked if there was anybody who knew everybody.'

I looked down at my boots. Saw the dirt in the footwell and the mud on the soles. 'You told him to see Fairfax.'

'The bloke I gave the lift to – can't remember his name – he said he thought he had recognized somebody. He wondered if there was somebody in the village who knew everybody. Knew the village like the backs of their hand. He said "backs". That was when I twigged his accent wasn't local. Said he was French, like I said.'

'And you sent him to Fairfax . . .'

He turned, looking a bit perplexed. 'Aye, love, like I keep saying.'

'Did Fairfax mention him to you?'

Loz chewed his lip, considering it. 'Aye, said he turned up and were as polite as you like. Described somebody he thought he'd seen out towards the camp and wanted to know if Fairfax could help. Fairfax told him he didn't sound familiar and the charver went on his way. Must have been mistaken or it were somebody from out of the area.'

I realized I was breathing hard.

'Did he describe who he saw?' I asked.

Loz turned the car left, over the little bridge. My stomach lurched and a solitary golden-brown leaf landed on the windscreen. Its stem was caught by the windscreen wiper and it swished back and forth across my vision.

'Nobody I recognized, from what I can remember. Bit older than himself he said. Bald head. Hard hands. Could be anybody.'

'And him?' I asked.

Loz shrugged. 'Blue suit. Wrong kind of shoes for the weather. Canvas bag. Not a film star but not a navvy neither.'

I stayed quiet. Let my thoughts ebb and flow like a leaf carried on water.

'Could I ask you to take me somewhere else?' I asked, making up my mind. 'I'd like to see a friend.'

He grinned, pleased to have helped a soaking, timid girl feel the need for company. I surprised myself by letting him enjoy the moment rather than treating his interpretation as a challenge. Perhaps I was growing up.

'Who'd that be?' he asked.

I found myself grinning. Found myself suddenly very eager to be in the presence of the one other person who had seen the dead man in the blue suit.

FELICITY

Transcript 0005, recorded October 30, 2010

B rian was going through his phase in '67. Trying it on, we used to call it. Testing to see what he could get away with. James hadn't been a bother at that age. Never been any bother any time. Brian were always that bit more trouble. He was the sort who would smash a plate just to see what sound it would make. In '67 he'll have been 11 – a couple of years younger than his brother and twice as bright. Had that fire in his eye that never seemed to go out. Always seemed a few steps ahead of you in an argument. Always seemed like he had an answer prepared for anything you might say. Don't know where he came from, I swear I don't. He could have become a lot of things, my Brian. Could have become something important if he hadn't been so dead-set on causing mischief. Loved to wind me up, he did. Always had a lie ready on his tongue. Couldn't answer the simplest question without needling one of us. So I didn't believe him when he said she were getting out of a car. Thought he were having me on.

'Lady from the big house,' he shouted from upstairs. 'Looks like somebody's drowned a film star.'

I was getting tea ready. Chucking potatoes in the fryer and talking to James about school. They were studying Henry the Eighth, he said. Was doing a sketch of one of his wives. I knew better than to look. His drawings were always a bit grisly. He used up his red crayons a lot sooner than the others.

'What did he say?' I asked, pointing at the ceiling as if the voice had come from the lightbulb.

'Said there's a lady from the big house.'

I dried my hands on a tea towel. The rain was still coming down and it was almost dark beyond the kitchen window. I had to look through my own reflection to see the back garden and the field beyond. Saw my own little kitchen with its soft warm light and its comfortable chairs and sturdy furniture and my children's clothes dripping dry in front of the fire. I remember that moment. Just one little heartbeat, one instant: a photograph I carry with me – seeing James's head bowed to his task and the curls of steam coming off the coats like they were souls leaving empty bodies.

'That's the door,' said James, in response to the knocking. 'I'd get it but I'm decapitating Anne Boleyn.'

'Good lad,' I said, smiling at him. I wasn't keen on the activity but I admired the big word.

I opened the kitchen door and stepped into the cool of the corridor. The kitchen was always hotter than a butterfly house but every other room took your breath away with cold. Brian had got there before me and opened the door. He was standing on the front step wearing a dressing gown. He was a short lad and it trailed on the floor. He looked like a wizard, with his floppy sleeves and the puddle of material behind him. And she was standing on the path outside, looking past him. Looking at me. Cordelia. She was paler than when I'd first seen her and her hair was stuck to her face like it were painted on her skin. There were dark lines under her eyes and her coat was soaked three shades darker than it was meant to be. I think she was smiling. Not a proper one – not a grin or the way you look when somebody says something that tickles your funny bone. But she was trying to make herself look a bit softer. She looked like a child trying to hold a pleasing face for a school photo. My heart went out to her. I'd been worried, to tell the truth. After what I'd found in the church and after what Pike and Pat had said, I'd been desperate to talk to Cordelia again. But we hadn't parted on good terms. It felt like I'd let her down. Told a fib and turned my face away from hers when she asked me to support her story of what we had seen when the tree came down. I'd had a nervous feeling in my chest at the thought of walking up the hill and knocking on her door. But she were here now. Here, looking forlorn and feeble and desperate to be invited in.

'Mrs Hemlock,' I said, like it was all normal and we were friends. 'Brian, let the lady in, she'll catch her death.'

Brian smirked. He shuffled sideways a little. He was only
wearing his underpants beneath the dressing gown. The material
hung like stage curtains across his skinny white body.

'Were that Loz dropping ye off?' he asked. 'Yer gev us a
start. Thought he were after me. I've had two bellyfuls of
petrol out that tractor o' his. Thought he'd worked it out.'

Behind Cordelia the rain continued to pour. There was only
one street light and it illuminated the sad shape of Fairfax's
cottage across the street. The light died before it reached Pike's
ragged cottage down the hill. The church, a little further down,
was no more than a square of darkness; an unlit furnace in a
coal cellar.

'I wasn't expecting you,' I said, feeling myself start babbling
as I stepped back down the corridor. 'I was doing mince . . .'

Her face fell. 'I should have rung,' she said.

'Wouldn't do no good,' said Brian. 'We aint got a phone.'

'We use Fairfax's, if it's an emergency,' I said, and I swear
it felt like somebody had my heart in their fist and were
squeezing it. 'Used it, I mean.'

'That'll have to stop,' said Brian, standing between us at
the foot of the stairs. He had one of his comics in his pocket,
sticking out like a truncheon. The Man From U.N.C.L.E.
maybe, or one of his old ones from when he liked cowboy
films. He was smirking, like he always did. I could smell
cigarettes on him. He liked to smoke while he tied his fishing
flies. Had a talent for it. I've pulled plenty hooks and barbs
out of his fingers over the years but the finished fly is always
something beautiful. Could have sold them if he'd had any
interest in making an honest living.

'Brian, take Mrs Hemlock's coat.'

'I'm not the butler,' he said, looking her up and down.

'Brian!' I snapped, wishing that he cared enough about my
feelings not to show me up. 'Do as you're told.'

He rolled his eyes. He'd started doing that. It drove John
up the wall. They came to blows a few times, in later years.
John never knew how to win those fights. Never knew whether
he was being a better dad by drawing blood or in letting his
lad work out his aggression on him. He could fight, could
Brian. Had a temper like an alley cat and used to bite and

scratch and claw like one too. But they weren't the right fights, if you get me. He never seemed to care about right or wrong or what were kind and what was mean. I'd tried with him. God knows I'd tried. Told him that unkindness was wrong. That cruelty was wrong. That bullying was wrong. He always wanted me to explain. *Why, Mam? Why is it wrong? Why is it good to be generous and friendly and welcoming? Why is that better? Who said, Mam? The animals don't worry about it. Birds neither. And that's all we are, aint we? Meat in shoes. Who set the rules . . .?*

'I hoped we could talk,' she said, and I noticed how wide her eyes were. Her pupils were like tadpoles; like spilled ink on blue writing paper.

'We're having tea soon,' said Brian. 'You won't want any. With the carrots chopped up it looks like sick.'

I were embarrassed. I swear, I don't know why he had to behave like that. I wanted to run into the kitchen with her and show her James and say, 'Look, I can make children who are nice and caring and who don't cause people grief'.

'We can be quick,' she said, looking at Brian like he were my dad and she was trying to persuade him to let me play out. She looked desperate, poor thing. It felt like I was seeing her properly at last. How young she was. Younger than me but for all her learning she were half-clueless when it came to people.

'We can be as long as you need,' I said, and glared at Brian. He looked at me like I were nothing. I thought he were going to spit on the carpet. He suddenly seemed tired of the game. Turned away from her and slouched back up the stairs to his wires and feathers and sharp little hooks. I hadn't been in the tying room for months. Last time I'd gone in I'd seen nowt but bones and skulls and dead things. Birds. Foxes. Little sad skeletons of field mice and dormice and a leathery, dehydrated toad he had found on one of his expeditions. I told myself it were normal. Boys liked gruesome stuff. Liked to know how our bits fitted together and what we were made of. I told myself it were all learning. All a different form of school. And he were so clever it was good to see him using his brain for something sort of scientific. But I didn't like the way the chemicals made his skin smell or the smell of warm, rotten meat that sometimes wafted under the door. John put a stop to it, in the end. But by then Brian had already learned enough.

'Come into the kitchen,' I said. 'I'll make tea.'

She followed me like a little girl. Stayed standing by the door until I invited her to sit down. I took her coat from her like she were an invalid. Handed her two clean towels from the drawer beneath the sink and she stood holding them as if she were a daft lass. She seemed like her batteries were running out.

'This is Mrs Hemlock,' I said to James. He turned and gave her a big smile.

'From the Winslow farm? Aye, nice place that. Sorry fer yer troubles.'

I saw a tower demolished once. All dynamite and dust and *three-two-one*. It were like that, the way she collapsed. Something just blew in her foundations and the next thing she were sliding down onto the arm of the chair and there were tears coming out of her like she were a squeezed sponge. James looked to me as if he were watching somebody die. I shooed him out of the room like he were a chicken. I didn't know what to do for best. She was half folded in on herself, sobbing and gulping as if she had a fever.

I fussed over her like she were made of glass. Patted her damp back, clucking out 'now now' and 'there there' like they were spells that could make her feel better. I didn't expect her to cuddle into me. I swear, but when she turned towards me and pressed her face against me it were like a baby looking for the nipple. That's what I thought, God forgive me. That's what it reminded me of. And I didn't know what to do so I just held her and patted her arm and tried to think of her like she were one of the bairns. We were still there when John pushed open the kitchen door. I had to angle my neck to see who it was. He were standing there with nowt on his face but rain. Didn't look shocked nor taken aback. Never did. Just dealt with things as they happened.

'Ye'll be wanting your privacy,' said John. His cigarette moved as he talked and in the light from the hallway and the mist drifting from his lungs he looked like a half-made thing.

She shifted at the sound of his voice. Sat bolt upright and rubbed her eyes and nose and gave this embarrassed laugh. She made all sorts of fussy little gestures and then took the towel from her lap and started rubbing it herself like she were a sideboard and it were sandpaper.

'Sorry,' she muttered. 'Sorry, just got upset . . .'

'It's nowt, love,' said John, not moving. 'This time of year it's all tears. And you've had your sadnesses. Dry your eyes, you don't want to get your dress wet.'

Cordelia and I shared a laugh at that, looking down at her soaked clothes. I loved him fierce. Still do.

'Nivver seen you dry,' said John, and he shrugged himself out of his black donkey jacket. He eased past us both and went to the kitchen sink. Washed his hands with the fat white soap. He liked to be spotless, did John. Scrubbed his fingernails and his wrists like a doctor preparing to do an operation. Then he combed his hair in the mirror by the sink. The ritual was always the same. Brushed the fine strands back across his head to cover the growing bald spot and then inserted a parting on the left. Half a dozen deft strokes left, half a dozen right, and he would declare himself satisfied. Only then would he kiss my cheek and squeeze my shoulder and sit himself down in his chair. His knees squeaked like the springs.

'How's the house?' asked John, as if it were a person. 'Bet the wind rattles in, eh?'

Cordelia held her hand to her nose. Seemed to be counting her breaths. When she looked at him she was herself again but her eyes still held the sparkle of tears.

'I don't use many of the rooms,' she said. 'It's a bit wasted on me. We didn't need anywhere that big really.'

'He'll be joining you afore long though, eh?' asked John. He found his ashtray beneath his chair and extinguished the one he was smoking while fumbling in his shirt pocket for a fresh one.

'We don't know what the future will bring,' said Cordelia, looking away.

'London he works, so I hear.'

'Yes. He's a Mandarin. Civil servant, I mean. Whitehall.'

John stuck out his lower lip, impressed. 'Knew he were

important. Only met him a couple of times but he were friendly enough. Generous too.'

'That'll do, John,' I said, filling the kettle. I knew well enough how many locals had taken more than their fair share of ready money from Mr Hemlock. It would do to not have his wife be just as familiar with the details as I was.

'The boys in their rooms?' asked John, undoing his shirt to the waist and making himself comfortable. He looked handsome, sitting there, like the chair were a throne and his damp work trousers a pair of velvet slacks.

'Brian's tying. James is probably drawing. Henry the Eighth this term.'

'That'll be a bloodbath,' said John, winking. 'Lock up your lipstick. He's a one for drawing, our eldest. I'm not sure you'd hang his stuff on your wall but it's got something to it. You got brothers and sisters Mrs Hemlock?'

'No,' she said, quietly. 'Only child.'

'And where is it did you say you were from.'

'All over, in a way.'

'Where yer mam, though?'

'Over in Durham,' she said, and I was surprised to hear that. It were only an hour and a half in the car to Durham. I wondered if she and her mam were close.

'Been there for work,' said John. 'Wanted to take Felicity with me but she won't go out if there's a chance of driving back in the dark. She's a nervous passenger. Nervous everything, ain't you, Felicity?'

Cordelia shuffled herself around on the seat. She looked uncomfortable. I suppose she weren't used to family life. I didn't know the first thing about her past and I didn't like to ask. John weren't as concerned with the look of things. He could be an old woman for gossip.

'Had a chinwag with yon charver from Bewcastle on walk from village,' said John. 'The estate's already asked him to fix the headstone and tow the tree. No time for Keith to get his lazy backside to the table. Shame having somebody from outside getting the job but the money were there so no point hanging about.'

I was busy with teacups and drying spoons. It took me a second to pay attention.

'Harper, is it?' I asked. Harper was an Irish mason with a premises a few miles away at Bewcastle. He had more work than he needed but it was hard to begrudge him. He was always full of laughs and tales. Fairfax was always fond of him.

'Aye, Ronan Harper. Came over to build the base and nivver left.' He rubbed his big broad chin. 'The Kinmont solicitor's had a call. Said the money were there to fix the place up. It'll have to wait until the weather clears, like.'

Cordelia's eyes burned into my back. I felt like a translator.

'Kinmont tomb was the one got taken out by the tree,' I said. 'There's only one Kinmont left and he lives away so local matters are handled by his solicitor. He'll be relieved, no doubt. Last time he came up it had no happy memories for him. Said flat out he wouldn't want to be buried in the thing. Got a life in Oxford, so I hear. Left the village before the war so it's no loss.'

'And somebody's paying to have it fixed?' asked Cordelia, quietly.

'Aye, somebody with a big heart and big pockets. Said it was wrong to have him or the church pay out for what were an act of God. I were hoping to get a name out of him but he had to be off and I only lets myself have one pint after work. I likes to be home. Felicity and my fireside, that'll do for me.'

Cordelia's lips had become a line. She was staring at the floor like there were a stain on it.

'Chivers aint been up to you yet,' said John, cigarette hanging at his lip and his hands on the edges of his chair. 'Man's an imbecile.'

I'd never heard him say 'imbecile' before. He might have been trying to impress.

'I'm not sure I've much to tell him,' said Cordelia. She looked at me enquiringly, daring to be contradicted. Was it a test? What did she want me to say?

'He won't put no more hours in than he needs to,' said John. 'Not exactly Sherlock Holmes. And it all seems pretty straightforward about poor Fairfax. There'll be an inquest right enough but that'll be open and shut. You're as well to stay out of it. Felicity's said she'll make a statement but what's it going to say? He left in a rainstorm and never came back? Doubt that will be much help.'

I stayed where I was, facing away from them both, watching her in the reflected surface of the window. She seemed to be struggling with herself. Looked like she was having a fight inside.

'There were all sorts of funny stuff in his house,' I said, and it was out before I could stop it. I suddenly heard myself speaking. Opening up. And it felt like I were getting lighter as I did so.

'Funny stuff?' asked Cordelia and John, as one.

'You know he liked writing. Well it were no secret he'd scribbled all these stories down and had most of the village's memories on paper. But I had no idea how hard he'd worked at it. Honest to God there were boxes and boxes full of scribblings and gibberish. No system to it. Just chaos. I'm good with handwriting and I could barely make much sense of it but it was like he had the whole village's thoughts pinned down on paper. And Keith's wife Pat said he had one of those recording things. I've nivver seen him with that, have you, John?'

Cordelia whipped her head in my direction. 'A recording device? Like a Dictaphone?'

'If that's what you call them. I never seen him with one. John?'

John shrugged one shoulder. 'He liked his toys. I mebs thought it were a music machine. I'll ask. Graffoe's into all that lot.'

'Graffoe?'

'Sorry love, friend of mine. Gives me my lift in. He knows about that stuff.'

'Did he know Fairfax.'

'Doubt it. Can't see as how they'd have crossed paths.'

Cordelia looked angry now, as if she couldn't work out how the conversation was supposed to flow.

'John works in Carlisle,' I said, filling in the gaps. 'Plumber for the council. Graffoe comes in daily from Haltwhistle and picks John up on the main road. You might know his car. Passes you daily.'

She didn't seem any less tense. Just sat, waiting for more.

'Aye, well, mebs it's no help,' said John, a little sniffily. 'What were you wanting our Felicity for any road?'

I passed her a cup of tea, complete with saucer. She took it without a word. She looked at its surface as if reading the leaves.

'I was up at the camp today,' she said, suddenly. 'By the castle. Mr Nixon told me about its history and I suddenly wanted to see it. A man called Loz picked me up. We talked. I wanted to tell Felicity what we spoke about.'

For a moment the only sound in the kitchen was the shifting of coals in the stove and the soft rhythm of rain on glass. Then John cleared his throat and extinguished his cigarette.

'Spit it out then, love,' he said, sitting forward. He would normally be reading the paper at that time. He was going to be entertained come what might.

'I tells John everything any way,' I said, and at the time, it was still true.

We waited for longer than was comfortable. Then she told us. Told us about the man Loz had seen and spoken to and sent to Fairfax's house. A man in a blue suit with a recording device and a canvas bag. He'd seen somebody he recognized and wanted to be sure. Wanted to know so badly that he went straight to a stranger's door.

I left it a moment after she finished. Wanted to give John his chance to say something. But he never. It were me as spoke.

'I found a page of writing paper in the church,' I said, quietly. 'Under a stone, in a locked box. There were footprints in the dust. It looked like somebody had tried to burn it. Just a page. Why would he do that? Why keep it there then make it so easy to see where it might be?'

Cordelia played with the collar of her jumper, pulling the moist material away from her skin. There were newspapers beside her on the sofa and she scanned the headlines as she thought. I remember seeing her eyes as being like a blur but I probably imagined that. Doesn't make it any less real.

'If he knew who the man in blue was . . .' she said, softly.

'He might just have had the time to move him. To move him and grab whatever else was in the floor.'

I looked at John. He seemed energized now, his thoughts keeping pace with Cordelia's.

'He looked startled,' said Cordelia, glancing at me. 'Think about it. When you told him what we'd seen there was a look on his face and then he went straight back out the door . . .'

'I don't know,' I said, shaking my head.

'He could have moved the man we saw. Could have grabbed whatever he had hidden. That might be what caused the accident. He might have been so shaken up . . .'

'He might have lost control of the car.'

'Or he might have been to see whoever shared his secret,' finished Cordelia. She and John looked at one another, half-smiling, faces flushed. I felt like the outsider. Felt like a silly woman in an apron with the smell of potatoes and gravy on my hands.

'Fairfax were as good a man as I've known,' I said, refusing to believe it.

'This doesn't mean he weren't. We don't know anything,' said Cordelia. 'But we have to ask questions. This place,' she muttered, frustrated, 'it's got something in the earth. It's seen so much blood and misery. People do things they might not want to. We're not all wicked. Sometimes it's just circumstances.'

They looked at me as if I were both their mams; as if they needed me to acknowledge what was being said before we could move forward.

'Here,' I said, at last, and I pulled the burnt paper from my apron. It was folded across the middle and some of the words were illegible but there was no mistaking Fairfax's handwriting or the smell of burning that marbled the air as Cordelia unfolded it.

'Can I?' asked John, and he pulled himself out of his chair and sat down beside Cordelia, squashing the newspapers. Their knees touched. Their shoulders touched. I swear it were all I could do not to stick a knife between them and pull them apart like frozen sausages.

John's lips moved as he read. Cordelia's didn't. She finished first. They looked at me together.

'We should just tell Chivers,' I said, in a last desperate attempt to jump off whatever road we were on.

'We will,' said Cordelia. 'But not until we have something to tell him. Felicity, there's something here. Some secrets that need to be dug up. Fairfax is dead and I know it's to do with what we glimpsed when the tree came down. It has something to do with the war. With this Frenchman. A boy on a car bonnet. We need to know more. Can you look through his boxes? Get us into the church again? And John, you need to find out who's paying for the restoration work . . .'

I turned my back on them but couldn't help staring; staring through my own silly reflection as my husband and my new friend talked about how to find whichever one of my friends or family had put a well-dressed Frenchman in a tomb and closed the door.

CORDELIA

The words on the burnt paper stayed with me all night. I left Felicity's just before nine p.m. and resisted John's persistent offer to walk me home. I wanted to think. Wanted to feel rain on my face and cold air on my cheeks and see if the hunter's moon would be red or blue. I never found out. The sky was too clogged with grey to offer a view of any lunar spectacle and in truth, the rain and the cold produced little in the way of sensory pleasure. I just ended up sniffly and damp. Two cars passed me on the way back up the hill. Neither one slowed down. The village seemed even quieter than usual as I trudged past the old vicarage, already beginning to go to seed, and past the Bridge Inn. The place was silent. No clinking glasses, no muffled songs or mumbled back-and-forth. Left, past the garage with its fleet of buses standing idle at the kerbside; their paintwork gleaming with a gloss of raindrops. Round past the church. The new church. Pretty little place built on a slope: a curve of old graves around the entrance and long, straggly grass and weeds. Newer headstones further away from the door – smaller, whiter, sadder. Children. Babies from the hospital on the hill.

I didn't let myself linger there. The headstones were teeth, waiting to take a bite out of a part of me that was starting to come back to life. I quickened my pace. Up past the big old houses. Slender trees to my right; an inadequate fence for the miles and miles of green that stretched away to my right. Up to the hospital. The locals still called it that. It had been a convalescent home for nigh-on twenty years but during the war it had been taken on by the authorities as a safe haven where expectant mothers from bigger cities in the north east could come and give birth without fear of any bombs dropping. Close to 5,000 women did just that. Those that didn't survive were buried, quietly, in the grounds of the new church: another layer on the endless strata of bones and blood upon which the whole vale seemed to have been constructed.

Work was going on at the spa. There was talk of it becoming a hotel. It was certainly a splendid old building; a colossal white edifice that would have looked more at home on the seafront at Brighton or Scarborough than in that little wooded area by the river. I barely looked up as I passed. I slouched my way down into the damp woods and slithered down the muddy footpath; the smell of the sulphurous water mingling with the scent of churned mud and mulched leaves. The river was raging. It took an effort of will to force myself over the bridge, placing my feet carefully on the wooden slats. Rain splattered hard and heavy on the few leaves that the autumn had not stolen and I squinted in almost total blackness as I dragged myself up the footpath on the far bank towards home. Was I afraid? I don't think I was, no. The worst thing I could imagine had already happened to me. There was nothing more fearsome in the darkness of the wood than there was within the shadows of myself.

For the first time since Stefan died I felt almost pleased to be home. The house looked as it always did – old and sturdy and totally wrong for me. It was too symmetrical – too splendid. I wanted chaos. Mess. I wanted patterned wallpaper hung upside down. I wanted floral curtains and polka-dot drapes. I could have had it, if I'd asked. But I think I preferred wanting it than having it. However it looked, I was pleased to see it that night. Happy to push open the back door and bathe myself in light. I drank a measure of sloe gin then poured another into a mug of boiling water. Went to the library and pulled a book at random from the shelves. I couldn't concentrate on the words. Every time I tried to focus I would again see the burnt paper and Fairfax's scribbled words and my vision would fill with images of frightened men and women herded like cattle and a young boy draped across a Nazi vehicle like a stag.

I woke where I was; stiff and cold in a high-backed chair. I don't know if I dreamed but when I opened my eyes I was glad to have left wherever I had just been. I was cold to the marrow. My clothes had dried to my skin and the moisture from them had seeped into my bones. I stripped and wrapped myself in a blanket while I waited for the water to heat up then ran a bath. There was only enough hot water for a couple of inches but it still felt good to ease myself over the lip of the white, wrought-iron tub and scrub the goose pimples from my skin. I washed my hair and shaved my legs and lay with a hot flannel over my eyes until the water began to grow cold. I felt better for it. The towels I used to rub myself dry were rougher than I would have wished but I had not really got the hang of doing the laundry. I brushed my hair for a while, sitting at a dressing table in one of the spare rooms and looking at myself in the burnished surface of an old Victorian mirror. Where had he found all this stuff? Who was it for? Did he know me at all? I tried not to think upon it. My marriage was not meant to be a union of souls. It was an arrangement – a solution. I was grateful to him for all he had done but there were times I felt I would have been better scratching a living by myself than trusting my whole future to the charity of a man who only needed me in his life as camouflage. If I dwelled too long upon such thoughts I grew angry. Angry at myself for being so dependent; angry at my body for making a lie of my promises to Stefan's father. I hadn't expected to get pregnant. Hadn't thought my body could so blatantly disregard my wishes.

It was just after ten the next morning when I finally headed back the way I had come. Out the door, down the hill, over the swollen river. When I had first arrived I had been told to turn left at the riverbank and make my way to the Popping Stone. It was a local landmark: three rounded boulders beside the river and a popular place for courtships over the years. The poet Sir Walter Scott proposed to his sweetheart there, though local legend had it that he only did so out of spite towards a previous lover who had turned him down. He had made her a promise he would find a new object for his affections before the year was out. The spot was as popular with locals as with tourists who all put great stock in the sulphurous water's healing powers. Several bottles of gunpowder-scented water had been left on my doorstep during my time in the village though I had barely taken more than a sip. It tasted of rotten eggs and while it may have offered long life to those who imbibed, none of the stooped, gnarled old folk who shuffled around Gilsland looked as though they were gaining much from the experience.

It took twenty minutes to reach Felicity's. The rain had eased off but the air was still wet and the sky had the look of uncooked bread. I saw two women at the bus stop and said hello to a man I half recognized outside the post office. He seemed a little taken aback but knuckled his flat cap as if I was somebody important. It was all I could do not to curtsey in return.

There was no answer at Felicity's so I presumed she had already made her way to Fairfax's. I crossed the road and peered in at the kitchen window. Felicity was on her knees, surrounded by papers, like a mug on an elaborate doily. I was cautious with my knock on the window but she still jumped like a teenager caught looking at a magazine. When she turned to me her face was white; the veins in her neck standing out as if she had just escaped the noose. One hand held to her heart, she gestured me to the back door. I went inside, into chilly air that smelled like forgotten fruit and liniment.

'Gave me a start,' said Felicity. She seemed as cool as the room; her whole manner stiff.

'I'm always doing that,' I said, trying to raise a smile.

'I don't know if I'm doing any of this right,' she said, leading me into the kitchen through the passageway. It was quite a nice space, designed like Felicity's, but the table was made for two, not four, and the pictures on the walls were in better quality frames.

'He kept it nice,' I said, taking my coat off. The sofa was also covered in paperwork so I just held it in my hand.

'Ha!' said Felicity, sharply. 'This room maybe. The room for visitors. For me! But you wait until you see the rest of the place. Bloody pigsty.' She had made herself a space in the centre of the papers and went back to her knees, folding her pleated skirt beneath her backside and holding it there with her slippered feet.

I was surprised to see her angry. She looked pale, as though she were fighting a bout of seasickness. I wondered if she had slept last night. Whether the thought of looking deeper into the dead man had filled her sleep with terrors.

'Probably too proud to ask for help,' I said, as softly as I could. 'How were you to know, eh?'

'Aye, well,' said Felicity, and she shifted, painfully. 'Bloody knees are killing me. Curse in my family. Our bones go to seed after we hit thirty.'

'It's temper in mine,' I said, moving closer to her. She shuffled herself. She looked suddenly like an Arab at prayer.

'Your mam quick with the stick, is she?' asked Felicity, turning to me. 'Mine were a terror. Kind-hearted but knew that she shouldn't spare the rod. She were right to do it. There's plenty in the village could still do with a hiding but we've all gone soft. I should have given my two a belting years ago.'

I found myself reaching out. I put a hand on her shoulder. Tried to comfort her the way she had done for me. She stiffened under my touch but gave the tiniest nod of thanks.

'Our Brian,' she said, rocking back on her haunches and huffing a strand of hair from her face. 'He'll be the death of me. Took a tanner from John's wallet afore school. What for, eh? What hasn't he got? Oh he says it weren't him, looks so bloody innocent you find yourself wondering if your eyes are the ones telling lies.' She looked down at the paperwork and I saw her head fall forward: a horse stooping to eat. 'I were harder on him than he's used to. Gave him a right telling off. He looked so upset. Stomped out the house like he were nivver coming back. And God forgive me but I went into the room where he ties his flies. I thought the money might be in there. Thought I could put it back and make it like it nivver happened. But by God I forgot the money as soon as I opened the door. He's been collecting things. I knew he liked bones. Frogs and birds and stuff. But it were like a museum. Skulls. Big ones from rams and foxes. I swear, he had a half-dead cat hanging from a string. Where did he get that, eh? And in the corner . . .'

I waited for more. Saw her fight with the tears that filled her eyes.

'He had this bucket with a lid on it. There were something in there, in among all this water and scum and rotten meat that stunk like chemicals. He had these big plastic gloves and wooden tongs, like you use for salad. It scared me. Scared me half to death. My own son.'

I stood where I was, wondering how best to comfort her. Truth be told her sudden bout of extra misery was inconvenient. I wanted to get on with what we were here to do. Wanted to make sense of a dead man's ramblings. I needed her to be useful. I felt for her, of course I did, but sometimes children are just born wrong. The sisters taught me that. Some children are wicked. It doesn't matter how you teach them and slap them and prophesy an eternity in the bowels of Hell – sometimes a child just needs to pull the meat from the bone and take a look inside.

'It'll be for a school project,' I said, brightly. 'They do a lot more advanced kind of science at school these days. It'll be an experiment. We did similar things when I was at school, which was more recently than you. Honestly, you're worrying for nothing.'

I saw hope flicker in her face. Saw her lower lip wobble and two spots of colour light her cheeks.

'Would that be it, d'you think?'

'More likely than anything else. And even if he took that money, who's to say it isn't for a school trip or something else. He seemed a clever kid. Bit precocious but that's no bad thing.'

She clung to my words like they were a rope thrown to a sailor. She wanted things safe. Clean. Wanted the week of the hunter's moon to draw to a close without any more violence slipping into her world.

'Don't think on it just now,' I said, in the voice I used for bedtime stories. 'How've you done? What have you got?'

She put her hand out to me and I closed my soft palm over her rough fingers. Helped her to her feet. She leaned back against the counter and managed a smile.

'You got home safe, then? John were worried.'

'Fine, no problems,' I said, a little impatiently.

'You didn't go by the river, did you? Went the long way, I hope.'

'I went by the river, yes. It's quickest.'

'Don't know how you dare,' she said, aghast. 'I'd shiver

meself to death. There's all sorts in the woods. Caves in the cliff, so they say, but I wouldn't go looking for them. Me mam would have gone berserk at the very thought.'

'It was fine,' I said, gesturing at the papers and indicating we should stop wasting time. 'Bit cold and muddy but I'm not scared of the dark.'

'The dark doesn't know that,' she said, and I swear I actually saw her shiver. 'One of the popping stones was taken away after the war. Kissing Bush too.'

I think my face gave me away. I found myself half-laughing, unsure whether to simply let her finish or to push her into some useful answers. It felt like talking to a little old lady: a superstitious crone in a Highland cottage. She wasn't more than thirty-three but she had the sudden air of somebody who should be wearing candlelight and cobwebs.

'Used to be an extra stone,' she said, wavering. Behind her, beyond the glass, the rain had started up again; delicately tapping on the glass like the pecking of countless birds. 'Nobody knows where it went but it were the biggest. There one day and gone the next. Somebody cut down the bush too. Ancient hawthorn tree, all gnarled and twisted. Dug up and taken away and a great hole in the ground. Ye'd have thought it would tek a giant to shift it. Scared us half to death. It were Mrs Parker's man who said it were a coffin stone.'

'A coffin stone?'

'Somewhere for the pall-bearers to rest their burden on the way to the church. Smooth, flat stone. You can imagine what some of the locals used to use it for after they'd asked their lovers to marry them.' She twitched a nervous smile. 'Parker, from farm next to yours – he'd only just moved here when the stone vanished, though at that time there were so much coming and going it were hard to keep track. He and Mrs Parker had already wed but he wanted to do things properly, like. Wanted to be a proper part of the village. Took her to the Popping Stone and turned white as a ghost. Told us all sorts of stories about how those old stones were centuries old and how in his country they were thought of as something to be feared – like they'd soaked up all the dregs of all the bodies who'd rested there over the years. Said the stone were like a cork in a bottle, holding bad spirits in. You can imagine what that did to us.'

'How do you know this?' I asked, unable to help.

'He gave a talk at the school not long after. The headmaster had asked him special.'

'And he spoke about proposing to his wife?' I asked, confused.

'No, that were just gossip, the sort of thing you pick up. But he told us about the coffin stone and what it meant and when it vanished like that we were all scared to sleep for weeks.'

Behind Felicity a tiny shaft of sunlight was trying to find a gap between clouds. A thin line of illumination cast a sudden yellow glow onto my face and the left side of my body and then was just as quickly snatched away.

'He's foreign?' I asked. 'You said "his country".'

'Aye, Swiss. Where the cuckoo clocks come from. You've not met him?'

I tried to remember. I think he waved hello shortly after I moved in: a distant stick-man in green. And perhaps I had seen him and his wife in their car once or twice. I'd never paid them any attention. I just knew him as the man who wanted to buy the house and his wife as the mousy, miserable woman who had knocked on my door.

'I don't really know anybody,' I reminded her.

'Aye, suppose. Nice man. Gave money to the Reading Rooms when it needed a new roof and always sponsors stalls at the wrestling and the cattle market. Turned that farm into a money-spinner. Her faither would have been proud.'

I clicked with my tongue; a sudden, unexpected clucking noise that betrayed my impatience.

'Her faither?'

'Dad. Mr Parker.'

'Same surname?' I asked, baffled.

'No, look, sorry, I always forget how little ye know. It's a horrible word but Audrey Parker were a spinster. Past thirty and not married. Quiet lass. She'd been away to school and not settled. Her faither was a military man, proper old-fashioned colonel-type though I don't know if he was an actual colonel

– that's just what people called him. Was already a soldier
before the first war. He bought the farm next to your place
about 1910. Married a lass from Greenhead who didn't want
to move to wherever it were that he were from. Audrey came
along during the war when he were off fighting. Her brother,
Loveday, the year after. Aye, I see you looking! He paid the
price for the name his family lumbered him with. Can't say
the local lads were too kind to him when he were home for
the holidays. The colonel came home after the war to be a
farmer though from what Mam told me he weren't the same
man who left. He'd gone grey and looked old and weren't fit
enough to lift a spade. It were his wife who made a go of the
place and then Audrey and her brother took it on when she
died. Always a bit touched by tragedy, so Mam said. Two of
Audrey's brothers didn't see their fifth birthdays. And Loveday
had an accident that took his arm at the elbow, though it didn't
stop him working like a Trojan. The colonel died not long after.
Farm was doing OK and Audrey had come back from school
and was happy to run the place with her mam and her brother.
But brother went off to war . . .'

'With one arm?'

'Oh aye, they'll find work for ye if ye're willing. Well, he
nivver came back. All those years studying at the posh school
and at university and he goes and gets blasted to bits. Her
mam died not long after and Audrey were alone with a great
farm to run on her own and she were already the age I am
now. We all thought she'd end up a bit dotty, all alone. That
were mebbe why she wrote to all the old POWs and sent them
bits and bobs when they were going through hardships. Bit of
company, even if it were miles away. Then next thing she's
got herself wed. Met some Swiss man while in Ireland buying
a breeding bull. Were a proper local romance. There were
those who reckoned she were one of those who had no interest
in marriage but it just shows what little people know. He were
a gent, Mr Parker, even if he weren't the prettiest. And it
were a lovely tribute, what he did.'

'What he did?'

'He took her name! What a thing, eh? Whatever he were
called afore he were happy to be a Parker if it meant keeping

the name of her faither on the deeds. Parker's Farm it were and is still and he's made a profitable business, like I said. Quiet man but kind and though you don't see Audrey smile over much there's a happiness in her that weren't there when she were young. No children but they works so hard they've probably no time.'

I rubbed my lip and realized how still I had been holding myself. My joints were aching. I'd been cold too many times. Shivering, I glanced back down at the mess of papers. The words looked like so many squashed lice: a jumble of scrawls all scribbled in the same hand.

'I'm sorry I wasn't here earlier,' I said. 'You must be going blind.'

Felicity sucked at her teeth, rolling her eyes. 'Wouldn't have made a difference, even with a big brain you need to be able to read the writing and I swear Fairfax has just done this to give me a headache. I've tried as well as I can to put it into order but there's no headings and it's only when I can make out a word that I've been able to make any kind of system. That pile by your feet seems to be the earliest stuff. It's in pencil and the handwriting makes some kind of sense. It's neat and there are initials. I reckon I've worked most of 'em out. Armstrong. Irthing. Sawyer, Lightfoot. Some of 'em have gone but others are still alive and I don't suppose many of them will be worrying about their secrets being shared. It's all just memories of school and the jobs they used to do and their mothers and faithers giving them a hiding for this or that. Just pages of how lovely things used to be, though I've no doubt when I'm old I'll say the same about now.'

'Right, well, that's a start . . .'

'Middle pile have the occasional date on them. Maybe ten years ago. Chats with the navvies, the lads who drained the bog, the charvers who built the base. Lots of people talking about how times are looking up and there's good money to be made and wouldn't it be a thing if it were true what people were saying – that Gilsland would be a terminus for the moon.'

'That lot?' I asked, pointing at the most chaotic of the piles.

'I'd say that's round about the point he lost his wife, God rest her, and there were nowt to keep him focussed. I can barely make any of it out but it's not as faded as the other stuff and it's in pen, not pencil and he's using more pages and not cramming everything in so it must have been after rationing stopped . . .'

I found myself grinning. 'That's proper detective work,' I said.

She shook her head at that but seemed pleased. 'Stuff about local landmarks. The wall. The fort.'

'The fort?'

'Roman fort. Chats with somebody whose name I can't make out, page after page talking about types of stone and architecture and gargoyles and the sort of stuff you'd only read if you had bugger all else to do.'

I looked a little disappointed. 'Nothing about a Frenchman?'

'If there is I can't make it out. I'm disappointed, despite myself. The page under the church floor was at least legible. Like he'd made an effort with it.'

I breathed out, rolling my head this way and that. I felt stiff and cold and hungry but had no desire to warm up or eat anything. I just wanted to understand.

'The tape recorder,' I said, closing one eye. 'If he'd started recording conversations then he could listen to them back and not have to scribble it all down as people were talking. Maybe the page you found was a transcript. Something from a recording.'

Felicity opened her eyes a little wider. She twitched, like Bogart, as though something suddenly pained her.

'There's no tape recorder here,' she said.

'Have you been through the whole house? Top to bottom?'

'No, of course . . .'

'Well, let's do that.'

It took better than three hours and by the time we had finished the house looked as though a tornado had blown through. We found no tape recorder. It was a sad, dispiriting trawl. Felicity went very quiet when we found ourselves in Christopher's old room. Little had been touched since his death. It looked as though he had simply popped out. There was a notebook on the windowsill, next to some battered paperbacks and a chunk of rock. The bed was made up with a sheet and brown woollen blanket. The cupboard and the chest of drawers were different types of wood and a sketch of Lanercost Priory hung on the chimney breast against a cold blue wall. I couldn't bring myself to open the notebooks. Nobody had disturbed the dust in years: the thoughts of a boy dead for twenty years still safely imprisoned beneath the covers.

We were standing on the upstairs landing, looking dejected, feeling grey, when the bird hit the window. There was no warning. There was just a sudden, startling bang on the glass and then the window on the landing erupted inwards in a sudden geyser of flying glass and feathers.

I jumped backwards, my hands coming up to protect my face, shrieking like a child. Felicity's noise was something else entirely. She gave a low, tremulous growl: the noise people make in the seconds before they die. A death rattle, they call it, and that's the only sound I can liken it to. I felt her hands dig into my arm hard enough to draw blood. I swear I think she believed she was about to be carried away by whatever spirit had won her soul.

'Felicity, it's OK, it's OK, it's just a bird,' I said, looking down at the sad, blood-spattered creature that was twitching on the threadbare carpet. It was brown and yellow with an eye that made me think of polished black stone. 'It's just a bird. A bird came through the window . . .'

But Felicity was scurrying down the stairs, her legs half buckling as she slithered against the bannister and dragged herself toward the front door.

'Felicity, it's fine, I'll tidy up, it's nothing . . .'

She pulled open the front door and ran out onto the road.

I heard a screech of brakes and then the crunch of metal hitting stone.

And then there was just the pitter-patter of the ceaseless rain.

FELICITY

Transcript 0006, recorded October 30, 2010

Noise and speed and flashes of colour. That's what I remember. A sudden blur of red and green and a rush of air and a howling, angry screech as tyres fought for grip on the wet road. Metal hit against metal and then against brick and I was just laying there, wet and shaking and cold and watching dust rise into the sky like a volcano had erupted and not knowing whether it were a Tuesday afternoon or Christmas morning.

'Felicity. Oh God, Felicity . . .'

I heard me name but it meant nowt to me. Not at first. My heart was hammering inside my chest. It didn't feel like mine. It made me think of a crazy person headbutting a wall, over and over. I might have giggled a bit, like the lunatic had taken over. It was all just wet air and wet road and grey sky and hard stone beneath my head. What had happened? Why was I laying in the road, arm under my body like it belonged to somebody else. And then I saw the bird. A flicker of it; an insinuation of feathers and spindly bones, fluttering into my mind as if it were an eyelash caught on the edge of my vision. It was the rhythm, I think. The swift pat-pat-pat of my pulse turning into a peck-peck-peck of a sharp, angry beak. Everything flooded back. Hit me like a wave. I was on the ground outside my house. Grazed knees, bleeding palms, a pain all down one side. A bird had come through the window at Fairfax's. It had stripped the years from me; made me a child, wrapped up in ribbons by a terror beyond reason. I'd fled, Cordelia calling my name. The wagon had been slowing down, ready for the turn down towards the church. The driver saw me just in time, swinging the vehicle to the left. I'd stood still. Just stood, motionless, like I had roots sunk into the earth. Something had hit me. A sudden blur of speed and power and I had hit the ground as the wagon struck the side of Fairfax's house and sent slates tumbling from the roof and scattered the birds into the clouds.

Groggy, I looked to my left. He was on his knees, breathing slowly, like he'd run a race. He was looking at me, face pale. Looking as if I had done this on purpose. As I had let him down.

'Jaysus, where did ye come from? My God, I thought I'd squashed you flat. Are you hurt? Mother Mary, you're bleeding so you are.'

It felt like I was underwater. The voices were muffled. Everything was moving slowly. I opened my mouth wide. Stared up at the slow-moving clouds and thought they looked soft and warm and comfortable.

'Mrs Goose. Can you hear me? Oh Jesus she's bumped her head . . .'

'She had a fright. Ran straight out . . .'

'Christ, Ronan, ye've tekken half the wall down.'

'Never mind that, how's the other? Who were it?'

Something popped behind my jaw and suddenly everything sounded clear. I saw myself, laying on the road, skirt all pulled up, one shoe missing and cuts all over my skin. I started to blush. What a fuss . . .

'Jesus, you saved her life. She'd have been under the wheels . . .'

'Brian, are you OK? Can you hear me?'

I watched him shake them off. His school uniform was ripped down one knee and there was dirt on his face.

'Who is he?' asked Ronan Harper.

'This is her son. Brian.'

'Well you saved your Mammy's life, boy. Christ you're a hero.'

He still hadn't spoken. Was still staring.

I heard my own voice. 'Brian. Why aren't you at school?'

Then Harper was laughing; a loud, pleasant sound. 'Jesus aint that like a mammy? Almost squashed flat and saved by her own lad and first thing is a telling off for bunking off. Jesus, wait until I tell the wife.'

Cordelia loomed over me, face full of concern. 'Felicity. God you nearly killed me. I thought . . .'

'I'm fine,' I mumbled, embarrassed. 'Fine.'

'You're bleeding.' I was amazed to see tears in her eyes.

'It's nowt. Get me up, it's soaking.'

Between them they levered me upright. My left leg was sore and it hurt when I put weight on my hip but somehow the pain wasn't important. I hobbled to Brian. He was standing there, face a little moon against the dark of his jacket and the gloomy sky. I didn't know what to say. I wanted to look into his eyes and ask a thousand questions but people were looking and I felt so silly and tattered that all I could do was pat him, vaguely, on the shoulder and mutter something about the state of his shoes. It would be different nowadays. We'd have cried and hugged and had a big long talk about meaning everything to each other. But you didn't do that then. It wasn't the way we behaved.

'I reckon you'll be getting out of doing the washing up tonight,' said Harper, grinning at Brian. He didn't return it. Just stood there, staring off into the distance.

Harper checked me over again. I hadn't been this close to another man who wasn't family. He smelled different to John; all aftershave and onions. He was bigger than John too. Big square face with deep lines and fleshy lips and skin the colour of wet sand. Brown eyes and two days of beard.

'This is your place, yes?' he asked, pointing over the road to my house. 'Shall we get you in? Get the kettle on? My lad will sort out the mess, ain't that right, Sean?'

A smaller version of Harper appeared beside him; a copy of his father but washed on too high a heat. He had a bright smile. Might have been twenty but no more than that. It took him an effort to take his eyes off Cordelia, I remember that. Even now, I remember feeling a bit slighted that even in the midst of all that chaos, a young lad found the time to look at her and like what he saw.

'Oh what a mess,' I said, turning to look at the scene outside Fairfax's. The wagon had shed its load. Scaffolding poles hung from the side and the cab was at an ugly angle from the bed of the wagon, like a chicken with a broken neck. A huge stone tablet lay smashed on the kerb.

'Never mind all that, would be worse with you under the wheels,' said Harper.

I felt Cordelia's hand on my arm. She kept squeezing me softly, telling me I'd be OK, I'd be fine, that I'd given her such a fright.

They got me into John's armchair without much difficulty. I was burning with embarrassment but they wouldn't hear any of my protests. Cordelia propped me up with cushions and then started taking my shoes off like I was a child. I couldn't stop her. Couldn't stop Harper walking around on the kitchen carpet with his muddy boots on either. I let them get on with it. Put my head back and closed my eyes and listened to them fuss and chatter like monkeys; the story getting grander and bigger with each re-telling.

'Where's the boy gone?' asked Harper, over the bubbling of the kettle on the stove.

'I told him to go wash his hands or the cuts would get infected. Felicity, do you have a medicine box? We need to clean up some of these grazes.'

I sighed, shaking my head. 'I'll sort it myself. Like I keep saying, there's no need to fuss.'

Harper laughed again. 'Tough lasses round here, did you not know that,' he said, and as I opened my eyes I saw him winking at Cordelia. 'You'll be Mrs Hemlock, yes? I did some work on your place. Repaved the lean-to.'

'The what?'

'In the low orchard. Lovely summer house up against boundary wall.'

'With the ivy? By the pear trees?'

'Aye. Old flags were like a jigsaw. Re-set the lot for you. Did your man a good price. He happy?'

She shot a look at me. Gave a tight smile. 'It's great. I don't spend as much time there as I should.'

'Aye well, we've not had the weather for it. Been a bugger this week getting jobs started. Thought we spotted a break in the weather and hoped we could at least sink a couple of foundation poles on the Kinmont grave but I reckon the heavens will open again soon.' He twisted to look at me and smiled, rubbing his hair with a big dirty hand. 'And o'course, the wagon's stuck in the house yonder.'

I felt myself warming up. My heart was becoming my own

again. My thoughts had been a roundabout pushed too fast; all blurs and gale. Now it was slowing. I was still sick and dizzy but I felt as though I knew where my feet were at last and I knew they didn't belong where they were – bare and mucky and sitting on the floor in front of John's chair. Unsteadily, I stood myself up.

'Sit back down,' urged Cordelia. 'The tea's nearly ready . . .'

'I'm grand, Cordelia. Honestly, there's no need to fuss.'

'Please, Flick, for me, just . . .'

She stopped and I found myself smiling. It started there, really. That's when we became friends. It was a nice moment, like deciding on the right name for a pet or a child or clearing a debt. It was a subtle shifting of labels; a re-adjustment of my centre. I was Flick. She was Cordelia. Cordy, in a rush. And we were friends.

Harper walked from the kitchen and returned a moment later, rubbing his hands. 'Barely a scratch on the wagon and the house has had nowt more than a bang or two. Needs a few tiles and might need a bit of pointing but I've got two apprentices'll value the work. Could be worse. Could be a lot worse.'

'Yes, Flick could be under the wheels,' said Cordelia, with a little giggle that I hadn't heard before.

'Aye, well, that would have been hard to explain to John.'

'He'd probably thank you for it,' I said, rolling my eyes and trying to make light. In truth I was imagining John's face in that moment. Wondering how he would have lived the rest of his life. Whether he would be all right. If he'd marry again. Whether some bit of stuff would turn his head and whether he'd lay in our bed telling her about how his first wife didn't know how babies got in bellies until she was already a few months pregnant and had no clue how they got out again until she started in labour. I coloured at the thought but kept myself focussed. Things were OK. Things were good.

'John dotes on you,' said Harper and I turned my face away to hide the smile.

'You said you were going to the church,' said Cordelia, and without being asked, she hopped up onto the counter by the sink and sat there with her bum on the draining board. She did it so suddenly and so naturally I found myself torn between telling her to get down and querying why I'd never thought to sit up there myself. She looked so stylish, like she was in one of those films with Terence Stamp; sort of dishevelled but beautiful; a rose crushed in a fist.

'Aye, I was telling John just last night. Got the contract for fixing the mess the tree made during the storm. He said you ladies saw it.'

Cordy didn't look at me. Swung her legs like she was a nipper.

'We were in the graveyard when the storm hit. Tree went right into the crypt.'

'I'll correct you there, love,' said Harper, raising his mug and gesturing at the air in front of him. 'A crypt's subterranean. Underground, I mean – usually under a church floor.'

Cordelia's jaw tightened. 'I know what subterranean means.'

'Yes? Good for you, love. What the Kinmonts have is a mausoleum, of sorts, though they're usually a damn sight bigger. They were all the rage for about twenty years but there aint many of 'em up here. Bit showy, I suppose. But this one were well built. I'd spied it long since. You couldn't see 'em but the figurative work would have been stunning in its day. You look close enough you could see there was a death's head above the first inscription.'

'Death's head?' I asked.

'Aye, people have always had funny ideas about symbols and what stuff stands for. Death's head is a real old one but the idea is you would scratch it on to keep evil away. People still ask for them nowadays, which shows you that people are the same no matter how far forward and back you go.'

'What else was on there?' asked Cordelia.

Harper started scratching, rummaging in his pockets. He unfolded a piece of paper with a black and white picture on it and handed it over to Cordelia. She stared, not blinking, then handed it to me. I didn't know if I wanted to see it but took it anyway. It showed the crypt as it had been just after the war. It looked little different to the structure I had passed a hundred times while laying flowers at Mam's grave, but for the first time, I found myself really studying the sculptures that had been wound into the grey stone.

'Work of art really,' said Harper. 'Half a dozen different religions in among that lot. Must have been a hell of a job for some seventeenth-century mason with a chisel and a wooden hammer.'

'What's that?' I asked, gesturing at the face above the door.

'Green man,' he said, peering at the picture. 'Pagan symbol. There's grapes and peaches woven in too, and I doubt there were many Reivers around these parts got to feast on them that often. Down there, but the name of Meg Kinmont: that's what they call an intaglio, an engraving on a flat surface. Two fish suspended from an anchor. That were the sign of the early Christians so the stone they used must have come from the wall. That little shape there – I'd say that's meant to be a horse – and there's carvings of a full moon and two running hares below the worst of the moss. Going to be a major job to make it like it was.'

'Is that what you've been asked to do?' I asked.

'No, they just want a bodge job. Tidy it up and salvage what I can. But I'll try and put it back best I can. Seems important. It's stood 400 years, I don't want to be the mason who couldn't get it back on its feet.'

'Have you cleared the site?' I asked, and I moved closer to Cordelia. Our shoulders were almost touching. It felt nice, like there were two of us and one of anybody else.

'Had the lad up yesterday. Dragged the tree free with the tractor and I'm sad to say that'll be getting the saw. Rotten through. Hollow, like an Easter egg. We've stacked it at the top of the field down to the river if you want any firewood. With that out the way it's not as bad as you'd fear. Table slab across the top is still in one piece and the door held up better than I feared. Lock snapped clean off but that's these new locks for you, I suppose.'

'It had a new lock?' asked Cordelia. It sounded an odd question, even to me, but Harper was like any other man when it came to talking about the things he was an expert in and just seemed glad to be asked.

'Aye, new lock, new hook, new bracket. First thing to break. Two of the supporting slabs have gone too.'

I coughed, sounding feeble. 'And the bodies?'

'No bodies, love. It's just a monument. You might think there are shelves in there with corpses laid out but it's empty inside save dead birds and a few rat skeletons and empty lager cans.'

Cordelia turned to me. Her hair had become entangled with an earring and I had to fight with myself not to tidy her up.

'Somebody's looked after it, then,' I said, focussing on Harper. 'Honest, I always thought the bodies were inside.'

'A lot of people do,' he said, finishing his tea. 'But the bodies were more likely buried under the church or elsewhere in the grounds. There could even have been cremations now and again and the pots of ash would have been buried instead of a body. That's more of a Roman tradition but it's stayed in these parts through the centuries.'

'Why did the Kinmonts even have a mausoleum?' asked Cordelia.

'Status symbol,' shrugged Harper. 'Maybe first Kinmont had a nagging wife who wouldn't let him sleep soundly until he promised to bury himself in something to rival Tutankhamun. Maybe he were superstitious and wanted to honour whichever of the gods on the stone meant most to him. I just know it's a fine piece of work.'

'You're pretty well informed,' said Cordelia. I think she meant it to sound flattering but I heard it as an accusation. How did he know all this when he hadn't read as many books as she had. She was a one for those kind of assumptions, back then. Thought she were the only one who knew which way the world span.

'I had the university commission three or four years back,' said Harper. He had perched himself on the arm of the sofa and was looking at the teapot with the expression I know too well. He wanted somebody to pour him a fresh mug. I would have done it had Cordelia not been there. Somehow I felt she would have judged me.

'University?'

'Aye, the archaeologists. Pulling Birdoswald and Housesteads to bits. They reckoned there was a Roman cemetery just by the top of the ridge. Over the river.'

'More bones,' muttered Cordelia, looking down. It seemed a strange thing to say.

'Urns, actually. Ash from the pyres. Old Billy turned up a load of artefacts with his plough back in 1950, and it took until lately to persuade him to let the experts in with their trowels and their graphs and the like. They went away happy.'

'What were you doing?'

'Pointing them in the right direction, I suppose. And there was a lot of heavy lifting to be done. Locals have been dismantling the wall and the forts for centuries. You'll be hard pressed to find an old property around here that isn't partly built from stones taken from the wall. Load of local masons got themselves on a sweet number before the war, helping rebuild bits of the wall to make it pretty for the tourists. There's a lot of kids around here can tell you with absolute honesty that their dad built Hadrian's Wall.'

I was feeling dizzy again. I could hear Brian moving around in the tying room. I could imagine him in there with his bloody hands and dirty fingers, playing with hooks and feathers and reflecting back at himself in the dead eyes of a bird. I saw his coat hanging over the back of the chair. Suddenly I wanted to scrub it clean. I wanted to cook him his favourite tea or buy him a copy of whatever magazine he wanted. I wanted to make him happy.

'They had a look in the churchyard too,' said Harper, crossing to the teapot and pouring himself the last of the tea. 'Every bit as interesting as the wall, they reckoned. One of them had notes by the bucketful on the place and I swear it was an education, even to Fairfax.'

I stiffened. 'Fairfax knew them?'

Harper guffawed. I thought people only did that in books but that was the noise he made, I swear. It sounded like a donkey had wandered into the kitchen.

'Fairfax knew every bugger, I thought you of all people knew that.'

'Me of all people?' I asked, and I heard my tone change.

'A friend, I mean,' he said, waving his hand. 'You were like family to him.'

I turned away and felt Cordelia squeeze my shoulder. I didn't know what I wanted next, truth be told. It was Cordelia who kept at him.

'I'm a bit rusty on my local history,' she said, and you wouldn't have thought it was the same girl. 'You look like you're good at keeping facts in that big handsome head. What was it you learned?' Suddenly she was looking sheepish and flirty and asking the big strong man to share his big brain with poor little her. I thought I were going to blush myself to dust.

'Been there since before people wrote stuff down,' he said, looking like the cat who'd got the cream. 'I might have my dates wrong but I have it in my head it was 122 AD when they started building the wall and there's plenty sign there was a church down the road there even before that. There's been all sorts of oddities found locally over the years – altars to the gods of Greece and Rome and plenty of native pagan deities too. Jove, Jupiter, Mars – I forget them all but it boggled my mind to imagine these soldiers and natives and wives and all their camp followers getting on with their lives just like we do.'

'Go on,' said Cordelia.

'Aye, well, first mention of the church as we know it was in 1190 AD. Just you think how many centuries had gone by since the Romans left. What were here? What were life like? The experts didn't know and nor do I. But I know that long before Lanercost Priory or Westminster Abbey, there was a church 300 yards from where we now stand and when you think of all the life and death it's seen it's a brave man who doesn't feel the urge to say a prayer.'

'I'm not one for praying,' I said, and I felt Cordelia nip me, like we were sisters. She wanted me to hush.

'It's a really good example of its type – that's what they told me over a beer. Fairfax was there, scribbling away. They reckoned that folk were simple then. Not simple like dull-witted, but simple like they understood things in more black and white than we do now. So they thought Hell was just below them and Heaven just above. And the church was built

to reflect that. God was the light and the Devil was the darkness. That's how the church looked. Those about to be baptized
came in through the small doorway on the north side and after
the ceremony they left into the bright lights of the south. It
was very literal. As a craftsman I like that. But they were the
same with representations of darkness. I got a chill when they
told me of the bones.'

She made an extra effort with her breathing. Wouldn't let
herself alter the casual way she was talking with her new pal.

'Bones?'

'Years back the church was being repaired and the flagstones
were taken up. There were more human bones found under
the floor of the church than they were able to count. The
archaeologists have made plenty guesses who they were but
nobody knows. They were centuries old though and they died
hard. The Saxons buried their honoured dead in stone coffins
and there are plenty of those in the churchyard. More bones
under the font too. Robert the Bruce ploughed his way
through this land after the Battle of Bannockburn and there
were locals who saw it as their duty to defend it. They were
buried where they fell. Honestly, we think we know about
where we live but we're just passing through really. The land
knows more than we do.'

'Fairfax interviewed you?' I asked.

'Time and again,' laughed Harper. 'Loved a yarn. Broke
my heart to hear of the accident. He'll be buried there, will
he, Mrs Goose? In the yard?'

I ignored him. The pain in my hip was getting worse. I
wanted a hot bath and some time to think. I wanted to see if
my son was OK and find out why he hadn't been at school.
I wanted to say thank you and tell him off all at the same
time.

'He's with the undertaker in Haltwhistle,' said Cordelia,
when she realized I wasn't going to answer. 'I think he'd like
to be buried there from what little I knew of him.'

'Buried with his secrets, no doubt,' laughed Harper. 'That
book of his – shame it never saw light of day.'

I tried to persuade myself to smile but my face wasn't obeying
me. I was tired and cold and everything ached. I moved myself

over to the table and picked up Brian's jacket. It was damp and dirty and smelled like him – that strange mingling of chemicals, meat and cigarette smoke. I carried it to the sink and picked up the nailbrush. I started scrubbing the dried-in grime from the elbows.

'Did anybody mention what we thought we saw?' asked Cordelia, and I promise you she flicked her hair when she said it. The girl knew what to do with men. Forgive me, but I don't reckon she were a virgin on her wedding night. She's told me as much since. Told me more than I really asked to know.

'I heard a whisper,' smiled Harper. 'Not to worry, you had a fright, so I heard. The mind's a funny thing. I remember looking at a cloud when I was sick with tonsillitis and I swear I saw Christ on the cross in among the ripples. Don't feel silly.'

'Thank you,' said Cordelia. Honestly, she had no shame.

Then two things happened. They might have been at the same time or they might have been moments apart but I remember them as happening at once. I heard John open the back door and come running in like he was being chased. He was saying my name. Saying it like a daft lad, over and over, like a pecking bird.

And then I found it. Patting the pockets, feeling embarrassed, muttering that I was fine and he didn't need to make a fuss. I put my hand in Brian's jacket pocket and it took an effort not to jump back like I'd been bit. I turned my back to the room to look at it properly. My lungs felt like they were being squashed. My arms went all chicken-skinned. It felt like there were crumbs under my clothes.

It sat there. Just sat there – glinting up at me from the blood and grime on my palm.

Bullet-shaped. Solid. Smooth. Smiling up at me.

A gold tooth.

CORDELIA

I could see from the shape of her that something had changed. She'd gone stiff, like all her joints had lost their elasticity and she had transformed into a shop-window dummy. John was trying to get her to look at him. Was digging at us both for answers. He'd had a call at work. Harper's lad. There'd been an accident. Felicity was fine but he might want to get himself home . . .

'It's fine, John,' I said, and his name seemed to fit the shape of my tongue. I liked saying it. Wanted to say it again.

'Mrs Hemlock,' he said, and I could see the battle in him. It was manners versus the moment. He wanted us all gone. Wanted to hug his wife without anybody seeing. It was like that, then. People cared about losing something of themselves if too many people saw them for what they were.

'Shall we give her a moment?' I asked, and it surprised me as much as him. 'I haven't seen the mess since we got in. Is the house OK? We'd be as well to take a look, don't you think?'

I pitied him for so many reasons. I saw the confusion in his face. He wanted answers and he wanted to hold the woman he loved. But people were watching. It was a rare, peculiar situation and he didn't know what he was supposed to be. I could have made him do anything in that moment. He was so directionless that all it would have taken was a slight pursing of my lips and I could have blown him to the four winds. I'd have done it, too, were there anything to be gained. I'd have climbed inside his head and pulled things apart if it hadn't been that Felicity was so much more important than anybody else within a thousand miles. It had almost killed me, seeing her laying there on the road. How had she become so important? When? All I knew was that I needed to save her from this moment and leave her to deal with whatever had caused her spine to turn so rigid.

'Ah, 'tis good to see you,' said Harper, and I noticed that his portrayal of a genial Irishman became more pronounced in the face of awkwardness. He was a clever man, there was no mistaking. Almost as clever as me.

'Your boy . . .'

'Ah, I told him not to worry you. Did he call from the house?'

'I don't know. It came through to work.'

'And you came running home. Aye, you're a good man, you mark my words. I'll be leaving you to it, I suppose. Best check on the youngster, see he hasn't pulled the rest of the house down while reversing, eh?'

They shook hands at that. Something passed between them that said this would be the end of it. Harper had done no wrong and John hadn't shown himself up. I think I envied them. Envied them the ridiculous simplicity of their association.

'I'll be docked a half day,' said John, when there was just the three of us in the kitchen. He seemed relieved at being able to immerse himself in the simple comfort of grumbling. 'I'll owe Graffoe a few good turns too. Dropped everything to run me home. Bloody hell, Felicity, but you scared me.'

She hadn't turned from the window. Her whole body seemed to be a cocoon, as if she were holding something precious within herself.

'You'll be wanting to say thank you to your youngest,' I said, and I almost laughed at how unlike the locals I sounded as I said it. 'He pushed her out of the way. Brave lad. Good boy.'

It sounded ridiculous against my lips. I'd read *Ulysses*, for God's sake, and here I was, dealing in monosyllabic platitudes. I repulsed myself. Repelled, now I think on it.

'Is he all right?' asked John.

'Scratches, but he's tough. Like his mam. His dad.'

John nodded. Gave his wife a look and then nodded, more to himself than to either one of us. He turned and I followed him down the corridor to the front room. It was a cold, unwelcoming space. The sofa was a brown and grey leather with tartan cushions which clashed spectacularly with the pink and apricot swirls of the wallpaper. An electric fire sat in an unlit hearth, edged with beige tiles. The coffee table in the centre of the room was made of cheap wood varnished to a gaudy gloss, and the dresser against the wall contained good china cups and saucers that looked as though they had never been used. With the curtains drawn it looked as miserable as the kitchen looked inviting.

'Is she really all right?' he asked, turning to me like he was being controlled by strings. 'They said not to panic, but I've got myself in such a lather. And Brian. Bloody hell, is it true? Did he push her out the way? What were he doing there? It were school today, weren't it? That lad'll be the death of both of us . . .'

I let him talk. He needed it. Needed to rail against the inadequacies of his life and the failings of others so he could avoid staring at the horror of what might have happened that day.

'She don't need this,' said John, hands on his hips, looking at the floor. 'I thought she did. Thought it might bring summat out of her. But it's gone 'tother way. That'll do, eh?'

'What do you mean?'

'This stuff with Fairfax. With this body she reckons you saw. When she told me there were a sparkle about her. Some life. It were nice to see. She can be such a one with her nerves. She won't cross water, did you know that? Won't walk over a stream and can only go over one on the bus with her eyes closed and her hand gripping mine down to the bone. She jumps at every noise. Fairfax, God rest him – he wanted to interview her loads over the years but was frightened to ask in case she got herself in a tizzy about it. That's what she does. She's a bag of nerves. But she were different last night, did you not notice? Talking about things that normally would have turned her stomach. I thought it would take her out of herself. But we didn't even get through a day of it and she's on her backside in the street.'

He pulled his cap from his pocket. Twisted it like he was killing an eel. Ran a hand back over his head and managed to raise his head enough to look me in the eye.

'That'll be the end of it, yes?'

My breath came out in a rush. There may have been laughter

in it. I was disgusted with him. How could he make a decision like that? Just tell me that he'd made up his mind and his wife could no longer come out to play. It felt like I'd been pressed into the pages of a book written a hundred years before. I glared at him, silently repeating my vows to myself – I would never be told what to do. I would never be controlled. I would never be shackled by somebody who did not love my independence as much as they loved the idea of us being together. It was the way I felt a lot back then. For all my cleverness I never really opened my mind or my ears to anything other than the bits of a sentence that stood out. I just heard John being some patriarch; some brute of a husband who found his wife weak. Looking back I wish I'd said something more comforting. He'd had a shock. He knew his wife better than I did. And by God he loved her. I was upset for myself – upset that he'd said that we were done.

'That's her decision to make,' I snapped. 'She was enjoying herself. She's really very clever and I don't know people like she does. I can't do this on my own.'

'You shouldn't be doing it at all. Fairfax had an accident and there was no bloody body.' He didn't raise his voice but I could see he was getting cross.

'There was!' I shouted. 'A blue suit and good shoes and a bag hanging from one strap. Sprawled on the grass with his head turned to one side. I saw him. Felicity saw him!'

Temper flashed in his face. 'Well mebbe he were there for a reason! You thought of that? There's a bloody rocket base up the road. There are criminals from London running a casino not more'n a few miles away. Pike's put his hands around enough men's throats and he lives twenty yards from the church gate. Do you want to dig into all that muck? Do you?'

I was breathing hard. I felt like I was being told off and that immediately made me aggressively defensive.

'If somebody's done something wrong . . .'

'You don't care about the living!' he snapped, jerking his head forward. 'You walk past people like they're stones. You've never come and knocked on a door and asked after a soul or even stopped to have a natter in the street. Yer walk past with your nose sniffing the clouds and now yer talk about what's

right and what's not. Yer doing this for the thrill of it and to
tek yer mind off yer lad.'

I wanted to hit him. I could see myself doing it – slapping
my right hand across his face and feeling the sting on my
palm. But his face changed before I could get to him. Regret
rippled across his face. Shame.

'I'm sorry . . .' he muttered, dragging his hand back across
his scalp. 'I'm het up. There were no need.'

I felt like my legs were going to give out on me. I slumped
down onto the armchair and felt the cold leather against my bare
arms and the back of my neck. The hairs on my arms rose like
sails and I found myself shivering, even as my cheeks burned.

'She's not like you think,' I said, surprised to hear
myself speaking so quietly. 'She's not some fragile thing.'

'I know that,' he said, whispering now, as if he was trying
to make up for shouting so harshly. 'She's got iron in her soul
and she can be stubborn when she needs to be. But there's a
difference between finding a bit more toughness, a bit more
spark, and digging into a bloody murder, love.'

'If Chivers had just come to talk to me . . .' I began.

'You ever think Chivers might know more than you, love?
More than all of us?'

I didn't reply. In truth, it hadn't occurred to me. Did Chivers
have an agenda of his own? Might he already know about the
body and be deliberately avoiding taking a statement from
me? Could he be in the pay of somebody a lot more powerful
than the silly snotty girl up the hill?

'Look, I've been thinking about this,' he said, and he came
nearer, standing over me. I must have shrunk back a little
because he instantly changed his pose and squatted down in
front of me like he was going to take my boots off.

'Love, I'll admit it – you got me interested last night,' he
said, and I saw for the first time how attractive his eyes were.
They reminded me of the colours at a pigeon's throat. 'What
you said about prisoners of war and papers under the church
floor. It got me blood up and I saw in Felicity that she didn't
want to let it go. But I feel like I were drunk on it last night
and I'm sober right now and there's no way I want either of
you messing about in this.'

'It was an accident,' I said, shaking my head. 'The wagon came out of nowhere. She'd run because a bird came through the window. She'd had a fright.'

'A bird?' he asked.

'Yeah, it came through the landing window and shattered the glass.'

'It dead?' asked John, standing up.

'Of course. What does that matter?'

'You won't understand,' said John, shaking his head. 'We must seem like peasants to you, love. I don't mean it cruel but you don't know life as it's lived here. They're a superstitious lot.'

'They?' I asked, temper rising again. 'You're not one of them?'

'I'm from Brampton, love. Compared to this place that's the big city. I don't walk under ladders and I try not to spill the salt but I don't worry about omens and old prophesies or drawing a cross on my shoe if I see a white horse. But they do, love. Felicity's from that. And a bird coming through the glass the week of the death of a loved one – that means they're not at rest. To Felicity that means Fairfax is somewhere other than at peace. No wonder she ran.'

I could see then how much he wanted me gone. He wanted to go and hold his wife and it would have been wrong of me not to let him. But I needed more. Had to push.

'Doesn't that mean she'll want to help me keep digging?'

'Aye, it might, but it's not what's best.'

'You, then,' I said, a little desperately. 'You could ask around with me. Read Fairfax's papers with me. You know the locals. You said about Pike . . .'

'Pike's a nutter. Always has been. Put more men in hospital than the flu.'

'And Chivers would know that?' I asked.

'Chivers knows plenty but you don't need to be a policeman to know about Pike. I said as much to Brian. I know Pike can seem reasonable sometimes and he's got that, I dunno, that badness about him which people want to get close to. But he's no good. When he fights he goes for the eyes. He's wrong.'

'And he lives directly opposite the church?' I asked, incredulous.

'Aye with his mam. Been here and there and did some time with the army though I wouldn't trust him with a wooden spoon, let alone a gun. He's dangerous. I dunno why Fairfax put up with him.'

'He knew Fairfax?'

'All his life. Was friends with Christopher, Fairfax's son. Felicity told me, years ago. Pike always seemed a bit more respectful with Fairfax, but you shouldn't poke a sleeping dog no matter how friendly they seem.'

I stayed silent. Screwed up my eyes as if trying to swallow toast with a sore throat.

'They're at it again,' said John, sadly, cocking his head. We could hear banging and shouting coming from upstairs.

'Brian and Felicity?' I asked.

'Aye. He's not a bad boy. Just needs his brain tweaking a bit. It's not easy, having a soul that don't fit yer surroundings.' He smiled a little. 'You'd know better than I.'

'Is that what he is? A city kid in the country?'

John shrugged. 'Sometimes I think so. Others I don't. He loves nature but I think he loves the wrong bits. He don't worry overmuch about sunsets or full moons. He likes getting two rats in a bucket and watching them fight. He can stand for an hour watching a spider eat a moth it's caught in its web. He can seem such a big mouth one minute and the next he's crying on his own in his room. His older brother weren't like him. Felicity worries.'

'You must too,' I said.

He seemed puzzled at that, as if I was the first person to realize that his son was more than just his wife's business. There was the sound of footsteps and then the slam of a door. A moment later it opened and closed again. John turned and crossed to the window, pulling open the curtains.

'She's gone after him,' he said. 'Limping like she's been in a bullfight and not a coat on.' He shook his head. I wanted to put a hand on his shoulder or say something kind but he had the same stiffness to his posture as Felicity had taken on in the kitchen and suddenly it all seemed too impenetrable.

These people had something I didn't – they could turn themselves to statues when the pain became too great. They could make a steel rod of their spine while people like me bent and twisted and spiralled into nothing but sobs and tears and wishes.

I was quiet as I gathered my things from the kitchen. Didn't say goodbye as I closed the door.

Felicity had gone running down the road towards the church. To my left, Harper and his son were sitting in the cab of the wagon, eating sandwiches and smoking. The lad waved his hand in greeting and I might have managed a nod in return.

I turned right. Back towards Gilsland. Back towards home.

Felicity wasn't going to help. John neither. Chivers had his own reason for ignoring me and Fairfax's soul was battering at the glass of the fragile world in which I had found myself. I couldn't leave it alone. John was right in what he said. It was distracting me from Stefan. But there was more to it than that. I felt like I'd been shown the body in the blue suit for a reason. I felt, to my very bones, that the body had been put there for me.

As I walked, I made a decision. I was alone here. I had nobody whom I could lean on or ask for guidance. But the reason for that was because I came from a very different background. I was an outsider here because of my associations elsewhere. I knew people. I had friends in high places, or at the very least, a husband in Whitehall. He owed me like I owed him. And he had influence to spare. It would not be a failure, an admission of inadequacy, to use all the tools at my disposal. And my husband was most definitely a colossal tool.

I quickened my pace, lost in my thoughts.

I didn't know it then, but I was watched all the way home. And the eyes that burned my back were as pitiless as rain.

FELICITY

Transcript 0007, recorded October 30, 2010

He were standing by the church. Had to be, didn't he? Smoking a cigarette under the branches of the big evergreen by the gate.

'What yer running for, Mam? Yez'll hurt yer self.'

He looked so pleased with himself. Looked like a bad lad. If he weren't my own I swear I'd have been frightened of him. Too cocky for his own good, curling his lip and smirking at me in his vest and his jeans and his boots with the laces undone. He looked like he were made of bone. Pure white, he seemed, like a statue come to life.

'Why'd you run?' I asked, and my voice sounded like a penny whistle; all high and trembly and out of tune.

'I never ran. I said I were off. Thought we'd finished talking.'

'You know that's not how it was.'

'No? Ah well, I'd stopped listening then.'

Twelve years old and talking to me like that? My dad would have given me a wallop for it and I'd have had no cause to complain. Maybe I hadn't walloped Brian enough, or maybe too much. Or maybe all the wallops in the world would have made no difference.

'You should have been at school,' I said, and it sounded proper pitiful.

'Aye,' he smiles, all swagger. 'And then you'd be flat under the wheels of that Paddy's truck.'

'But why weren't you?' I asked, and I felt the tears stabbing at the backs of my eyes again.

He ground out his cigarette on the damp trunk of the tree and turned to me as if I were wasting his valuable time.

'I weren't feeling well,' he said, like I should have known. 'I had one of me headaches.'

'Did you tell the nurse?'

'That bitch? She couldn't care less. Just wants to put her fat hands on you.'

'So you just walked out?' I asked.

'Aye. Got an early bus. I only missed a bit of spelling and I can spell good enough.'

I felt a sudden stab of pain down the side I'd landed on. It showed in my face and suddenly his whole self changed.

'You hurting?' he asked, and though he didn't come toward me he did move aside to allow me under the protection of the branches. Up close he smelled different to how he used to. It used to be biscuits and soap and that earthy scent you get when you pull back the bark from a silver birch. Now he smelled like *them*. A man. Cigarettes and sweat and a rancid, unscrubbed tang that caught the back of my throat.

'Me old bones,' I said. 'Came down a clatter.'

'Sorry,' he said, and maybe he meant it. 'Didn't have time to put a pillow down.'

I was holding my hands in fists. I wanted to put out my hand and rub his hair but the mood he was in he could have reacted like my hands were on fire.

'It were good timing,' I said.

'Aye,' he says, smiling. 'Just saw the truck and then saw you, running like you'd got dogs after ye.'

'I'd had a fright,' I said, and I felt sick at remembering the bird.

'At Fairfax's?' he asked, and I could see his brain working things out.

I nodded. He was looking at me with eyes like conkers and it went through me. I had to look over his shoulder or I'd have given in to a shiver. Harper were right – they'd tidied up sharpish. The slabs of the old mausoleum were laid out on the long damp grass around a large patch of dirty earth. The churchyard looked a little bare without the old tree. What remained of the broken trunk stood where it always had; a finger that had pointed skywards for centuries now cut down to the first knuckle.

'Bird came in,' I said, quietly. 'Gave me a turn.'

He nodded, understanding. 'Doesn't seem right, does it? He were OK was Fairfax.'

I nodded. There didn't seem much else to say about it. Fairfax had known the boys their entire lives. I should probably have talked to them both about his passing but it just wasn't what you did. People lived and people died and you got on with it because tomorrow it might be you that did the dying. That's changed now, of course. Folk can't lose a pet without acting like they've had their whole family burned to ash. Maybe it was the war that made us hard or maybe we just knew that death was as much a part of the circle as life was. You get that in farming towns. You see the changing of the seasons; crops rising and leaves falling; berries bursting into life then being crushed in the beaks of the birds who need them for their own squawking, desperate young. I suppose you don't weep much for the death of one tree when you're standing in an orchard.

'You really think it weren't an accident?' asked Brian. 'You and Lady Muck?'

I was going to say something that would answer his question without really giving anything away. But I was no good at that. My face let me down. And if I'm honest, I wouldn't have known the difference between my truth and my lies at that moment. So I shrugged and said I didn't know.

'I heard what she was saying,' he said, scratching his chest. I noticed how filthy his fingernails were. 'Last night. About the camp and the tapes and stuff. Sounds like she's mad.'

I understood, then. That's why he'd come home early. He'd heard us talking and wanted to snoop. He wanted to know what we found. He'd sneaked away from school to come and spy on his mam and her new friend.

'We found nowt,' I said. 'There was nowt to find.'

'You didn't look in the right places then,' said Brian, and his smirk was back. It got my back up and I wanted him to know it.

'That tooth,' I said. 'Where'd you get it?'

He didn't even blink. 'Just found it, I told ye.'

'Found it where?' I asked.

'Don't remember?'

'When?'

'While ago. Mebbe longer.'

I got frustrated then. Started on at him. 'Brian, you can't go around with a tooth in your pocket. It's worth something. Somebody might be asking questions . . .'

'Doubt that,' said Brian, with a look I didn't like. He was staring past my shoulder and I suddenly knew there was somebody behind me.

'Go get a coat on, Brian,' said Pike. 'Ye'll catch your death.'

I turned around. Pike was standing with his feet in a puddle; his welly boots covered up to the ankle. He had on tight jeans and his bomber jacket, open at the waist. He was bare-chested. No hair on him. Not a single one. He had a gold necklace, like twisted rope, at his throat and an ugly patch of skin below his belly-button, like he'd had an operation. He'd got dressed in a hurry. Pulled his jacket and boots on without bothering with owt else. I felt my thoughts catch fire. What had got him so excited? And why was he talking to Brian like they were old pals?

'Pike,' I said. I hoped more words would come out of my mouth but nothing happened. He just stood looking at me with those eyes I could never read.

'What were that about a tooth?' he asked, angling his head like a bird who has heard a worm. 'You have something, lad?'

'Nah, Mam's off her rocker,' said Brian, and the lie didn't even make his voice waver.

'Mucking about, were you?' he asked, while I stood there like a lemon, wondering what to say.

'Aye, that's it,' said Brian. 'You see the wagon in the wall? Mam were almost under it.'

Pike nodded. Pulled at his necklace. I noticed that his neck and the skin on his chest were almost different colours. His face was all grimy and stubbled but the other parts of him were pale, like a young girl.

'Games,' he mused, chewing his cheek. He turned to me. 'Saw you limping past the window. You hurt?'

'Scrapes,' I said, shrugging.

'Bumps and bruises,' said Brian.

'Me mam heard the wagon hit the house. Fucking Paddy. Can't drive.'

'It were my fault,' I said.

'No,' decided Pike. 'It were Paddy. You want me to have a word. I saw he were still up there. Not right. Could have hurt you.'

'Honestly Pike, it's nothing. I ran out.' I was gabbling. Wanting it all to be right again. Nice again.

'This tooth,' said Pike, rolling his eyes back in Brian's direction. 'Were it gold?'

'There's no tooth, I told you,' said Brian, and he sounded impatient. Pike didn't like it.

'Don't be answering back, lad. I'll put you over my knee.'

'We were finishing off anyways,' I said, and I realized that I still had the tooth in my hand, digging into my palm like it were trying to bite through.

'They rebuilding the tomb, are they?' asked Pike, staring at the patch of dead earth and not seeming to hear what I'd said. 'I'll be watching 'em. Mekking sure they do right by Fairfax.'

I couldn't help but ask him what he meant. 'Fairfax? But it's the Kinmont plot.'

He looked at me like I was daft. 'Fairfax were the only one gave a damn about the place. He let me mow between the stones when I were little. Me and Christopher. Meant summat to him.'

I gave him a proper looking over. There were raindrops landing in the muddy puddles at his feet. There were dozens of ruts in the shabby, muddy track and the one that ran behind him caught my eye. It weren't big thick trenches like you'd get from tractors or proper cars. They were fancy thin treads, like you'd get on a modern car. In places they were filled with rainwater but elsewhere it was clear to make out that a snazzy, sporty car had driven down the muddy track and then reversed out the same way.

'We'd best get in before it starts again,' I said, and it was an effort to sound like meself.

'Nah, ye've got something to do first,' said Pike. 'Brian, give us that tooth, lad.'

Brian shook his head, all cross again. Exasperated. 'I haven't got a tooth. It were a game.'

'We'll not be having any more games, then,' said Pike.

I'd seen him like this before. He were no different to the lad he was at school. He could turn on you like he had rabies. One minute he'd be quiet as a mouse and the next he'd be trying to get his thumb inside your eye.

'All right there Pike? You dressed for it? It's gonna be coming down.'

He turned at the sound of the voice. Harper's lad. Big smile on his face and a box of tools in his hand.

'Away now, Paddy,' said Pike. 'The bogs are over the river if you're feeling homesick. Nowt here for you.'

The lad kept the smile in place. I looked at Brian and saw, for the first time in years, a look of fear on his face. I swear I wanted to hold his hand but the tooth were all I could think of. I don't know why I didn't just give it to him, now I think on it. Maybe it was fear of what would happen if Brian was caught out in a lie. Or maybe it was because there were some things that were better off in anybody's hands but Pike's.

'Mrs Goose, you look soaked through,' said Harper's lad. 'Will I walk you both back up the road?'

That set Pike off. 'You got potatoes 'tween yer ears, Paddy? I said there were nowt for ye.'

'Da's just parking the wagon,' he said, ignoring Pike. 'Bit better parked than an hour ago, eh? Shall we be ganning along?'

The lad was only a few paces away from me. He was bigger than Pike but it didn't matter. If Pike went for him it would be like watching a terrier with a rat.

I felt Brian's hand touch mine. For a second I felt a kind of warmth in me – a feeling of connection. It meant a lot to me – him wanting to hold his mam's hand. Then his little dirty fingers prised open my own and he seized the gold tooth as if his hand was a beak. I looked down, and my lungs betrayed me. I gave a gasp, loud enough for Pike to hear. And then Brian was off. He could move fast when he needed to and next thing he was just a streak of white, dodging through the gravestones and over the fallen tree then disappearing over the iron railings into the field beyond.

'Little bastard,' says Pike, proper livid. He turned his back on Harper's lad. He stomped past me, fury on his face and it

wasn't in me to stand in his way. He reached into his coat
pocket and he started moving fast as he approached the church
door. Then he pulled a big silver key from his pocket and
stuck it in the lock.

I looked at the young lad and he were as dumbstruck as
me. Then Pike was coming out of the church with a shotgun
over his arm.

'No, Pike, don't . . .'

He glared at me as he climbed over the iron railings and
stamped away across the grass. The field sloped down to the
river and beyond it was the forest that sloped up to the Roman
fort a mile away. If he followed the river right he'd reach
Gilsland. He'd have to pass Halpin's place. The Heron had
Pike's number, there was no mistaking it. He was a big old
hardcase and he would see Brian safe home. And Pike were
just after scaring him. If I'd gone running down that hill after
him he'd have shot Brian just to show he were the type that
would. Better to stay put. Let the boy lose him in the woods.
He would be twice as nippy as Pike. He'd be grand. I told
myself that. Told myself like it was a prayer as I watched Pike
vanish into the gathering dusk as the hunter's moon started to
rise above the trees.

I only had one thought in my head, truth be told. Not for
Brian – I knew he'd be safe enough in the woods. No, I wanted
to know why Pike had a key. He'd entered the church without
a gun and come out holding one. He knew its secrets. Its hidey
holes.

I entered the church like it was on fire. I followed the boot
prints to the third pew from the front. I felt around in the grey
light and found a hole big enough to fit my finger in. The
panel slid back like it had been greased. I reached inside as
if it was full of mouse traps. My hand touched something
cold. Metal. I knew the barrel of a gun well enough. Knew
that cool sensation on my fingertips.

I sat back like I'd been shot. Caught something with my
boot. It felt like a dead thing; a rotting fox. But the rustle of
paper cut through the pounding in my head and my chest.

A prayer cushion. Red and frayed. The stitching half
unpicked and a picture of a robin coming apart upon the front.

I picked it up and felt paper crinkle beneath my hands. Reached inside and felt the familiar texture. Paper, half-burned.

I peered at the opening page and saw Fairfax's scribble. Date. Time. Name.

I'd have read it all there and then were it not for the sudden sound of a shotgun blast and the terrible, terrible screaming of a thousand crows.

CORDELIA

'I want to speak to Cranham Hemlock.'

I hesitated before saying anything else but it was part of our agreement that I always remind people of the little woman in his life.

'And to whom am I speaking?'

I bit the inside of my cheek and scowled at the wall.

'I'm his wife.'

'Hello, Mrs Hemlock.' The voice was Home Counties. Some skinny thing with a scrawny throat and a ruffle-necked blouse who drank her tea from a cup and saucer and thought that young girls who seduced influential older men should be hanged from the nearest tree. 'Your husband was in a meeting with the minister but I'm sure if it's urgent . . .'

'Quite urgent,' I said, then tried to put a smile in my voice. 'But I know how busy he is. I don't like to trouble him but, well, it's a personal matter.' I dropped my voice a little and became her confidante; two wives gossiping over their hopeless husbands. 'It's a silly thing, I know, but, well . . . I could use some advice.'

'Of course,' she said, understanding completely. I don't know what she imagined but it made sense in her world. 'I'll ask him to call as soon as he is available. I do hope you're keeping well. Will we be seeing you at the gala in November?'

'Thank you.'

I hung up the phone. Sat for ten minutes staring at the damn thing. I was cold again. I dashed upstairs and rummaged through the horribly sensible clothes that Cranham had insisted I accept as a gift when I was pregnant. I had to keep the baby warm, he said, as if he knew anything about what I needed. I never wore a stitch of his pre-approved garments. Wore my own clothes and revelled in my own tastes and wrapped myself in a blanket instead of giving in and doing as he suggested. God but I was a stubborn thing. Unexpectedly, none of that mattered any more. I just wanted to be warm. I slipped into some crisp turquoise-coloured slacks with a neat seam down the front and a black polo neck beneath a cream, chunky-knit cardigan. I had a glance at myself in the mirror on the back of the wardrobe door and didn't find the reflection too revolting. I looked a bit like a folk singer. Stefan would have laughed.

He called back forty minutes later. He sounded as he always did – flustered and shrill. He was constantly afraid I was going to tell him I didn't want to do this anymore. Divorce would mean scandal and he had wed me with the sole aim of avoiding it.

'Cordelia,' he said, breathily. 'Lovely to hear from you. Is all well?'

'Fine. All right.' I bit my lip. 'I need a favour.'

He laughed at that. Taken aback, I suppose. He'd never heard me ask him for anything. All that I had, he had offered without demand.

'Are you a little short?' he asked. 'I can wire the post office a money order for whatever you need. Are you getting the parcels?'

I closed my eyes. I felt sick. Hated being this pitiful, kept thing.

'Cranham, your department has good ties with the police, yes? That comes under your umbrella?'

He paused. I could hear him trying to work out where I might be heading.

'It's nothing to worry about,' I said, brightly. 'I'm just a bit concerned about somebody. I made a friend, you see. A nice lady who lives in the village. She's been very helpful and I rather want to do something nice for her. She rents out a room at her house and a few months back a man came to stay. He went out walking. Birdwatching, so she thinks. He didn't come back. I'm sure he just got called away but she's been worried ever since and the people up here are a bit reluctant to make things official so I thought that perhaps you could see if there was anything suspicious about it? Perhaps a business that reported an employee missing?'

I could hear him frowning. 'I'm not sure I can involve myself . . .'

'She's been such a help. I really would like to take the
weight off her mind.'

'Does she have a name for him?'

'That's the thing – she's not kept very good records. She
just knows that he was a middle-aged chap with a foreign
accent. Maybe Swiss or German or French. And it was
some time this year.'

'That's very vague,' he tutted. 'You must get a lot of people
passing through. For the air base. For the spa. I can't imagine
that any of my contacts will be able to help.'

I rather enjoyed the lying. It was good to feel as though I
was doing something I was good at. I hadn't even planned the
story when I made the call – I just knew my tongue would
come up with something.

'It's lonely here, Cranham. You do so much for me and I'll
always be grateful but sometimes I need somebody to talk to.
And I'm so out of practice I might say all the wrong things.
All sorts of stuff might come spilling out . . .'

He cleared his throat. He understood.

'I'll certainly try, my love.'

I heard the clinking of glasses behind him. He was in a bar.
People were listening. He was trying to make it sound like
we were a real couple. It sounded as false as the way he spoke
his vows or the kiss he gave my damp cheek when the vicar
said I was his.

'I think I'll head back down to the village,' I said, breezily.
'I've been in and out a lot these past few days. I'm starting
to get to know a few people. They're saying kind things about
Stefan. Asking after you . . .'

'How lovely. Now, I suppose I must get on.'

'Of course. How long should I give you?'

'Oh, you just do as you will and leave it all to me.'

I think I hung up before saying goodbye. I feared that if I
opened my mouth I would tell him what a patronising bastard
he was, though with the wisdom of the passing years I will
admit that he was not such a bad stick. It wasn't his fault.
None of it was. He liked men, that was the thing. And he
needed to look respectable while he enjoyed their attentions
and built his career. It had all worked out rather well, truth be

told. Stefan's father could never acknowledge Stefan was his – he had too much to lose. But when I told him I was pregnant he did what he was so very good at and solved the problem. Found a junior civil servant with a secret he wished to hide and arranged for us to be introduced and wed. Then he funded my disappearance to the country. He sent flowers when Stefan died. I still have them, pressed into the pages of a poetry book I had sent him when I was still a student and which he had in turn returned to me, stating that the gesture had been inappropriate. It wasn't his fault that he fathered a child. Not really. He just wasn't strong enough to keep saying no. And my goodness he said it plenty before I got him into bed. I love hard, that's what Flick says. I fall for people like they're going to fill some great gap in me. I grow consumed by the thought that if they could just become mine, my life would fit the shape it should always have fitted. And when they let me down – when they fail to be what I need them to – that love turns into a bitter, acid thing.

I pulled on my woollen hat and stepped into the evening air. It was a little after seven. The clouds had cleared just enough to give me a glimpse of the promised moon amid a sugar-sprinkling of stars. The moon looked like an orange split in two. I had never seen its craters and patterns so pronounced. It was the kind of moon that I could imagine prehistoric people worshipping with fire and sacrifice and it would not have surprised me if I were to hear chanting or saw a procession of flickering torches heading towards some forest clearing where a virgin in a white dress was staked to a tree.

I lost myself in daydream for a while, trying to keep my feet steady on the slippery path down to the river. The moon gave me a decent amount of light to see by and as I made my way towards the river I noticed that winter was beginning to steal across the woods. It was a sensation more than anything – an intuition that the trees were preparing for change. I caught it in the whispers of the softly moving branches; a crispness, a rustling, the way old people's voices can take on a new, more mortal timbre, in their final years. It was as if I could smell the coming of the end; the transformation and death of the remaining leaves which were already turning to mulch and decay beneath my boots.

I heard the river before I saw it. It didn't roar but it had raised its voice in recent days and the stones that were usually visible from the bridge were now more deeply submerged. I wondered about the Popping Stone. The Kissing Bush. I wanted to shake my head dismissively at such superstitious nonsense but I'd altered in some inexplicable way over the past couple of days and I suddenly felt less inclined to dismiss such things as the preserve of the uneducated. I found myself willing to listen. To open my mind a little. I wish I'd done so before. The hope of Heaven would have been comforting when Stefan died.

There was a light on the far side of the river. I glimpsed it through the trees and stopped where I stood. It was a soft kind of radiance; little more than a flash of colour amid the khaki and black but it was enough to catch my eye and cause me a moment's pause. I strained my hearing, listening for voices, but could make nothing out. Where was the light coming from? I tried to get my bearings. The bridge would take me to the footpath that would lead up the slope to the spa. The light was coming from a little further away, downriver, in the part of the forest that I had rarely investigated. There had been houses there, at one time. Little cottages, inhabited by the artisans who made money from the tourists, selling their wares from carts and barrows along the footpath. What was the name? Green something. Green Grove, that was it. The authorities had started dismantling the little cottages a decade back and only a couple remained; blocky, miserable affairs covered in ivy and littered with mud and leaves.

Quietly, my feet making no noise on the wooden planks of the bridge, I crossed the river and headed away from the footpath. Cautiously, I made my way through the trees towards the light.

I heard the voices before the shapes came into proper focus. One voice raised in temper – the other soft and low, like the confident growling of a dog that knows it rarely needs to go to the trouble of biting anybody.

'Yer don't understand! I just need to talk to him! We're pals. It's none of yer worry.'

'I'm not worried. But you'd be as well to move on.'

'Hiding between your legs, is he? Little shite. Led me a fucking merry dance up and down the bloody ridge. But yer not as clever as ye think yez are, ye little bastard. Found ye, didn't I!'

'No you didn't. Because he's not here. I've told you that. The only thing here for you is trouble and I'm too tired to dish it out. But if you're going to push . . .'

'I'll blow yer bloody face off.'

'Yes, Pike, you'll huff and you'll puff and you'll piss off. You're no big bad wolf.'

I stayed where I was, pressed against the damp trunk of a slender tree. The man I knew as Heron was leaning in the open doorway of one of the abandoned cottages. In front of him, propped up on a branch that he had sunk into the floor, hung an old oil lamp. It gave off just enough light to see his backpack and a wooden crate. Craning my neck I could make out the contents. Detergent. Milk. Bread. Tins of food. Matches. Whisky. Home-made jam. I recognized the contents at once. Such gifts had been arriving on my doorstep ever since moving in. Did we have the same benefactor? I frowned, unsure what to make of it. Then a thought occurred. Had Heron been providing me with the helpful parcels? And if so, what on earth for? I thought of the boot prints by the bed and stared at his big, brooding silhouette. I suddenly wished I could better see his face.

'Ye've never scared me, Heron.'

'I know that, lad. That's what baffles me.'

'I could come down here any night. Could stick a knife in yer guts while ye were sleeping and decorate the trees with yer insides.'

'Aye, you could. Tell you what, I'll go get some shut-eye now and you just let me know when you're ready.'

I found myself grinning. Heron's voice barely rose above a whisper. There was no fear in him. In contrast, Pike sounded like an angry adolescent.

'He's got something I need,' whined Pike.

'He's just a boy. And he belongs to John and Felicity. They're all right. They don't deserve you.'

'But Fairfax . . .' shrieked Pike. 'The tooth . . .'

'Fairfax is gone, lad. And I know you don't know how to deal with what you're feeling. So I'm being kind. I'm keeping it gentle. But if you're not on your way you're going down the fucking well.'

For a moment there was complete silence. I held my breath, wondering which of Felicity's sons had fallen foul of Pike and what any of it had to do with Fairfax and the dead man. I knew at once it would be Brian. He had that badness to him. I recognized it as soon as I saw it. The sisters at my school would have called him wicked.

'You can't protect him forever,' threatened Pike.

'No. But if I hit you hard enough you'll forget why you're after him.'

I shrank into the darkness of the tree as Pike stomped past me. He had a shotgun in his hand and I could make out mud upon his face. I waited until he was out of sight before I let myself breathe out properly. Then I smelled cigarette smoke. Close, beside my left ear.

'Hello Miss,' said a voice, so close to me that I could feel warm breath upon my skin. I jumped the way Felicity would have; the way a silly girl would have. I laughed and it came out reedy and frightened.

'I wasn't spying,' I said, before I could work out what else to say. 'I'm sorry, I heard voices . . .'

'I don't like you being out in the woods in the dark,' he said. 'There are poachers. Traps.'

'I'm fine,' I protested, instinctively, but stopped when I sensed him moving. He appeared in front of me as if he had been made from shadows and trees. He had a square, handsome face with thick lips and two days' growth of black beard upon his cheeks. His hair was a tangle of black curls and he wore a dirty white scarf tied around his neck. He was dressed in black bomber jacket and army trousers that disappeared into tall, lace-up black boots.

'I'll bring you your food by in the morning if that's all right,' he said, and his voice was melodic, as though it was used to telling campfire tales and singing old folk songs.

'It is you who's been bringing them . . .?' I began.

'Aye.'

'Why?' I asked, unable to help it.

He gave a half smile and his cigarette rose an inch. 'Saw you and your boy not long after you moved in. Liked how you were together. Figured you might need a hand. Hope it wasn't a liberty.'

I wasn't sure how to appear. Was there any reason to be displeased? I had never met a man who gave something away without expecting payment and I think my doubts showed in my gaze.

'I'll leave off then,' he said, shrugging. 'No bother if it's a worry. I'm the same myself.'

'The same?'

'Independent. Don't much care for other people's help. They always seem to want something in return.'

We shared a smile. I found myself liking him. Then a thought occurred.

'You just helped Felicity. Was that Brian that Pike was after?'

He nodded. 'Pike's all bluster. Never had a dad. Just needs a couple of reminders what's OK and what's not.'

'And that's where you come in?' I asked, looking sceptical. 'Why?'

'Who else? Every bugger else is scared of him.'

Behind him I heard a sudden rustle and an instant later Heron's hand was across my mouth. He pressed himself close to me and I was suddenly overwhelmed by his nearness. I could smell the fire and the gunpowder and the paraffin upon his fingers and with my face pressed into his jacket I got the whiff of the skin beneath the mingled scents: an earthy, woodland smell, like dew the night after a bonfire. My eyes widened at the suddenness of it and then his face was a shade from mine – his blue eyes growing bigger and smaller and blurring as I tried to make sense of it. He jerked his eyes right and I followed his gaze. There were six of them. One great, majestic stag with antlers like hawthorn trees. Two smaller does. Three youngsters. They moved through the trees like liquid.

'Don't speak,' breathed Heron. 'They can't smell you. You smell of me right now. And they know me.'

I found myself suddenly aware of myself and where I was – pressed against a tree and pinned beneath this strong, mysterious man as these forest creatures slunk between pockets of shadow. I felt him relax his grip and I gave a tiny nod, promising not to make a sound.

'There's two rich bastards from the castle been tracking that king for weeks.'

'King?' I whispered.

'The buck. King of the woods.'

There was no mirth in his voice as he said it. He meant every word.

'You were a gamekeeper once, so I heard,' I said, under my breath.

'I were all sorts. And none sat well. Now I keep them safe.'

'The animals?'

'Those I can.'

We watched the family of roe deer flit past the abandoned cottage and after a moment I let out a breath. 'Thank you,' I said, and it may have been the first sincere one of my life.

'Not a bother,' he said, shrugging. 'I'll walk you up the spa path, if you like.'

I was going to tell him not to worry about it and reassure him I would be fine on my own. But I also wanted to enjoy an extra moment in his company. Under that moon, on that night, there was something ethereal and otherworldly about him. It would not have surprised me to look down and see that he had furry legs and cloven hooves.

'That would be nice,' I said.

He nodded and we set off back towards the path. He looked for a moment as though he was going to offer me his hand as we crossed a particularly slippery area but he did not. He walked in silence and I followed behind.

'Is Brian all right?' I asked, as we reached the path.

'Can't say,' said Heron, shrugging. 'He's nowt to fear from Pike. It's just piss and wind.'

'But he had a gun . . .'

'Everybody has a gun. Difference is, most of us know how to use them. Pike's a boy. He plays at being something else but he's got a scared soul.'

'Why did he want Brian?'

'He said Brian had something that belonged to him.'

'Like what?'

'Didn't matter to me,' said Heron. 'Brian gave him the slip a dozen times but Pike saw his footprints by the bridge. Caught up with him near the grove. It's as well I was home.'

I smiled, enjoying the idea of the ramshackle cottage being 'home'.

'So where's Brian now?'

'Slipped out the back while Pike and me were having a chat. Can you smell the sulphur water? You're not far from the true well.'

'The true well?'

'Not the one where the tourists drink. I mean the true spring, straight out of the earth. Stinks like gunpowder and rotten eggs and looks like day-old coffee but it's the reason for this whole place existing. Romans blessed it, did you know that? And there hasn't been a religious movement that hasn't come up with some ritual or another based on the importance of the waters.'

'You're from here?' I asked. 'You seem to know a lot about the history.'

'I were friends with Fairfax,' said Heron, without looking at me. 'Told me a lot.'

'I'm sorry,' I said.

'Thanks. Sorry for your sadness too.'

We walked on in silence and it was with some disappointment that I saw the great white shape of the spa appear out of the woods. Two vans were standing in the car park and a sleek dark vehicle was parked in the shadow of the furthest trees. There were lights on at the spa but I couldn't hear a sound.

'Be a nice hotel,' said Heron, nodding at it. 'Be good for more people to see this place before it goes.'

'Before what goes?'

'Gilsland. The river. The way things were.' He said it without sentiment and it seemed wrong to press him. I thought he would leave it there but abruptly he spoke again. 'Things change and they stay the same. Fairfax said he'd found that out. That's why he wrote our stories down, you know? Wanted

a record of this place and this time. He knew better than
anybody what this little part of the world has seen. All the
blood and bones beneath our feet. But happiness too. Laughter.
Think of all the love that's sunk into the ground and you can
almost trust it to stop the hate. We're built on more than our
dead. He told me that. He missed his son. That's all there is
to say on that. But he loved Gilsland and its people. It were
a sadness for him to die like that. Seems wrong to think of
him laying in a drawer somewhere, cut up and lonely. Wish I
could lay him in the ground and pull the earth over him like
a blanket. That's what he'd want. Took death serious did
Fairfax. Knew where we belong and where we go.'

I stayed silent as he spoke. When he finished I didn't know
what to say. I felt an overwhelming urge to thank him again.
He gave me a smile, and raised his knuckles to his forehead
as if saluting the lady of the manor. I watched him turn. Was
still watching when somebody called my name.

I spun at the sound. A man was walking towards me from
the parked car. He wore a grey suit and a brown hat and his
collar and tie were fashionably modern. For all that he was
well dressed, his face was nothing special. His features were
gathered together in the middle of his round countenance, the
way posh restaurants serve fancy meals.

'Mrs Hemlock,' he said, again.

I felt the absence beside me. Heron had disappeared down
the track. Was he watching? Was I alone?

'I'm Cordelia,' I said, stiffly, as he came to a halt a little
closer to me than I felt comfortable with. 'Can I help you?'

He looked me up and down. He made no attempt to disguise
it. I could see the wheels turning in his head as he worked
me out. I couldn't tell whether he would make a good poker
player or a poor one. Perhaps that was the intention all along.

'Been for a stroll, have you?' he asked. He had no accent.
Kept his hands by his sides as he spoke. He had schooled
himself in giving nothing away. 'That would be your bodyguard, I presume.'

I didn't turn my head as he glanced at the path down which
Heron had disappeared. I took an instant dislike to the man
and refused to give him any information.

'Would you mind telling me how you know my name?' I asked, and the sisters would not have recognized me. Suddenly I was the wife of a senior civil servant – a respectable woman in sensible clothes and enough starch in my voice to stiffen a clown's collar.

'I'm Dingwall,' he said, and his face remained expressionless. 'You had rather hoped that your husband could assist you with some research, am I right?'

I looked at him hard. He had grey eyes and there were ugly, bristly hairs between his eyebrows and emerging from his ears and nose. I looked him up and down, as he had done me. There were white dog hairs on his shins and his shoes were wet at the tops.

'My discourse with my husband is my own affair,' I said, and it was hard not to blush at how prim I was pretending to be.

'Affair, you say?' he asked, and his cheek twitched in a way I did not like.

'What is it you want?'

'I want to help,' he said. 'As you requested. Information. Names. All manner of little secrets, untangled, just for you.'

His whole manner oozed with contempt. I didn't know what it was that he took particular objection to but I got the impression he would never have tired of rubbing the heel of his shoe into my eye.

'My husband sent you, did he?' I asked, and I found myself wondering if I should tell Cranham just how unpleasant his messenger had been. I decided against it. The man was presumably some office underling – a rank-and-file everyman who objected to running errands for a man several tiers his superior.

'In a manner of speaking,' he said, and his cheek twitched afresh.

'Well,' I asked. 'Shall we go back to my house and you can tell me what I want? I must say, you were very prompt. It can't be two hours since I asked . . .'

'I shan't,' he said, flatly. 'I don't wish to linger here. Ghastly place.'

I looked shocked. Showed surprise and irritation in my face. 'Gilsland has a lot going for it,' I said.

'I have no doubt,' he said, though as he looked around him it seemed he could smell something distasteful. He looked at the spa. 'This place, for example. I'm sure it will be splendid. Though I do wonder if the guests will allow themselves to dwell on the more unsavoury elements of its past. Its time as a convalescent home, for example, when men scarred by war would fit and cry and scream long into the night. Or its time as a maternity hospital, perhaps. All those women from the north east, driven here by the coachload to open their legs and spew another pink, round-faced little bastard onto crisp white sheets.'

It seemed as if the world was slowing down. I felt my legs weaken. Felt sick rise up my throat. Could he *know* . . .?

'Your mother, for example,' he continued, smoothly. 'What was she? She told the doctors eighteen, but who could say, eh? Which of the men from the base was it, do you think? She enjoyed her fair share, so it goes. It was almost a crime giving you back to her, no more than a girl herself. She wanted to kick up her heels and throw off her petticoats and she was lumbered with a baby, howling and crying and getting in the way. No wonder she forgot to feed you. No wonder she'd lock the door on you and go away for days and never once think about you, snivelling in the dark. It's a shame what happened to her. But some women just can't say no to it, and that "it" could be all sorts. Drink. Opiates. A bit of hows-yer-father. She liked the lot. It's amazing she kept you so long really. But them nuns wanted you, didn't they? Bloody shock to all when you passed those grammar school exams with the best marks in the county. But they didn't see into your soul. Not properly. They wanted the credit for taking a poor little girl from a broken home and turning her into an Oxbridge scholar and they put up with what they knew about you because it was worth it for the reward. The people who know you properly – they always knew it would go wrong. You had your mother's ways. And you proved it, didn't you? Opened your legs like there was no tomorrow. Made yourself popular as the whore on campus. And then you set your sights on the big fish . . .'

'Stop it,' I whispered, and I felt as though I was going to sag to my knees. 'Please . . .'

'A peer of the realm, no less. A rich, powerful, elderly gentleman and honorary faculty member at your college. You saw him, you seduced him and you got yourself pregnant by him. Oh you played well, my girl.'

'How . . .' I begged. 'How can you know?'

'What was it, eh? Love?'

He was mocking me. I couldn't find my voice. I wanted to scream the truth at him. I fell for him. He was kind and clever and his eyes sparkled when he laughed and he made me see things in a way I hadn't seen them before. He had done so to be generous to a girl who did not know where she was supposed to fit in the world. I had tried to reward him in the only way I thought men wanted. Rewarded him as I had so many of Mam's friends when I was young. He had turned me down. He wanted none of what I had to offer. So I pushed. Promised him secrecy and pleasures beyond imagining. I was wicked, like they'd always said. I hadn't expected Stefan to arrive. But even then, he fixed things. Found Cranham for me. Even now, I would give myself to him if he wanted it. He was the only person to have ever shown me kindness for its own sake and I had corrupted him in my desperation to show gratitude.

'You asked your husband to look into something for you. He called my department. And my department called me.' For a moment, something close to pity crossed his face. Later, I wondered how much of what he did was an act. 'You won't be asking anything else, Mrs Hemlock. Not if you want your secrets to stay hidden. And not if you want your husband's second life to stay that way. You are the wife of a man who might one day be powerful and for that reason it's important we know the kind of person you are. Can I report back that you are the kind of person who knows when it is important to close their mouth and open their ears and not do the kind of things that could prove very embarrassing for people so much more important than you?'

I looked at the floor. I could feel tears at my cheeks. I refused to give in to them. Something defiant and vengeful was beating tiny wings in my throat and I could feel myself growing furious. How dare he!

'I'll tell Cranham,' I hissed. 'Tell him what you've said . . .'

'Cranham is not our concern,' he said, silkily. 'Cranham could be controlled as easily as an old dog. But for form's sake, it would be wise to thank him for his help and not to mention our conversation. It would be a shame if he were to learn the truth.'

'He knows!' I protested. 'He agreed to the marriage anyway . . .'

'Oh, Mrs Hemlock, there are so many truths. And he will hear the one that best suits our needs.'

He turned at a sound from the vehicle. I peered past him. Had that been the sound of the passenger window winding down? Was somebody else in the vehicle?

'I'll bid you goodnight, Mrs Hemlock. I do not want us to meet again but something tells me there is little I can do to influence that matter. Please, do place some flowers on your son's grave for me, should you choose a resting place where those other than yourself can pay their respects. I know the boy's father would dearly love to have been able to send lilies. Perhaps he will yet get opportunity to do so. Good night.'

I managed to stay on my feet until he had climbed inside the vehicle and driven away. His car purred as he backed out of the parking space. He did not switch the lights on until he was out of sight. I could not make out the registration plate or the identity of the passenger.

Only when the car was out of sight did I give in. I slid to the floor as if made of wet paper; hands upon my face and my knees drawn up like a child's.

I didn't respond when Heron said my name. Just scrunched up my eyes and shook my head and thought of my boy. Smiling. Playing. Laughing. Then fading. Dying. Dead. My boy. Dead. Taken. Gone . . .

He scraped me off the floor like I was an injured doe.

'Don't worry, lass,' he said, and his nose touched my damp cheek as he whispered into my ear. 'I heard nowt. And that which I did hear will go no further. You were a good mother to that boy and there aint no wickedness in you. You were sent, lass. That's what I knew first time I saw you. This place. This time. You didn't choose it. You're here to do right. And I'm glad to know you.'

This time, when the tears came, I thought of the water gurgling at the foot of the cliff.

And in my mind it carried an accumulation of miseries; a surging crimson torrent containing all the sticks and all the bones; all the stones and all the tears, of all the years. These were tears I shed for people unknown. For lives I had never touched and which were no more to my own existence than pebbles in the water. And yet I wept for their pain and their absence.

I huddled into him as he carried me. I didn't feel the rain until it had already soaked him to the skin.

FELICITY

Transcript 0008, recorded October 30, 2010

There wasn't enough hot water for a proper bath. It were only an inch deep when the hot ran out. I boiled the kettle twice and did my best to make it a bit more comfortable for him but I don't think he'd have cared if he were frozen or scalded. He just sat there, all pink and goose-pimpled and naked, hugging his legs and resting his face on his knees.

'I can leave you alone,' I said, and the steam rose from the water to form a little cloud below the ceiling. I didn't want him feeling funny about being naked in front of his mam. They can be like that, can boys. 'Brian? Good scrub. Feel better.'

He gave the smallest shrug. He looked like he did when he was small and the fever nearly took him. Dark under his eyes and skin that looked like he'd been slapped all over. He looked at me the same way then, too – as if something awful was happening to him that I should have the power to prevent. It broke my heart when he were small and it broke my heart that night too.

'Shall I do it then?'

He nodded again, and I decided not to notice the tears that trickled from the corners of his eyes and dripped into the water.

I took the flannel and rubbed it against the soap. Big, chunky soap, the size of a sandwich. Got you proper clean and turned your bathwater the colour of October skies. Scrubbed his back and his neck and both arms and legs. Lifted his arm and did his armpits. Handed him the flannel without a word so he could tend to his own business. He did as he was bid. When I stood up my knees cracked and I felt a sharp pain down my side.

'Do you want in after me?' he asked, quietly.

I smiled, pleased that he had thought to ask. He wasn't sulking exactly, though John had given him a telling off that would have stripped the skin off some people. He just looked fragile. He'd been gone the best part of five hours and I'd spent most of it with my fingers gripped tight around the material of the sofa. I was like a bird perched on a branch. I had to hold myself still or I swear I'd have shaken myself to bits. It's a terrible thing is that kind of fear. Everybody knows what it is to be scared but until you've imagined never seeing your children again, you don't know the half of it. Thinking rationally, there was no way Pike would have risked prison just to teach a young lad a lesson. But terror isn't rational and as the time ticked away in the aftermath of Pike's warning gunshot blast, my imagination started playing pictures. I kept seeing him with blood coming out of his nose and his mouth – all broken and twisted on the riverbed. I saw him with a tree branch stuck through his middle and his head hanging forward on his chest. I saw him with bulging eyes and lolling tongue with a rope burning his skin beneath his jaw. I saw him dead on the grass outside the church: blue suit and brown shoes.

He'd been with Heron, he said, when he finally came back. Talking, down by the river. Pike had come for him but Heron had seen him off. He reckoned he was safe now. He stood with his head bowed as he spoke, like he were a praying choirboy. I didn't know whether to hug him or slap him but the relief that flooded through me as I helped him out of his wet clothes was so powerful I half thought I was going to come apart at the seams. John put the kettle on and made him a ham and tomato sandwich. Good white bread and thick butter with a smear of mustard. He didn't start telling him off until he'd eaten it and drank two mugs of hot tea. Then he told Brian this would have to stop. He couldn't keep putting his mother through this kind of thing, though there were redness in John's eyes each time he came back from walking the woods and said there were still no sign of him. He couldn't tell Brian that, of course. Wouldn't have been right to tell the boy his dad were in tears over him. I hadn't expected John to get so angry but it didn't take him long to work up a lather. Brian didn't even answer back. Just sat there, nodding, wrapped in a blanket covered in crumbs while I stood at the sink and watched the rain put tiny bullet holes in our reflection.

'Mam? You getting in?' he asked again.

'I'll leave it. Not enough water to bath a rabbit,' I said, and handed him the big towel from the top of the set of drawers. I turned away as he stood up. He got himself out. I wrapped the towel around him properly and started scrubbing him. I tried to be gentle but the towel was rough as sandpaper and it took him an effort not to let on it were hurting.

'He didn't mean it,' I said, under my breath. 'About you being good for nothing . . .'

'He did,' muttered Brian. 'You could see it in his eyes.'

'Pike went after you with a gun,' I said. 'It was horrible.'

'He wouldn't have done owt. Not really.'

'So why did you run?'

Brian looked at me thoughtfully. He was mulling it over. Chewing on it, like stale bread.

'I thought he might take it,' he said, at last.

'Take what? The tooth?'

He nodded, closing his eyes.

'Why would he take it?' I asked, and I kept drying him just so I had something to do with my hands. In truth, I think I wanted to put my palms over my ears and start singing at the top of my voice. I already knew more than I had ever asked to.

'He takes things. That's what he does.'

I turned him to face me and for the first time in my life I put my finger under his chin and made him look straight into my eyes. I'd seen it done in a film and always thought I would be too embarrassed to do it myself. But it felt like it was the right thing to do and I didn't even think about it until later.

'He steals, you mean?'

'He takes what he wants. He's taken a fishing reel and a pocket magnifying glass off me. Tom from school – he took this buffalo-skin wallet that his uncle had sent him from America. That coin that James said he'd lost playing football? The one we found at Birdoswald and was hundreds of years old? Pike took that off him.'

I stayed quiet. I were as guilty as Brian. Everybody knew

you had to keep your hand on your purse or your pocket near Pike. He'd been no different at school. Took your lunch or the laces from your shoes and swore blind he'd stick his thumb in your eye if you told a soul.

'Where did you get it, Brian?' I asked, quietly. 'It's not a nice thing to have . . .'

His face creased up and I could see he was fighting with himself.

'I won't take it,' I said, when I realized that was what was scaring him most.

That seemed to clinch it. He gave a little nod and I stopped drying him. His pyjamas were on the rail in front of the fire and I wasn't sure if I should go get them before he started telling me so I just stood there, a bit daft, waiting for him to talk, with one foot in the bathroom and the other on the landing. That's where I see myself when I think of that night. Half-in, half-out, like I'd been cut in two.

'It were in the collection box,' said Brian, and there wasn't any emotion in his voice. 'In the front of the church. The wooden box on the wall. I looked in the slot at the top and it was glinting up at me and I took it.'

I didn't know what to say. We'd never been religious but stealing from the collection plate was something that bad people did. I gave him a hard look before a dozen questions rippled my features into an expression of pure bafflement.

'The church hasn't had a collection in years,' I said. 'It's not held a service while we've been here. And what were you doing in the church anyway? Did Fairfax let you in?'

He raised his hands as if I were hitting him.

'I'd seen Pike going in. I never meant any harm. He had a key. Why would Pike have a key, Mam?'

'Brian, I don't understand.'

'I were hiding in the churchyard. Playing, I suppose. And Pike went in and he had a bag with him and he opened the door with a key. He was in a minute then came out again. I don't know if it was a mistake or if he heard something but he legged it out of there sharpish and didn't lock it properly. I'd never been inside and I couldn't help it. I had a little nosey. Have you been in, Mam? It's spooky and cold and your breath

doesn't go anywhere when you breathe out – it just hangs in
front of your face. I could see Pike's boot prints on the floor.
There were prayer books and cushions and pews all scattered
and turned over. I don't know what I was looking for, I just
wanted to see. And I looked in the collection box by the door.
I could tell there was something inside. I opened it with my
penknife. There were some old coins and this tooth. I took it.'

There was colour in his cheeks, as if he'd been running,
and I didn't like how shiny his eyes were becoming as he
spoke about it.

'Brian, that must have been a donation. Or something for
Fairfax. It wasn't for you to take . . .'

'No, Mam, there's no services. And the letter would have
said, wouldn't it?'

'Letter?'

He shook his head like he was telling himself off. He
looked cross and started rubbing at his arms.

'Just a note,' he said, all sullen, like. 'A bit of paper, folded
over. Nice handwriting. And a reel.'

'A fishing reel?' I was getting agitated at how many answers
I needed him to share. I wanted to shake him suddenly.

'No, a tape reel – like a recording machine. Just one of
them. It looks like what you get ribbons wrapped around at
the market.'

'Did you take that too?'

He didn't look sheepish now. He was starting to smirk again.

'I thought I'd better take it all, just to be safe,' he said,
getting cockier with each word. 'Like I said, Mam, it weren't
there for anybody specific. It didn't make any sense.'

'The reel,' I said, interrupting. 'Where is that?'

He rolled his eyes at me and rubbed his hand across his
mouth like he was a man checking if he needed a shave.
'Reckon Pike had it, don't I?'

'How do you think that?'

'I've got a place for stuff like that. Somewhere nobody
looks. I put the tape in there and the note and the coins. I kept
the tooth on me 'cause I liked it.'

'And Pike took the reel?'

'Must have. Went back to the tree and it weren't there.'

'Which tree?'

'Doesn't matter now,' he said, back to being a bugger. 'The sweet chestnut just over the boundary wall. Climb up and look inside and it's hollow, Mam. I kept a few bits in there. Pike must have seen. Took it.'

I could hear my breathing was becoming shorter. I felt like I'd been running.

'What did the letter say?'

'It were foreign,' he shrugged, as if this made it little more than nonsense. 'Just a couple of lines.'

'So how do you know what it said?'

'I asked, din't I?'

I rubbed my hands through my hair, exasperated. It was like pulling teeth, but that's an awful thing to say, considering.

I heard John's voice drifing up the stairs then felt the draft that meant the front door was open. I felt like screaming. A few days ago life had felt like it had a rounder shape. Things led back to themselves. All my friends and family and the things I had to do – it was like they were all connected to me with wool and they twisted around each other as if we were all Maypoling. Now my life was jagged edges and sharp lines and it felt as though the wool was tangling me up and cutting in.

'Get your pyjamas on,' I said, trying to sound stern. 'We're not done.'

I left the bathroom before he could think of a clever reply and as I came down the stairs I saw John was talking to Heron in the doorway. Heron had that look about him. Looked like a soldier or a cowboy or somebody who rides a horse and swims in waterfalls in the films. If he'd given a damn about such things he could have been in any one of the magazines. He was the sort who would make your tongue twist over your words and I honestly couldn't think of a single thing to say as I stood still on the stairs.

'Thought it might be better to bring her 'ere,' said Heron, and John must have heard the stairs creak 'cause he turned around. He was wearing his cardigan over his vest and braces and holding a mug of tea in his hand. From where I stood I could see how thin his hair had got on top. He seemed smaller, too, though

everybody looked small next to Heron. I felt such a cow for
thinking it but you can't help your instincts, can you? And I'm
shamed to say it but that were the first time I thought that John
were starting to look a bit knackered. Starting to look like he
was going to look when he got old.

'Felicity,' said Heron, and he touched a knuckle to his
forehead. 'Your friend. She could use a bit of company if
that's all right. Bit of a run-in with somebody passing through.'

I changed my position and saw Cordelia. She seemed
somehow less solid than I had seen her before. I got the
impression that it would take weights in her shoes to stop her
floating away. She was like a breath that hung in the air in a
cold church. I hurried down the rest of the stairs and pushed
past John.

'Come in, come in, you'll catch your death,' I muttered and
Heron gave me a nod, like we were the grown-ups, as he
handed her to me. I had my arm around her and folded her
into me. 'You've been wet a week! You're costing me the last
of my towels! Goodness it's a job you're not made of sugar.'

I fussed her down the corridor to the kitchen. She made no
protest. Her hair was soaking against my cheek and her coat
squelched against my arm. As I steered her into the kitchen
she stopped and looked at me. 'Thank you,' she said, and it
was an effort not to let myself down. I could have cried for
the sadness in her.

'You coming in, Heron?' I asked, over my shoulder.

'No, I'll away, thanks love. Leave you to it, eh?'

'Thanks for Brian,' I said, looking back at the bulk of him
in the doorway. 'He said you saw Pike off.'

'Don't think on it. I'll be away. Talk to you when you're
settled, eh?'

I left him talking to John. Brought her into the warm and
sat her down at what I was starting to think of as her chair.
There was tea in the pot and I poured her a mug. She watched
me the whole time and for once, I think she would have liked
to have offered to help. She just didn't know any way to
contribute.

'Brian got home safe?' she asked, all sad and small.

'Aye. That's boys for you.'

'No trouble with Pike?'

'Seems like it's done.'

We made small talk as I pottered about. There was so much to talk about and yet it somehow seemed as if there were things that should be left unsaid. I had run from Fairfax's house like a child. She'd seen Brian save my life and the last I'd seen of her I'd been limping off after him. Where had she been since? Who had frightened her?

'I phoned my husband,' she said, out of nowhere.

'Yes? Is he well?' I didn't know what to say so just tried to be polite.

'I don't know,' she said, and she started nibbling the skin around her thumb. She had lovely nails and I almost wanted to tell her to stop it. It was beginning to feel like having a little sister. A little sister who was cleverer than me and prettier than me but who always managed to get me into trouble.

'A man spoke to me,' she said, at last. 'I think he was security services.'

I turned, me eyes like teacups. 'A spy? Like from the films?'

'I don't know. But he knew things. Said things about me. Where I'm from. How I got here.'

I wanted to push her but she seemed so wrung out it would have been cruel. I started drying the dishes that had been left on the draining board. She spotted a way she could be helpful and picked the hand towel off the back of the pantry door and joined me at the sink. Close to, she smelled of her nice perfume and rain. Smelled a bit like Heron too. I wondered if she would be the one to turn his head. Heaven knew she was good at it.

'Can I tell you something?' she asked, her voice not much more than a whisper. 'Something that I've always thought was a secret?'

I nodded. Wiped the tea towel around the inside of a mug and looked down at the metal draining board so I wouldn't have to stare into those big eyes of hers as she spoke. I was glad I did. I know for sure I'd have cried. When she were finished I had a hand on her forearm and she was stiff as a statue: both hands flat on the counter and her whole body rigid. I think it half killed her to tell me who she was and where she'd come from. I've wondered many times since whether the words I chose to say next were the right ones, but I know they put a bit of life in her eyes and that was better than seeing her as she was.

'I've found some more of Fairfax's writing,' I said, under my breath. 'In the church. Under the floor.'

It was as if somebody had lit a fire in the attic window of a deserted house. Whatever she had been through, all that mattered to her in that moment was a chance to read the words on the sheaf of papers.

'Have you read it? Where were they hidden? Exactly? Show me, oh please, Flick, are they here?'

I found myself smiling. It was wrong of her to be so gleeful about such a thing but her excitement was contagious. I pulled a face of admonishment but couldn't keep it up.

'I haven't read them. I thought I should wait . . .'

'Wait for me? Oh, that's so generous of you. I don't think I could have forced myself to wait for you.'

I didn't tell her about the panic that had been gripping me during Brian's absence and that it took an effort not to throw the damn papers on the fire. They hadn't seemed important, as I sat waiting for my son to return home. Yet in Cordelia's company they represented another piece of a puzzle and I was becoming as keen as she was to see what the finished picture would look like.

'You thawed out?' asked John, opening the door. Cordelia flashed him a look of annoyance and I found myself breathing a sigh of relief. I'd had it my head she was a little soft on him and there was no way I could stop him if he took a fancy to her. She had that quality – men just can't do anything about it, or at least, that's what it seems. Sometimes I wonder if they don't just like pretending to be weak so we don't expect more from them. Brian was like that when I asked him to mow the lawn. Did it dreadful just so I'd stop asking.

'Heron's got a long night ahead,' said John, sitting down on the sofa and looking at Cordelia without showing the annoyance I knew him to be feeling about her presence in his chair.

'Aye?' I asked, refilling his mug.

'Thon hunters that were in the paper. Reckons the moon'll have them out in droves.'

Cordelia looked to me for explanation and I obliged.

'Dead deers being left in the river. Nasty business. They reckon they've suffered plenty. Legs cut off before the poor beasts had died. Hearts and lungs taken too. Been in the papers, surprised you didn't hear about it. Heron's taken it awfully personal. He not tell you?'

She shook her head and water ran down her neck. I watched it disappear into the throat of her jumper.

'I wouldn't fancy being in their shoes if Heron does catch them. He says there were a stag he found up Crammel Linn had his antlers hacked off with a saw. Caught in a wire snare, see. Heron had to end its misery, poor sod. I reckon he'll do worse to whoever done it.'

Cordelia sat back in the chair and looked up at the ceiling. I was conscious of Brian up there, just a few feet above. James too, though he'd no doubt be drawing or having one of his adventures in his head. He'd been the only one of us who looked a bit disappointed when his brother came home safe.

'I've been thinking,' said John, and ticked his thumbs into his braces as he spoke. Cordelia and I shared a little smile and it was a nice, sisterly moment. I instantly felt bad for what I'd thought about her. Of course she knew what men wanted. Of course it showed in the way she was. Poor girl had been through more than I could tell you.

'Thinking, John?' she asked him, a bit flirty. 'No need for that.'

'Yer a cheeky one,' said John, wagging his finger. He seemed in a better mood for his chat with Heron. Or perhaps it was the way I walked down the hall that set him right – I wasn't too badly hurt from my brush with the lorry. He could stop worrying.

'Go on then, we're all ears,' I said.

'Ye're both convinced of what ye saw,' he said. 'And don't tell me ye've been in 'ere talking about knitting patterns because I won't believe you. So, tell me honest – were there a body on that grass after the tree came down?'

He said it so simply, so flatly, that I had no time to prepare an answer. I simply spoke honestly. Yes. Yes, there was.

'Hmm,' he mused. 'And you, Mrs Hemlock, you came here to get out the rain and told poor Fairfax what you'd seen, yes?'

'Aye, that's right,' I answered for her.

'Then he gets his car and sets off for goodness knows where and he crashes and dies, God rest him, and the body in the churchyard has gone when you go back to check, yes?'

We both nodded. I didn't want to speak in case I spoiled it.

John kept sucking on his thoughts like they were boiled sweets.

'Fairfax has spent years asking people for their memories and their stories and writing down people's secrets, yes?'

'Yes,' said I, wishing he'd get on with his point.

'So . . .' he said, musically.

Cordelia and I were both looking at him but there was a smugness I didn't particularly like so I shook my head and gave my attention to her instead. She was looking at me earnestly, as if waiting for permission to say what was on her mind. Then I realized that was exactly what she wanted. She wanted to say something unkind about Fairfax and she didn't want to upset me. I gave the tiniest nod.

'You know what I'm driving at,' said John.

'Aye,' said Cordelia, and it sounded odd in her accent.

'Go on,' I said, sighing.

'Fairfax moved the body,' said Cordelia, and for a moment she stared at the bare wall and it was like she were watching it all play out on a cinema screen. She had a mind like a rocket.

'It's the only explanation,' said John.

'It's not,' muttered Cordelia. 'There are lots of explanations. But that's the one I believe. He knew who the body was. He knew he didn't have much time. So he got in his car . . .'

'There were tyre tracks by the church,' I said, quickly. 'Thin ones, like from that silly car of his.'

'Well he drove to the church, took the body and grabbed whatever it is that was so important in the church. Then he put it in his car and headed off through the storm. He got himself on the Spadeadam road. The peat bog. Miles and miles of ground that will hold its secrets forever. But the storm got too much and he had the crash that killed him.'

I didn't like hearing it but I couldn't stop her. Not now.

'The man who spoke French,' she said. 'The one with the recording device. He went to Fairfax's. He matches the description, give or take. He must have told Fairfax something he shouldn't have. Maybe he upset somebody by accident. Perhaps he fell or something . . .'

She shook her head, angry at herself for sounding so vague. She took a breath like she was trying to order her thoughts.

'Fairfax doted on Christopher, yes? Never got over his death. Well perhaps this Frenchman had something to say about the war that Fairfax didn't like. So Fairfax loses his temper and the man in blue ends up dead. Where would he stash the body? How about a mausoleum that won't be opened for years and that Fairfax has the only key for . . .'

'No,' I said, sharply. 'No, Pike had a key. He's been storing stuff there. I found guns. Not shotguns. Military rifles.'

She looked confused. 'Pike? Why would he . . .?'

'Fairfax might have given him it?' said John.

'Why?'

'He thought the best of people. And he and Christopher were pals, near enough.'

It looked to me as if Cordelia were reading lots of different books all at once. Her eyes seemed to be darting everywhere as she spoke.

'Could you imagine Fairfax hurting somebody?' she asked, directly.

'No,' I said, and meant it.

'But he would protect somebody, yes? Somebody he cared about?'

I could see what she meant. I'd been able to see it before she even started speaking.

'Where was Pike when the storm hit?' she asked. 'Could Fairfax have been going to warn him?'

'Probably up to mischief,' I said, trying to make light of it. 'He deals in cigarettes. Beer. Has some friends who are up to no good. Over Newcastle way.'

'So Pike's been either storing guns in a safe place for some bad men, or he's been ripping them off. They send some heavy to ask around and he ends up dead. Can't you see it?' she asked, and it was like there was energy fizzing off her.

'I dunno,' said John, shaking his head. 'I don't know if Fairfax would cover up something like that. He cared for Pike but not to that extent. He knew right and wrong and that'd be wrong. But there doesn't seem any other way to account for the body going missing. Do you think he might have taken something from the church? Something he wanted to keep safe?'

I looked at the swirling pattern on the floor and listened to the rain on the glass. It felt as though I were listening to a hundred conversations. I knew it would only be a matter of time until she put it together. I saw it happening – saw her thoughts moving and drifting into a picture that she could clearly define.

'His car,' said Cordelia, at last, and it was all I could do not to close my eyes and hang my head. 'Who has Fairfax's car?'

'It were towed,' shrugged John. 'After the accident. It'll be at the garage, like as not. Be sold when the solicitor gets it all sorted out, though it were in a bad way as I hear it.'

'It wasn't taken for evidence?' she asked, hopeful but appalled.

'There's no case, love. Chivers said so. It's just junk now.'

'So there may be something in the boot,' she said, eagerly. 'Something that could help. God, there could be a body . . .

John shook his head, like she was going too far. 'You can't sneeze in Gilsland without somebody telling you they've heard all about it. And I know what you're thinking and I'm not having it.'

'We could do it quietly . . .' she began.

I shook my head. 'This has gone far enough. We should just tell Chivers what we think. Or his boss. Tell the other office. Or go to Carlisle . . .'

Cordelia flushed red. 'They threatened me,' she said, like a hissing cat. 'I can't let anything trickle back to this Dingwall. Not until I know for certain what's happened. Please, Flick, let's just poke about . . .?'

'Who the bloody hell's Flick?' asked John, indignant.

'We haven't read the papers I found,' I protested, trying to stop her from persuading me to go with her. My heart felt like it was falling through my body. I wasn't right for this. I should just step back, I knew it. And yet, a part of me didn't want to end the game. And though it was superstitious nonsense, the bird had truly unsettled me. If Fairfax did die wrong, he deserved some help in putting it right.

'What's these papers then?' asked John.

He looked a bit clueless, sitting there in his vest. He looked like he'd intruded into something that were nowt to do with him and I suddenly felt an urge to tell him to bugger off and mind his own business. Goodness, what was I becoming?

'Please,' she said, again. And that were what sealed it. The way she looked at me and made me feel like I was the only one in the world who could fix the gaps in her. I've seen her do it to other people plenty times since but it's never changed how good it felt when she did it to me.

'I'll fetch them,' I said, and went to the coal bunker in the passage. The papers were in a biscuit tin by the door. I should have opened the back door and given them to the breeze. Should have tossed them on the fire. Instead I returned to the kitchen and handed the tin to Cordelia. They were typed out neatly. No mistakes. He'd done it a few dozen times. There weren't many pages but from the way he had laid it all out, you could tell he was proud of the job he had done. This was the story he had always been searching for – the one his son would have written if he could have done. When I saw the second name that had been inscribed beneath the title, I felt something reach into me and squeeze my lungs flat.

Cordelia took the words and pulled herself out of the seat. She crossed to where John sat and plonked herself down next to him. Then she patted the empty cushion beside her and I sat down too.

She removed the papers from the tin and took them in her pale hands.

We read, and everything changed.

SECRET HERO

By Fairfax Duke and Christopher Duke

They told me their story because they couldn't keep it to themselves any longer. And I'm telling you because somebody, some time, deserves to know. It won't be in my lifetime, I know that. It won't be in theirs. These words will go somewhere safe. Under the flagstones, beneath God's gaze. I think of them as a time capsule: something to be opened for future generations at a time when we are all just names and the wars we fought in are memories.

I won't name him. That would be wrong. I'm sure if somebody truly wanted to know they could put the pieces together and make sense of it all, but I promised I would not tell, and I am trying to keep that promise. At the same time, I have a vow to keep to Christopher. When he went to war I swore I would keep him informed of life back home. I got into the habit of asking people questions. People started telling me their stories and I would write them down and send them to Christopher. When he died, I didn't stop. It somehow became more important to keep asking. Keep writing. It helped me to continue to feel his presence. Eventually, I knew I would find the tale that would have inspired him to write the book that would have made him famous. Christopher was destined to matter. He had a gift with words that I cannot replicate. War robbed me of my son but more importantly it robbed the world of a true talent. It is in his memory that I write these words

and you will forgive an old man for crying as
he writes.

They came to me in early spring. They brought
a bottle and a fruit loaf and we talked, as we
had so often. Crops. Birds. Plans for the hall
and whether the river would flood again this
year. We talked as old friends. And then he said
it. Told me he had something he wanted to get
off his chest. I wince, thinking about the way he
said it. That little smile of acknowledgement at
his poor choice of words.

He told me that all I knew of him was a lie.

How do I start? Perhaps I should simply repeat
it the way he said it to me. His name had been
Abel. He was a Frenchman. Was apprentice as
a printer in a little town called Les Papillons in
the Dordogne. He told me that meant The
Butterflies. His home was in a commune of cliffs
and caves in a pocket of the world that I will
never see. I have looked at the area on maps
and seen photographs but I cannot truly imagine
how it would be to grow up in that place of
fossils and bones. His childhood was simple, his
ambitions no different to that of any other young
man. He played in the caves. Played football.
Drank wine and coffee and sang songs with his
friends. Then the Germans came.

It was with disgust that Abel witnessed his
government give in to the Nazis. Their collaboration turned his stomach and like so many other
brave young men and women, he searched for
a way that he could help liberate his country.
He became a member of the Resistance. He joined
the Maquisards. Brave men and women who
refused to surrender to an occupying force.

For long months and years he lived in constant
expectation of death. He learned to kill. To live

with the knowledge of having taken a life. He
considered himself fortunate each day that
he was not captured or shot. But his luck ran
out. Fleeing the Gestapo, Abel suffered a terrible
fall and was left with terrible injuries. Despite
his wish to fight the Germans he could no longer
be thought of as a fighting man. Instead he was
sent to a town in Correze where he could be
involved in the passing of information and could
use his knowledge of the printing press to ensure
that even the remotest villages received information about the Resistance.

He was a useful asset, but his fighting days
were done.

In 1944, the year that my son was taken from
me, the Maquisards had become the scourge of
the SS. They won countless victories against the
Germans and it was Hitler's personal command
that all possible measures be taken to stamp
them out. Their primary tool in this was the
Milice. These men were a unit of paramilitaries
created with the express instruction to obliterate
the Resistance. They were brutal extremists and
many were recruited from prisons where they
had been serving sentences for terrible deeds.

The Milice frequently used torture to extract
information or confessions from those whom they
interrogated. The French Resistance considered
the Milice more dangerous than the Gestapo and
SS because they were native Frenchmen who
understood local dialects fluently, had extensive
knowledge of the towns and countryside, and
knew local people and informants.

Among them was a man called Jean Favre. He
was known as Le Tanneur due to his ability to
skin a man without killing him.

In June 1944, three days after the D-Day
landings at Normandy, the Maquisards had
passed through a town in Correze. They had been

victorious in seizing key towns from the Nazis but the arrival of the 2nd SS Panzer Division forced them to retreat to a town known to be loyal to the cause. The SS followed them. So too did the Milice.

Abel was mute witness to what occurred next. As the tanks rolled into the square, he saw the horror of what had already been done in the search for the Resistance men. He recognized the young man strapped to the hood of the commanding officer's car. The young Maquisard had suffered almost beyond endurance.

The Mayor of Correze stepped forward to beg for mercy and was killed with a single shot. Then the SS commanding officer began to shoot the inhabitants of the town. Men aged 16 to 60 were strung from lampposts for daring to aid the Resistance. And then the young man on the front of the tank found the strength to speak.

Despite his pain, despite his suffering, he cursed the Nazis as dogs. From among the ranks of soldiers and the huddle of Milice bastards, emerged Favre – Le Tanneur. He tortured the boy. Branded him with flaming coins and took pieces of his skin.

It was a miracle that Abel survived. He had already accepted that he was to die. There was already a noose around his neck when the commander declared that ninety-nine corpses were sufficient. Abel would have been the hundreth man. It was Abel who cut free the young Maquisard who had been dropped, on the verge of death, on the blood-soaked road as the Nazis retreated. It was Abel who nursed him back to health, even as news of fresh hells from nearby Oradour trickled through.

Das Reich had cut a bloody swathe through the resistance. Hundreds were killed. Abel spread such stories. With his printing press he shared word of the atrocities. Even towns that had collaborated began to resist.

Within months the Nazis had capitulated and the war was over.

It was men like Abel who gave evidence at the trials demanded by the people. His testimony helped secure justice for countless men. He stood bravely in the courtroom and fixed his eyes on Jean Favre and told the court what he had seen him do.

Favre was sentenced to eight years imprisonment. As he left the courtroom, he promised Abel that he would find him. He would hurt him. And he would take his skin.

That threat has been with Abel every day since and I admire him so vehemently for making something of his life in spite of that which he has seen. He has tried to live a good life, and that is no easy thing to do. I, too, have always hoped to be thought of as a good man, but in truth, I cannot truly call myself such.

I believed in liberty when I fought in the first war but three decades later, the echoes of that conflict took my son. I believe in working hard for a living and not taking from your fellow man, and yet my soft heart insists I help my young neighbour with activities I know to be illegal, due to the loyalty he showed my son.

Should anybody find his guns and tobacco and brandy in the flagstones of this church, I trust you will say a prayer for his soul. He is not a bad person, I believe that, and Christopher always felt very fondly about him. Do not think too harshly of an old man who wanted to help him.

Abel's life has taken many turns since that day. I know him as a good man, and I understand why he has been so quiet about his past. I am honoured he chose me as a confidante.

I do not know when these words will be read

or what small part I have played in their preservation but I hope in some distant time, they are studied by somebody who will say a quiet prayer for the souls of a brave man, and for my son, whose loss I still feel as keenly as if somebody had removed my soul.

FD, 04.04.67.

CORDELIA

I slept on Flick's sofa under a crocheted blanket that her mum had made and which I couldn't resist twisting my fingers through. The pillow she gave me smelled of baking and rain. I didn't sleep much. The curtains in the kitchen didn't close all the way and it seemed that wherever I put my head, the shaft of pinkish moonlight kept finding my face. It was like a persistent lover. At first I enjoyed the delicate kisses and soft caress but as I grew tired and cold and grouchy it became another annoyance, alongside the creaking pipes and the settling stones in the fire. I heard one of them get up for a pee in the night. It might have been John, based on the heaviness of the footsteps. At one point I felt eyes upon me but by then I was in that half-asleep state where nothing feels fully formed and the edges of things seem to bleed into one another and by the time I sat up and looked around I was completely alone.

The clouds seemed to have blown themselves out overnight for a while and there was a pleasant violet hue to the sky. I opened the front door and sat myself on the front step wrapped in the blanket. It was a fresh, chilly morning and the mist had lifted enough for me to be able to see all the way down the road to the church.

My thoughts turned to the man in blue before they turned to Dingwall and the things he had said to me. Maybe I was distracting myself on purpose but as far as I saw it, I had little choice. If I stopped thinking about the dead man I would have to begin thinking about all the other aspects of my ragged life.

As I sat there I thought of the stranger's words, painstakingly transcribed in Fairfax's hand. Was the man of whom he spoke to also the man whose corpse I had seen? Could a man who had survived so much truly have met his end in such a tiny, faraway place?

I thought upon all of the different lives that would have

had to bounce off one another in order for Flick and I to gaze upon his dead body beneath the broken stones of the Kinmont tomb. Was it possible? And if Fairfax had been aware there was a corpse in the mausoleum that shouldn't have been there, was his complicity an act of cruelty or kindness? Could he have been protecting Pike? And if he was, how would Pike respond when he learned that his neighbours had been digging into his crimes?

I heard the rumble of an approaching train. It wouldn't stop. No trains would stop in Gilsland ever again. The line cut the village in two as precisely as the Romans did two millennia before but the station itself had been closed down on the orders of Dr Beeching. A team of navvies had come in the night a few months before and dismantled half the rural stations on the line.

I watched the engine as it trundled past: steamed up windows and a few glimpsed faces – pink circles scribbled with blurry features. Could the dead man have been sitting on the train and seen a face from the past? Somebody he once knew? Is that what persuaded him to get off the train and go speak to the man who knew everybody? Had that decision cost him his life? Had he been trying to protect his own identity or revenge himself upon a past abuser?

More than anything else, I wanted to know whether it was possible that a wartime sadist had found his way to this tiny part of the world in order to inflict revenge upon the Resistance fighter whose evidence had secured his incarceration. Was there even the slightest chance of such a thing? I needed to know more. Needed to learn what had happened to the man called Favre after Nuremberg. And what of Abel? Was he our victim?

My head span. I tried to focus on what I could see. Broken down houses and damp stone; tatty outbuildings and the distant grey blur of the church. Somewhere a bell chimed the hour. The distant bleating of a sheep carried on the wind and the cold breeze played with my fringe.

'Tea?'

I turned and saw James. He was dressed and ready for school. He'd combed his hair and fastened his tie right to the top. I could smell toothpaste coming off him. He handed me a burgundy mug and I shifted up to let him sit on the step.

'Sleep OK?' he asked, getting comfortable.

'Bit chilly but I got a few hours.'

'I'd have brought you more blankets.'

'I don't think there's enough blankets to keep me warm at the moment,' I said, watching a little bird, sharp as an arrowhead, flitting into the eaves of Fairfax's house across the road. 'Feels like the cold's got into my bones.'

'You need to run about more,' he said, watching the bird with me. 'That's a wagtail. Pretty isn't it?'

I shifted my position to better look at him. He had lovely manners and his accent didn't sound like either of his parents. He wasn't overweight but there was a roundness to him, a fleshiness, that suggested he would always battle with his weight. He didn't seem shy, not exactly – just slightly removed from things. He was the sort who could leave a party and nobody would notice them go.

'You ever draw birds?' I asked, making conversation. 'You're the artist in the family, aren't you?'

He smiled and looked away, embarrassed at being pleased. 'I don't draw things I can look at. I just draw the things I see in my head.'

'And that's all the gruesome stuff?' I asked, a little surprised.

'It's not gruesome,' he said, thoughtfully. 'Not really. You're watching a bird and thinking it's lovely and I'm seeing the worm in its beak. That's all.'

I was a bit surprised at how mature he sounded. He was a clever lad, I could see that, but it was the sort of cleverness that rarely brought happiness. It was a restless, questioning intelligence that would forever leave him dissatisfied. I knew it well.

'And you see people having their heads cut off, do you?'

'Most of the stories you hear around here involve death. You know the ghost story? The castle?'

I shook my head then settled against the doorframe, wrapping my hands around my tea.

'Centuries back the baron of Featherstone Castle arranged for his daughter to marry a man she didn't love. She wanted this other man who had no money but a good heart.' He paused at that to make sure I was listening and not laughing at him. Satisfied, he continued. 'She refused to go through with the marriage but her father insisted. After the wedding, he instructed his daughter to ride out with the wedding party to see the new lands she had inherited through the marriage while he oversaw preparations for the banquet. When the wedding party reached a clearing in the woods, the bride's lover and a group of his friends tried to rescue her and ride away. It was all very romantic. But her new husband was a warrior as well and there was a battle. In the midst of it all the bride was struck by her lover's sword and died in his arms – as did her husband, *and* the man she loved, all mixed in together and their blood soaking into the ground.'

I looked at him and saw he was staring off into the distance as though the story he was telling was playing out in front of his eyes.

'You're good with words,' I said, hoping for a smile in return. He barely noticed me.

'Back at the castle the baron became worried,' James continued. 'He sent out riders. Where were they? Finally he heard the sound of horses and rushed out to greet his returning guests.'

He turned and looked at me and his eyes reminded me of wet pebbles.

'They rode right through him,' said James. 'Ghosts. Spectres. The whole lot. He was found weeks later by the king's men who had come to see why he had not been paying his rents. He was white-haired and babbling and quite mad with fright. I heard that story when I was not much more than four. Like I say – it's what you're raised on.'

I wasn't sure what to say in response. I liked the energy in his eyes and the fire with which he spoke but there was something about his glee as he described the deaths that I found a little unsettling.

'I don't know if I'll sleep tonight now either,' I said, trying to make light of it.

'Maybe just as well,' he said, quietly, then dropped his voice further. 'There's something you might want to know. Look, I'm probably going to get into trouble for this . . .'

'You sitting with a girl, Jimbo?' came a voice from the top
of the stairs. 'Honestly, can't leave you alone for a moment.'

Brian was mooching down the stairs in his dressing gown
and pyjamas. His hair stuck up on his crown and his lip
was curled as if he was smoking a pipe. Immediately James
stood up.

'What you talking about?' asked Brian, jerking his head.
'Causing trouble, Jimbo? Or storing up a few pictures to enjoy
in your head at bedtime?'

He blushed and turned away, reaching past me and grabbing
his coat from the peg by the door.

'Tell Mam I got the early bus,' he said, teeth together. 'It
doesn't matter.'

I wasn't sure whether to stop him or to say something sharp
to Brian. It was hard to imagine them as brothers. There was
a nastiness to Brian but it would be wrong of me to say that
James was his entire opposite. It wasn't sweet benevolence
that oozed out of him – just a kind of harmless nothingness.

'You can thank me later,' said Brian, knocking me in the
back with his knee as he leaned over me and watched his brother
walk off down the road. 'Saved your ears from bleeding.'

'He was telling me a story, actually,' I said, and it felt strange
to pretend to be a grown-up with somebody who would respect
me no more for the act.

'Aye, like I said. You want more tea? Your hair looks nice,
by the way. You're pretty when you're not soaked to the skin.'

I found myself grinning. For all that he was absolute trouble
there was no doubting that Brian was a disarming boy. I could
imagine him growing up to be the kind of rogue that always
managed to persuade other people to cover for him or take
the blame.

I followed him into the kitchen and watched as he built the
fire up. He filled the kettle afresh and sawed a loaf into inch-
thick slices which he placed under the grill. He poured himself
a glass of milk and made no attempt to wipe the moustache
away. He sucked his teeth and looked at the table then went
into the back garden and came back a moment later with a
handful of wildflowers which he placed in a small crystal vase
he half-filled with water. I leaned against the wall, watching

him work and slowly the kitchen filled with warmth and life. At seven thirty, Flick and John came downstairs, dressed and washed.

'Sleep OK?' asked Flick, and her eyes scanned the room as she spoke to me. She took in the vase of flowers and the hot toast and the pot of tea and gave the tiniest of smiles. As she passed Brian I saw her brush his hand with her knuckles: the lightest of touches, two petals bumping together on their fall to earth. Whatever they had argued about, it was now forgiven.

Brian left for school just before eight. He was well-behaved in front of his mother and father but he caught my eye as he was leaving the kitchen and I'm sure there was something devilish in the grin he shot me. I would never know how to read Brian. Nobody would.

'I thought about it all night,' said Flick, when there were just the three of us. 'It was like I could see them. Bodies, full of holes and burning. Why did they choose Fairfax? He was just a nice old man who wanted to write people's stories down. And the thing with the coins!' She shuddered. 'Those poor poor people.'

'There's nowt to say you'll ever know any more than you do,' said John, lighting a cigarette. His reluctance to continue investigating had died in the face of the words on the singed pages.

'We can ask,' I said. 'That's all we can do.'

'If it were Pike . . .'

'We'll cross that bridge later.'

'You still don't have anything that isn't just guesses and imagination. It could just be a story. Fiction, written by Fairfax to keep himself busy. There's no body.'

I didn't argue with him. He was talking to the air, not to me or his wife. He wanted his objections heard so that if it turned out we were fools at least he would be able to remind us he had not been taken in.

'I don't like lying,' said Felicity.

'It's not lying.'

'It's not the truth.'

'You're getting into difficult territory there,' I said, and was pleased to see her smile.

'Howay then,' said John, and some Geordie crept into his accent. 'I'm off to work. Try not to get run over by any wagons while I'm gone, eh love?'

She gave him a little flutter of a smile, like a butterfly beating its wings. He kissed her on the head as he pulled on his cap. He paused for a moment, uncertain whether he should do the same to me.

'Look after her, eh?'

'I will,' I said.

He looked at me for a moment too long, then his eyes flicked to his wife and back to me. 'I wasn't talking to you.'

CORDELIA

Flick and I didn't talk much as we walked. I could hear her breathing harder than she needed to and I'm sure she could hear the little waver in my voice as I said hello to a man in green fishing waders and a waterproof coat who was walking his Labrador on the opposite side of the road.

'Know him?' asked Flick, as he returned my greeting with a grunt.

'Just his face. Saw him in post office. Why?'

'Making conversation.'

'Oh.'

There weren't many cars on the road and the gutters were still gurgling with muddy puddles and mulched leaves. I felt like I could hear Flick's mind making noises like a waterlogged motorcycle engine. I couldn't think of very much to say.

'Meg Merrilies' cottage,' said Flick, half to herself, as we followed the path into the village. She nodded at a little house on the bridge. 'You read Walter Scott?'

I was a bit taken aback by the question. 'What? Well, some, yes.'

'Don't know any myself,' she said. 'But there's one book of his – *Guy Mannering*, it's called. Lots of this area in it, though different names and such. There's a lass in it called Meg Merrilies. Bad old sort and landlady of the alehouse. She were based on a local lass. A real lass. Reiver, like I told you the other day.'

I thought back to our brief conversations. The day of our meeting felt like an age ago. Where had I been? A grave. Laying there, thinking of my son and wanting the world to leave me alone or swallow me down.

'You were in her grave,' said Flick, flatly. 'Hundred years old and they probably put her in there kicking and screaming. There's some say that that was her house yonder but others reckon she were actually from Mumps Hall, up the road. Who's to say, ehh? Oh, there it is. That's the one. You can see the sparks.'

She was right about that. The road curved to the left before it entered the bulk of the village and the garage stood to our left. It was a large building with half a dozen coaches and minibuses parked up on the forecourt. The front bonnet of an agricultural vehicle had been lifted up and a short man in blue overalls was leaning into its guts. Red sparks were dancing around his head. Nearby, a fat man and a thin man in matching shirts and ties were leaning against the front of one of the coaches eating sandwiches from greasy paper bags. They both waved at Flick as we approached.

'That's Hopper and Mont,' said Felicity. 'Bloke with his head in the tractor is Gordon.'

'Which is which?' I hissed.

'Hopper's the fat one.'

It took a moment for them to place me. They looked at Flick the way the locals tended to look at one another – as if they were reading words off a card that was slightly too far away for them to see clearly. It took me a while of living there to realize that you weren't truly local until you had mastered the squint.

'How's you, Felicity?' asked the one called Hopper. He had a plump face with dimples and a fat neck. With his round spectacles and pudding bowl hair he gave the impression of being made up of water lilies. He was sweating lightly, despite the chill.

'Mustn't grumble, Hopper,' said Felicity, and her voice sounded deeper and more heavily accented. 'Enough rain for you?'

'Cats and dogs,' said Mont. He was older, with no teeth at the front and a perfect meringue of white hair on top of his heavily lined face. 'You hear about Haltwhistle? They're looking to evacuate and that didn't even happen during the war.'

'Something in the stars,' said Hopper, sagely. 'Were never rain like this when I were a bairn.'

'Nah. We had summers too. The ground don't know whether it's February or midsummer.'

I stayed silent. Flick had been quite clear about that. She needed a favour from somebody who didn't give them freely and she didn't want him thinking that there was anything fishy about her nosing about in the boot of a dead man's car.

'You'll not have met Mrs Hemlock,' said Felicity, as if she had just remembered me.

Both men gave little nods of greeting. I think one of them began to say something about being sorry for my sadness but lips stuck together as he said it and I got a jumbled sequence of syllables instead.

'Nice to meet you both,' I said. 'They didn't tell me the weather got like this when we moved in.'

'Aye well, you've got a good house to shelter in til the sun comes back,' said Hopper. 'My brother Wilf helped the contractors with the brickwork on your front wall. Charged a fair price.'

'Your James was on the early bus,' said Mont, turning back to Flick. 'Hard worker that one.'

'Aye, likes to get in early and spend some time in the art room.'

'Sits on his own still,' said Hopper, a little sadly. 'I always tell him to come sit at the front by me but he won't have it. Stares out the window. I reckon he's happy enough. Not like your youngest. By he's a handful. Keeps you on your toes, eh?'

'Am I paying you to chatter?'

We looked up as a sudden harsh Geordie voice replaced the sound of sparks falling on wet ground. Gordon had removed his head from the tractor. He was probably fifty years old but there was so much grime on his face it was hard to say. He was a squat, round-shouldered man with close-cropped red hair and a moustache that reached to his chin and which was so darkened with grime that it looked like a horse had left a hoofprint on his face. He had welding goggles perched high on his head so that he took on the appearance of a fly and as he gave a curt nod at Flick, I saw him poking his tongue into his cheek as if trying to dislodge some food. I realized a moment later that he was actually trying to better situate his false teeth, which appeared to have been designed for somebody with a smaller mouth. They slurped and rattled and whistled as he spoke. If he'd had a pet budgerigar, it would have died from the stress.

'Good to see you, Felicity,' he said, rubbing his hands on his overalls. 'You'll be keeping my lads from their work, I see, eh pet?'

Hopper and Mont grinned at their boss.

'Cig break, boss,' said Hopper. 'Starting the Longtown run once the weather's been on the wireless.'

'You'll get that bloody coach there even if there's an iceberg in the way,' said Gordon, giving them a stern look. He turned his attention to me. 'You're from the Winslow farm,' he said, without much enthusiasm. 'Your husband have owt to do with shutting the railway?'

I stared straight at him, wondering what was best to say. I had no idea whether it was anything to do with Cranham.

'I don't think that's his department,' I said, apologetically.

'Well if it were his doing then shake his hand fer me,' he said, grinning. 'Best thing to happen for me business in years, though there'll be plenty who'll moan and whine that it's going to kill the place off. Kill it off, I tell you! Like the government hasn't been trying to do that for years!'

'Don't get him started,' said Hopper, smiling, and it was clear that they had heard his opinions on the matter before.

'I'll start if I like,' snapped Gordon. 'Twelve coaches I've got, love. Started out with a knackered old bus and now I'm one of the biggest employers in the region. There were four butchers in Gilsland when I were a boy. Four! Were all go once upon a time. Boom and bust, that's what they say now. That's what we've had for as long as people have been writing down. Good times and bad times, like the writer used to say. But people always need to get about and for as long as I'm able, they'll be doing so on Temple Coaches.'

Talking to Gordon was like being in the front row at a political rally. Not all of what he said made sense but he said it with gusto and it was hard not to be carried along by his pride in himself.

'You tell yer husband that next time he's having a port and a cigar with the ministers that there won't ever come a time when I don't see a way to make money off of their bad decisions. Were same in '56 when Wimpey came to build their bloody rocket site. 3,000 men they had working there at one time and nigh-on all of 'em needed transporting to the site. Who did it for 'em? Me. Brampton, Carlisle, Hexham, Gretna – every place that could make up a busload sent men to work on that blasted rocket. Did it help Gilsland? Did it buggery. All it meant were the local lads took jobs that paid a fortune and which gave 'em ideas they oughtn't have had. Thought it would last forever. Went to their heads and spoiled a lot of good lads. Then the government decided it didn't give a damn about the moon and it were all over. Of course there's still a site and still jobs and you still hear them testing their weapons and dropping their bombs but we won't see four butchers again in Gilsland in my lifetime – not unless I get out of the coach business and into meat, eh?'

He gave a huge laugh at that. I laughed along, looking to Flick for help. She was way ahead of me.

'Give over, Gordon, we didn't come for a rally. It's a sad business we're here on, if I'm honest. Could you spare us a moment?'

He looked at Flick quizzically and his smile faded. 'Fairfax's car?'

'Aye.'

'I were sorry for it, Felicity. Were a bad thing to happen. I heard he'd just seen the tree come down and were off to get help at the base. That right?'

Hopper and Mont were still hanging around, listening in. Felicity gave a little shrug. Her lips looked grey.

'We think that were it, aye,' she said. 'Who's to say? That car . . .'

'I told him not to buy it.'

'We all did. Were an expensive mistake.'

'There's parts to be saved,' said Gordon, and he rubbed the sleeve of his overalls across his face as if rubbing a peephole in a dirty window. 'You'll be helping sort his estate I'll imagine.'

'Not much estate,' said Felicity. 'But aye, I'm helping with the mess of it all.'

'Interviewed me half a dozen times, did Fairfax,' smiled Gordon, wistfully. 'Always scribbling. Bet I used up a dozen notebooks for him.'

'That were the thing of it,' said Felicity, guilelessly. 'He'd been writing Cordelia's story.'

'Aye?'

'Aye. Been talking a fair bit these past weeks. She gave him some papers she found in the house and she's a bit concerned she may have given him something that belonged to her husband.'

I tried to look like a silly wife. I gestured at myself, indicating that I was a bit scatterbrained and feather-headed and that I would be in trouble with my influential husband if he didn't come to my aid.

'She gave it to Fairfax as he was getting into his car,' said Felicity, her voice full of reprimand. 'She saw him put it in the boot. Would we be able to have a little look and see if we could get it back. Would mean a lot to the both of us.'

Gordon looked from Flick to me and back again. He was clearly an intelligent man and I could see him weighing up if there was a way to turn it to his advantage.

'Back often is he?' asked Gordon. 'Your man?'

'As often as he can,' I gushed.

'Mebbes you could bring him down the social club for a chinwag,' he said, scratching his chin. 'Got a lot of ideas he could maybe pass on to those what makes decisions.'

I nodded, eagerly, and it seemed to sway him. He sucked his lower lip and there was an obscene slurping noise as he struggled with his false teeth.

'I aint opened it up, I don't think,' he said. 'You won't want to see it, I doubt. Be a bit hard for you, I'd have thought, Felicity. But tell me what you're after and I'll go look.'

I shook my head, urgent and severe. 'No, it's fine, I really would rather look myself . . .'

'There's blood,' he pointed out. 'It's a state.'

'I don't mind blood,' I said, and it sounded so much like the wrong thing to say that I shot a glance at Hopper and Mont to see if they were pulling faces. They weren't. They just squinted.

'Well, whatever you like,' said Gordon, sighing. 'But you'll remember me to your husband, yes?'

'Of course.'

'Righto. This way.'

I followed Gordon into the dark confines of the garage. It was a dark, cold space that reeked of damp and engine oil. One long wall was obscured by stacks of huge tyres and there were pigeons cooing in the steel girders high above. The light came from a row of bulbs that hung from straggly wires.

Gordon led me behind a large white vehicle with a hook on the back and nodded at the crumpled remains of Fairfax's car. It looked like an old running shoe. It was battered both at the back and the front and the windscreen was completely missing save for a few jagged teeth of glass stuck into the metal casing.

'Were a bad one,' said Gordon. 'Pleased I didn't have to see him, and I've seen a lot.'

He crossed to a metal box on the wall and removed a small set of keys. He handed them to me with a little nod. 'I'll leave you be, then,' he said, and disappeared into the darkness of the garage.

My heart was thumping. It felt as though the past few days had all been leading to this moment. I was making fists with my hands – the key digging into my palm. I was shaking as I put the key into the lock and at first I couldn't turn it. Then finally it gave and as I opened the boot I was hit with an unmistakable reek. It caught my throat and seemed to stuff its fingers down my throat. It was the smell of rotten meat and corrupted earth; fouled water and decomposing tissue. It made me gag. I had to force myself to look into the dark space and I swear the smell was so strong I truly expected to see a mangled, rancid body laying there in the darkness.

There was no body. The boot was almost empty. All that lay inside was a spare tyre and a fine covering of dirt. *There has to be a manuscript*, I thought, as a pulse began to beat in my temple. *A Dictaphone. Something!*

'All right back there, love?' shouted Gordon, from somewhere nearby.

I forced myself to look closer. Surely there had to be something. A logbook. Leaflets. Something that showed this car had belonged to a real person with a real life. I closed my eyes and forced myself to think. Fairfax had been in a hurry. He needed to hide those secret words of his before anybody saw what lay on the grass. So he ran to the church and stuffed the papers into a prayer cushion that he thought nobody would ever look at. And then he bundled the body into the boot. Where was it now? Where were the other pages?

At once I knew how I would have behaved in such a situation. He would have shoved whatever he found onto the passenger seat . . . or under it! I darted to the front of the car and looked inside through the open window. Even in the half-dark I could see the blood on the dashboard. I tried to blank it out. Hurriedly I reached in and felt around on the soft leather of the luxurious car. Nothing on the seat. I reached further and felt around . . .

My fingers curled around the handle of a small case. At full stretch I pulled it free and it was all I could do not to yell with triumph as I stared upon the Dictaphone. I stuffed it into my jacket and hurried back towards the light.

'Find it, love?' shouted Gordon, as I nodded to Felicity and moved swiftly towards the road.

'Yes, thanks so much! I'll tell Cranham how much help you were!'

He gave a little salute and I looped my arm through Felicity's – hurrying her up the road and breathing heavily. When we were out of sight I opened my coat and showed her what I had found.

'Open it!' she said, excitedly.

I did as I was bid. Slid open the soft leather of the case and stared upon the smart plastic device with its speaker and earphones – its wheels and plastics and dials.

'There's a reel inside,' I said, softly.

She nodded but said nothing. She was staring at the inscription, written in black ink, on the soft white inside flap of the case.

I read it aloud, lips barely moving; voice softer than the breeze.

For my dear friend Fairfax. Thank you for listening and for helping me bury what belongs beneath the earth. Please keep this memento of our friendship, with my deepest gratitude. Your comrade.

FELICITY

Transcript 0009, recorded October 30, 2010

There were an imprint of a bird on the kitchen window. You couldn't see it at first – it was just a smudge on the glass. But if you angled your head you could make out the shape of wings and beak and eyes. It was too big for a hedgerow bird. Cordelia thought it might have been a pigeon. We checked around in the back garden in case the poor thing was in misery but we didn't even find a feather. That seemed important, somehow. All these years later I can't really tell you what we were thinking but I do know it mattered to both of us that we didn't listen to the recording until we had made sure we weren't about to be interrupted by the sudden grisly flapping of broken wings.

'Maybe it's been carried off,' said Cordelia, peering under the big leaves of the rhubarb bushes. 'Cats, maybe. A fox?'

'I hope not,' I said, and I felt a shudder ripple through me as I imagined sharp teeth crunching through brittle bones. 'Maybe it's flown away.'

'Yes,' said Cordelia, deciding to believe me. 'They're tough, birds. And it's bigger than that other one that came through . . .'

I held my hand up and shook my head, hunching down into myself. I didn't want to think about it. The pain in my hip was reminder enough of what had scared me so badly I had to run from the house and into the path of the wagon.

She turned from the rhubarb plants and looked at me with those blue eyes that always seemed to be staring into the very centre of me. You know those lights you get at the optician, when they're looking into the centre of your head and you can see your own veins floating in your vision like a plant without flowers? It made me feel like that.

'Are you ready?' she asked, softly.

I looked at my watch. It was mid-afternoon. We had a couple

of hours until the boys came home. There was nothing to stop
us. No interruptions.

'If you're sure . . .' I said, and it was just something to say,
really. Just noise.

Cordelia nodded and stood up. We trudged back into the
house. For once, we weren't soaking wet. The shower on the
way back from the garage had barely lasted a moment and
we had been able to stroll in relative comfort beneath a cold,
pinkish-blue sky. We'd talked the whole way. Talked about
the inscription on the recorder. I still don't really know what
I believed. It seemed too extraordinary – too removed from
the world I knew. I had grown up in wartime but my war
had been very different to the one experienced by millions
upon millions of poor souls. Few of the people I knew went
away to fight and of those who did, most came home. My
childhood wasn't full of air-raids and falling bombs and
houses blown to bits in front of me. Food was a little more
scarce and there was always a sensation that the world was
wrong, somehow, but the battles and massacres and brutality
barely touched us. Even when the prisoners of war arrived
it was hard to associate the polite young men who worked
in the fields with the stories we heard of the evil done by
Hitler far away. I couldn't make sense of the idea that a man
who had seen such evil in a tiny place in France – a place
not that different to Gilsland – could meet his end a stone's
throw from my front door.

'Sit down,' said Cordelia, pointing to the kitchen table. The
recorder was already sitting there. It reminded me of a
Christmas present, wrapped so expertly that its contents were
completely obscured. There was something thrilling about not
knowing what we would find. I remember my heart beating
faster than it should have done and the hairs on my arms rose
up like the sails of a ship in a bottle.

'Whatever we find . . .' began Cordelia.

I nodded, though I didn't truly know what I was
agreeing to.

It was Cordelia who pressed the buttons that started the
reels rolling. I don't think I could have done that.

At first there was just a hissing noise, like the brakes of a lorry. Then the sound of footsteps started bleeding out through the speaker. After a moment there was the unmistakable sound of running water.

'That's a river,' I said, unnecessarily.

'Ssh,' said Cordelia, patting at the air.

The sound of the river continued for almost five minutes. I began to wonder if that was all we would hear. Then there came the shrill chirruping of a bird. It was a high sound; a collection of whistles, trills and clicks, like somebody fixing an old church bell. It evolved into a sound like a flute; a solemn noise, like an old hymn. If I had to describe what the bird was saying I think the word was something like 'pioo' but that doesn't really sound right either. It was the noise of a child firing a pretend ray-gun.

I realized I could feel Cordy against me. Whether she had huddled closer to me or I had done it to her I really don't know but there was no mistaking that we were now pressed together like dolls on a shelf.

The sound of the bird continued. At length it became a river and footsteps again. Were we listening to the steps of the dead man?

'That can't be all,' said Cordelia, and I could see the confusion in her face.

I had nothing to give her save my own mask of disappointment. I was about to offer her some pointless consolation about it maybe being for the best, and then we heard the voice. A short, clipped 'hello'. I almost jumped out of my skin.

'Hello. Hello, sir. Sir. Monsieur!'

I closed my eyes. Every inch of me felt like there were spiders crawling all over it. It was a Frenchman's voice, of that I was certain. And it contained something that made me think of a smith's forge; all steam and steal and danger and sweat.

'Sir. Stop. Arrretez. S'il vous plaît. S'il vous plaît. Il n'est pas ce que vous en pensez. Savez-vous de moi, monsieur? Je sais que vous. Mon Dieu, je sais que vous . . .'

All these years later and I remember the shape and sound of those words. Sound daft in my voice, don't they? But I remember them like the sound of me own bairns saying me name. It sounded as if they were being carried along on the water.

'Don't run. Sir! Damn you, I know you! And you know this face. I must speak. S'il vous plaît. There are secrets . . .'

The recording suddenly became muffled. There was banging and sudden steps and then the sound of voices. It was impossible to make out the words but it was the sound of an angry exchange. We listened to two minutes of unintelligible argument and then without warning the recording stopped.

Cordelia sat forward in her seat, peering at the machine. She threw herself back, exasperated.

'That's it? The end of the tape. For God's sake . . .'

I saw my face in the glass of the picture frame beside the table. I looked pale, like scrubbed stone.

'Did you know what it meant?' I asked, softly.

Cordy pulled a face and shrugged. 'Some,' she muttered. 'He wanted him to listen. Asked him if he knew him . . .'

We sat in silence, consumed with our own thoughts. The story that Fairfax had written down made it clear that a man called Jean Favre had done terrible, terrible things during the war. But we only know the name Favre because of Fairfax's story. Was the man with the tape recorder Abel? It seemed likely from the tone of Fairfax's papers. How, then, could their paths have crossed in the woods near Gilsland?

'You know everybody,' said Cordy, suddenly. 'Who saw service in France?'

I shook my head. 'Don't start thinking that. So many people pass through, don't they? It must have been a stranger.'

'A stranger who told Fairfax their deepest secret?' asked Cordy, scornfully.

'Sometimes that's easier . . .'

'You must know who went where,' protested Cordy. 'Who fought where. Fairfax's son! Could he have seen what happened at this little place? Could he have told Fairfax before he died?' She scowled, knowing that there were too many missing pieces. 'If we could just hear what they were saying!'

I was staring into the wood of the table top. I felt cold and sick. I felt let-down, more than anything else. I don't think I'd ever imagined myself solving a crime or anything like that but it had become important to me that I make sense of what we had seen during the storm and now I had nothing but loose threads and confusion.

'Who speaks French?' she asked, suddenly. 'If the man spoke to somebody in French he must have expected them to understand. We know he could speak English so why would he address them in French?'

She started playing with the machine. Spooled it back and started playing the conversation again. The second time around it was no clearer. We could make out the tone of the words but not the content.

'This is madness,' said Cordy, frustrated.

I heard the pantry door suck in as cold air blasted down the corridor. Somebody was coming in the front door. I started forward, my heart in my mouth, but Cordy was too intent on listening to let me hide the device or silence the voice. A moment later the kitchen door opened and Brian was standing there, head cocked. His face was red, as if he'd been running, and he was narrowing his eyes at the tape recorder.

'That a Frog voice?' he asked, and his question was to Cordelia and not me.

'Go get changed, Brian,' I said, standing up. 'I'll make you some tea.'

He shook his head at me and focussed on the tape recorder. He was angling his head like he was moving the aerial on the TV, trying to get a better reception.

'They're having a ding-dong,' he said. 'Who is it? Fairfax's mate?'

We both span towards him. Cordelia stopped the recording.

'Which mate?' asked Cordelia, in a rush.

'Bloke who stayed with him a few months back,' shrugged Brian. 'Was out here recording birdsong. Some friend of his back home was here during the war and missed the sound of the local birds and the river and stuff. He was here recording it for him, so Fairfax said.'

'You met him?' asked Cordelia, voice rising.

'Not met. Not really. He was reading headstones in the graveyard and Fairfax was leaning in the gateway to the church.

I had a natter with Fairfax and he told me. That his tape recorder, is it? He must have left it for Fairfax.'

Cordy turned to me, eyes full of accusations. Had I been keeping this from her? Did I know?

'When was this?' I asked him, trying to stay steady.

'May sort of time, I reckon,' he said, without much of a care. 'Few months anyways.'

'What was he wearing?' I asked, and Cordy asked at the same time.

'Blue suit,' he shrugged. 'Had curly hair parted here.' He pointed to the side of his head. 'Who's that he's arguing with?'

'We don't know,' said Cordy, and her face looked like thunder.

'Why didn't you say?' I asked him. 'When you found the tooth you must have known it was this man's.'

'Tooth?' demanded Cordy.

I ignored her. Kept staring at Brian and I think he knew he'd proper done it this time. I would have gone for him if he hadn't spoken up.

'Aye, it made sense it was his but you never asked me about any French bloke,' said Brian, squirming. 'It was just a letter and the tooth.'

'What letter?' asked Cordelia, and I swear she was ready to swing for one of us.

I told her. Told her what my son had found and how it had led to Pike chasing him through the woods with a shotgun.

'Where's this letter?' she asked, when I was done.

'Binned it,' said Brian, unconcerned. 'He said there was nowt to it anyways.'

'Who did?' I asked.

'Cuckoo,' he said. 'The clock man with the birds. Came to school and spoke to us and I asked him to read it because he said he spoke French and German.'

'Who the bloody hell is Cuckoo?' asked Cordelia.

I found that my mouth was dry. I couldn't unstick my tongue from my teeth. It felt like somebody had sucked all the moisture out of me.

'Your neighbour,' said Brian, untying his tie and enjoying knowing more than both of us. 'The farmer. Swiss man. Mr Parker.'

Cordy said nothing for a moment, then her face creased.
'The man with the birds, you said.'
'Aye, I told you. He's Swiss. They make cuckoo clocks,
don't they? That's what everybody says. And that's why he
must want the birds.'
'What birds?'
Brian rolled his eyes. 'He collects them. Traps them.
We've seen him, out towards the castle. Uses lures and traps.
He came in to school to talk to us about crop rotation but
when it got to the "any questions" bit we all asked about the
birds. He said he didn't know what we were going on about
but we've seen him. His missus took him away after that so
I had to grab her to ask about the note. Her husband had a
quick glance and told me it was nowt but gibberish. Why?'
I felt Cordelia's eyes boring into me. It was like she was
poking around inside my head.
'My neighbour,' she said, teeth locked. 'That funny little man.'
'Aye, Mam knows him to say hello to. His missus too. She
were at Fairfax's all the bloody time last winter.'
Neither Cordelia or I spoke. We just let the silence stretch
out. I found myself staring through the outline of the bird
on the window. Suddenly it was all I could see. The image
beyond the glass was just a grey and green blur that seemed
unfamiliar to me.
'We have to,' said Cordelia, jerking her head in the vague
direction of her house across the river.
I nodded. There was no way she was going to stop now.
And there was no way I was going to let her go alone.

CORDELIA

The Parker farmhouse had a reddish sheen to the brick in daytime but the sun had long since settled behind the hills when Flick and I cleared the treeline at the edge of my property and looked upon the large, L-shaped building. The moon was full in a cold, clear sky and in the darkness around the house was the colour of deep, silent water.

'You need anything from home?' asked Flick. Her voice broke on the first word. She hadn't spoken at all on the walk and I could tell her throat was dry.

'I'm fine.'

'I just thought . . .'

'What?'

She shook her head. She was wearing a headscarf and the knot at the back wagged like a tail.

I stopped where I stood and she must have noticed I was no longer beside her as she turned around, looking guilty.

'Your husband,' she said, all trembly and pathetic. 'He might have left you something to protect you, in erm, emergencies.'

'No,' I said, flatly. 'I haven't got a gun. If you wanted a gun you knew where they were. You could help yourself.'

'They're Pike's . . .' she said, vaguely.

'And that's what's stopping you, is it? The fact they're Pike's?'

'I'm sorry I spoke,' she said, and her face was flushed.

I was angry at her. Angry at everybody. I could see fragments of a picture coming together, finding one another like droplets of spilled mercury, but there was so much I didn't understand. Who did I think I was? We were two people with no business poking about in another person's grief and perhaps we were causing a greater injustice by doing so. I was horribly aware of the absurd picture I was about to present; a stranger in this place, knocking on my neighbour's door and demanding answers about their knowledge of a dead man.

'Should we go?' asked Felicity. 'Really? Should we just go?'

She was standing between the high brick gateposts at the edge of the Parker Farm. She looked like a goalkeeper, all hunched and agitated. Behind her the farmhouse was a sullen, brooding mass. There was only one light on: a solitary red and yellow blur. I knew from my walks how the house looked in daylight. The front door and the windowsills were painted dark green and the driveway was made of large paving slabs with weeds growing between the cracks. Spiky bushes lined the drive as it curved around towards the front door. One part of the house was three storeys high but the shorter part – the foot of the boot – was only two storeys and was topped with a tall chimney, higher than a man. To the rear were outbuildings and the bower where the cattle were milked. On days when the wind blew towards my house there was no amount of burning paper could disguise that scent. Right then I found myself listening to the sounds of the night. The only sound was of the rustling of the leaves all around us.

'Cordelia?' she asked, again.

'You can go if you like,' I said, and knew as I said it that I would have been devastated if she had taken me up on the offer of a way out. 'I'm just going to ask some questions. The worst that happens is they tell us to get out and I don't think I like them anyways.'

She lowered her head but seemed to accept my decision. I slipped my elbow through hers and we walked up the driveway to the front door. I didn't remark upon the car that was parked a little way off, down towards the barn. My mind was too busy.

'Shall I?' she asked, and we climbed the three steps to the door.

In the end, neither of us knocked on the door. As we waited, a light flicked on. A line of yellow light appeared around the edge of the door. A man's voice, muffled like the words on the recording, told us to hang on. There was the sound of keys in the lock. It struck me as odd. Who locked their doors? In all my time in the area I had never known anybody go to the trouble of locking up and yet it sounded as if deadbolts and at least two locks were being manhandled. Then the door slowly swung open.

It was Mr Parker. He was two steps above us but he still only seemed to be my height. With the yellow light of the hallway turning him into something more like a silhouette than an actual being of flesh and bone, I had a sudden vision of a creature from a fairy tale. He was Rumpelstiltskin. He was a gnome of a man. He had the appearance of a jockey turned to drink. His skinny legs disappeared into big workboots and the shabby coat he wore on top of his overalls had patches at the elbows. His collar was held shut with a tie knotted so tightly that it looked like it had been used to restrain an angry bull. His face was all creases and folds and his huge nose made me think of a bird's beak. His blue eyes were set deep into his head – holes in snow. His wig was not the same colour as his eyelashes. They were fair but the mop of hair atop his round head was dark. It looked like he had ripped somebody else's hair from their scalp and elected to wear it as a hat.

'Mrs Hemlock,' he said, and the 's' sounded like a 'z'. He cocked his head, quizzically. Looked at me for a moment more than he needed to and then did the same to Felicity. Wheels were turning in his head. 'Mrs Goose. Is all well?'

The silence stretched out for a time. I was chewing my lip. I wanted there to be a sudden moment of clarity; a coming together of half-formed thoughts into one perfect sensation of comprehension. But as I looked at Mr Parker I saw only the same funny little man who had tried to be kind to me after Stefan had died.

'Could we possibly have a moment with you, Mr Parker?' asked Felicity, and I was amazed to hear her speak first. 'It's a silly thing but it's about Fairfax.'

'Fairfax?' he asked, straightening up a little. 'A tragedy. But please, please, do come in.'

I paused for a moment, gathering myself, and then I did as instructed. Mr Parker stood with his arm out, pointing down the hallway, and I went in the direction he instructed. Felicity came behind. As I passed him I smelled nothing that I would not associate with a middle-aged farmer. Just cows and sweat, fresh air and cold.

The hallway was a pleasing space. Wide, with wooden dressers all along one side, stocked with porcelain ornaments and animal sculptures. The other wall was hung with oil paintings in gaudy frames. Rural scenes. Hay wagons and sunset harvests. There was no carpet on the floor but two threadbare rugs had been trodden into the wooden boards.

'Second on the left,' he said, and I turned the handle of the white-painted door.

I found myself in a large, comfortable parlour. If the house were mine I would have called it the red room. That's how it struck me as I stood in the doorway. Three of the walls were papered in a pillar-box shade and the curtains that covered the windows on the far wall were a rich crimson. The three-piece suite was cherry coloured, enlivened with cream swirls. Even the sideboards that stood against the wall to my left seemed to have been varnished with a red-tinged polish. It felt as if I had climbed inside somebody.

Mrs Parker was sitting in the high-backed chair beside the fire. The coals glowed scarlet, melding with the pinkish light that emanated from a lamp by her elbow, veiled with a ruby shade.

'Mrs Hemlock,' she said, turning, and she let the surprise show in her expression. She glanced at the carriage clock on the tile mantelpiece as if confirming her suspicions that this was not a civilized hour for visitors. Her face showed displeasure, which became more pronounced as Flick followed me into the room. 'And Mrs Goose. Good heavens, are we under attack?'

Had I said it, I'd have made it sound sarcastic. But Mrs Parker did not seem to be joking. Her face was horribly serious. I suddenly felt as though I had been called to see the Mother Superior for a lesson in wickedness.

'We're so sorry to intrude,' said Felicity, looking around her. She moved to stand beside me and I felt her fingers brush the back of my hand.

'And what's this about?' asked Mrs Parker, beginning to stand. She was wearing a cream cardigan over a blue dress. She clashed with the room.

'It's a silly thing really,' said Flick, nervously. She wasn't used to such places. In her life, people greeted visitors with tea and cake and warm towels. We felt like intruders about to be told off for our thoughtlessness.

Suddenly Mrs Parker's face softened. It was an incredible transformation. One moment she had been stern and brittle and the next she seemed to unstiffen at the edges. Her face became rounder, plumper as she smiled and then she was crossing the room and extending her hands to me as if we were friends.

'I've been thinking of you,' she said and I found she had taken my hands in hers. She spoke into my eyes, intense and deliberate. 'Has it been terrible? I so wanted to come and call but you seemed so insistent on being left alone to grieve and we never once saw your curtains open. I'm so pleased you have found a friend. But truly, there's no need to thank us for being there at the end. We did all we could.'

For a moment my face showed incomprehension and then that was burned away by the open furnace of my anger. Did she think that's why we were here? To say an overdue thank you for her presence at Stefan's bedside when the fever took him? I hadn't even wanted them there. They were ghouls, hanging around in the corridor outside Stefan's room and disturbing the air with their low words. They wanted to bring me things. Kept asking if we needed water or blankets or extra pillows. They wanted to be in the room with me and I was too overcome by my emotions to keep them out. They had been standing against the bedroom wall as his heart finally stopped. They were breathing in the air into which his soul departed. It had always seemed they had taken something of him away with them.

'That's not why we're here,' I said, and my voice was barely more than a growl. I turned to Flick, eyes blazing.

'What's the matter then?' asked Mrs Parker, dropping my hands. She turned to Felicity. 'Is it your Brian? Really, there's no need to pay us back. He's not had much.'

'Much of what?' asked Flick.

'He's been siphoning the tractor,' said Mr Parker, behind her. 'Don't know where he's selling it but it's next to nothing to be honest and I don't mind a bit of ingenuity. He's a bright boy.'

I heard the accent in Parker's words. Forced myself to take control.

'It's Fairfax,' I said, flatly. 'There are some things we'd like to know.'

'About Fairfax?' asked Mrs Parker. 'I don't see as I would be able to tell you much. And Mrs Goose was closer to him than me. But I'll help how I can.'

She pointed to the sofa and Flick and I sat down, shoulder to shoulder. Mrs Parker resumed her seat and her husband took the other chair. We listened to the ticking of the clock and the sound of the settling coals.

'We've been going through his things,' I said, talking to Mrs Parker instead of her husband. She seemed to be the dominant force in the room so it seemed right I address her. 'Some of his writings.'

'Well, he was always a one for his scribblings,' said Mrs Parker with a faint smile.

'We found a story among his things. Not one of his local history bits or bobs. This was like a real memoir.'

'Yes?' she asked, brightly.

'It was about something that happened during the war. Something that occurred in France.'

She kept looking at me. I didn't find it remarkable, at the time. Whatever she knew or didn't know, surely she would have glanced at her husband.

'It wouldn't have seemed so important if it wasn't for something else that we stumbled upon,' I said, holding her gaze. I didn't want to tell her about the body. Not yet. 'We heard a story about a man who came to see Fairfax. A Frenchman. He said he was here to record local birdsong. And we have it on pretty good authority he went to see Fairfax to ask questions about somebody he used to know . . .'

Felicity butted in, sitting forward on her chair.

'Our Brian said he asked you to translate a letter in French when you came to his school and that got me thinking about last winter when you were at Fairfax's all the time . . .'

Mrs Parker shook her head and her face hardened again. 'All the time? What are you implying?'

'No, no, nothing like that,' protested Flick, colouring.

I turned to Mr Parker. He was staring at his wife. He caught me looking at him and gave a sad little smile.

'I don't think I want this conversation to continue,' said Mrs Parker. 'I think it's a bit rich you coming here and upsetting us when all we've done is try and help you.'

That tore a hole in my veneer. I rounded on her, furious.

'Help me? You've only been to my door twice. Once to try and take advantage of the fact I didn't know what my land was worth and the second time to watch my boy die!'

'How dare you,' she snapped, as angry as I was.

I turned back to Mr Parker. 'Are you really Swiss,' I demanded. 'Or are you a Frenchman from a little place in Correze? Did Fairfax find something out about you?'

'Don't tell her anything,' said Mrs Parker, throwing him a hard look. 'You don't have to. She's mad. Mad with grief . . .'

'Are you?' I asked again. 'Your accent doesn't give anything away. It's foreign but it could be from anywhere. You arrived here after the war, yes? Was it Ireland where you met? Fresh start, was it. I can't blame you. What you saw . . .'

Mrs Parker hauled herself out of the chair and came to stand above me. I thought she was going to slap my face but instead she stood with her hands on her hips, bristling with rage.

'Ask yourself what you're doing,' she hissed. 'Just think about it!'

I felt Flick's hand on my shoulder and for a moment I took a step out of myself and realized just what I was attempting to do. I was bullying this small, fragile man into reliving something that must have been beyond endurance. If I was correct in my suspicions, he had witnessed true horrors. And I needed him to face them afresh.

I closed my eyes for a moment and when I spoke again my voice was more calm.

'There was a body in the Kinmont mausoleum,' I said. 'A man in a blue suit. He left a little present for Fairfax after they spoke.'

'Please . . .' said Mrs Parker, despairingly. 'Please stop.'

'Did you kill him?' I asked, staring at the small, shrivelled husk of Mr Parker. 'Was he Jean Favre? Did he see the man you used to be? A Resistance fighter named Abel? Did you kill him and ask Fairfax to cover it up . . .?' I was pulling at my hair, desperate for answers. 'I need to know!'

I felt a chill on my neck as the door to the room opened. I spun, unable to help myself.

'Do you?' asked the man in the doorway. 'Do you really need to know?'

Beside me, Felicity's hand flew to her mouth.

I looked hard at the face of the newcomer and suddenly understood who I was staring at.

I was looking into the face of a dead man.

FELICITY

Transcript 0010, recorded October 31, 2010

The last time I'd seen Fairfax's son he'd been eighteen years old and heading off to war. His dad hadn't wanted him to go. Christopher was never a strong lad and he had poor eyes and a weak chest but he'd been dead set on doing his bit. He'd made his dad proud, even if Fairfax would have given his right arm and both legs to stop him from signing up. Christopher nearly got safely through it. We'd already stormed Normandy and were closing in on victory when the bomb fell on the radio post where he was working as a wireless operator.

It was Leslie, the young girl from the post office, who hand-delivered the telegram to Fairfax's house. The way she told the story, Fairfax had turned whiter than milk before she'd even knocked on his door. Saw her through the window and knew his world was about to fall apart. Knew, with some horrible cold certainty, that his boy was dead.

'Christopher,' I gasped, looking at the man in the doorway, and if I'd been a Catholic I would have started crossing myself and never stopped.

He'd changed a lot in the years since he went off to war. Looked more like Fairfax than he used to. There was a paleness to him, as if he was too used to an indoor life. He had a greyness to him, and it wasn't just the suit and overcoat that hung on his thin shoulders like it would on a hanger. He had the same long, rectangular face I remembered and the hair at the front of his head still flopped forward like it would on a pony. He had a scar on his chin now and there was a lot of silver at his temples. He wasn't smoking and yet he still seemed to be wreathed in a fug of fumes.

'Christopher,' said Mrs Parker, moving towards him, hands out like she was greeting the Pope. 'It's fine, you don't need to . . .'

Mrs Parker stopped talking as Christopher shot her a look. I noticed how wiry his eyebrows were. He didn't seem to have any lips – his mouth just a gill in his face.

'Don't let me stop you,' said Christopher, to the room in general. 'I was enjoying the masterly speculations.'

Cordelia's hand was in mine. We were both twisted, staring at the figure by the wall. He gave me a quick glance.

'It's nice to see you Felicity,' he said, polite as you like. 'All grown-up, I see. Two children and just the one husband. I was sorry to hear about your mother. Brian and James, your boys, am I right? Youngest one's got spirit.'

I was finding it hard to breathe. How did he know about my life? Where had he been? Why had he let us all grieve for him?

'You're Christopher,' said Cordelia, beside me. 'I'd heard you were dead.'

He flashed a quick smile, showing perfect white teeth. I glimpsed the metal points of the bridgework. They were dentures.

'You're Mrs Hemlock,' he said. 'Quite the character.'

'Yes?' she asked, and through the fear I felt a thrill at her defiance.

'Shall I share your story?' he asked. 'Would you mind awfully?'

'I've never hidden any of it,' she said, and she even found the strength to give a little laugh. 'I've only one friend in Gilsland and there's nothing I wouldn't tell her so if you think you can shut me up with threats you're very mistaken.'

I looked from her to Christopher, who had taken out a silver case and was lighting himself a long white cigarette.

'And your husband?' he asked, breathing out more grey.

'He can fight his own battles.'

Christopher considered her, chewing at the skin below his mouth.

'It's worth it, is it?' he asked her, and barely sounded interested in the question, let alone her answer. 'Nowhere to live. No more money. Without him you'd have nothing.'

She laughed properly at that. 'What have I got?' she asked, looking like she was ready to fight. 'Somebody else's house.

Somebody else's life. I did what I did for Stefan and the world took him from me, so to be honest, I don't give a damn about your threats. I want to know why there was a body in the Kinmont tomb.'

There was silence in the room as Christopher smoked his cigarette. At length he jerked his head at Mrs Parker and she returned to her seat, meek as a scalded dog. I looked at her husband. He had shrunken into his chair. He was playing with something in his hands, moving his fingers like he was washing up. I glimpsed something yellow and a black beady eye. He was holding a dead bird in his hands, thumbing its feathers and staring into his cupped palms.

'Dingwall said you were hard to scare,' said Christopher, and twitched a smile as he walked to the front of the sofa and stood with his back to the fire. 'But I'm scarier than Dingwall.'

Cordelia looked at him with insolence written all over her face. She flicked her hair behind her ear and looked at his cigarette. 'Got a spare?'

Christopher seemed delighted with her. He lit her cigarette and passed it over. She took a drag. I'd never seen her smoke but she didn't cough as she breathed out. Just looked at him like she could do this for as long as he wanted.

'I should be cross,' he said, at last. 'I've had to drive a long way for you. I've had to look at things I didn't want to look at again. I'm fairly agog with nostalgia.' He made the word 'agog' sound like he was gasping. Then he smiled. 'I'd made my peace with not coming back. But you've made it very difficult for me to stay away.'

'Your dad,' I said, and it hurt my insides to say it. 'Are you back for Fairfax?'

'A sadness,' he said. 'But I'd been dead to him for a long time. It would seem wrong to grieve.'

'You can choose that, can you?' asked Cordelia, scornfully. 'Whether to be upset?'

'I learned to control my emotions a long time ago,' he said, neutrally. 'It's a shame what happened to Father and I can't help but feel a little responsible. But in truth, I'm several rungs down the ladder on that one. People like you are a lot closer to the top in terms of who should be feeling guilty.'

'That's not fair,' I protested, and he shushed me with a wave.

'You're right,' he said, and his cheek twitched. 'I'm never sure when I'm being myself and when I'm being the job.'

'The job?' I asked.

Christopher nodded, staring straight at Cordelia as he answered my question.

'They found I had certain abilities not long after I signed up,' he said, and there was no smugness to him. 'Apparently I had a way of seeing things that was useful to some of the less celebrated combatants.'

'I don't understand,' I said.

'The intelligence services,' said Cordy, without turning her head. 'You're a spy?'

He shrugged at that. 'We all serve our country in different ways. I had a gift for finding things out. I could plant false trails and keep the enemy so confused they would twist themselves into the ground trying to untangle the wisdom from the lies. They don't give you many medals for it but it wins wars. It was just a pity I had to die.'

For a second I thought he was about to admit to being a ghost. I fair feared he was about to put his hand through his own chest.

'Operational decision,' he explained. 'My section commander needed men who did not exist on paper. He needed men willing to become deniable assets if caught by the enemy. And I was happy to oblige.'

'But Fairfax,' I said.

'He was a kind man,' said Christopher. 'A good father. But I had a chance to be more than a weak lad from Gilsland and if I had to make Mam and Dad cry to do so I was willing to do it.'

'And?' asked Cordelia, coolly.

'And we arranged it. A telegram home, a notice in the paper, a death certificate. And then I was a ghost. I could operate where I was needed. And after the landings I was needed a lot of places.'

'France,' said Cordelia. 'Correze.'

He looked at her like she was a child. 'You're going to ask about the massacre,' he said. 'About Jean Favre. Le Tanneur.'

'Was he the man in the mausoleum?' asked Cordy, straight out.

Christopher pinched the bridge of his nose and then looked at Mr Parker. I followed his gaze. Parker gave a tiny nod and Christopher sighed.

'Favre was the person the Maquisards feared,' he said, eyes closed. 'The Resistance hated the Germans, don't misunderstand me. They knew the Nazis to be evil of a kind. But the Milice were something else. They were Frenchmen who had chosen to side with the enemy. They spoke the language. They blended in. They had a capacity for horror that eclipses anything the SS could imagine. Their weapon was terror. When they caught Maquisards they made sure they made examples. And Le Tanneur was the best at that. Favre could cut a man's skin off from the neck to the ankles without letting him die. The SS loved him. He was a weapon. He'd been a leather-worker before the war. They say that he gave a handbag made of Maquisard's skin to the wife of one of his commanders. He saw it as a gift.'

In the armchair, Mrs Parker dropped her head. She shook herself, not wanting to hear.

'He was requisitioned by the 2nd SS Panzer Division. Das Reich. It was an elite unit, the pride of the eastern front, and it had a very specific set of orders. It was given the task of wiping out the Maquis. Obliterating the Resistance. And after the Normandy landings they had only one goal. They were to maintain order, no matter what the cost. So they made examples. Villages that sheltered members of the Maquis were viewed as one entity. Be you man, woman or child, you were a Maquis sympathizer. And therefore you were liable for the consequences.'

I realized Cordy's hand was tightening around mine. I didn't really feel as though I was in the room any longer. I was in a brightly lit square in a French village, listening to the rumble of tanks.

'They wiped out whole communities. They mowed villagers down for sport from the backs of their vehicles. As they passed through rural France they left nothing but misery and grief and at the centre of it all, standing by the sides of the SS commanders, was this local man who had discovered a talent for brutality. Favre. He liked them to watch. Enjoyed nothing more than the screams as he slowly went about his work in full view of villagers whose only crime was to offer bread and beer to the men and women fighting for their country.'

'You sound like he sickens you,' said Cordelia, and there was surprise in her voice.

'Of course it sickens me,' he said, and he displayed a touch of annoyance at her doubting him. 'They were acts of evil. But his crimes were small beside the atrocities committed by Das Reich. June seventh. A place called Tulle. 100 men between the ages of sixteen and sixty were hanged in the main square in retaliation for the actions of some Resistance members. Favre hurt people for the sport of it. A sharp curved blade and a furnace full of coins.'

Cordelia said nothing. Just stared.

'June tenth, 1944,' said Christopher, looking at nothing. 'Das Reich pressed on into Limousin. They rounded up the inhabitants of a small village. 650 people. They were herded into the square and separated into groups. The women were taken to the church and the men to the barns. The order was given for the soldiers to open fire. The church was set alight. There were only a handful of survivors. The entire place was destroyed.'

'The gold,' said Mr Parker, softly, from his armchair. 'It dripped like candle wax.'

We turned as one. He was stroking the head of the dead bird. He was all folded into himself – tucking in his elbows like they were wings.

'You were there,' said Cordelia, and her voice was so quiet it would not have disturbed a candle-flame held to her lips. 'You're the man . . .'

'Mr Parker used to be called Abel,' said Christopher, smartly. 'He was one of the first men into the village in Limousin after the reports started coming back about the massacre. He saw what was inside the church. He found the bodies. Hundreds of bodies. Human shapes made of ash. Gold and lead, mingled together into great shapes of twisted liquid. The heat in the church had been so ferocious it had melted the bell. Melted

the tabernacle and candlesticks. Melted the chalices in the
strong box. Turned that whole place into something no man
should see.'

We looked at the little man in his chair. He grew smaller
under our gaze. He was staring into the fire. There were
shadows upon his face.

'After the war it was important that justice be found for the
victims of these atrocities,' explained Christopher. 'Our allies
in France needed men to testify against the Nazi soldiers who
perpetrated the massacre. Abel was one of the men brave
enough to do that. But to do so nearly cost him his life.
Members of the Milice were now responsible in part for
running the country. Some had fled abroad but others were
now powerful members of the government and they did not
want the past being raked over. My network heard that an
assassin had been sent to deal with any witness thinking of
testifying at Nuremberg. We needed to get Abel out. By this
time, Abel was working for a fertilizer company in Alsace.
He was doing well in his life. But he knew what he had to
do. My unit relocated him. He gave his testimony and started
a new life. Favre was arrested and imprisoned. Abel did the
right thing. He should have been left alone.'

Cordelia narrowed her eyes, shaking her head.

'That doesn't add up,' she said. 'Why Gilsland? Why
Mrs Parker? Why here?'

Christopher showed his irritation. 'I am already breaking
the Official Secrets Act just telling you this much. But you
would not leave things alone, would you? Can't you just accept
it is as I say?'

I could see Cordelia was battling with something. A light
had come on in her eyes when Christopher mentioned the
Official Secrets Act. She screwed up her face as if something
didn't fit.

'This is all a bit cosy, isn't it?' she asked. 'How did Mrs
Parker here end up as Mrs Parker? How did Abel end up in
your own little village? That's asking for trouble . . .'

My mind was on fire. I was jerking my head like a horse
plagued by flies. Taking it all in, trying to make sense of it:
my eyes flicking this way and that, taking in the pictures, the

horse brasses, the ornaments . . . the photograph above the dresser. A young boy with sad eyes and a gap where the bottom half of his left arm should have been.

Cordelia was about to speak but I beat her to it. I blurted it out before I even realized the sense of staying quiet.

'Your brother,' I said, turning my gaze on Mrs Parker.

'Was he a part of your little unit?' asked Cordelia, catching up and pointing at Christopher. 'Your old friend from Gilsland? What was his name?'

'Loveday,' I said. 'Suffered for it too.'

Cordelia glared at Mrs Parker and I don't know where her fury was coming from. All I had heard was convincing me that the people in the room were decent people. She seemed to be listening to a different version of events.

'I can't talk about that . . .' began Christopher.

Mrs Parker shifted herself. Her posture changed as she looked up at the old photograph on the wall.

'He'd been through so much,' she said.

'Your brother?' I asked.

She shook her head. 'Abel. My husband. He was so fragile. Broken.' She gave a warm glance at the small, goblin-like man. 'And we've been good, haven't we, my love? I never wanted any of the things I now have but we've found a happiness. A happiness we deserve. Loveday gave us that. Loveday and Christopher – two dead men.'

I found myself thinking of the slight, hobbling figure of Audrey Parker's brother. He'd lost half an arm in an accident with a harvester but his father had pulled some strings and found him a role where he could serve his country. That was the story everybody knew. He never came back from the war. I suddenly realized what that role had been. Intelligence Services. He had recruited an old friend from Gilsland and persuaded him they would both be better off dead.

'We were approved, you see,' said Mrs Parker. 'Because of what we'd done in the war. The authorities knew he would be safe here. No questions would be asked. And I'd done my bit.'

Cordelia rubbed a hand across her nose and glanced at Christopher.

'The prisoners of war,' she said, flatly. 'The care packages.

The letters from home. You're one of his spies, aren't you, Mrs Parker.'

'Don't speak,' said Christopher, sharply.

'Is that it?' I asked. 'The men who worked the land here. All those soldiers who you sent your food hampers to and who you write letters to. You use them, don't you? You gather up titbits of information to pass onto your brother and his spies.'

'We all serve in our own way,' she said.

Christopher lit himself a cigarette. Wordlessly he lit a second one for Cordelia. He passed it to her and she smoked in short, angry puffs.

'Favre,' she said. 'The killer. The sadist. He'd tracked you down.' She looked at the tip of her cigarette, putting the pieces together. 'You knew, Mrs Parker. You knew he was coming . . .'

Mrs Parker smoothed down the front of her skirt. 'I received information that the man we once knew as Jean Favre was travelling under a passport belonging to a Marcel Defouloy. He'd applied for the paperwork to come to England. One of the families I wrote to in Alsace – they told me. We told Christopher. We'd tried to put that life behind us and now it was walking up to our door.'

'He was coming here to kill me,' said Mr Parker, pulling his arms in tighter. 'To skin me. To burn me with coins . . . He saw me. Out in the woods as I took my walk. I ran. Came home. Hid, like a child. But he went to Fairfax.'

I understood, then. Fairfax was the man in whom the Parkers had chosen to confide.

'Fairfax knew Abel's story,' said Mrs Parker. 'We told him everything, even though we knew it was wrong. He was a good man, always wanting to learn about the people around him. Always asking questions. We told him who Abel was on the promise his story was not told during our lifetime. It seemed right, somehow. He was Christopher's father, after all. And then this monster, this terror whom we had spoken of – he walked up to Fairfax's door. When he realized who he was talking to he contacted us.'

'And?' asked Cordelia, staring at the side of Mr Parker's head.

'I took care of it,' said Christopher, from across the room. There was silence for a time. Cordelia was thinking. Mr Parker was playing with his dead bird.

'How did he die?' I asked, and I was shocked as anybody to hear me ask.

'As well as could be expected,' said Christopher, and I think he might even have given me a little smile.

'Why the crypt?' asked Cordelia. 'Outside your own father's front door?'

Christopher had the grace to look reproachful. 'It was only meant to be temporary. Opportunity would arise to remove him properly. He seemed safe where he was. Then the tree came down.'

'And Fairfax knew?' I asked. 'That he was in the crypt?'

'He saw Favre die,' said Mrs Parker. 'When it happened. When he died. Things got difficult. Pike might have seen. Fairfax understood. He said that Favre was an evil man and that he deserved to lie, unmourned, somewhere that nobody would ever find him. The day Fairfax died he was coming to tell us that the crypt had been compromised. He needed us to know that the body had been discovered. That must have been what killed him – the shock of it. He crashed without ever telling us what had happened.'

Cordelia was looking at Mr Parker.

'Why did you tell him your story?' she asked him.

He shook his head at her and his wig slid a half inch to the right. He was a pitiful figure. He'd been broken by what he had endured.

'He tortured you?' I asked. 'Favre?'

He said nothing.

'Why did he burn your story?' she asked, puzzled. 'Was that after Favre was killed? And why did Favre leave him the recordings? What did he mean when he called him his comrade?'

Christopher waved a hand: his patience fraying. He'd heard enough. I turned to Cordelia and she had her fingers wrapped tight around the hem of her skirt. She looked white.

There was silence in the room. The clock ticked. Steam rose from our damp clothes and the hot coals clicked in the hearth.

'He got what he deserved,' said Cordelia, at last. It seemed like a hard thing for her to say.

I saw a delighted smile ripple across Christopher's face.

'Your father,' she said, looking up at him. 'He acted the right way. Did nothing but good. And nobody's mourning this butcher from France. Nobody here has done anything wrong, have they? And we're all good at keeping secrets.'

I suddenly realized what she was saying. This was over. We had our answers. We knew the identity of the man in the grave and he was exactly where he was supposed to be. I was about to ask what had happened to the body after Fairfax retrieved it but then realized I didn't want to know.

'Is that it, then?' I asked. 'We just forget?'

Christopher looked from Cordelia to me and back again. 'You thought I was dead half an hour ago. Can you do so again?'

I nodded, knowing that I truly intended to try.

'You can forget what we know, can you?' asked Cordelia. 'Just pretend we never met?'

'That's how my world works,' said Christopher. 'It's all secrets and lies and pretence. I spin the plates and juggle the balls and try to keep friends from falling out and enemies from making up until it can be made to serve the interests of Her Majesty. This little incident? Nobody even cares. A bad man is dead. A good man got caught up in it. And two women from Gilsland know nothing that can cause embarrassment. My department brought a brave soldier to England and he has made a life here. And when an old enemy came knocking, we dealt with that as well. So, I will not do anything as demeaning as request a handshake, but could we all, in good faith, agree to draw a curtain around this week's strange events? I fear the alternative would be to nobody's liking.'

I looked to Cordelia. It was she who would have to decide whether this could be left alone. After a moment, she gave a slight nod.

'I will remember you, but for different reasons,' said Christopher, as we stood up. He was talking to Cordelia and she shot him a puzzled look. 'We are always eager to find new recruits. I sense you would be an asset.'

He held out a business card. It was a square of white. It did not even display a name. There was merely a PO Box stamped upon it in black ink.

'In case you wish to maximize yourself,' he said.

She held his gaze for a second then took the card. She turned on him and led me out of the parlour and down the corridor. We did not look back. She opened the door and walked slowly down the steps and I realized I was hissing after her to stop.

She never did. She kept walking. Walked right across the grass and turned right onto the lane and stalked away from me, heading for her own house.

'Cordelia?' I shouted after her, and I realized she had no intention of turning back.

I walked home alone, jumping at every sound, startled by every flicker of cloud across the moon. John was waiting for me at the bottom of the lane. He'd been there for a while.

''Ow were it?' he asked.

I didn't answer. It would be a long time before I felt able to speak about it, and by then, all the lies had changed.

CORDELIA

There was a light covering of snow the morning of Christmas Day 1967. It wasn't deep enough to get anybody worked up but it was enough to make the place look a little more festive. The weather had gone to more trouble than I had. My own attempts at decorating for Christmas were feeble. I'd hung some paper streamers above the fireplace in the library and my paltry selection of cards sat on the mantelpiece. Three of them were the same and carried identical pictures of glittery robins. The inscriptions from my old university friends were as saccharine and bland as I had feared. They were thinking of me, they said. Hoped to catch up soon, they said. It had been all I could do not to throw them on the fire.

I'd received a nicer card from Felicity. We'd seen each other only once since the night at the Parker Farm. She'd been walking towards the post office in the village as I was making my way back from sending a telegram to Cranham. He was holidaying in Italy and had urged me to get in touch if I needed any extra money for the festive season. Instead I had simply sent him my best wishes and told him to have a lovely time with his friend. There was a little grin on my face as I imagined him receiving it. It had been both a kind and a malicious act and the sisters would no doubt have called me wicked for such a thing.

She seemed strangely nervous as we drew closer. She had a wicker shopping basket over one arm and she'd had her hair restyled. Her skirt also seemed a little shorter and there was a new colour to her lips. She looked good – even if the hairstyle did seem a little too familiar to my own. I found myself aware of the changes in my own appearance. I was wearing boots more at home in a stable than in any of the pubs I frequented at Oxford, and my waxy jacket had been chosen for its water-proof qualities rather than anything to do with style.

'Flick,' I said, and I swear she seemed to sag with relief that

I was still content to use the nickname I had bestowed. If she'd called me Mrs Hemlock I think I'd have burst into tears.

'Cordelia,' she said, smiling.

We didn't hug. This was still Gilsland. Spontaneous displays of affection in the main thoroughfare would have made it into the *Hexham Courant*.

'You're looking well,' I said. 'Love the skirt.'

'So does John,' she said, and I think she may have tossed her hair a little. She looked good. Happy, even.

'How are the boys? Brian maimed anybody this week?'

'Not yet,' she said, smiling. 'Been knuckling down, actually. The school wants to have him tested and apparently that's a good thing not a bad one. Reckon he might be clever.'

'He's got something about him,' I said, nodding.

'I hear you've been courting scandal,' she said, dropping her voice. 'Seen out walking with Heron. Picnics by the river. And there's a rumour he's brought you a Christmas tree.'

I smiled at that, rolling my eyes. 'We talk. He listens. He's not the sort for indoors.'

'But you'll not be alone for Christmas, eh? He'll be coming up? Your husband?'

I shook my head. 'Already sunning himself in Lake Garda.'

'Be better if he were drowning himself in it,' said Felicity, and appeared shocked at herself. We shared a smile.

'There's a card for you,' she said, remembering, and started rummaging in her basket. She handed over an envelope. On the back, James had drawn a squirrel with its head cut off. 'There's a plate for you at the table if you want company.'

I took the card but ignored the request. There was no way I could go. I'd planned a Christmas Day in front of the television. I'd been learning how to cook over the past few weeks and reckoned I could handle a Christmas luncheon of scrambled eggs with Alphabetti spaghetti and white toast, provided I washed it down with one of the bottles of sloe and damson wine that Heron had left on the back step next to a spindly silver Christmas tree and a carving of a bird. None of the gifts had come with a card and we had not spoken about them on our walks but there was something between us. It would never become more than it was, but it mattered to me.

'I'm here if you need me,' she said, and I was grateful to her for not making a big deal of it.

'Me too,' I said, though I figured I would be less use.

I opened the card when I got home. It showed a little church against a fading sky; snow on the ground and a robin sitting on a cross. Inside she had written something that made me feel like I had already drunk the wine.

*To Cordy. The Strongest person I know. I am proud to
be your friend. Flick (and family) xxx*

It sat in the centre of the mantelpiece. I still have it, all these years later. Still can't look at it without feeling a little giddy and nostalgic.

I woke early on Christmas morning. I could hear church bells. We'd never had much in the way of Christmas mornings when I still lived with Mam and in the convent school we were lucky if our presents weren't a cold shower and a slap around the face. But I still felt oddly pleased with the world as I opened the curtains and looked out upon fields that had been turned a muddy white by the soft snowfall. I lit the fire in the hearth and pulled on warm clothes, filled the kettle and spooned real tea into the pot. I'd stopped bothering with the coffee machine. I'd lost the taste for it. Then I switched on the wireless and ate thick bread with jam and felt absurdly happy with myself. Even now I can't fathom it. Perhaps it was simply that I had made it to Christmas. Stefan had been gone for nearly eleven months and I had managed to keep on breathing. Last Christmas it had just been him and me and we had delighted each other with crackers and silly hats and stuffed ourselves with chocolates and clementines, brazil nuts and lemonade. This year it was just me. There would only ever be just me, of that I was certain. But it didn't mean he hadn't lived. It didn't mean that all was for nothing. He'd lived a life full of smiles and though it had ended decades earlier than it should have done I could take comfort in the knowledge that none of his life had been anything other than glorious. I couldn't think of anybody else who felt the same.

After breakfast I made a decision I had been avoiding for

some time. I should go and see the Parkers. We had only
glimpsed each other fleetingly since that night in November.
We'd exchanged waves across the boundary wall and Mrs
Parker had honked the horn of her car as she passed me on
the lane. But nothing real had passed between us. Christmas
Day seemed the right time to make a gesture. I opened the
box of Christmas cards that I had bought and then not bothered
to send to my university friends. I wrote a simple, heartfelt
message inside and placed it in the envelope. I had a box of
ribbons in a button box in the dresser and I carefully selected
a neutral spool and wrapped it around one of my bottles of
wine. The finished product looked rather fetching and it was
with some remarkable *joie-de-vivre* that I set off to my neighbour's house. I suppose I felt like a grown-up. I don't think
I'd ever felt that way before.

I left footprints in the snow as I walked and it was all I could
do not to run in a circle just to enjoy the image they punched
into the pristine surface. It was a little before twelve. The Parkers
would no doubt be at church. Everybody else would be too.

Nobody answered when I knocked on the door. In many
ways, that was a relief. I wasn't really sure what kind of
conversation I was expecting but I knew there would be
awkwardness aplenty and my shoeprints in the snow would
be a better indicator of my gesture of friendship than any
amount of stilted conversation. I decided to leave the gift where
it would be easily seen. The front step seemed the obvious
place but I had seen plenty of magpies and crows pecking at
food parcels and shiny bottles and could imagine nothing more
likely to send the wrong message than the Parkers returning
from church to find smashed glass and a puddle of red against
the pristine whiteness.

I wondered if the back door might be better. I crunched around
to the side of the building and towards the courtyard that led
down to the outbuildings. I could hear the distant sound of a
cow making a racket. I wondered if the calf it mourned was
currently laying in a roasting tin surrounded by onions and
potatoes, then shuddered when the cruelty of the notion hit home.

The back door was set back into a rough-hewn wall of grey
stone. The red slates that made up the porch had been turned

into a stripy Christmas scarf by the fine dusting of snow. And through the glass I could see the little room where the Parkers would change into their workboots and hang up their damp clothes. I decided it would be a good place to leave the gift and reached out for the handle of the outer door.

I can't remember exactly how it happened but one moment I was lost in a haze of thought about Christmas and cattle and whether or not I had been right to send Mam a card when I had received none in return, and then I was staring at a set of boot prints that were so familiar to me I could just as well have been staring into a mirror.

The prints led away from the back door and towards one of the outbuildings. The pattern was unquestionably the same as the one that had been left on the floor beside my bed several weeks before.

I stood perfectly still. The pattern was perfect. Whoever had walked across the courtyard had done so purposefully, with neat, even steps. I thought of the shuffling, shambolic Mr Parker, dragging his leg behind him. Thought of his wife. Her feet were surely too small. Could it be Christopher? Surely he would be back in London by now, squatting at the centre of his twisted web of lies, spies and secrets.

I took a step towards the window and peered through the glass, hoping I could work out who the steps belonged to by examining the shoes within. I saw only a further array of wellingtons and a stand for umbrellas into which somebody had deposited a dozen different walking sticks and a gaudy brolly.

Before I had even realized it, I was following the footsteps. I wasn't sure whether to walk beside the prints or on top of them but as I looked back at my own steps I realized there was no way of disguising my presence here. And besides, it suddenly seemed important to me that I preserve the prints. I would need to show them to somebody later. I would need to photograph them. I would need plaster casts made for comparison against the prints that were still a dark stain against the wooden floor of my bedroom.

Should I have gone straight for Sergeant Chivers? Should I have gone home and called the exchange and demanded to be put through to the first available police officer? Should I have run down the hill to Felicity and John, or stood still and shouted Heron's name until he came to my aid. Probably, yes. But I was a stubborn thing and it seemed absurdly important that I do this by myself. I needed to know. Needed to see if I had been the worst kind of fool.

The footsteps sloped gently upwards towards the nearest field. To my left were outbuildings with big open doors and high roofs. The floor was muddy and the space had been sectioned off into what looked, to my inexpert eyes, like individual cells. I passed them by. There was a tight feeling in my chest and I was gripping the wine tight in my right hand as I walked – the knuckles turning white against the green of the bottle and the deep red of the liquid.

The footsteps carried on past the metal gate that marked the entrance to the field. They doubled-back slightly. Whoever had made them had opened the gate and then retreated back into the courtyard as they swung it open. There was a small area of smudging and mess and then the steps carried on, across the field, where I could make out the shape of a small stone building with a brick roof.

That would have been the time to turn back. There, under the cold blue sky with its pale, liquid sun and the playful fingers of the frosty air pinching at the areas of exposed skin.

I walked quietly, deciding, without really knowing it, that I would be best served by standing in the existing footsteps. I had a fear of putting my foot in one of the trenches made by the cow's hooves and twisting my ankle – leaving myself immobile and vulnerable on the cold hard ground.

I smelled the building before I reached it. The reek was almost physical: a ghastly, chemical tang that seemed to reach into my mouth and nose like tree roots and which made tears instantly spring to my eyes. I stopped where I was, a dozen steps from the entrance; that rectangle of complete blackness set into the old, lichen-mottled stone.

There was a noise from within. It was a soft, damp sound, like a boot being pulled from thick mud. There was a rhythm to it. As I stood there I found myself able to count the beats between each occurrence. I stayed perfectly still. Heard it half a dozen times.

There was nothing inviting about the little stone structure. The stench, the sound, the sight of it, all spoke to me of something from the most menacing of fairy tales. And yet I needed to know. Despite everything, despite the risk, despite the damn stupidity of pressing on, I had to know what was inside.

Softly, barely lifting my feet from the ground, I crossed to the door of the building and peered inside.

It took a moment for my eyes to adjust. The smell that emanated from the darkness was almost unendurable. My eyes started streaming immediately and I felt a cough start to tickle at my chest and throat. It was through a blur that I saw the thing within. It was through a veil of tears and dread and against the surging of my own blood in my ears that I saw the figure in white standing, bent-backed, in that room of skulls.

My senses were flooded. It all came at me like a shotgun blast. The shelves, floor to ceiling, with their hideous array of perfect, moon-bright bone. Horns. Teeth. Eye sockets. Grinning smiles and jutting jaws, all denuded of flesh, feathers or fur. The soft, blood-red light of the gas-lamp, giving off only a whisper of illumination at the figure's right hand.

He stood with his back to me, stirring the great wooden pot like a witch with a cauldron; the metrical thump of his large wooden mortar sploshing through the liquid to create the sound which had frozen me where I stood.

He was naked from the waist up. His skin was as white as the skulls that lined the wall and bore the scars of a life lived hard. His spine curved slightly, like a rat's tail in repose.

His head was a thing of horror. The skin looked like it belonged to a dead creature; all patchy and stippled with patches of purple and red.

In the centre, beneath the crown of his perfectly bald head, were the livid red lines of the swastika that had been carved into his skin more than two decades before by the countrymen he betrayed.

Jean Favre.

Le Tanneur.

I don't know if he heard me breathing. But he stopped moving. Stopped stirring the pot. Then he reached out a pale white hand and picked up the light.

The shadows changed. I turned to my right and saw how he had decorated the wall. At first I thought it was a tapestry; a motley assemblage of different threads and colours, swirled together into an abstract wall hanging the length of the room. It was only as I peered closer that I made out the details. Saw, with cold terror that the hanging was made up of skin, stitched to skin, stitched to skin.

I couldn't move. Just stood there, staring at this collage of flesh; this confusion of different leathers, and tried to keep myself from sinking to the floor as the sheer horror of what I was seeing flooded my senses. This was not just animal skin. I could make out great patches that were unmistakably human; unfolded features, flattened out as if their owners had melted into vile puddles of membrane and tissue, then stitched to the flanks of cows and calves, pigs and deer, birds and fish and foals.

There was movement to my left and then a sudden swift blur. I was on my knees before I felt the pain. Then there was wetness on my face and filth in my hair as I collapsed forward onto the damp floor. I tried to stand but my legs wouldn't work. Far away, I heard the smash as the glass bottle hit stone. The light in the room had changed. Through the flashing colours I could see a round, flat stone, the diameter of a cart's wheel. Laid out on the smooth surface was a corpse. The entire torso had been stripped of meat. Beside it was an older body; grey and green and putrid. The top of its head was missing.

I looked up and into the face of Mr Parker. Without his wig, and with the battle scars carved into his bare chest, he looked like a child's drawing of a monster.

He raised the paddle a second time. There was no emotion on his face as he brought it down once more.

My final thought, before everything went black, was a kind of sad, scared acceptance. I had what I wanted. I had revelation and truth: reward for my perseverance and stubbornness.

And now I had the consequences.

FELICITY

Transcript 0011, recorded November 1, 2010

B oth boys had got bikes for their birthdays. We'd started paying for them back in January and had made the final payment with two weeks to spare. Brian probably didn't deserve his but we'd spent so long paying for them that it would have felt daft not to let him have it. And to be fair to the little sod, he was grateful. He was first down the stairs, as always. Came bouncing into our bedroom like he was still six years old and announced that it had snowed overnight and that he'd been awake since not long after midnight. He hurried us out of bed like there had been a fire and woke his brother by hitting him on the head with a pillow until he opened his eyes. Then it was dressing gowns and slippers and Brian led the way downstairs and into the kitchen where he found the Schwinn Sting-Ray 'muscle bike' that he had been going on about for the past three years. James had one too, along with a set of pencils and paints and three new toy cars. Brian got some marbles, a book on fly-tying, and a Meccano crane. Between them they had plenty of chocolate and a distant auntie had sent them a Napoleon Solo gun for them 'to share'. Before breakfast, Brian had shared it with his brother by shooting him half a dozen times in the back of the head.

John got me some new slippers from the posh shop in Carlisle. I'd got him some aftershave and a new hat. Brian did me a sketch of a cowboy being trampled by a horse (he'd seen it in *Bonanza*) and James got me a necklace with an amber amulet. I didn't ask him where he'd got it or how much he had paid but it was a lovely thing and he had smiled when I said I liked it.

I got started on the dinner while John was still washing up the breakfast dishes. We were having turkey. It was a big bugger and had arrived two days earlier in a hessian sack. It had taken an age to get the feathers off and even longer to scoop them all up. Feathers always made me sneeze. I was doing it with roast potatoes, mash, three types of veg and bread sauce. We were having half a grapefruit each for starters and there was enough brandy in the brandy butter to put a scorch mark on the roof when we lit the Christmas pudding.

I wanted them out of my hair and John was itching to go and see if there was enough snow out towards Talkin to get the sledge out so they all cleared off mid-morning and I had a bit of peace to work in. It was nice, standing there at the sink with my apron on and some carols from the posh choir-boys dribbling out of the wireless. I was chopping and peeling and mashing like somebody with a dozen hands. Mam used to cook the meat the night before but that had always seemed a bit like cheating, and the kitchen was full of the smell of roasting meat and softening onions and my mouth was fairly watering by the time I stopped for a little rest not long after eleven. I sat myself down in John's chair and switched on the telly. Bob Monkhouse was grinning in that way of his and I watched him laugh and wink and twinkle for a while as I sipped my tea and thought about what an odd year it had been. This would be the first time Fairfax hadn't popped around just before lunch with some poor story about not wanting to intrude but needing to borrow something, and John would tell him to get himself sat to the table because there was enough for every-body. We'd been doing that every year since he'd been widowed. For some reason, the tradition had become so important that we all preferred the pretence of his turning up uninvited, rather than actually inviting him along. Don't ask me why – that's just families and friends for you.

I spotted two little feathers down by the plug behind the telly. Black-and-white with little pretty speckles on them. They were belters; downy but firm, with a little touch of shimmer to the pattern. They would make for perfect fishing flies. I'd forgotten to save any of the turkey feathers for Brian and though he hadn't said anything I'd felt bad that they'd all gone in the bin. These two might be a nice surprise for him when he got back. I pulled myself out of the chair and got down on my hands and knees and reached behind the spindly legs of the set. They were a bit

out of reach and I had to push forward, static making my face
tingle, before I could close my fingers around them. Maybe I
overbalanced. Maybe that was when my knees started playing
me up. But I know a sharp pain went from my ankle to my hip
bone and it made me lurch forward like somebody had kicked
me up the backside. I gave a yelp and tried to stop myself
but the telly was just too heavy and it went over backwards
like one of those chimney stacks that they blow up with
dynamite. The set hit the wall and as I wrapped my arms
around I heard the sound of wood hitting wood.

It took me a moment to wrestle everything back into place.
I was sweating and sore and Bob Monkhouse was still prat-
tling on but there seemed no harm done. I heaved the telly
back onto the stand and put the feathers in my pocket and
stepped back to push my hair back from my red face. As I
did so I looked down, half-remembering the unexpected noise
of wood on wood. I peered down the back of the telly and
saw the little patch of empty space in the skirting board and
the wooden panel on the floor. I had a sudden memory of the
false panel in the church; the recollection of the gun against
my fingers and the burnt pages in my hand. I should have left
them all where they were. No good had come of looking into
the forbidden spaces. I hunched down, pain in my legs, and
reached inside the hole.

I knew what I had found even before I looked at it. The
cassette felt cool and plastic against my fingertips. I dragged
it out of the wall and held it up. The words written in black
ink upon the paper strip at its centre were simple and direct.

For Fairfax – and whoever else needs to know.

For a moment I just stood there, swaying slightly, hot and sore
and sweaty with the sound of 'Hark the Herald Angels'
warbling out of the radio to do battle with the sound of water
boiling on the stove and hot fat sizzling in the oven.

I think I already knew. Looking back, it's hard to say for
sure. But as I bent down and checked the hole for its other
secrets, I understood. It was chock-full of a boy's private things.
The magazines that I pulled out of the space in the wall weren't

as filthy as the sketchbook. The pages and pages of naked ladies weren't enough to turn my stomach. They were pretty girls with their tops off. Stockings and suspenders. Big smiles and lots of make-up. The pictures that James had done in his secret jotter were the ones that turned my stomach. It was all just so ugly. Naked ladies made up to look like animals; made up to look like birds. Naked forms with feathers stuck into their skin or bull horns emerging from their foreheads. Women stripped of skin clutching flowers to their bloodied chests. Each one had been signed in my son's neat hand.

My legs went a bit and I had to reach out for the counter. These were James's sketches. I recognized the style. They all had the same kind of feeling to them and they all made my skin rise like turkey flesh as the room span around me. This was his secret place; his hidey hole. He'd stolen the tape that I held in my hand from his brother's own treasure trove inside the old tree. The one he'd stolen from the collections box inside the church. He'd taken it – and in doing so he'd ensured that the only story that the dead man wanted Fairfax to hear, was the one he never did.

With my hands shaking and my bones seizing up, I went to the cold living room and found Fairfax's tape recorder. I'd placed it in the bottom drawer of the dresser, hidden beneath some old papers.

I wish I'd had somebody to talk to as I placed the reel in the device. I wanted to mutter something to make it all seem less important. But I was alone, listening to Christmas carols and the sounds of my home.

I pressed the 'play' button like Cordelia had. Closed my eyes as the voice, slightly accented, emerged from the tape recorder. I remember every bloody word.

'Fairfax, mon ami. I had to think very hard about whether or not to leave this recording . . . I may have imposed on you enough already. I may have loaded you up with a grief you can never be free of. But I need you to know something that you will never learn unless I say these words . . . forgive me, my voice must sound strange to you. I am bleeding. A sick man, hurt by one bigger and younger and stronger . . . I'm

sorry, I must say this right . . . he said his name was Pike and that I had no business near his 'stash'. Forgive me, I do not know what this word means.

'This recording, yes . . . I noticed you admiring the Dictaphone as we spoke. I believe it will be my gift to you. That seems right, somehow. It will be very useful in your work. And useful work it is. You are a storyteller and your son would be very proud of the way you honour him. But you are a splendid listener too. Is that the word? The English word? Splendid. That is how I would describe you, mon ami. A splendid fellow. We talked for only a short while but I found in you a man who understands what it is to be one thing on the outside and another within. When I knocked on your door I was in distress. Though I had come here to offer forgiveness, the sight of my abuser almost undid me. I wanted revenge. But that is not why I came here. I have carried such hatred inside me, Fairfax. That hatred has made me ill. I know you saw that illness in me. You remarked upon it – my cough, my pale skin, the sweat on my head. What a sight I must have made at your door. And yet you invited me into your home. You spoke with me of Gilsland and its history and you listened as I spoke to you. I was not certain I was right to do so and I was – how do you say it? – cryptic? Evasive? I told you much without telling you anything at all. I saw distrust in you, even as you offered friendship.

'So I tell you now, mon ami.

'My name is Marcel Defouloy. During the war I was a member of the Resistance. I was a Maquis. A proud man, willing to die not so much for France but simply to stop a movement I knew to be against goodness. A movement I knew to be wrong and which had ripped a blade into the belly of my comfortable life.

'Where to begin . . .? In the final weeks of the war I was in Correze. That is where I am from, Fairfax. A quiet, pretty place, not unlike your own little part of the world. Such horrors had been committed there, mon ami. The people were dying. The Nazis, Das Reich were sweeping through like disease. My unit was sent to liberate the town of Tulle. We blew up a bridge. We engaged the occupying SS and we defeated them. And then *the Nazis came back. I was captured by the Milice. Do you know the Milice by reputation, Fairfax? These men were zealots. They were criminals and madmen who believed in Hitlerism as much as any German. They scared us more than the SS. How were we to know which among us was a traitor? They were our neighbours. Our brothers and sisters. Among them was a man called Favre. He had been a leatherworker before the war. He had been in prison when the Nazis invaded. The story was that he had been imprisoned for taking the skin from a young man's back after a dispute over a girl. He was picked out by the Milice as a man with special skills. He became their interrogator.*

'Favre was set to work on me, Fairfax. He hurt me in ways I could not imagine. I was stretched across the bonnet of a German military vehicle and in the centre of Tulle, as the whole village watched, he heated a handful of coins in a brazier. These he placed upon my skin, one at a time, as he softly asked questions about Maquis movements. I smelled my skin cooking. The pattern of the coins ate into my skin. I heard women and children sobbing and men pleading for mercy. I told him I knew nothing and he did not seem to care. Eventually I gave him a name. A town I knew had no Maquis. A safe haven that the Germans would soon see as no threat. He seemed pleased with my choice. He told his commander. They left me there to watch what happened next. I still see them. See those ninety-nine men hanging from the lampposts in the square.

'Fairfax, what happened next will never leave me. The things that happened in that town, that town which had no Maquis and which posed no threat . . . Das Reich wiped them out, Fairfax. The Nazis and the Milice – they destroyed an entire town. Hundreds of men, mown down with machineguns. Women and children, packed in the church and the church then set ablaze. The heat was so intense that the bell melted. It dripped upon the floor and onto their corpses. The treasures of the church became puddles of gold. One of my brothers in the Maquis was among the first men to see the devastation. He said he could never imagine such horrors. He did not believe men capable of such brutality. In the doorway of the church he found soft gold, still steaming, still half fused to the ashes and dust

that had once been a person. He took it, Fairfax. Not for its value but because of what it meant. It had been something real – an emblem of a life. It had seemed important.

'*Later, he gave the gold nugget to me. Whether he knew of my betrayal I do not know but one morning I found the gold on the doormat of my home. The note told me that it was to ensure I would never forget. Can you imagine it, Fairfax? To carry the weight of so many deaths? I had the gold fashioned into a tooth to replace the ones smashed out by the Nazis who passed by my bloodied, half-cooked body as they exited Tulle. That tooth was pushed deep into my gums – a memorial that I would taste and feel for every second of every day.*

'*Last year the doctors told me I was dying. My thoughts turned at first to vengeance. I needed to find Favre – the evil man who had burned me to the bone and directed the Nazis to unleash bloody vengeance on innocents. I had succeeded, after the war, Fairfax. I found a good job in a paper mill. A bookkeeper, far from the scene of my terrible betrayal. But I had never found love, nor had children, or allowed myself friends. For twenty-five years I lived a solitary life as those who had served in the Milice prospered or fled. Many were forgiven. They formed part of the new government after the war. But those who had committed atrocities fled France to new lives in new countries. Favre was among them. I asked questions, Fairfax. I dug and I bribed and I begged until I came across a man who told me a story I could hardly credit. After the war, the British had helped war criminals escape. Those with specialist skills or special knowledge were given a free pass. A new life. A new career. A new identity.*

'*It pains me, Fairfax. You spoke so wisely about the import-ance of forgiveness and you spoke with such passion about your friend, the man whose wife had been telling you of his great deeds during the war. I came here to make peace with my torturer and when I saw him by that river, capturing that beautiful bird, I was filled with nothing but a need for blood. He ran from me, Fairfax. And then I came to you. But you spoke so beautifully. You listened and you counselled and in your eyes I saw what God wanted from me. He wanted forgive-ness. Wanted me to forget the past and make peace before my*

death. I cannot shake my abuser's hand, Fairfax. That would
be too much. But I leave you the tooth that I have carried with
me for so long. It seems right, somehow, that it be here, in this
quiet, peaceful place – within sight of you and your wisdom.

'I have never been a religious man but I have always felt
there is something more – some battle to be fought between
good and evil and that symbols could be made to serve any
purpose that man invested them with. The tooth was just a
hunk of gold but I turned it into something more. Now, as I
sit in the cool doorway of your little church and taste my
blood, I realize I have been wrong these many years. I needed
no emblem. I needed no insignia of my guilt. It seems appro-
priate that your young friend be the one to see to its removal.
He had the same bullying swagger as the men who took so
many lives. When he struck me and I felt the gold wrenched
free from my gums I thought my heart was being tugged out.
But as I sat in the cold gloom of the archway and licked my
wounds, I realized he had done me a favour. He had made up
my mind for me. He had set me free.

'I think you know what I am telling you, Fairfax. The stories
you have been fed by your neighbours are the worst kind of
lies. They are truths made deceitful by their theft. They are
the stories of many men and women and they have been woven
into one cruel charade that has been used to bind you to their
cause.

'Favre has been in your home many times, Fairfax. He has
drunk your wine and eaten your food and made himself
the cornerstone of your small community.

'I saw something in your eyes as we spoke, mon ami. Some
understanding of who I might be. And I realized that my fate
was no longer in my own hands. You asked me to wait as you
drove away. I think I understand where you are heading.
Perhaps I should have shouted out and told you the truth but
in the end, my life and my death have never been mine to
dictate. You have gone to fetch him. Favre. Mr Parker, as you
call him. And when he returns you will see who he truly is.
You will see whether he is the man he pretends to be now, or
the man he was.

'I am leaving you this confession to help you deal with

whatever comes next. Your young friend, Pike. He caught me hanging around the church. I don't know who he thought I was but he believed me to be chasing his possessions. He hit me. Left me bloodied. My tooth fell onto the dirty stone. But as I sit here, I feel a peace I have not felt in a long time. My judgement is beyond my control. And there is a comfort to be found in that.

'*Thank you for your hospitality and friendship, Fairfax. This morning I did not know you but now I believe I have found a man who will be a safe place for what I know. Favre is Parker. He is a cruel and terrible man. Whatever you do with this knowledge, you have my blessing. And if our paths cross again, I hope you will embrace me as a brother and without regret. Thank you Fairfax. Au revoir.*'

The recording clicked off after that. And I just stood there. Stood listening to the pans on the stove and the hissing of the fat and the drone of the bishop. His words had been drowned out by the confession of Marcel Defouloy – a good man who had been murdered by the same monster who had tortured him all those years before. Tortured him until he made up a lie that would cost hundreds of innocents their lives.

Cordelia.

I think I said her name aloud. Suddenly, nothing mattered more than being by her side. The Parkers were her neighbours. She was all alone up there. Alone in the world.

I was running down the hill towards the village before I'd even made up my mind to go. I left the pans rattling on the stove. Left the turkey cooking and the sermon droning on. I left the Dictaphone on the counter. I wanted to fetch her and bring her home. Wanted her to be safe with me and mine as we made the call to the police and finally made sense of it all.

I ran like the bloody wind.

CORDELIA

It was the smell that brought me back to myself. That chemical, ammonia-rich reek. It worked like smelling salts and I opened my eyes to an explosion of pain above my ear and behind my eyes. I tried to move and discovered that I had no strength in my limbs. I was laid out on a cold, dank stone. I had a sudden image of da Vinci's Vitruvian Man; my arms outstretched and my legs splayed against the perfect round circle of rock.

'I thought this was enough,' muttered Favre. 'Truly. I stopped for so long. I lived right. Did well. Earned my right at a second chance . . .'

I tried to raise my head and fresh agony seared down my spine and into my hips. I felt as though my head was caved in all down one side. I don't know what I felt. Confusion. Fear. Dread. I was in a place between sleep and wakefulness; between life and death, and my thoughts were a churning mess of fragments. I tried again to lift my head and he seemed to notice. A face appeared above me; repulsive and twisted: blobby, purple, wormlike lips and deep-set eyes. He looked at me with nothing readable in his expression. He saw me the way the slaughterman sees the next beast into whom he must drive the killing blow. This was almost work to him. This was what he was for.

'I didn't kill for more than twenty years,' he said, his lips barely moving. 'You might not believe me but after the war I made a decision not to draw any attention to myself. The loss of the war was a shock, Mrs Hemlock. You might not remember that but the Nazis were supposed to win. I had chosen a side that would allow me to do that which I was good at and that decision cost me my liberty. I hid in some terrible places as they hunted me. But Christopher knew my value. I had been a Milice elite. I had been close to the men who would form the new government. I was a man that

mattered. Christopher's unit reached out to me. Made an offer.
He had persuaded his people that it was better to use what I
knew than to add my name to the list of the damned. There
were those who sought my execution for the events of '44 but
when Christopher caught me and I shared all I knew, he made
the correct decision. I could help him. I knew things nobody
else did. There were many like me. Men who could be valuable to the allies, whether it be for their skills or their secrets.
It was my secrets that he needed. For countless days I fed him
information. I proved my value. And he was as good as his
word. He provided me a new life. He is one of the Old Boys,
remember? A good chap.'

His voice twisted at that, as if he was saying something so
revolting that it made his gorge rise.

'Audrey was already one of the team,' he said, and his voice
was without cadence or song; just flat monotonous crochets
that fell upon me like hail. 'She is an exceptional woman.
Throughout the war she had helped spread counter-intelligence.
Her brother – he is an important man. Loveday. A silly name
for one so skilled. He read my file and chose to place me
somewhere he knew to be impenetrable.

'A word in an ear here, a polite letter there. You English
are so . . . well-connected. Our story was a cover. We did not
begin as true man and wife. But something grew between us,
of that I am certain. We have lived a true marriage, Audrey
and I. She has learned so much from the prisoners of war she
befriended and who write to her with such glorious titbits each
week. Christopher uses her the way a surgeon uses a knife.
She sends her old friends the messages that the world needs
to hear. She receives replies rich with confidences. She is
valuable, and we have been well rewarded. We never spoke
of my crimes.'

I tried to speak. Even through the fog I had to understand.
'Did . . . she know . . .?'

He smiled at that – a fleeting thing, like the flash of an
axe-blade in the dark.

'What she knew, I cannot say. But when news came last
year that the Maquis bastard in France was asking questions,
it was she who thought of Fairfax and a way we could protect

ourselves. The old fool was always so interested in stories. Such a busybody – always scrabbling around asking questions as if he were a writer or somebody who mattered. Christopher may have suffered at the thought of his grieving father but he never did a thing to stop his pain. He did what he had to, and that is all I have ever done. Audrey fed Fairfax such a tale. Fed him such a wonderful tapestry of lies. Told him I was this heroic figure by the name of Abel. A hero of the Resistance, tortured by the devil Favre. And so when Defouloy sniffed me out and slithered into this place, Fairfax knew he was looking at a bad man who had done bad things. He got him talking. Acted friendly even as he plotted his end. And then he came and told us.'

He gave the tiniest smile at that. Seemed to like the memory.

'It pained him, of course. He was such a gentleman, you see. Could not stomach the idea of handing a man over to those who might have done him harm. But he had experienced grief. He hated the Nazis as they had robbed him of his son. I enjoyed that – enjoyed knowing that the man he grieved for was the same who had brought me to Britain.

'Marcel was just sitting there when we arrived at the church. It was dark. He had fallen asleep, huddled in on himself, and there was blood on his chin. That idiot Pike had thought him to be interested in his pitiful possessions.

'When I addressed him I did so as an equal. He had been brave beneath the knife all those years before. But the spirit had gone out of him. He did not want conflict. He wanted judgement and told me I should demand the same.'

As Favre spoke, the shadows behind him lengthened. The sound of the flapping leather and the hunch of his back made it seem as though I were trapped in the gloom with a colossal bird.

'Killing him brought me no joy,' said Favre. 'I didn't know I had done it until he was at my feet. It was over in seconds. It brought me no pleasure. Audrey didn't turn away as I did what I had to. And when it was over it was she who fetched Fairfax and told him that Defouloy – the man he thought was Jean Favre – had attacked her and that I had no choice but to defend her. Fairfax chose the tomb. He said it would be years before it would be needed. Perhaps we should have demanded that the body be put in the bog but at that time, we needed the body stashing away as quick as could be. We dumped him in the old Kinmont tomb. We set fire to Fairfax's transcript of our conversations. We demanded all evidence of his visit be removed.'

Favre wiped his forehead, running his delicate fingers back over his smooth scalp.

He sighed, displeased with people's inability to do what they promised.

'I know now that Marcel had a tape recorder and that Fairfax kept this for his own purposes. I know too that he did not burn all the papers as instructed. But none of that mattered these past months because killing that bastard Maquisard set something free in me. The man I was – the man I hide inside this pitiful shell. It felt good to be him again.'

He turned at that, staring at the hideous skins along one wall. Slowly, he gazed along the mound of skulls which were stacked like fine china behind me.

'This is who I am,' he said, with a note of triumph. 'Le Tanneur. The torturer they despised and feared. For years I have been practising my skills on animals. I have satisfied the craving within me by watching the agonies in the eyes of God's creatures. Have you heard the sound a deer makes when you stake it down and open its guts and it slowly empties onto the forest floor? Do you know how it feels to take the skin from cattle as the beast still bucks and lows beneath the blade?'

He moved quickly, towards the pot, and reached inside. He pulled out what at first I took to be a heavy coat. Slowly, the dreadfulness of the truth filtered into my understanding.

'He has been softening for months now,' said Favre, looking at the skin of Marcel Defouloy. 'I find it pleasing – this idea of working again on a skin that I last played with so many years ago. There is a pleasing symmetry to it, is there not? If you look carefully, you will see the pattern of the coins which seared his flesh.'

I tried again to move. Managed to half slide and half shuffle into a position that allowed me a glimpse of the light that bled in through the open door. I saw a flicker of movement. A flash of colour against the grass and the mud and the snow.

'Fairfax brought him to us after you found his resting place,' said Favre, shaking his head, as if it had all been too perfect for words. 'There was something in his eyes. Something I hadn't seen before. He told us what had happened. A tree had come down and you and that stupid Goose woman had seen Marcel's corpse. So he gathered him up and stuffed him in his car and drove him here. To us! I helped him remove the body from the boot. That was when it happened. Defouloy's shirt tore open and we both looked upon the damage I had done to him in '44. He still had the imprint of those burning coins against his skin. And Fairfax suddenly knew he had been lied to. He had not helped a victim avenge himself upon his persecutor. He had helped me – the Milice's chief torturer – finally murder the man he had abused years before.'

I was coming back to myself. Could feel the blood in my veins. Could hear my own heart.

Keep trying, I demanded of myself. *Don't give in. Live. Live! They call you wicked. They call you stubborn. So be both. Fight. Fight!*

'He drove away before I could stop him,' said Favre, and he reached down to his left and picked up a wooden frame, and a wicked-looking implement with two handles and a curved blade. 'He was heading for the camp. Looking for a military man he could tell everything to. It was the storm and his own guilt that killed him. I don't know whether he drove into the tree on purpose or whether fortune was simply on my side but his death was a pleasing thing. And now I have Marcel to myself again. I took his body from the boot of the car and have enjoyed every moment of his transformation. Did you know I once made a Maquis into a handbag? I can tell you while I skin you, if you wish . . .'

I had been feigning utter incomprehension as he spoke. I had ensured my eyelids fluttered and that my breath had been shallow. I looked like somebody nearly dead. He did not look like he was expecting me to suddenly scramble to my feet and launch myself at him. But whether he was prepared or not I was too weak to capitalize. He caught me by the arms as I sprang for him and with strength I did not expect him to possess, forced me back onto the stone like he was forcing a reluctant lover onto his bed.

'No,' he said, and the light caught his tiny black eyes. 'You do not get to escape from this. Soon you will be with your son – the son who died so magnificently; whose soul I watched depart. But first, there is pain. So much pain . . .'

I didn't need to fight him off. Didn't need to push him back or try to get my fingers in his eyes. All I had to do was keep him there, hunched over me like a pecking bird; my fingers digging into his wrists and keeping him still, above me, distracted . . .

He never heard Felicity. Never saw the timid little woman scoop up the broken bottle by its neck.

He didn't make a sound as she stuck it in his back. Just twisted in shock and pain and let go of me to round upon her.

I pulled the glass from his back as he advanced towards her. It made a vile sucking sound as it popped out of his skin.

Favre half turned at that. Parted his grotesque lips to show the tiny row of sharp teeth. For a moment he blocked out all the light. The world beyond the skull room disappeared and there was just him and me and Felicity in a room that reeked of skin and blood.

And then I thought of Stefan. That moment, as I held him, and his soul went wherever it wanted to be.

This thing had been there. Had witnessed his last breath.

I lunged forward with the broken bottle.

And stabbed.

And stabbed.

And stabbed.

FELICITY

Transcript 0012, recorded November 1, 2010

Where do I even start with what happened next? It was me who stopped her stabbing him but by then he was long since dead and I only stopped her because it had gone on long enough. Most of the next few hours were a blur.

We supported each other as we made our way back across the snow. She was bleeding and couldn't hear out of one ear. She kept stumbling and didn't know which way was up nor down. And I was trembling enough for the both of us and if I hadn't kept telling myself that the blood on my wrist was Cordelia's, I think I'd have started scrubbing myself clean in the snow.

It was Cordy who insisted we go to the Parker house first of all. The door was open and Audrey wasn't back from church. I didn't like being back there. Told her we had to get down to the village before we were discovered. But she insisted. I can see her now; blood all over her face and clothes, picking up the telephone from the cradle and saying, bold as you like, that her name was Cordelia Hemlock, and that Jean Favre was dead. She didn't ask to be connected to a number. Just said it into the receiver. When I asked her why, she looked at me like I was mad.

'They're listening,' she said. 'They've always been listening.'

We holed up at her house. I wanted to call the police straight away but she told me to wait.

'They won't be long,' she said.

She looked at herself then. Saw the state of herself and I think she realized what had happened, and what she had done. I can see her still; half-nodding to herself, then wiping away the tears.

I ran her a bath. There didn't seem much else to do of any

use. I made tea, because that's what you do. Around one p.m., John and the kids turned up, frantic. The pans had boiled over and they had played the recording. What was I thinking of? What had happened?

They joined me in Cordelia's kitchen. She was upstairs, soaping herself human again.

The men who arrived mid-afternoon were smartly dressed and drove big, grey cars. One of them smelled of cigars. The one who knocked on the door was a slight man. He had a peculiarly-shaped head that was wider at the bottom than the top, so he looked like a lampshade. He had thinning red hair. He wore a pinstripe suit and a black hat and though it was bitterly cold on the doorstep, he didn't look uncomfortable. He asked to see Mrs Hemlock. John was at my side in a flash. The boys were behind us, like we were trying to form a wall of bodies between this man and Cordelia.

'She had to do it,' I said, straight out. 'He were killing her. Go up there. See what he's been doing. See what's been living among us!'

He let me rant for a while. Then he angled his head to see between myself and John and I turned to see Cordelia walking into the kitchen. She was pale and her hair was wet and the bruise in her hairline was an ugly, blue-black mound the size of a cracked egg.

'Let him in,' she said, quietly. 'Thanks for staying with me, Flick. But you can go now. Things will be OK.'

'Go?' spluttered Brian. 'We're going bloody nowhere, Miss. The second we're gone you'll be in handcuffs and they'll be dragging you off to one of their underground chambers for probing and prodding and all that, so if you think we're leaving you're off your rocker.'

She smiled at Brian. He'd barely stopped cuddling me since he arrived at Cordelia's place. John neither. James was a little more reserved. He knew I'd seen his drawings.

'My name is Tom,' said the man, as if we hadn't spoken. He looked around him at the warm, comfortable surroundings of the kitchen, then poured himself a tea from the pot in the centre of the table. He took it black without sugar and winced as he tasted the bitter brew.

'I don't care who you are . . .' began Brian, but Cordelia
shushed him.

'I believe we have a little situation to deal with,' said Tom,
smoothly. 'Your neighbour, Mr Parker. I understand he suffered
an accident in one of his outbuildings. You heard him screaming
in pain, is that right? But by the time you arrived he had
already lost too much blood. A tragedy, but farms are dangerous
places and one does hear often of people being dragged into
their machinery when not paying attention.'

Cordelia watched him, face unreadable. Me and my family
just stayed in the doorway, watching the discussion like it was
a game of tennis.

'Mrs Parker, too,' said Tom, and he took a long white
cigarette from a silver case and lit it with a gold lighter. He
lit another and passed it to Cordelia, who took it without
saying a word.

'Mrs Parker?' she said, at last, when she had blown out a
lungful of smoke.

'She saw his body and went quite mad. Grief will do that.
She has been taken to a facility that will treat her but I fear
she is unlikely to return home any time soon. Truly, it is a
terrible thing to happen to such good people. Thankfully, the
village has benefited hugely from their generosity over the
years and I am sure this will be the same when the will is
read out. I fancy the local area will benefit greatly.'

Cordelia pursed her lips.

'Did he know?' she asked. 'Christopher? Their handler?
Did he know the truth?'

Tom sucked at his lip, weighing up the value of discretion.
'He has been forced to make many difficult decisions,' he said,
holding Cordelia's gaze. 'He has done a great deal for Queen
and country. He is, above all, a good man. It was not his choice
for Mr Parker to be placed here. But there are those in power
who have different priorities. We all serve different masters.
I am sure the gentleman you spoke to at the farm will have
done all he could to prevent situations such as the one we find
ourselves in. And yet, it can sometimes be impossible to contain
a spirit that wants to get out. You can nail three coffin lids in
place and malevolence will still seep through the cracks.'

Cordelia chewed on this for a while. I could see her half agreeing with him.

'That stone. The one he placed me on. It was from the river . . .'

Tom spread his hands. 'Two Irish workmen and a hydraulic lift. It wasn't difficult.'

'And the workmen?'

Tom shook his head and my mind was suddenly full of skins and screams.

'And we go on, do we?' asked John, sullenly. 'Just forget what happened.'

Tom turned on him and dropped the soft voice he had been using for Cordelia. 'You don't know what happened,' he snapped. 'You have guesses and the word of your wife. I have evidence of a terrible farming accident. And that is all.'

'But Fairfax,' I began.

'Crashed his car during a storm.'

'And Marcel? A Frenchman, a decorated Maquisard – nobody will look for him?'

'I'm quite sure somebody will,' said Tom, 'but I'm quite sure you will all be alert for outsiders snooping around.'

Cordelia rubbed her fingertips on the wound upon her skull. 'And if we disagree with your version of events?' she asked.

'Why would you do that?' he replied. 'There are so many opportunities for advancement when one does one's duty.'

'Advancement?' asked Cordelia.

He smiled at that, I swear it. It was just a flash of a thing, like a bird taking a fish from still water, but in that moment he knew he had her. She did too. Standing in the kitchen of a house she never wanted, in the village where she was born to a mother who never gave a damn. I could see her working it out. Could see her trying to decide if she was selling any part of herself if she made this bargain.

And I don't blame her for the decision she made.

EPILOGUE

October 2, 2010

I t took forty-three years for Cordelia to finally find Loveday Parker. He had existed under a dozen different aliases in the decades since the war. None really suited him. He was no Guy Pevington or Simon Arbuthnot. He was no Tim Kernick or Emmet Trent. The only name that fitted him was a solitary letter. He used to use it as a signature, in green ink, on the top-secret documents that crossed his desk and which went straight on to the Home Secretary and Her Majesty once they had been properly vetted.

For a short while, in the late 1950s, Loveday Parker had answered to the name of 'X'. He ran a very specialized unit within MI6. He had the power to make decisions that changed the world, and he knew enough secrets to bring governments to their knees. He was not a good man or a bad man. He was simply the leader of a spy network that spanned the globe.

Cordelia and Felicity sit at his bedside in the comfortable, private hospital where Loveday lays dying. He is eighty-seven years old, though the chart at the foot of his bed declares him to be three years younger.

For the last four years he has been known as Patrick Bainton and has been living in a pleasant apartment on a leafy Victorian road in Weymouth. He has not had to suffer many hardships since leaving MI6 in 1969. His cover as a diplomat ensured he earned a good pension and he has received large dividends from the half-dozen global companies of which he is a major shareholder. He is also an honorary fellow of his old university and gives generously to Westminster School, where he spent his formative years and which gave him respite from the life he endured at the family home in Gilsland, where his elder sister tortured him without mercy whenever she found opportunity.

'Loveday,' says Cordelia. 'Wakey-bloody-wakey.'

He coughs afresh. It's a horrid, rasping sound; a match struck on brick, and then he starts to gag as the fluid in his lungs bubbles up to spill onto his chin and pyjamas.

'Cordy, he's almost gone,' says Felicity, shaking her head. She looks weak and old, sitting back in the hard-backed chair and starting to shiver.

She had been unsure whether to make this trip. John is in the first stages of dementia and she does not want to be away from him. He's still John, a lot of the time, but there are moments when he forgets that he's long since retired from work or that he doesn't live in Brampton or that one of his sons is dead. Brian killed himself in prison in 1977. He'd been Pike's accomplice in a post office robbery. The postmistress had been killed and Brian, overcome with guilt and terrified of Pike trying to silence him, had turned himself in and given evidence against the older man. Brian couldn't handle prison. He hanged himself the day they took away his radio for some minor breach of prison rules. Pike did his time without difficulty. Served eighteen years for murder then came home to his mam's house. He'd only been out a week when his past caught up with him. He was killed with a solitary blow to the head in an alleyway outside a Newcastle nightclub. The only witness described, a tall, dark-haired old man who smelled of wood-shavings and wore a gypsy-scarf around his neck.

'You in there, Loveday?' asks Cordelia.

She's peering at him like a specimen on a slab. She has little sympathy for the condition he is in. Old age strips the veneer from people – that's what Felicity used to say. And Cordelia knows herself to be a hard, stubborn woman. It is the face she wears for the world and it is the one she knows to be her true self. Half a century in counter-intelligence and she has yet to find any evidence that she is wicked. Difficult, yes. Unflinching, certainly. She has even been called 'ruthless' by certain broadsheet newspapers that have yet to make their mind up about her brief tenure at the top of MI6. But she is pleased to fall well short of wickedness. Her grandchildren would find it hard to hug somebody evil, she feels sure of that. And they dote on their fearsome, funny grandmother.

Loveday coughs again and then manages to wriggle upright. There is still an intelligence in his eyes and despite the watery lenses, the blue irises are sharp and focussed.

'Mrs Hemlock,' he says, and there is a slight smile to his lips.

'It's not been Hemlock for a long time.'

'She's a baroness,' says Felicity, from her chair. 'Retired now, though she still goes to meetings.'

Cordelia hides her smile behind her hand. The 'meetings' are the cross-party intelligence and security committee and her statutory attendance days at the House of Lords.

'You've come for me?' asks the man in the bed, wheezing. 'After so much time? Why?'

'Because you're dying,' says Cordelia, flatly. 'And I'm old and so is everybody who remembers what happened. And if I don't ask you now, I'll never know.'

Loveday wets his lips. He screws up his eyes.

'Was I talking? In my sleep?'

'German. Arabic. You cried out a lot. Said her name.'

He closes his eyes at that. Swallows, painfully. He wriggles his left arm free from under the covers. The pyjama sleeve is knotted at the elbow, just below the stump.

'She did this,' he says, quietly. 'Held my hand in the harvester because I wouldn't do what she wanted.'

'And what did she want?' asks Cordelia.

'Everything I had. She was just cruel. Just liked pain. Some people see a duckling and coo about how pretty they look with their brothers and sisters and their mother. Other people throw a rock. That was Audrey.'

'And yet you allowed Christopher to recruit her?' asks Cordelia, sitting back in her chair. 'Why?'

'We were made of the right stuff,' says Loveday, with a faint smile. 'Father was part of the right clubs. We knew the right people. It wasn't hard to be selected – you just had to be a good chap. I was good at codes. Good at strategies. It wasn't unusual for members of SIS – MI6, as it is now – to use their families for some operations. And when they started building the POW camp, it was a perfect cover for Audrey.'

'Christopher?' asks Felicity, quietly. 'How did he end up part of it?'

Loveday finds the strength to give a slight shrug. 'He had a flair for it. I did well in the early days of the war and was running my own unit by '42. I bumped into Christopher on a trip home. He was still scribbling in his notebook. Still writing stories. He wanted to do his bit and I was in a position to help him. We got him a position as a foreign correspondent for a news agency. Told them back home he was a wireless operator. He proved himself very useful.'

'Fairfax never said,' mutters Felicity.

'As far as his family knew he was a wireless operator, far from danger. In truth he was a valuable member of my unit. It was a huge sacrifice, pretending he had lost his life, but the job demanded it and he carried the pain without showing it, even as he knew the agony his father must be going through.'

'But you allowed him to corrupt the village he was from,' says Cordelia. 'You let him place Favre in your sister's house.'

Loveday blinks. Holds his eyes closed for several breaths. He seems to be making up his mind.

'When Christopher caught Favre, after the war, he saw the value in him. He knew names and dates and places. He was a survivor who had only worn the Milice uniform to be allowed to inflict pain. He would do whatever it took to survive. Vile as he saw him, he knew he was an asset. We wrung out every last piece of information from him and set him up with a new life in Ireland. He was Swiss, so we said. We got him a job as a numbers man at a cattle auction. He was never supposed to come to Gilsland.'

'But he did . . .'

'Audrey was struggling with the farm. She needed help. She was setting up networks of intelligence with her little postcards and her food parcels and we saw the potential for expanding it. Favre could be critical to that work. He knew people who could be persuaded to assist. And the farm would be the perfect cover.'

Cordy looks at him for a time. She is perfectly still. Her lips become a thin line.

'He was doing it again,' she says, without emotion. 'Killing.

Hurting. In Ireland. I've seen the press reports – mysterious disappearances, bodies vanishing from graves. He used what he had over you to get himself away from it and into yet another new life. After all you did to free him, he was going to cause embarrassment to your unit. A survivor like Favre would have sensed opportunity. He must have wanted more than the life you gave him in Ireland. He wanted a house and money and a little freedom. And you wanted to be able to keep an eye on him. You gave him your sister.'

Loveday swallows. He tries to hold Cordy's gaze and then turns to the wall. 'They deserved one another.'

Cordy looks over her shoulder to where Felicity is sitting, shaking her head.

'When Marcel went looking for his abuser . . .' begins Cordelia.

'I told them he was coming. Questions had been asked. He was digging around.'

'So Audrey and her husband told Fairfax their cover story. Favre said he was a victim and his torturer was on his way. You wrapped the poor sod's brain up with guilt and barbed wire.'

'Audrey's work was valuable. It had to be protected . . .' begins Loveday.

'And so did your little empire,' finishes Cordelia. 'You dumped a killer in the middle of a community that had no idea what was living in their midst.'

'Eventually, it would have been taken care of,' says Loveday. 'Christopher was already working on a solution.'

Cordelia breathes out, long and slow. She's nodding to herself. Her long white hair makes her look somehow spectral, in the light of the yellow room. She seems half-formed. She pulls herself up, and though the action pains her, she does not let it show. She can handle pain.

'That's all?' asks Loveday, and gives in to a cough. 'You've been looking for me all these years and you're just going to ask me a handful of questions and leave?'

Cordy gives him a tight smile. 'I haven't been looking for you,' she says. 'You never really mattered. A report simply crossed my desk a week ago asking whether we planned to reveal your true identity when you die, which will be in about six days according to your surgeon. My inclination was that we let your death go unremarked. But I did think it was a good opportunity to come and ask the one thing that has been pestering me for a long time, and which Flick here was keen to see resolved. I've dug deep and there's no doubting you did a good job in covering everything up. What happened to your sister?'

Loveday pushes back into his pillows. He starts to choke on the mucus in his throat and it takes a long time for him to be able to breathe sufficiently well to talk. Neither woman tries to help him.

'His death didn't touch her,' he says, at last. 'She saw the body and it was like she was looking at an animal hit by a car. She came with us willingly. Her network hadn't been compromised. She ran it from a new location for the best part of eighteen years. She stayed with the section longer than Christopher or I. I didn't go to her funeral but I know there were many there who spoke of the great service she did her country.'

'She was a cold, wicked bitch,' says Felicity.

'And she was one of the best,' says Loveday, before closing his eyes, exhausted.

Outside, a black Bentley is waiting in the car park. A soft rain is falling from a pale blue sky.

As the two old ladies approach the car, a tall man in a black suit emerges from the driver's seat and approaches with a large umbrella. Cordy gives a curt nod of thanks. Flick grins. They walk arm in arm to the vehicle and with a little difficulty and shuffling of limbs, climb into the warm, leather-lined interior.

'You already knew all that,' says Flick, under her breath. 'You told me all that years ago. You said.'

'Nice to have it confirmed,' says Cordy, settling back in her chair.

'You don't think it was cruel? Asking an old man to remember the things he did so long ago?'

Cordelia considers this then shakes her head. 'No. There's no time limit on accountability. You can change everything about yourself but the evil you did will always drag along behind you. And if you pretend it isn't there, it's up to somebody else to hold it to your face and demand you look.'

Felicity stares at her old friend for a moment, then gives a nod. She starts rubbing her sore knees. Checks her watch, as Cordelia opens her handbag and checks her sleek mobile phone for messages. There are too many to deal with so she scrolls through them until she finds the one she wants. It's from her grandson, Arthur. He will be graduating from university on the same day she is due to be presented with an honorary doctorate from her old college at Oxford. He wants to know if they could dress to match. He will be there to report on the day for the *Daily Telegraph*, though in truth, he is only using the job as a stepping stone to a book deal. He has always been a scribbler. Always loved stories. Arthur is her favourite grandchild. He makes her smile just by thinking about him. She was not around enough when her own children were growing up but she has been a doting grandmother, whatever her son and daughters might imply when they have had a glass of wine too many. Arthur always talks to her frankly. Asks her about the service. Where she was based, how she was trained, how many agents she recruited and how many spies she brought to the side of Queen and country. She rarely tells him the truth, and if she does, she makes it sound like a lie. She is very good at this.

'Will they drive me to the train station?' asks Flick, pointing at the driver and the large, surly bodyguard in the front passenger seat.

'They'll drive you all the way home,' says Cordelia.

'No, everybody will look if they see me getting out of a great posh car,' protests Felicity.

'Let them look,' says Cordelia.

Felicity shakes her head and sighs. 'You've a wicked side to you, Cordelia,' she says with a smile.

Cordelia reaches out a hand and takes her friend's fingers in her palm. She turns to her and gives the kind of smile that the staff at Thames House do not know exists.

'You're so much more than you let yourself believe,' says Cordelia. 'You're strong and loyal and brave . . .'

Felicity squeezes Cordelia's hands with her own and tuts, embarrassed at the fuss. They sit in silence, warm and comfortable, heads resting against one another's. Felicity does not speak for a time. She is thinking of Fairfax and Christopher and all the things that were and are and might have been. Finally she nods.

'Seems wrong to make that the end of it,' says Felicity, quietly. 'Seems wrong to just leave it at that.' She peers at her friend, all innocence. 'Your grandson. Arthur. He's a writer, isn't he? Have I got that right?'

Cordelia grins. Her eyes are bright and there's a blush to her cheeks. Then she switches off the recording device in her handbag and gives a nod.

She calls Arthur. Decides, on impulse, that the time has come.

Their story will go under the ground in the cool of the little church.

One day, perhaps, it will be read.